School's Out

An award-winning broadcaster and journalist, Sarah Tucker was a presenter on the BBC1 *Holiday* programme and anchored *I Want That House Revisited* on ITV1. She regularly contributes to women's magazines, the *Sunday Times Travel Magazine* and *The Guardian*. Sarah Tucker is the author of *The Playground Mafia, The Battle for Big School* and three romantic comedies published by Harlequin.

Praise for Sarah Tucker

'Scandal, backstabbing, illicit affairs . . . a fab, girlie read!' *New Woman*

'Mums will be able to see the truth behind this fun novel' *In The Know*

'A real laugh-out-loud tale' *OK! Magazine*

Also available by Sarah Tucker

Fiction
The Battle for Big School
The Playground Mafia
The Last Year of Being Single
The Last Year of Being Married
The Younger Man

Non-fiction
Have Baby, Will Travel
Have Toddler, Will Travel

Sarah Tucker

School's Out

arrow books

Published in the United Kingdom by Arrow Books in 2008

1 3 5 7 9 10 8 6 4 2

Copyright © Sarah Tucker, 2008

First published in the United Kingdom in 2008 by Arrow
Arrow Books
The Random House Group Limited
20 Vauxhall Bridge Road, London, SW1V 2SA

Addresses for companies within The Random House Group Limited can be
found at: www.randomhouse.co.uk/offices.htm

The Random House Group Limited Reg. No. 954009

www.rbooks.co.uk

A CIP catalogue record for this book
is available from the British Library

ISBN 9780099519782

The Random House Group Limited supports The Forest Stewardship
Council (FSC), the leading international forest certification organisation.
All our titles that are printed on Greenpeace approved FSC certified paper
carry the FSC logo. Our paper procurement policy can be found at:
www.rbooks.co.uk/environment

Typeset by SX Composing DTP, Rayleigh, Essex
Printed and bound in Great Britain by
CPI Cox & Wyman, Reading, RG1 8EX

Always to Tom . . .
And Jerry.

Acknowledgements

A very big thank you to Amanda and Luigi at LBA for striking the deal and for your unreserved support and wise counsel. To Nikola Scott and Emma Rose for your excellent guidance and expertise, and for helping me up my game. To the marketing and distribution teams at Random who are second to none, and Bill for your brilliant covers. To Diana for her incredible attention to detail and patience. And to Alastair McKenzie, who gave me my first break in the travel industry and whom without, I would not have seen as much of the world, and met the fascinating people I have. Thank you.

Chapter 1
Breaking Point

No sooner have I entered the large and brightly coloured reception of Dunsfield Infant and Junior School than Julian Warren's mum whose name I can never remember accosts me with a slightly manic-sounding, 'So, Amanda, what are your plans for the holidays?' There are already about fifty other fidgeting mums and listless dads waiting to go into the assembly hall to hear what Ms Gooden has to say about the school's achievements this year. All I can hear in the overcrowded foyer is the buzz of everyone anxiously discussing the latest hot topic, the summer holidays. It's almost July and already my three are starting to get excited with the thought of six weeks of no homework and no uniform, the two bits of 'school-dom' they dislike the most.

'Oh, hi! Erm, we're going to Cornwall for five weeks,'

I tell Julian's mum, still wracking my brain on the name front. I know it begins with an L – Linda, Lavinia, Lucy, Lottie? 'We're staying at our friends' bed and breakfast, well, it's more like a family-run hotel, really, as Skyler is endlessly feeding everyone and her afternoon teas and suppers have been a hit. It's down on the coast, in a town called Tremontgomery. Have you heard of it?'

Julian's mum shakes her head blankly.

'It belongs to George and Skyler Blue. Their eldest attended here a couple of years ago. George decided to take voluntary redundancy and they moved to the West Country. I wish my husband Nigel would cut back a bit too,' I say. 'We hardly see anything of him at the moment.'

'Will he be joining you in Cornwall?' she asks, concentrating half on the conversation, half on the assembly-hall doors, which everyone is now looking at expectantly as we wait to be ushered in.

'He's hoping to join us at some point,' I explain, trying to convince myself this will prove true, knowing he's worked the last three weekends running.

Salim Nayar's mum, Malika, has been listening in. 'Lucky you. I can only get two weeks off this year because the woman I work with is getting married. I've had to schedule the kids' activities like a military operation. They're going to Camp Beaumont for the first week, then they have a week at soccer camp, then a few days with their tennis coach, then they're both on a golf camp for a week. That just leaves the two weeks I can get off for our holiday to the South of France. I've had to liaise with Patrick Hamilton's mum to organise pick-ups and drop-offs. It's a nightmare, and it's the same every year! You'd think it'd get easier, but it doesn't, Linda.'

That's it, Linda! 'What are you doing for the holidays, *Linda*?' I ask.

'We're going to the South of France, too. We hired a canal boat last year – Julian was into boats at the time and we were told it would be more of an "experience" for the kids, but it was so painfully slow, we were all gagging for the beach by the end of the first day. So we've decided to go back to camping near a beach this year.'

'Could everyone please come in now,' beckons Ms Gooden's assistant.

As we shuffle through the doors, I can hear lots of other mums bemoaning the competitive-holiday syndrome: parents trying to outdo each other with the imaginative, fun-filled, action-packed breaks they're planning for the kids. Jessica Trent, sponsorship secretary of the PTA, says, 'I've given up on those kids' camps, I want to spend time with Joey this year. He went to one last year, cried all the time and had to come home early. He said they started at eight in the morning and it was archery, football, tennis and table tennis all day – I felt tired just listening to it. Seems better to just keep him home this year.'

'Well, I just feel so lucky this year,' says Cora Jones, who has twins in Jack's year. She's an immaculate suited-and-booted mum who regularly writes features in the national press about motherhood and parenting.

She's not exactly popular with the other mums but they seem to tolerate her, despite her writing last month that Dunsfield mums are 'frustrated underachievers'. 'Last year I spent a fortune on a nanny for holiday cover, but this summer I'm taking a break from work completely. Jerry's cashed in some shares, so for the first time ever I've got the luxury of not having to worry about holiday cover or signing them up for camps. And Jerry's managed to book August off. We've borrowed a friend's house in Majorca for the month so it'll be bliss. I've got to draft a book synopsis for my agent while I'm there but Jerry said he'll look after the children so I can focus on getting that done, which is sweet of him.'

Momentarily distracted from finding our seats, we all look at her with a mixture of envy, bemusement and fury. Oblivious to the reaction she's causing, she continues: 'I'm setting up another business to help mothers who need to find holiday nannies. It's such a pain when you can't get one, don't you think?'

I don't think she really expects an answer, just nods of agreement and possibly even applause, given the look on her face.

'I'm afraid I couldn't afford a holiday nanny,' says Jessica, nobly facing up to Cora, 'and even if I could I wouldn't hire one as it's the only chance I get to spend time with my children, being the frustrated under-achiever that I am.' I stifle a snigger. Another mum I've not spoken to before is about to give Cora an earful as well, when I recognise a voice calling my name across the room.

'Amanda, darling!' Suzanne's voice resonates loudly across the assembly hall, causing all heads to turn in her direction. 'I'm so glad you're here. Darling, I desperately need your help! Something dreadful has happened,' she says, rushing towards me and giving me a hug and three kisses on alternate cheeks. She's just come back from an art history and watercolour course in Toulouse, where they kiss three times, but I'm so used to two that she ends up giving me the last one on the lips. I haven't seen her look so anxious before. Is something wrong with her rather delicate son Orlando? Or has she discovered her husband Howard is having an affair? Knowing Orlando and Howard, either's possible. Perhaps they've lost all their money, although this is less likely as Suzanne is one of the wealthiest people in Whitlow and she wouldn't be broadcasting it if they had. In fact, she looks so anxious I suddenly am quite worried that something more serious has actually happened.

'Howard's monumentally fucked up,' she says, plopping herself down on the seat next to me.

Thought so, he's having an affair.

'I've just had the most awful news and you're the first person I thought of. Amanda, you must help me, there's no one else I can go to,' she says, looking genuinely needy, which is a shock to say the least.

'Needy' is a word I wouldn't normally use to describe Suzanne. 'Uber-successful PR exec' is more like it. And need doesn't ever come into it as while managing a team of twenty herself, she also has a full-time nanny, housekeeper, personal trainer and shopper at her constant beck and call.

'I need your advice about holidays,' she says. This is the 'something dreadful' that only I can help with? 'You know we booked a cruise around the Med for three weeks in the summer, with the wonderful kids' club that Orlando will love and which takes them all day?'

I nod, knowing the kids' club is probably more for her benefit than Orlando's and thinking that only your closest friends can try your patience this much. Maybe I should suggest Cora would be better suited to advising her, as whatever's happened, it really can't be all that serious.

'Well, the company's gone completely bust, bankrupt, kaput, and here we are left with two weeks to the end of term and a complete void in our holiday calendar. I had my assistant and the company travel agent hunt for holidays, but everything's booked up. They've looked everywhere; every continent, every tour operator, every villa company. Well, everything decent, that is,' she adds.

'What about your place in Umbria? I thought you tried to keep that free in the summer just in case,' I say, thinking of the rather splendid six-bedroom villa in Italy they happen to own. I have to concede that while for most of us this unfortunate problem wouldn't have conjured up quite the level of drama and anxiety, for Suzanne this is genuinely a disaster of monstrous proportions. She's an utter control freak and, in fairness, she gets so little time off work, it's not surprising this has thrown her into utter panic.

'Yes, I know, I know,' replies Suzanne, looking even more exasperated. 'We have this huge great gorgeous home in Italy, don't we? And what does Howey do? He lets his boss have it for the three weeks we're due to be on the cruise. He's not even charging him for it, the prat, and the guy is loaded. Not that we need the money, of course, but Howey thought it would go down well, and he says there are more important things than money, the hypocrite. Then Howey suggests we go with them instead, but I'd rather stick hot pins in my eyes, to be honest. His boss is a tedious, boorish letch who nit-picks about everything, and she's one of those hyper-hyper, up-at-dawn, run-and-cycle-and-swim types who wants to do something extremely energetic every morning and to boast about it for the rest of the day. I just need a proper rest. It exhausts me just looking at her. And she's so infuriatingly jolly all the time it makes me want to hit her, Amanda, it really does.'

I laugh, amused that there's someone who gets on Suzanne's nerves as much as she sometimes gets on mine.

'But you are my salvation. You have all your wonderful travel contacts to help me.'

'I only do the odd freelance piece now, you know that. My contacts just aren't as good these days, Suzanne.'

Suzanne looks dejected. 'But you must have some-one you know who'd be able to help? You can't have lost all you contacts! That's just not good business sense, darling.' Ah Suzanne, ever the PR gal.

But I genuinely feel I have lost touch with so many of my former colleagues and friends from my old days travelling the world. Settling down to have three kids, managing their day-to-day lives, and keeping the house organised and Nigel happy is a full-time job and leaves little opportunity for the freelancing I'd hoped to keep up. Unlike Suzanne, I've never been particularly good at delegating, not that Nigel and I have any money to hire anybody to delegate to. And I'm less than delighted about Suzanne reminding me that long ago I did have a successful career that I was absolutely passionate about and could have sorted her out with the perfect destination before you could even spell Mediterranean. I worked hard for over a decade to establish myself in a highly competitive industry that was as glamorous on the inside as it seemed on the outside. I travelled the continents, researching and presenting for radio and TV, and writing fun and inspired pieces for newspapers and magazines. I was sent on some wonderful assignments: bungee jumping in New Zealand, whale-watching off the coast of Newfoundland and dune-surfing in the Namib desert. No money in it, of course, but it was a wonderful and carefree life and I loved every single moment of it. In fact, I can feel myself getting a bit dewy-eyed.

'Amanda, are you OK?' says Suzanne, touching my arm.

'Yes, I'm fine, I'm fine,' I lie.

'So what do you suggest? She looks at me intently,

like a puppy dog waiting to be fed, ready to pounce on my every word. Oh, the pressure of finding an ideal holiday for the utter perfectionist that is Suzanne Fields. Suddenly I'm very pleased to have a real excuse for not having any good contacts.

'I don't really know what to say,' I reply as we finally settle in our seats. I look up at Ms Gooden, hoping she'll call us all to attention any minute, but she's deep in conversation with one of the mothers. 'All the bespoke tour operators I know that fit your bill would have been booked up a year ago. You remember how early you had to book for the Garden Route safari? I think it was two years.'

Suzanne's still looking at me like a startled rabbit, though it could just be the botox. 'I know, I know,' she wails. 'I thought about Marrakesh, but it's too hot at this time of year, and apparently all the quality riads are booked up or closed anyway. Egypt will be sweltering. I thought about Namibia after you told me about Etosha National Park, but that's booked up too. There are lots of activity holidays, in Slovenia and Finland and fresh-air places like that, but that's not really my thing or Howey's and I don't think Orlando would enjoy it . . .'

Realising she's not going to give up easily, I get my brain into gear. 'Have you thought about Brazil? Beaches, good weather, good fashion.'

'Booked,' she says, sighing.

'What, all of it?' I tease, struggling to hide an exasperated smile.

'Well, the bits worth going to. I wouldn't risk going

anywhere that's not come recommended by someone credible. I've already been to Vietnam, Cuba and Thailand, even though I hate Bangkok airport – an endless maze of shops selling expensive nonsense and food that looks as though it's been regurgitated. There're always such long delays that I end up spending a fortune in Ferragamo, and I hate Ferragamo.'

I can't help but nod in agreement at this. My memories of Bangkok airport are also not good and, as they are for Suzanne, are all too clear in my mind, but for very different reasons. It was the last press trip I took before I properly gave up work. We were travelling to Chaing Rai in northern Thailand, heart of the opium-growing region. Jenny was barely two at the time, and I didn't really want to go, but we needed the money. I was feeling so tired, but thought it was just stress. Then, on the Friday before I left, I went to the doctor and discovered I was two months pregnant. I'd been so busy I hadn't even noticed that I'd missed my period. I didn't tell Nigel because he was engrossed with work, and I didn't have any real friends back then as all I did was juggle work and Jenny.

On the morning I was due to fly out, I had the worst morning sickness I've ever experienced. For ten hours I had to sit in economy, squashed between the snotty, brittle editor of *Beautiful People* and a young, talkative reporter from the *Daily Echo* who had a serious body-odour problem. I'd been up and down to the loo so many times to be sick I'd lost count and I felt so dizzy I could barely focus on sipping from the bottle of water

I shakily clutched. I remember trying to listen to the young reporter drone on about her boyfriend and how all men were bastards and all I wanted to do was faint, throw up or both. Miranda, the PR girl, kept drifting past to ask if everyone was all right but never stayed long enough to listen to the answer. By the time we arrived at Bangkok airport I was dangerously dehydrated and had also developed worryingly severe cramps. I could barely stand and had to lie down on the floor of the Duty Free as Miranda, looking distinctly pissed off, went in search of a business-class lounge so that I would at least cause less embarrassment to her and the rest of the group. I think it was when I was lying on the floor, one cheek pressed hard against the cold white tiles and surrounded by shelves of Benson & Hedges and JLo's latest perfume, that I realised what was really important to me. I was passionate about my job, but what was really, really important were those I loved and the health of me and my baby. I vowed never to go on a press trip again.

'Any other ideas, Amanda?' Suzanne interrupts my train of thought. 'You must have some more.' She is almost whining like a lost puppy now. Ms Gooden still looks engrossed in conversation. Does she have nowhere better to be?

'How about South Africa? Children love it and there are wonderful vineyards,' I say. Finally, Ms Gooden steps up to the lectern and everyone falls blissfully silent.

Almost everyone.

'Went there last year, and wouldn't mind going again,' Suzanne whispers, 'but they don't have any first-class seats left and I'm not slumming it in cattle class.'

Thankfully, before I can utter any regretful words of exasperation, Ms Gooden begins to speak. 'Thank you, mums and dads, for coming this evening, in what I know must be one of your busiest times of the year.' Ms Gooden, sixty-something, twenty of those years at Dunsfield, is wearing her usual navy and cream M&S twinset and smiles graciously as she looks around the hall, waiting for the last few murmurings to quieten down. 'The summer term is the shortest of the year, but it's one in which we seem to achieve the most. Exams, sports day, speech day, the summer fête, the school play and that delicious barbecue were all crammed into ten weeks, but thankfully you have six weeks' holiday at the end of it to refresh yourselves and unwind.'

'Who's she kidding?' whispers Suzanne, as some of the other mums giggle.

'All those in Year Six have done extremely well, and Dunsfield continues to be the top-rated state school in the area. This is in no small part due to the support we get from you, the parents, so please will you all give yourselves a round of applause.'

Ms Gooden has been on one too many confidence-building seminars, but the assembly hall spontaneously bursts into applause anyway, including a few laughs and one loud 'whoop' from a dad in the back row. When the applause dies down she starts to talk about plans for the next school year, the new IT room and where the PTA funds are being allocated. I'm only half concentrating as I'm still trying to think of a holiday for Suzanne.

Skyler and I met Suzanne five years ago. It turned out that Orlando, the quietest and most polite little boy I've ever met, was in the same class as my Jenny and Willow, Skyler's eldest. Suzanne had adjusted her hours so she could pick Orlando up from school more often, and we clicked with her surprisingly easily, given the reputation that had preceded her. She was known as being hard-nosed and demanding, but recognising an undeveloped motherly streak in her, Skyler and I turned a blind eye to the playground comments about her and we quickly discovered a side to Suzanne that so often goes unnoticed. She has a wicked sense of humour, and, being in PR, can suss out someone out in moments. She fitted in well with Skyler and me, and joined us at our spot in the corner of the playground, giggling like wayward silly girls, and trying to dodge the PTA committee at the obligatory coffee mornings in the nearby café.

Coffee turned into the odd lunch while Suzanne was working locally, but when she moved to a City firm we started to invite each other to dinner parties instead. She is fiercely bright, independent and funny, but at the same time she can be infuriating in her frankness – sometimes downright rudeness – and her single-minded pursuit of whatever it is she wants. She already has everything most people would only dare dream of: a huge five-bedroom house with half an acre of garden

– unheard of in the centre of Whitlow – hot and cold running staff, a well-paid job and a meticulous timetable of health and beauty regimes, rounded off nicely with a catalogue of interesting and exotic holidays to indulge in. When a glitch occurs, she's able to guilelessly delegate the responsibility and worry to someone else. I'm not quite sure how she has managed it all; I guess she's just ruthless enough only to expect the best. But why does she suddenly think I should help her out? It's not as if I haven't got enough on my plate.

For a start, Hannah is moving to a new school after the holidays. She's a bright girl but she's very unhappy at school. I know she and her teacher, Ms Carter, who unfortunately will also be teaching her next year, don't get on too well. She wrote on Hannah's last report that she 'lacked emotional maturity'. I don't know many adults who have emotional maturity, so it's certainly not a quality I think you can expect in an eight-year-old girl. We kind of stumbled upon Hannah's new school, Dragons, as we'd not really worked out what to do about her increasing anxiety over going to school. When their prospectus dropped on to the doormat it just seemed the perfect answer, and before I knew it we were visiting the school with an enraptured Hannah in tow. Dragons is a private school about twenty minutes' drive from our home, as opposed to the ten-minute walk to Dunsfield, but it has class sizes of less than twenty. The decision to go private has added to our already overstretched financial burden, and since Nigel's deal is taking much longer than he'd anticipated, we've decided to put our house on the market to make sure we can afford the fees.

'How's Nigel?' Suzanne whispers, obviously as bored with Ms Gooden's speech as I am.

'Oh, he's fine, still busy with the deal, but hopefully it should all be sorted by the summer.' Nigel is managing director of a coffee-bar business that's expanded dramatically over the past few years. They went into Europe last year and want to go global next, but they need serious money to do it. Nigel has been in meeting after meeting with financiers, trying to organise a deal for what feels like for ever, and hopefully this year it will all come to fruition. Coffee has been giving me sleepless nights, but it's more through the stress of will it/won't it happen than actually drinking the stuff.

'Don't worry,' says Suzanne, 'the City's such a funny place at the moment, bullish one minute, bearish the next. They all play at being risk takers, but none of them are. It's not their money, after all. They're all like lemmings, following each other's tails.' She affectionately squeezes my hand, perhaps sensing the stress I'm under, although I'm sure she doesn't appreciate the extent of it. Still, she's probably starting to suspect things aren't quite right; she's recently invited Nigel and me to countless £200-per-head balls, operas and expensive restaurants, and we've had to politely decline them all. We're not in her league at all, and though she doesn't show off as such, she talks about money as though everyone has as much as she and

Howard do. Like Nigel, Howard works long hours in the City, but Suzanne's happy with the arrangement. She told me once that she gets on better with him when she doesn't see him much, whereas I miss Nigel when he's not around.

'What are you doing for the summer holidays?' she asks, although I'm sure I've mentioned it to her before.

'Staying at Skyler and George's place for five weeks,' I reply. 'I'm going down with the kids when school breaks up and Nigel is joining us as and when he can. The kids are really looking forward to seeing Willow and Rose.'

'Oh yes,' says Suzanne, clapping her hands together. 'Of course, Skyler asked us down too, but we'd already booked the cruise, and anyway we didn't want to intrude. They've had so much work to do on the house by the sounds of things, and the last thing they want are freeloaders coming down when they probably need fee-paying guests.'

Typical foot-in-mouth Suzanne and, as usual, I'm not sure whether she means to upset me or whether she is just being thoughtless. 'We're not going to freeload while we're there, Suzanne,' I whisper calmly. 'It's kind of a working holiday for us all. We're going to help out wherever and however we can, and anyway, it sounds as though they've got things running near perfect now.'

Ms Gooden's speech has come to an end and everyone is applauding. We clap too as Ms Gooden takes a little bow and leaves the stage.

'If you're really stuck, you could always take her up

16

on her offer, Suzanne, and join me and the children there for the summer. The more the merrier, I would say, and at least it will solve your holiday problems.' Suzanne's walking ahead of me now so I'm not even sure she hears this off-the-cuff idea, which, in fact, I'm now already regretting having said. I might have known Suzanne a long time but we've certainly never holidayed together and I know Nigel and Howey don't get on *that* well.

I follow Suzanne back through the reception area and out to the playground towards her new Land Rover. I walked to school, so we hug each other at the school gates. 'You know, darling, I don't know if Cornwall is really me,' says Suzanne as she kisses me three times again. 'The weather was utterly dire last year in the UK, hot one minute, freezing the next, and everyone was so crabby.'

'That's climate change for you,' I say. I feel I should defend the good old British holiday and, against my better judgement, find myself pushing for Suzanne to come to Cornwall. 'Your best bet is to go somewhere you like, whatever the weather, and be with people you love. That's why I think Cornwall will be so perfect for me this year.' That and it's going to save me a small fortune and my sanity.

Suzanne still looks doubtful as she opens her car door.

'And remember, Cornwall is extremely trendy these days,' I add craftily, 'home to many supermodels, entrepreneurs, musical impresarios and celebrity chefs.

It's not the backwater it once was, and Skyler wouldn't invite you if she didn't want you to come.'

'I'll think about it,' she says, climbing into her car. 'You're all very bohemian, Amanda, you can rough it if you need to. You've been on all these outward-bound adventures where you've lived off an ant for a week and trekked through jungles and stuff, but that's not really me, or Orlando – or Howard, for that matter.'

I laugh. 'Oh don't be silly, Suzanne, this is Cornwall, we're not talking the Sahara desert, for goodness' sake. I'm sure they even have Prada there.'

'Hmm, I'll think about it. Hopefully my travel agent will have turned something up. Someone's bound to cancel their holiday before we get to the end of term.' She's clearly not convinced by my Cornwall suggestion. Can't be *that* desperate for a holiday, then. 'Fancy a lift?' she asks.

'Very kind of you, but I've got to pop into the shop on my way home so I'll walk,' I explain, although I'm doing nothing of the sort. I'm popping into the estate agent's to drop off the spare set of keys so that people can come round to look at the house while we're away. Suzanne waves her hand in a queenly fashion as she zooms off in her car, leaving me to sneak off to the estate agent's.

It's a warm evening and I enjoy the walk, despite my worries. I'm looking forward to the holidays, and especially to seeing Skyler. She's the one person I can always talk to about everything, and I miss her. She used to live just up the road, so I could pop in any time. Then one day at pick-up time she announced: 'We're selling up and moving to Cornwall.' I was gobsmacked for a few seconds. 'One of George's best friends at work has just died of cancer. He was only thirty-eight and it made George think about lots of things. He hasn't been that well recently through stress, and the markets are particularly bad at the moment. He doesn't like the guys he works with, either, thinks they're a bunch of back-stabbing oiks, so we've decided to finally make the move and start afresh. Next month, actually, as George has been able to take voluntary redundancy!' I was shocked, but happy for her. I knew she'd been considering it for a long time. I just thought it would be one of those decisions that gets relegated to life as a pipe dream, along with a holiday house, an Aston Martin, chucking it all in and driving round Morocco in an old VW van with the kids. But Skyler and George had actually taken the plunge, and good on them, I thought. I'm so excited now about going down to see the house for the first time, and about seeing Skyler, who's the one person I can talk to about our financial worries. She'll understand.

I stroll down the leafy high street just five minutes from our house, knowing each shop window by heart. I've pounded these pavements virtually every day on the school run with the children. I can't believe this could all change and that our life as we know it depends on the whim of some financier. Nigel has tried to explain how these deals work and how investors make their decisions, but he usually loses me after the first ten minutes, which makes me cross and him frustrated. Perhaps motherhood and domesticity have made my brain go soft over the years. I don't feel I've challenged myself for ages. But at the same time, I feel more tired than I've felt in years. Nigel gave me a voucher for some reflexology a while back, which I only managed to use last week, just before it expired. The woman told me I had an overactive thyroid and that I was a mess.

'You've worked your body hard and now it's time for some TLC. You need to take care of yourself.' But I have four other people to take care of and I may be losing my home in the next few months, so I'm not sure how I'm supposed to do that.

As I walk up our road, I say out loud, 'God, I'm looking forward to Cornwall.' I wonder whether Suzanne will come. Now I think about it properly, it wouldn't really be all that bad holidaying with her, I'm sure. She's funny and feisty, a doer and decision-maker, so I know she'll have loads of wonderful ideas for Skyler's place. She's as bossy as hell, but she managed to get loads of publicity for Dunsfield's last school fête by bullying the local estate agent's into paying for most of it. And I know she's highly respected in her company. I think she's just been promoted, although she was a bit vague about it when I asked her at our last dinner.

Earnest Avenue, where we live at Number 8, is a cul-de-sac of a dozen or so houses, all quite pristine apart from Mr Durning, our neighbour, who's been building an extension for ever and still seems to be getting nowhere. I unlock our front door, hoping the children are all in bed and that Charlotte, our eighteen-year-old, £12-an-hour babysitter, is sitting in front of the TV watching reruns of *Sex and the City*. As I put my bag down, my mobile rings.

'Hello, Suzanne,' I say.

'Hi. Just wanted to say that Cornwall sounds lovely. I've called Howey and told him my thoughts and Orlando is happy about it too. I just called Skyler to check it was OK and she sounded very excited. Which day are you going?' I'm so stunned at the speed of her decision-making ability that I robotically answer.

'The day after we break up – the Thursday.'

'Well, Howey's working the first week, but he can come down some time after that. I'll drive down with Orlando when you go. I'm able to take three weeks this year because of my new job, which is one bonus. Anyway, must go. Lots to prepare, or rather get others to prepare. Cheerio.'

I hear her giggle as she hangs up, leaving me standing in my hallway suddenly hoping I've done the right thing. Yes, she's fun to be around, but I can't really say I know her *that* well – although perhaps this is the perfect opportunity to do just that . . . Then again, I was so looking forward to just being with my family and seeing Skyler. I wanted to be able to freely chat about my problems, Nigel's work, having to move, everything really, and now I don't know if I'll be able to. But I'm sure it will be OK, I think to myself as I go through to the sitting room, hoping I haven't inadvertently dropped myself and the children into a summer catastrophe.

Chapter 2
Cecile Dies

Two weeks later, we are due to set off for Cornwall. We're running late, of course, but the car is packed and the children and our retriever, Hunter, are ready to go. I'm just coming out of the house with the final bag when I see that Mr Durning's builder has parked another huge skip on the road which leaves me almost no room to get the car off our own drive.

'Bloody hell!' I shout at the top of my voice. I'm fed up with these ignorant and bloody-minded builders who hog all the road space. Added to that I've just about had my limit with all the dust, noise and dangerous equipment they leave all over the place, and holes seem to be appearing in the pavements for no apparent reason.

I notice Mr Durning's window is open and am tempted to knock on his door and give him a piece of my mind. I'm summoning up the nerve to go and knock on his door when I see Hannah walking towards me, singing happily for a change and carrying her backpack. Jack is leaping excitedly behind, ever the energetic five-year-old, and Jenny's trying to drag Hunter out of the house by his lead. 'Do you want me to close the door, Mother?' she calls out.

I wish she wouldn't call me that. Jenny is a lovely girl in so many ways: hard-working at school, good at sport, loads of friends, kind and generous, but she has an edge to her even at ten years old, and she knows which buttons to push. Calling me 'Mother' is one of them. It wouldn't be so bad, but that's what everyone called my mother, who was a difficult woman, so I can feel myself flinch at the words. I try not to let it show, as Jenny will only use it more.

'No, hon, I'll do it,' I reply. 'You get in the car and settle Hunter.'

I walk back inside to check we've got everything. Nigel will be returning to an empty house. His study is full of piles of paperwork, which I don't dare touch. We won't be seeing him for at least two weeks, maybe longer. He's been away from us before, but never during the school holidays as he always used to be able to keep those weeks free.

'Have a lovely time,' he said as he kissed me goodbye this morning, 'and give George and Skyler a hug from me. Still don't know why you suggested that Suzanne join you. She's funny enough, I suppose, but so high-maintenance. You do realise that, don't you?' He was grinning at me.

'It seemed like a good idea at the time and I'm sure she'll be fine,' I replied defensively. 'We get on well and I know she'll have lots of good marketing ideas for Skyler. Orlando's no trouble, either, he's so quiet we'll hardly know he's there.' But I was starting to get worried about how the holiday would work out and that I'd made a serious mistake suggesting Suzanne join us.

He kissed Jenny, Jack and Hannah goodbye, hugging them each individually and then having a family hug in the hallway before he left – even Hunter wanted to join in. I was quite tearful then and am still so now as I look around and realise it's not just a house I will be saying goodbye to if and when we sell this place; it will be my family's life story. Still, at least selling the house and moving somewhere smaller will release the capital we need for school fees. Our cost cutting has also involved letting go of the gardener and the cleaner, so everything is looking rather scruffy at the moment. And I looked in the mirror this morning and realised I hadn't been to the hairdresser for months and my hair now resembles a scouring pad. No wonder Suzanne keeps asking me if everything is OK.

Jack, of course, says he loves me whatever I look like. Always full of beans and smiles, he bounds about the house like some Duracell bunny, brightening every-where he goes with his mischief. 'I like the garden better now,' he told me when I looked out at it the other day and sighed at the overgrown mess. 'It's like a jungle, and I'm Tarzan and you're my Jane, Mummy, but don't tell Daddy because he might get upset.'

Hannah is rather like a cat; she doesn't care what the house and garden looks like as long as she's warm and fed and has somewhere to sleep at night. She seems very independent for one so young, although she still comes running to Nigel or me when she falls over.

Jenny is more vulnerable but won't admit it. She's always looking for praise and, as she's been a grade A student so far, she's always got it – but I feel occasionally getting it wrong would help her immensely. I don't want her becoming a know-it-all at so young an age or she'll be impossible as a teenager. At the moment she still loves me but I'm just waiting for the day when she'll start to hate and resent me for being her mother and for just, well, being.

As I wander round the house to make a final check and peek into the bedrooms, I realise that although I know we're doing the sensible thing, I really don't want to move. I know it's for the best, but Jack was born here and the house is all the children have known.

I double-check the kitchen, making sure Jack hasn't pushed one of the oven switches by accident. The fridge is well stocked with healthy ready meals for Nigel in case he forgets to eat, which he does all the time at the moment. No wonder his face looks so gaunt. He used to be so relaxed and healthy before work took over his life. He had time for himself and the family then. He would say that he's doing this for the whole family that hopefully, in the long run, it would mean that he could spend more time with us, not less.

My favourite room in our home is the sitting room,

with its huge cream sofas draped with our white and silver wedding blankets, which Nigel and I bargained hard for in Marrakesh. There are the stone and wood carvings from Africa and North America standing proud on the polished wood floors, exquisite paintings from South America, and lush red and deep orange rugs from Italy, all gleaned from my work travels. My favourite is one of Skyler's dramatic flower paintings she gave me for my birthday some years back, which always makes me think of her when I walk past. The bookcases are full of children's books and travel guides, a couple of which I wrote myself, and many of which are signed copies from the people I've interviewed. They're possibly worth something, but for me it's their sentimental value that counts: they're filled with so many memories, journeys and adventures.

I get a bit tearful looking round the dining room, remembering the parties we've had here. The children used to look down through the banisters at all the 'pretty people', as Jenny called them. As I check the windows and French doors, I smile, remembering some of the conversations we've had in this room over the years. I swallow hard, hold back the tears and tell myself everything will sort itself out and, who knows, we might not even have to sell up. I walk out of the dining room, through the hall, check that my note to Nigel is on the table and, with a last look around, close and lock our bright yellow front door.

Our people-carrier, a six-year-old blue Renault

Espace that's seen better days, is crammed full. I get into the car. Jenny is sitting beside me, Jack behind her, and Hannah in the back with Hunter. Jack is clinging on tight to his teddy, Fishbowl, with one hand while holding the portable DVD player in the other. Jack's teddy is the reason we are an hour late leaving. He lost it this morning and we searched the house and emptied the expertly packed car without finding it. Then, as we were repacking the car in a far less organised fashion, Hannah found it inexplicably trapped under her booster seat, looking rather squashed and forlorn. I notice Fishbowl has puffed up a bit now as I turn to make sure all the children are safely secured and Hunter is sitting comfortably with his blanket. I've given him my usual last-minute lecture about behaving on the trip.

'House secure, three kids in the car, everything packed, dog lectured, DVD player and Nintendo DS working, spare batteries, books, iPods charged, drinks and snacks that won't make a mess – right, I think that's everything,' I say briskly and then wonder how on earth I'm going to get this tank of a car past that skip.

Because we couldn't find Fishbowl, we're now in rush-hour traffic. I don't usually mind driving in London, despite the road rage that seems endemic these days. When I don't have the children I drive our red 1960s clapped-out Mini – being aggressive in something nippy and small is so much easier than throwing my weight around in this thing. When I drive the Espace, I get lots of hateful looks from people in their Smart cars. They scowl at me because I'm destroying their planet, which I probably am, but on the other hand I don't know how else I'm meant to ferry about three kids, one dog and all the assorted gear they require. Anyway, this year I figure I'm paying it back in full by not flying the whole family abroad – now that's got to be effective carbon offsetting!

In fact, I'd sworn that this would be the holiday when I didn't overpack, and would, for once, be able to see out of the back of the car. I called Skyler yesterday to ask what to bring and she'd said a little unhelpfully, 'Don't bring anything, just yourselves. We have loads of towels, beach balls, games and outdoor stuff to keep them occupied for the entire summer holiday. No need to overdo it on shampoos and stuff, either, because there's plenty of shops in the town if you run out of anything. We're so looking forward to seeing you tomorrow. George sends his love, he's out in the garden at the moment, and Rose and Willow can't wait to see Jenny, Hannah and Jack.'

'Do you mind that I mentioned the holiday to Suzanne?' I'd asked hesitantly.

'Of course not, I did ask her in the first place, remember? The more the merrier. Look forward to seeing you. Must dash: I've got lunch to prepare.'

And yet the boot is still packed to the roof. I adjust my wing mirrors and settle down to the steady stop and start of rush-hour traffic. Whitlow is on the borders of south-west London, so it's easy to get in and out of town if the traffic's good. Today, however, we are bumper to bumper with coaches, four-wheel drives, sports cars and Transits. There's a skip truck taking up two lanes, which slows us even more, but my pet hate bus drivers, who snootily use their bus lane when it suits, but otherwise seem to straddle two lanes. Black cabs use any lane available, but at least they drive relatively well. Now there's a grey-haired old biddy in a hat going at twenty.

'If you drive any slower you'll go backwards!' I shout at her impotently. I don't want to overtake her because only last week I had to attend a speed awareness course for getting caught speeding along this same stretch of road.

The weather is suddenly humid and the cabriolets are out in force. There are a few furtive-looking couples heading out to the countryside, Louis Vuitton weekend bags casually thrown on the back seats. Eventually we reach the flyover, although we're still only doing thirty. Jenny's happily listening to her iPod, Hannah is dreamily looking out the window and Jack is halfway through *Shrek the third*. Thankfully, I've brought a selection of about thirty DVDs for him to watch. There's been a crash on the other side of the dual carriageway and everyone has slowed down to take a look, but once we get past that the traffic finally starts to speed up, and we're finally on the motorway.

I've set the satnav – otherwise known as Cecile – to Tremontgomery, and now I've made the shortcuts I know out of London, I turn it on. Her voice starts to give directions. I don't really like using Cecile as I always think something's going to go wrong. Nigel got her on a business trip to Paris and she speaks English with a sexy French lilt. Nigel and I have different views on what the real Cecile looks like. Nigel imagines her as a twenty-something, size 10, 34D brunette in a bikini, stretching and contorting her lithe, leggy body over a huge glass map of the world as she pushes our Espace in the right direction with a long silver wand. I like to think of her more as a fifty-something moustached woman with halitosis and bad skin, who's taking her directions from an out-of-date *A to Z*. Cecile only speaks occasionally, getting particularly excited every time we come to a junction.

'Go to zee left and bearrr leaft arfterrr tree undred yards,' she'll say, rolling her 'r's provocatively. Usually, against my better judgement, I do as she says, but Nigel likes to do his own thing, especially in London. I suspect he likes to hear her repeat herself and get mildly agitated when we're disobedient.

I've decided to break the journey briefly at Avebury, near Stonehenge, where we're going to have a picnic. An hour out of town and we're heading happily towards the turn-off when Hannah decides she wants to go to the toilet. We stop at the next service station and while Hannah's in the loo I call Suzanne to see if she's making good headway.

'Hello, darling, on the hands-free so can talk. Where are you?' she says, sounding wired and focused.

'We're about ten minutes from Stonehenge,' I say, stretching the truth a little.

'Oh, we're already on the A30, darling. Left early.

Tiffs packed the car yesterday,' she explains airily. Tiffs is her cleaner-cum-domestic secretary. 'Should be there for a barbecue on the beach. It's all turning out so well, isn't it? Orlando's very excited about us all holidaying together and says it'll be a bit like having a play date every day, isn't that sweet? The weather looks wonderful here. What's it like where you are?' she asks.

'Probably the same,' I say grumpily, 'we're only a few hours away, Suzanne, not in a different country.'

'Do you want me to tell Skyler you're running late, or will you do that yourself?' she asks.

'I'll call her myself,' I say, slightly irritated that she'll be arriving before me and hoping she doesn't get the cottage. One of us has probably got to go in the main house, but Suzanne's only got Orlando, whereas I've got three and a dog. Surely Skyler wouldn't give her the cottage?

'OK. Ring me when you get close, although I don't know what the reception will be like. Bye, darling.'

I get the children back into the car, Hannah and Jack whinging for Maltesers – I'm not going to relent though, as I need the supplies to last longer than the morning. I'm also having a problem with Hunter, who's spotted a retriever in a Range Rover and is pacing outside it just in case the dog, which is barking manically, decides to get out. The owner, a grey-haired man in his fifties with a paunch and an attitude, scowls at me and shushes Hunter away as I come over to apologise.

'So sorry,' I say, catching hold of his lead. 'He's just very friendly.'

31

'Yes, well, you shouldn't let them loose in petrol stations. They could get killed with all these cars around,' he says huffily.

I smile, say nothing, but notice his number plate, HF1, as he gets in the car and hastily drives away.

'I know, let's play name games with the number plates,' I suggest as I round everyone back into the car. 'We can start with that grumpy man's plate.'

'How about Huge Fatso, Horrid Frump or Humpy Fartface?' Hannah shouts gleefully. Jenny and Jack find this hysterically funny and for the next five minutes we amuse ourselves with thinking up names for the rude man, deciding that Humpy Fartface is the most imaginative and accurate of all of the suggestions.

As we near Stonehenge, I start talking about the history and legends surrounding the stones.

'No one really knows for sure how the stones got here. You used to be able to walk around them and touch them, but now there's a barrier and you can only see them from a distance. On Midsummer's Day in June, you can watch Druids dancing round them; they think they have some connection with fertility rites.'

'What's fertility rites?' asks Jack.

'They give you babies,' replies Jenny before I have time to speak.

'Does that mean we'll all have babies if we start dancing round them?' Jack looks up at me wide-eyed.

'No,' interrupts Hannah, 'you have to have injections to have babies, Jack. My friend Julian says his mummy had to have lots of injections before she had him.'

I don't fancy going into the ins and outs of IVF at the moment, especially as I haven't had the birds-and-bees talk with Jack yet, although I'm sure Hannah and Jenny will have given him their take on it. Sure enough, Jack pipes up.

'Jenny says that the daddies give the mummies the injections,' he announces.

'Well, I suppose in a way they do,' I say, trying to be diplomatic without lying.

'When are we having lunch, Mother?' Jenny asks, thankfully changing the subject.

'Soon. When we get to Avebury. There'll be stone circles we can touch there. And crop circles.'

'What are crop circles, Mummy?' Jack asks. 'And why is everything in circles?'

'Crop circles appear in fields of corn or wheat. It's when the crop's been flattened down in huge circles and patterns. Some people think it's just done by vandals who come and stamp down the crops in the middle of the night with large planks of wood.'

'Why would they do that?' Jack asks, completely fascinated.

'To trick people into thinking aliens have landed,' I reply. 'A lot of people think that aliens create these crop circles as a sign that they've visited Earth and want others to follow. Others believe the circles are part of some magical ritual where witches come and cast spells.'

'Do you believe in witches then, Mummy?' asks Hannah.

'I think there are still witches about, darling, yes. In medieval times, they used to burn witches at the stake on huge bonfires.'

'But we don't burn people at the stake any more, do we, Mummy?' says Jack, looking a bit worried.

'No we don't, darling,' I say, realising I've scared him and feeling thoroughly guilty. We're nearly at Avebury, where I'm sure I'll get more questions about witches, magic and having babies.

I love Avebury. Nigel and I went there a lot before we had a family. We were like George and Skyler then; both quite bohemian. We even considered buying a house in Avebury, but bourgeois reality soon hit and we realised it was too far from his work and the airports I'd need to travel out of. Since we've had a family we haven't had the time to visit. I love the energy here, though, and remember a visit one midsummer's night years ago. It was a warm evening and for some reason we had one of the small hotels almost to ourselves, it was such a quiet season. We'd been going out for about three years at the time and that night we got very drunk in the nearby pub. We ended up running round the stones, not realising that there were loads of sheep droppings everywhere. Nigel managed to step in huge great wet piles of them as he chased me, half naked, calling out, 'I want to rip all your clothes off and fuck you senseless, Amanda Elizabeth Curran.' He didn't rip all my clothes off – well, not until we got back to the bedroom anyway – but there was a telltale trail of sheep droppings in the hotel lobby and up the stairs. The next morning at breakfast we were served lightly poached eggs, well-cooked vegetarian sausage, an edible flower and a £90 bill for carpet cleaning. I was just relieved I didn't have to face many other guests that morning.

We arrive at the car park and I unpack the kids, Hunter and a huge picnic of M&S and Waitrose nibbles that I know Hunter will finish off if we don't manage to. We wander over to the stones to find somewhere to sit.

'This one looks friendly,' says Hannah pointing at a looming stone. 'It looks as though it's winking at us.' I unpack the picnic blanket and food beside it as Jack asks about witches again, and whether I know any more stories about being burnt at the stake and did it hurt much.

'Well, some people think these circles are people who were turned into stone many, many centuries ago,' I say, breaking some baguette and laying out the ham and cheese slices for them. 'Legend says they were dancing round in circles when they were enchanted and turned to stone.'

'Will there be any stone circles and witches in Cornwall?' asks Jack, biting into his bread.

'Oh yes, Jack, there are loads of stone circles in Cornwall. And probably loads of witches and ghosts and pirates,' I promise.

'Pirates!' says Hannah, clapping her hands in excitement. 'How wonderful! Do they all look like Captain Jack Sparrow?' She's grinning from ear to ear.

'No, I doubt if they look like Johnny Depp,' says

Jenny, nibbling at a piece of cheese. 'Do you know what pirates used to do to their prisoners?' she continues mischievously.

'No. What?' say Hannah and Jack together, both looking fascinated.

'They used to tie them to the top of their mast and get a long, thin, red-hot poker, then they'd burn their eyes out and tear their skin off—'

'Now stop that, Jenny,' I say, seeing that Jack is about to cry and even Hannah looks horrified.

'Well you started it,' she says cheekily.

'And don't you answer back, young lady.' I glare at her. Jenny gets up and walks away, sulking. To change the subject, I tell the children the censored version about Daddy stepping in the sheep poo and getting told off, which they all find very funny.

Hannah looks after her sister who's still walking off aimlessly in a grump.

I call Jenny back over and suggest that we all go to the gift shop. We buy Skyler some crystals and a divining rod, which the children are so fascinated by that we end up buying one for each of them, and for Rose and Willow. We also get some aromatherapy oils and a bag of crystals for Skyler and the girls, and a few aquamarines for me, which are supposed to be good for patience. I sense I'm going to need a lot of it on this journey, and perhaps for the duration of the holiday.

As we make our way back to the car park, the kids try out their divining rods and head off in different directions, with Hannah ending up on the edge of the road before I manage to stop her. Then the humidity that's been building all day suddenly breaks and large drops of rain start to fall. It's pouring by the time we get back to the car, and we're all sodden.

I bundle the children in and go round to the boot to find dry clothes. I don't want them to start their holiday with colds. Jack and Hannah have no qualms about taking their clothes off, but Jenny's becoming more self-conscious and almost strangles herself trying to change her top without showing any flesh. I get an old towel and rub Hunter down. When they're all settled I realise I'm the wettest and smelliest of the lot, but looking at the time I discover we've spent well over an hour at Avebury already, and I want to get to Skyler's before dark.

I start the car. Cecile immediately announces in her prim tones that we have three and a half hours to go till we reach our destination, then asks me to bear right after two hundred yards, which I do. But as I'm turning I'm hit by the most awful stench of sick, followed by squeals from the back seat.

'Yuck,' howls Hannah, 'Hunter's been sick everywhere, Mummy, all over me.'

Over the next ten minutes I dig out another new set of clothes for Hannah and take a very sorry-for-himself Hunter out of the car, all in the pouring rain. I look accusingly at Jack, who admits that he gave Hunter a bit of bread with some hummus on it because he looked hungry. 'Well, he's got an empty stomach now,' I scold.

I can feel myself getting tense, which may be the result of too much coffee and Green Black's chocolate en route, or the more likely fact that I'm cold and wet, it's pouring with rain, the dog has been sick and we've still got a long way to go. I use some of the aromatherapy oils to mask the stench after I've cleared up, then throw away the old towel, some papers, old books and maps that Hunter's thrown up over and settle everyone down again. With a strong smell of lavender oil and only a faint whiff of dog sick, we head off through increasingly torrential rain towards the motorway.

We pass Bristol a few hours later, the children now sleeping or dreaming out of the window. As we finally reach the junction for the A30, the rain suddenly stops. Hannah and Jack are now on *Ghostbusters II* and Jenny has recovered from her sulk and is able to break into a smile as I comment on how beautiful the surrounding countryside looks in the late afternoon light.

I haven't been to Cornwall for decades; the last time I visited was on a press trip with the Cornwall Tourist Board. It was one of those trips where journalists can bring partners along, which is a bad idea. Partners behave as though they're on holiday whereas journalists, no matter how laid-back they try to appear, are acutely aware that they're not. They know they are on show and any bad behaviour will get reported straight back to their editor, and advertising revenue could be dramatically cut as revenge – something no publisher wants.

On this particular trip, a dashing, arrogant male journalist got off with the pretty but dim PR girl and his partner found out. Subsequently there was a lot of luggage thrown about in the couple's bedroom on the third night and a lot of name-calling. The PR girl promptly resigned the next morning and abandoned the group in a hotel in Falmouth, taking the dashing journalist with her. I think they now have a family and live in Kent. Despite all that, what I saw of Cornwall was wonderful: the beautiful gardens in Trevarno, Tregrehan, Trelowarren, Tresco and Trewidden – in fact, I remember a lot of places beginning with 'Tre', so I'm hoping Skyler's place is signposted.

'What's Willow and Rose's house like?' asks Hannah, and I'm suddenly aware that the skies are darkening and we're still not there yet.

'I've only seen a few photos of it. It's called Silver Trees and it looks beautiful and it's just by the beach,' I explain. 'And I think we've got a cottage to ourselves, which will be good.'

'And when will Daddy be coming down, Mummy?' asks Jack.

'In a couple of weeks, darling,' I say. 'Do you remember, I told you that he has to do a lot of work?'

'*Oh*,' Hannah and Jack say in unison. Even though I've explained to the children that he won't be down, they're still disappointed.

'You know he's working hard for us, darling, so that he can spend more time with us and buy you new things when you want them,' I say, arguing a case I'm not utterly convinced of myself.

'We don't want new things; we want him,' says Jenny, voicing my thoughts exactly.

'He says he will call us every day to let us know when he's coming down and you can speak to him, if you like,' I say, knowing full well that once they're there, they'll have so much to do they will completely forget about calling their dad. For now, though, they all nod, seemingly appeased.

In fact, I'm not really sure what Silver Trees looks like myself. I've surfed for it on the Net loads of times but they still haven't got their website up. Skyler's described it and sent me pictures as it has gradually taken shape, but I haven't seen anything recent. In the end I looked up Tremontgomery, which is the nearest town. It looks charming, although it reminds me slightly of the place in *The Wicker Man*, which is a bit creepy, especially as the Internet blurb mentions that the area is famous for its pagan festivals and spiritual fairs during the summer. As Cornwall has become the playground of London's middle classes, I wonder if they ever end up as the sacrifice.

On the same website I noticed a rather swanky hotel in Tremontgomery called the Elysian. It looked stunning, with a luxurious spa described in flowery prose. It had an indoor and outdoor swimming pool, golf course and tennis courts and looked very sophisticated. I wonder idly whether Nigel and I might go for a romantic dinner there when he's down, but

Cecile interrupts and I concentrate once more on the road.

An hour later, aware of the fact that the sun is setting and we still haven't seen a signpost for Tremontgomery, I disobey Cecile's instructions, which seem to be sending us in completely the wrong direction, and take a road to the left. Cecile is not amused: 'Bearrr rrright in tree 'undred yarrrds . . . bearrrr rrright in too 'undred yarrrds . . . bear rrright in one 'undred yarrrds.'

I don't and Cecile sulks for ten minutes, then starts up again. 'Bearrr right in tree 'undred yarrrds . . . bearrrr rrright in too 'undred yards . . . bear rright in one 'undred yarrrds.'

I still don't bear right.

'Why aren't you doing what Cecile says?' asks Jenny, aware that I'm being disobedient.

'I know a short cut, darling. Cecile doesn't.'

'But she doesn't like it when you go another way. Daddy says she gets quite cross.' Jenny shakes her head at me.

'She's a machine, Jenny. How can she get cross?' I say, continuing on the road Cecile desperately wants me to leave.

'Daddy says she gets all cranky and won't speak to him when he disobeys her, that's all. I'm just telling you,' she says, replacing her iPod earplugs and looking straight ahead.

I decide to turn Cecile off before she starts swearing

at me. Ten minutes later, still with no signs to Tremontgomery, I start to regret my decision and turn her on again. There's no sound, and then the satnav quietly switches itself off and I'm left staring at a black screen.

'See, told you so, Mother,' says Jenny triumphantly. 'Cecile's dead.'

At a crossroads, which is not signposted at all, I stop and reach for the road atlas I keep in the car for just such emergencies. Then I remember I threw it out after Hunter was sick all over it in Avebury. Oh well, I think to myself, it can't be that hard to find. Yet another half-hour later I'm still driving, finding myself on narrower roads, with no pavement or street lamps and no sign of buildings, let alone villages, in sight. I tentatively ask everyone if they're OK.

'Hunter looks as though he's going to be sick again, Mummy,' says Hannah, 'and you need to go to the toilet, don't you, Jack?'

Jack nods enthusiastically in reply.

'We should get to a town sooner or later,' I say hopefully, 'and then we'll ask directions.'

'Do they speak English in Cornwall?' asks Jack.

'Yes, they do, darling,' I say, hoping I don't meet another tourist as lost as I am.

After another fifteen minutes, with Jack and Hannah listening intently to Jenny telling them stories of pirates and witches and unhelpfully suggesting that Silver Trees may be haunted, I realise it's after seven, we're running out of petrol, Jack still hasn't had a toilet stop, and Hunter's making very disconcerting whining noises. We come to a village signposted Trethornan and I try to phone Skyler, but before I can press 'call', the phone dies. Never mind, I'm sure we can find someone who'll let us use their phone.

The village has one pub and four houses, all of which look very dark and unlived in. I stop the car and get Hunter and Jack out as quickly as possible. Hunter splutters up something that looks suspiciously like Maltesers and Jack sneaks behind a tree for a long and patiently awaited pee. Unfortunately he's found a tree surrounded by stinging nettles. He starts to cry, and as I hug him, I feel truly pathetic. I've travelled the world extensively, navigating my way round some of the most confusing cities, but now I've managed to have a spat with my satnav and get lost in my own country.

I see a house with some lights on and knock on the door. No answer. I knock again and finally hear footsteps. An old man opens the door, stares at me and says nothing.

'Hello, I'm sorry to disturb you, but I'm completely lost. I'm looking for Tremontgomery. Do you know where it is?' I ask, smiling, trying not to look too much like a desperate tourist.

'Ten miles up the road on the left,' the man says, 'but I'll just check with my wife.' A woman comes to the door; she's taller than her husband, with long jet-black hair and close-set eyes. She looks like Winnie the Witch.

'Yes, it's about ten miles up on the right. You can't miss it, there's a big signpost, but the road's flooded at the moment after all this rain, so I doubt you'll be able to get through.'

'It's on the left, dear,' the man interrupts.

'No, it's on the right,' she replies, looking at her husband, who shrugs his shoulders and walks away muttering to himself.

'OK,' I say, 'do you know anywhere we can stay this side of the flood tonight? I've got three children and a dog and we're running low on petrol, so if you know of a bed and breakfast where we can stay that would be wonderful.' I realise I now sound completely desperate.

The woman looks at me sympathetically. 'There's a bed and breakfast just a few hundred yards up the road. I don't know if they take pets, but I'm sure they'll have room,' she says with a smile. 'I would put you up here, but we have a full house tonight; my parents are staying. There's a garage just outside Tremontgomery you can get petrol from, should be open tomorrow.'

I thank the woman and return to the car, where Jenny is terrifying Hannah and Jack with tales of Blackbeard. We head up the road to a farmhouse with a small lit sign saying 'Bed and Breakfast – Vacancies' and stop in the car park. This time I get everyone out, hoping the B&B will take pity on us and let Hunter in too. I ring the bell, which clangs solemnly at some far corner of the house.

'I don't like it here,' says Jack, whispering loudly by my side.

'We haven't seen it yet,' I say, 'and anyway, we don't have much choice if the road's flooded, so it's better we have a good night's sleep here and then head for Silver Trees early tomorrow morning. We can leave in time for breakfast,' I add, reassuring myself as much as Jack.

'I was looking forward to the beach barbecue,' says Jenny unhelpfully.

'Me too,' chips in Hannah, gripping her DVD player.

The door creaks open and an old lady with piercing green eyes, a deep look of suspicion and a strong whiff of whisky greets us. It's going to be a long night.

Chapter 3
Last Night I Dreamed of Silver Trees

'You better come in, then,' she says after I've told our woeful tale and she's decided we don't look too threatening.

We all troop in, tired and bedraggled, Hunter bringing up the rear, and make our way to the small reception desk. While the woman looks through the register, I glance round the room. The furnishings are dated, but at least it's clean. It reminds me of the sitting room in my nan's house, where everything was immaculately tidy, despite ornaments in every nook and cranny. She used to make my mum walk on newspaper when she went into the sitting room to save the carpet. The carpet here is frighteningly similar – huge, swirling red, black and orange flowers. There are two orange sofas and a coffee table on which there are lots of heavy, brightly coloured glass ashtrays emblazoned with pictures of maracas. On the mantelpiece are two Spanish flamenco dolls, one a foot high with a red and black skirt, the other half the size wearing yellow and black. I smile: I haven't seen one of those in ages. The children, however, are fascinated by two bees ingeniously made out of yellow and black pipe cleaners that are sticking out of an expansive arrangement of dusty-pink silk tulips.

'We have two double rooms available,' the woman says. 'It's fifty pounds per room. We don't take pets usually, but the dog can go in the garden if you tie him up and he'll cost ten pounds. You have to share the bathroom. Breakfast is served between seven and nine.' She says all of this matter-of-factly, her whisky breath wafting across the reception desk.

'We'll take them,' I say quickly, half relieved, half exasperated. It isn't exactly what I'd envisaged for our first night in Cornwall. No warm welcome, cosy cottage or beach supper, only cold comfort from a woman who looks as though she needs to get a life.

I turn round to find Jack pulling the pipe-cleaner bees so that they are now one long line of yellow and black. The woman eyes Jack.

'And the bees cost an extra ten pounds,' she adds.

I take Hunter out to the garden, which even in the darkness seems to be a fair size.

'You can put the basket here,' the woman says, pointing to the corner of the porch. 'I may have some old blankets, too,' she adds. 'We had a dog once.' She pauses. 'It died.'

'Oh, I'm sorry to hear that,' I reply.

'Yes, Eric killed it by accident when we were out shooting rabbits last year.'

I don't bother to ask who Eric is, but I hope that he's not staying the night. Hunter looks slightly less peaky, so I leave him tied up and go back to the children, who look exhausted.

'Follow me,' says the woman as she walks up the stairs, which are carpeted in the same lurid pattern as the living room. She shows us to two rooms opposite each other. They're simply furnished, with a large old-fashioned oak wardrobe and a queen-sized bed in each. The beds have sheets and blankets, which the children aren't used to and which they are intrigued by. There's a TV and bedside lamps, the shades of which have long dangly bits, perfect for Jack to pull. Everything looks very clean, though, so I'm happy.

The girls take one bedroom, and Jack will sleep with me. Thanks to Jenny's terrifying storytelling in the car, all the children want to sleep with their clothes on, so I have a difficult time getting them into their pyjamas. We're all so full on leftover picnic food and chocolate that no one even thinks to mention dinner. It's too late for baths, so they each have a catlick in the small bathroom at the end of the landing, which has pink knitted dolls covering the toilet roll and stale pot pourri in glass dishes. The bathroom light has one of those energy-saving bulbs that hasn't been fitted properly and flickers on and off as though a fly is caught in the wiring.

After a goodnight kiss and cuddle from me, they each lay their heads on their pillows and fall straight to sleep. I go downstairs and out to the car to fetch Hunter's basket and blanket, returning to the porch to settle him.

Back in my room, I rummage around in my bag, as quietly as I can so as not to wake Jack, until I eventually unearth my phone charger. I dial my voicemail and listen to increasingly frantic messages from Skyler, Nigel and Suzanne, plus one from an estate agent saying he's showing someone round next week and is that all right. It's after eleven but I decide it's still best to call everyone, except the estate agent, obviously.

'I was worried sick about you, darling.' Nigel's voice sounds anxious and relieved at the same time.

'Sorry,' I whisper. 'My phone ran out of juice and we couldn't get to another one, and then it got dark and we were running out of petrol and the dog was sick and Cecile died.'

'She died?'

'Yes, I killed her. I didn't do as I was told,' I say.

'Oh, I'm sure she'll be all right. Typical woman, very temperamental.'

I smile. It's good to hear a friendly voice, even though he's teasing me. I tell him the kids are fine and missing him, and about the musty bed and breakfast we've found ourselves.

'I know Skyler's worried sick, so give her a quick call before she sends out a search party or calls the police,' Nigel advises. 'I miss you,' he says softly.

'I miss you, too. How is everything? Do you know when for sure you'll be down yet?' I ask hopefully.

'In a week or two, that's all I can say at the moment. Only one more person to convince and then I'll have the funds we need. It's my make-or-break week, darling. Pray for me,' he says rather charmingly.

'I always do,' I reply, and suddenly become tearful.

'Have a lovely time, Amanda. And keep the bed warm for me. It's lonely in the house by myself.'

I ask if he's found the meals I left him, and he says he has. We stay on the phone for a few more seconds without saying anything, just listening to each other breathing.

'Love you,' he says finally. 'I'll speak to the children tomorrow. I expect they're all fast asleep. Send them my love.'

'I will, and I love you too, Nigel.'

I sit on the bed for a few moments and have a quiet little cry. Silly really, as I don't know what I'm so upset about. I've been more tired than this in my life, I've had worse journeys, and I've been away from Nigel for longer. I think it's a culmination of everything and the fact that I'm feeling so unsettled at the moment. If only I'd listened to Cecile earlier, then we wouldn't have ended up in this awful place and started our holiday so badly. We all need a holiday desperately. Even the children are feeling the tension between Nigel and me, and this was meant to be a wonderful rest for all of us. With all the worry, I seem to have forgotten how to have fun, and I'm sure I don't laugh as much as I used to.

I snap myself out of my bad mood and call Skyler.

'I'm so happy to hear from you,' a desperate voice answers. 'But why are you whispering?'

'Jack's asleep and we're sharing a room.' I explain about the phone and Cecile, which Skyler finds very funny. She tells me that Tremontgomery is about an hour away from where we are, so it's not as close as we were told.

'Everyone gave us different directions, and in the end we thought there was a conspiracy to get tourists lost.'

Skyler laughs. 'Well, there are some quaint folk round here. We'll see you in the morning. Willow and Rose are desperate to see the children. How are they?'

'All sound asleep but they were desperate to get to Silver Trees tonight, like their mum. I'm so looking forward to seeing you, Skyler. I miss you,' I say, feeling myself getting emotional again. What is the matter with me at the moment?

'I miss you, too,' she says, her voice starting to break as well. I wonder if she's having a tough time at the moment too.

'We can talk properly when I get there,' I say.

'Yes, that would be lovely. We've got a full house, but we'll find time to catch up. I'll *make* time. Well, better let you get some sleep. I'll tell George and Suzanne that you're OK; Suzanne and Orlando have settled in nicely and the forecast for tomorrow is great. Call me tomorrow morning and I'll give you directions from there, OK?'

'OK,' I reply.

*

I don't remember when I fall asleep, but the next thing I know, I wake, still fully clothed, to a sharp knock on the door. I stumble to it and open it a crack.

'We do fried eggs, poached eggs, scrambled eggs, boiled eggs – soft and hard; we do beans, sausages, fried bread, toast – brown, white or malted. We have muesli, fruit juices – orange, grapefruit or tomato.' The woman has woken me at seven to reel this all off at me. Thankfully, the children have all slept soundly.

'Thank you,' I say, still half asleep.

'Like I said last night, we finish serving at nine, *on the dot*. Would you like to order now?' she asks, pen and pad in hand. I wasn't planning to stay for breakfast but now I know how much further it is to Tremontgomery, I figure the kids will be too hungry to wait till we get there. I try to guess at what they'll want to eat.

'Hannah will have beans and sausages. Jack will have a soft-boiled egg with toast. Jenny will have muesli and I'll have a poached egg,' I say, feeling slightly more with it.

'With or without toast?' she asks pointedly.

'Oh, just by itself, that will be fine,' I say, not really caring either way.

I go back to bed and collapse, calculating in my head that I can have another hour in bed and manage to get the kids up and dressed and down for breakfast before nine and still have an early start. But soon there's another knock on the door.

'Hello, hello, Mummy?'

It's Jenny. 'Yes, darling, what is it?'

'It's half past eight and I think we're supposed to be down for breakfast now.'

I sit bolt upright and wake up Jack, who's lying in a deep sleep next to me. He jolts up to join me and promptly bursts into tears.

'Oh, I'm so sorry, darling,' I say, giving him a cuddle.

'That's OK, Mummy,' he says, trying to snuggle back to sleep in my arms.

'Did you sleep well?' He peeps open an eye again, looking suddenly alarmed.

'I dreamed about pirates cutting my eyes out and witches burning me at the stake and then ghosts trying to drown me,' he says.

I really must have a word with Jenny about her storytelling. I hurriedly get Jack dressed and run a brush through my hair.

Thank God the girls have managed to get their shoes on and have washed their faces. We head downstairs, and I half expect, half hope that breakfast is over because then we can make our excuses and head off immediately. But in the small dining room I see three tables have been laid out for breakfast. There are two other couples sitting at the tables. One couple are in their twenties and look disgustingly bright-eyed. They're dressed in running gear and look as if they've already been out. They nod and smile at us but say nothing. The other couple are in their sixties and slurp cups of tea noisily but don't look up.

'Are we too late?' I ask, seeing the woman coming towards me.

'You are late, but we've already prepared breakfast so we'll heat it up for you,' she says with a sigh and turns towards the kitchen.

The children sit at the spare table, by the window. The day looks as though it's going to be a good one. I leave them tucking into some toast and go out to check that Hunter hasn't been shot in the night. The woman has obviously let him run about the huge garden, which backs on to fields, so he's very happy when I greet him, bounding up and licking me to death. When I return to our table, the rest of the food has arrived; it all looks a bit tired, but we've only got ourselves to blame. I tell the children quietly they don't have to eat anything and they play with their food while I say goodbye to £100. So much for a cheap start to the holiday.

Outside, even in the warm glow of morning sun, the house looks tired, with paint peeling off the walls. After we've collected Hunter, we wave goodbye and make our way back to the car.

'I'm still hungry, Mummy,' whines Jack. 'My tummy's rumbling.'

I sigh. 'Well, let's find a place to stop on the way,' I say. I realise Skyler won't be wanting to make breakfast for us all when we arrive; she'll have her guests to deal with.

'Something nice,' says Jack, 'not like here.'

'Yes, something nice,' I say.

After everyone's settled back in the car, I call Skyler. 'Hello, we're on our way, but we thought we'd get some breakfast first. How do we get to you, and is there anywhere we could stop?'

'Well, I have got lots of people to feed this morning, and George has a lot of guests who want to go surfing because the weather's good, so that would probably be easier. You could go to the Elysian. Carry on along that road for about an hour and you'll come to a signpost for Tremontgomery and the Elysian Hotel. Just follow the sign, and tell whoever's on the desk that I sent you. Deborah, the owner, is lovely, so I hope she's there so you can meet her.' I hear her name being called and she tells me she's got to go, then the phone goes dead.

We set off, and after filling up at the first petrol station we come to, I make what turns out to be a silly bet with the children. 'The first one to see the sea gets a pound,' I say, in the hope that they'll start to take note of the wonderful countryside we're driving through and stop burying their heads in the DVD player and Nintendo. Alas, my plan backfires as they spend the next forty-five minutes shouting over each other, 'I can see the sea! No, I can see the sea!' when all they really can see is the sky. For an hour, we drive up and down hills, around sharp bends, past woods, through meadows, some with cows, others with sheep marked with blue, pink and red. Then, before I can tell Jack why the sheep are painted rainbow colours, we drive round a particularly sharp bend and find ourselves looking down over a spectacular vista. The children and I simultaneously scream at the top of our voices, 'I can see the sea!'

'This *must* be Tremontgomery,' I say.

Bordered by rolling hills on all sides, whitewashed stone cottages tip over into a gentle harbour sheltering about ten yachts, some of which look quite grand. It looks very pretty in the morning sunlight and as we wind down the steep road into the town, I can make out a sprawling market just setting up in the square and surrounding lanes. I love markets, whether in France and Italy, where they are colourful and pungent, or in the Far East, where they have an overwhelming vibrancy. Perhaps this won't be quite as exotic, but I can't wait to explore it.

As we turn the corner I lose sight of the town and, in the same moment, Jenny spots a signpost to the Elysian Hotel. I turn the car and head up the long steep drive, bordered by pine trees.

The Elysian is a spectacular, perfectly symmetrical Georgian house with an intimidating front door and two stone lions standing guard. We enter through heavy revolving doors. Jack wants to keep going round and round but I pull him out firmly and frogmarch him into a spacious hallway, with plush beige carpet and oversized cream sofas. On the over-sized round table in the centre of the hall there is an elegant glass vase filled with arum lilies. There are two doors on either side, with a lot of noise coming from what must be the dining room. Four huge, round mirrors cover the walls to our side, and in front of us a Scarlett O'Hara-style staircase sweeps up to a minstrel's gallery above. Dramatic abstract paintings hang on the walls on the second floor and the ceiling rises to a skylight, through which I can see the blue sky with puffs of white cloud beyond. The children follow my eyeline, looking up to the sky and marvelling at the size, drama and grandeur of the place – it's all in such striking contrast to the musky shabbiness of the bed and breakfast we've just left.

Looking down again, I notice there's a long white reception desk to the right with a young girl standing behind it. She looks up, stares at us briefly and then looks down again, probably thinking we'll go away if she ignores us. She's a bit horsey, dressed in tailored black trousers and a thick white cotton shirt, with the collar up. She has a short, neat ponytail tied loosely at the back.

'Why couldn't we have stayed here last night?' whispers Jenny, who prefers luxurious to homely.

'Because it would probably have cost Mummy what Daddy gets paid in a week,' I reply.

The horsey young girl walks up to us. 'Are you all right?' she asks, managing to sound as though she doesn't particularly care if we are or not.

'Would we be able to have breakfast here?' I ask. 'Skyler Blue from Silver Trees said you were the best place to try.'

'I'm not sure if they're still serving breakfast,' the girl pouts.

'Hello, may I help you?' says a rather more genuine voice behind me. I turn to see an elegant woman in her early forties with long blond hair, athletic limbs and a graceful frame. She has a gentle aura about her, although her face is a little hard. She wears a smart, stylish cream linen suit and discreet make-up.

'Oh, thank you. We're staying with our friends the Blues at Silver Trees, but we got waylaid en route yesterday, and—'

'I know Skyler and George,' the woman interrupts. 'I'm Deborah Banks, co-owner of the Elysian. Very pleased to meet you all – Skyler had mentioned you were coming down for the holidays. I'd introduce you to my husband, too, but he's already headed off with some guests to play a round of golf.'

I turn round to introduce the children. Jenny's biting her lip, Hannah's pulling flowers out of the arrangement on the table and Jack's jumping about because he's desperate to go to the toilet. I left Hunter in the car, knowing this would be the sort of establishment that, understandably, wouldn't be keen to welcome dogs.

'We'd were hoping you might still be serving breakfast,' I explain, regaining my composure.

'Of course, but do freshen up first, then I'll show you through to the dining room. Would you like that, children?' She turns to Hannah, Jenny and Jack, who all nod vigorously.

'Thank you,' I say, delighted that I've met a friendly, helpful person at last.

'I'm Amanda Darcey,' I say, offering my hand. 'And this little rabble are my children, Jenny, Hannah and Jack.'

Deborah shakes my hand. 'Well it's a real pleasure to

finally meet you all. Just pop along the corridor to the cloakrooms and I'll wait here. Then we'll have Samuel show you to your table and take your breakfast orders.'

'Erm, is there somewhere I can let our dog out too? We left Hunter in the car but I know he'll need to have a run around.' Deborah doesn't even falter her smile as she graciously nods and turns to the snotty reception girl.

'Lauren, could you take Hunter into the garden, please, and ask Thomas to look after him?' She turns back to me. 'He's the chef's son. He loves animals and he'd be delighted to look after your dog while you have breakfast.'

Lauren nods and smiles; she obviously has a lot more respect for her sweet-smelling boss than she does for us foul-smelling visitors.

Giving my car keys to Lauren so she can let Hunter out, we follow Deborah to the cloakrooms, which are larger than the entire downstairs of our home. The children run into the cubicles – they're obviously more desperate to go to the toilet than I realised – while I check myself out in the floor-to-ceiling mirrors. I look old, tired and scruffy and I smell of musty bed and dog sick. Deborah must have thought she was greeting a bunch of hobos and yet she still managed to be gracious and charming.

'Isn't Deborah lovely?' I say to Jenny as she comes out of her cubicle. 'I'm pleased Skyler's met some nice people round here.'

'Oh Mother, she's got George and Willow and Rose.

And anyway, she's good at making friends,' Jenny replies, a ten-year-old going on twenty.

When Hannah and Jack have finished washing and managed to dry their hands under the automatic dryer, we leave and, at Deborah's direction, walk across the hallway towards the welcoming clamour of the dining room.

It is a large sun-filled room, with floor-to-ceiling patio doors along one side looking out on to ornate manicured lawns. The walls are painted a lemon yellow but are completely bare. The room is filled with about ten round tables, each heavily draped in white linen tablecloths, with a small vase of lilies on top. In the middle of the room there's a grand table laden with the usual breakfast things, plus fresh and dried fruits, all sorts of breads, cheeses, cold meats, smoked salmon and even a tureen of miso soup, Japanese, pickles and steamed rice. A tall, smartly dressed man, whom Deborah introduces as Samuel, shows us to a table on the patio side of the room.

We sit and look through the menu. I smile, because there are eggs – scrambled, boiled, poached and fried – but also egg-white omelettes, duck-egg omelettes, goose-egg omelettes, and the added options of mushrooms, cheese and fresh local ham. I allow the children to order whatever they want and choose the continental for myself. It's expensive, but this is a timely bit of luxury after yesterday's horrendous journey and this morning's cold, limp breakfast.

While I'm helping myself to cereal and dried fruit, I

indulge in a little people-watching. I'm sure I recognise some of the faces and I can imagine somewhere like this would be exclusive enough to lure the rich and famous. Some faces appear well lived in, while others look as though they've had a lot of work done – the skin on their faces plumped up and pulled back, their lips too full and their eyes in a permanently startled expression. I'm sure I recognise one of them as Mr Humpy Fartface from the car park, as the children now call him. Everyone is dressed casually but immaculately, as though they're about to go sailing or running in the latest designer gear. The air smells of all things nice: newly baked bread, freshly ground coffee and just-blooming lilies.

'This is more like it,' Jack says suddenly as his soft-boiled egg appears with toast fingers already cut. We all laugh because he sounds just like his dad.

After we've finished and done a bit more people-watching, I ask for the bill. Handing over a £50 note, I try to think of it as a necessary expense, even though we haven't yet made it to Silver Trees and I've now spent nearly £200, if you include the petrol.

Deborah is smiling and chatting briefly with guests as she greets them at their tables. I watch her slowly make her way over, every inch the consummate professional and natural hostess.

'May I show you around?' she says, coming up to our table.

'Well, that would be lovely,' I say, although I really want to get to Silver Trees now.

'It will only take ten minutes, I promise, and then perhaps you could come back for longer while you're staying with Skyler.'

Leaving a too-generous tip for Samuel, who has eagerly entertained Jack while us girls took our time over finishing breakfast, we follow Deborah back into the hallway and through another door into a sitting room, which also has patio doors looking out on to gardens. There are groups of large, comfortable-looking sofas and long glass-topped coffee tables, piles of the latest glossy magazines, lush pot plants and some stunning abstract paintings and sculptures. Deborah explains that they come from both local and London artists who have lent their work for display. We go through into what she calls the winter sitting room. It doesn't have as much natural light, but there's a large fireplace and more enormous sofas, these covered in ochre throws.

'We also have a spa here offering reflexology, all the usual massage treatments, spiritual healing, and Pilates or yoga sessions with our personal trainer.'

She walks us past the spa and swimming pool without stopping for breath, then outside to the tennis courts.

'We have three grass courts as well as an eighteen-hole golf course, and in a couple of weeks' time we'll be opening our cookery school, launched by Allison Norfolk. We're very excited about it, as you can imagine.' She claps her hands again, as though we should all applaud and Jack, bless him, starts to clap too. 'We have our own vegetable and herb garden and bake all our bread fresh on site each morning,' she continues. 'All the fish comes from the local fisheries, although there aren't many fishermen still fishing round here.'

'Oh, that's a pity,' I say.

'Yes.' She sighs. 'There are still two families, and we buy from them whenever we can.' She nods seriously and we all nod back.

'We have twenty bedrooms, including four suites. Alas, we can't see the sea from here, but the views are rather special anyway.' She turns to me, smiling. 'Silver Trees has sea views and we're very jealous of them.'

'I've never been,' I say. 'This is the first time we've visited.'

'Oh, Skyler and George have done wonderful things with the place, but I won't tell you too much or I'll spoil the surprise. It's quite stunning up there,' she says with a glint in her eye.

We follow her back into the hotel, while Deborah tells us all about the renovations and how they hope to bring more investment to the area. She talks about the Elysian very much as her baby, a project that she's put a lot of love into, and I find myself warming to her. It's much the same way that Skyler talks about Silver Trees. I can't help feeling, though, as I walk around the luxurious hotel, that it feels almost sterile in its perfection and that it is lacking in soul. It has luxury, but its grandeur doesn't substitute the obvious lack of character.

'Well, I think that's everything,' Deborah says as we

return to the reception area. 'Lauren, have you got the directions to Silver Trees?'

Lauren appears from a back room, and hands over a map and some typed directions, which seems excessive, given that Silver Trees is just on the outskirts of the town. Thomas has brought Hunter round to the front of the hotel, and hands him over to Jack with a grin.

'Now, please say hello to Skyler and George, and give Rose and Willow a hug from me, won't you?' Deborah says as we walk towards the car.

'We will,' I say. 'Thank you so much for everything. The food was wonderful – just what we needed.' We pile ourselves back into the car and wind our way down the drive. At last we're on our way to Silver Trees.

Chapter 4

Cabin Fever

The sign for Silver Trees is a large hand-painted wooden panel half covered by brambles at the end of the road. The drive is long and bumpy, the hedge high; I expect to see the house round each corner, only to find yet another long stretch of hedge. Finally, on the third turn, the wall of green gives way to a large courtyard and a beautiful old stone house that takes my breath away.

Silver Trees is about half the size of the Elysian. It's built of warm red and ochre stone and has a pretty light-blue front door topped with a fanlight. There are the original sash windows on each side and the whole of the front is dripping with wisteria and white and pink roses. Two huge old oak trees stand on either side of the house and in front is a small lawn covered with daisies. To the right of the house, leading from the courtyard, there's a stone path that splits into three. One heads towards a small wood, another to what looks like a vegetable garden, while the last leads behind the house, probably to the sea. On the other side of the building is a small gravelled car park bordered by silver birch trees, where I spot George's Land Rover. Gazing back at the house and remembering the early photos, I can see how hard they've worked. With its tall windows and warm stone, smelling the flowers and feeling the wonderful sense of space and cosiness, I can understand why Skyler and George fell in love with it. I think I already have too.

It was a derelict old schoolhouse when George and Skyler first found it. It wasn't even on the market, but the estate agent's friend was thinking of selling it and they just happened to be in the right place at the right time. Skyler being Skyler believes it was fate, but I believe it was luck and determination on their part. They had vision, tenacity, time and, more to the point, George's redundancy money – although I know they had to borrow a lot more money to restore it. I have always admired Skyler's sense of style. In Whitlow she managed to transform her four-bedroom mid-terrace Victorian house into a wonderland of colour and texture. It looked good enough to eat, but not so perfect that it didn't feel like a family home. Having visited her Whitlow neighbour's bland but tasteful house, I was amazed at how two structurally identical houses could be so different.

The children are as transfixed as I am.

'Isn't it lovely? So much nicer than the Elysian,' says Jenny, whom I had assumed would prefer the grandeur of the hotel. She has frighteningly expensive tastes for one so young.

'Yes it is,' I say. 'Do you prefer this to the Elysian too?' I ask the other two.

'Yes, plus Willow and Rose's mummy and daddy own it, so of course we do,' says Jack, while Hannah nods in agreement.

'And I'm sure their breakfasts are just as good,' adds Hannah hopefully, knowing from play dates of old that Skyler is a brilliant cook.

We all clamber out of the car and walk towards the front door. As we approach I hear music, although I can't quite place it. It's only when I walk through the door that the waves of violins flow over me and I recognise the soundtrack of *Pride and Prejudice*, when the young lovers meet and kiss at the end. I'm so overwhelmed and relieved to finally be here, I feel my eyes well up yet again. Thankfully, Jack burps loudly, which brings me straight back to earth. The entrance hall is empty and our shoes are loud on the stone-flagged floors. A beautiful wooden staircase leads up right in front of us, with two entrances on either side, both covered by loose red curtains rather than doors. Between the staircase and the right-hand doorway is a small table on which are photographs of the children sailing, surfing, riding and swimming. On the walls are a selection of Skyler's paintings, all of which I've seen before in her Whitlow house, although they seem smaller now. Beside the table is a wonderful chair in the shape of a jester's hat.

'Look, Mummy,' says Jack, running and jumping on it. 'It has feet on the end of its legs,' he says, and so it does.

I look up to the left of the door, where a brass bell on a pulley hangs halfway up the wall. This must be the old school bell, but I don't dare touch it.

All the lower interior walls are of the same warm stone as the outside, and the floors are polished wood. I gaze up at the ceiling to see a small chandelier with curtains of crystals hanging down like waves of raindrops reflecting light off the walls. There are three huge circular mirrors opposite us, leading up the stairway. They look just like the ones at the Elysian, and I wonder who thought of the idea first. They certainly look more in keeping here.

We can hear voices to the right and pull back the curtain to find a large dining room. The round tables are covered by cream tablecloths and simple vases of jasmine, its glorious scent filling the room. Sitting at the largest table are three women in their forties. One of them, who's all tits and lips, is clearly eyeing up George, who's oblivious to the attention as he serves toast to one of the other tables. Two smart-looking men sit opposite the women at the same table, and on another sit a couple of unhappy-looking fifty-something women, both wearing bright yellow sundresses.

Skyler is serving breakfast to one of the miserable women. She looks up and when she sees us she nearly drops the plates.

'Amanda! You've made it!' she calls out, just managing to put the plate on the table before dashing over to us. Willow and Rose suddenly appear behind their father with dishes of jam and marmalade. They all look up and smile broadly, but continue to serve the ladies, who also look up to see who's receiving such a warm reception.

Skyler gives me a huge hug, then bends down to hug Jenny, Hannah and Jack in turn. She's wearing a small orange apron around her waist, at least three cotton tops in varying shades of green and brown, and a petrol-blue chiffon skirt that could easily double as a petticoat. She looks like a rather splendid, funky fairy. It's so good to see her again. Rose and Willow are mini versions of their mother in little chiffon skirts and tops in brown and green, while George is wearing loose grey cords and a smart dark-green T-shirt. They all look very happy, healthy and tanned; in fact, I've never seen George look so well. All this fresh air must be doing him good.

'We're still serving breakfast, but we're nearly done.' Skyler smiles. 'I'll get George to finish off, though, so that I can show you the cottage and get you settled in, OK?' she says, looking down at the children and grinning. 'Have you eaten?' she asks.

'Yes, we ate at the Elysian,' I say.

'Oh, good. Did you meet Deborah? She's so nice. The hotel's swanky and a bit pricey, but lovely. She's worked very hard on it,' says Skyler, smiling at me.

'I'll tell you all about everything later on; we'll just

wait here to say hi to George,' I say, looking over Skyler's shoulder and realising the two women she was serving are trying to attract her attention again already.

Skyler heads back over to them. It seems they want to complain about the eggs being overdone. I can hear Skyler apologise and say she'll make some more if that will help, but the ladies refuse, saying they'll be fine but not to let it happen again. From their accents I detect they're American, possibly West Coast. They're both very thin, with pointy noses and chins. Skyler turns back to me, still smiling, and winks.

'The customer is always right,' she whispers as she walks past me, 'even when they're wrong and rude.'

George comes over, brushing himself down.

'Hello, everyone,' he says, and gives us all a hug. He's lost some weight but doesn't look gaunt, just healthy. In Whitlow he always looked grey and tired.

Rose and Willow run up and the children all jump up and down with excitement and hug like long-lost friends. Willow and Jenny used be to best friends when they were in the same class at school and it seems that time hasn't faded their bond as Jenny's face lights up more than I've seen in weeks. Rose gets on with Hannah like they're twins, as they're both eight and on the tomboyish side. Of course, both Willow and Rose adore Jack too, and I suspect he has a crush on them both as he follows them around like a lovesick puppy; he'd never pay that much attention to Jenny and Hannah, that's for sure!

'I'd love to stop and chat, Amanda,' George says,

kissing me on both cheeks, 'but I've got to sort out the outdoor activities for the guests. We're doing a bit of coasteering today.'

'What's that?' asks Hannah.

'It's a lot of fun; it's walking, jumping and running by the sea and along the cliffs and rocks. It's ever so slightly dangerous but very exciting. I think you're just about old enough, so your mum might let you have a go while you're here if you fancy it.'

I can tell by Hannah's face that she does, but before she can ask to join them, Jack is already asking about the beach.

'Can we go, Mummy? Can we go out and play on the beach now? Oh, please can we?' he asks, not stopping for breath. Skyler's returned from the kitchen and is smiling at him, waiting to take us down to the cottage.

'Not right now, darling,' I say. We follow Skyler out of the dining room and into the hallway. 'Let's find Orlando and Suzanne first and then we can have a walk later to get our bearings.' The children don't look convinced, but walk along behind me anyway, chatting away to Rose and Willow, who're grinning from ear to ear and have already linked arms with Jenny and Hannah.

Willow has long wavy brown hair like her mother, tied up in bunches today. She's the same age as Jenny, but is very feminine and floaty. Rose is darker and very pretty, with large blue eyes like her father.

As we walk, I think how much George has changed. I remember when, about a year before they moved to

Cornwall, Skyler asked to meet me in the local coffee shop. She was in tears when I arrived.

'George isn't the man I married, Amanda,' she said, sipping her herbal tea. 'He always comes home late from work, tired and stressed. He's short with the children and irritable with me. We had an argument last night about whose responsibility it was to remember to buy the toothpaste. Isn't that petty? He was shouting, I was tired and had had a long day with school and the girls, and I shouted back, but then he suddenly started to cry. He just broke down and collapsed on the floor. He's gutted about Charlie dying of cancer and he told me if he carried on like this he feared he'd end up dying of a heart attack or something. He told me he didn't know what life was about any more. That he wasn't having any fun.'

It wasn't long afterwards that Skyler told me about their move. Strangely, I can sense that whether Nigel's deal happens or not, it may be the right time for a change for us as well. I don't feel like I've had fun for a long time and I'm certainly not seeing enough of Nigel. Things are starting to feel very reminiscent of what Skyler went through with George.

We're walking down one of the stone paths through the woods now.

'This path leads to the two cottages,' Skyler explains. 'We let them throughout the year. The other path on your right leads to the vegetable garden.' She points to where I can see some runner beans on bamboo poles.

'We've been growing our own vegetables since we arrived. Everything grows well in this climate. We thought we knew a lot about plants before we came here, but we've learned so much more. To be fair, though, we've spent a lot more time than we thought renovating and setting up the business.' She sighs. 'But we've started to focus on the gardens this year and it's been fun.' She smiles, obviously proud of her little vegetable patch.

'Have you visited much of the area while you've been here?' I ask. 'Minack or the Eden Project, or the Tate in St Ives?'

'None of them; we haven't had the time,' Skyler replies sheepishly.

'That happens everywhere, Skyler,' I say, putting an arm round her. 'I know people who live in the West End of London and have never been to the theatre in their lives. Tourists sometimes see more of places than the people who live there.'

Skyler laughs, her eyes sparkling in the sunshine as she brushes her hands through her gypsy-like hair. She looks back briefly at Willow, who's listening to Jack recount the story of Fishbowl nearly being left behind. Rose is telling Hannah where the best climbing trees are to be found, and Jenny has broken away from the group, trying to catch hold of Hunter's lead. He's full of energy and desperate to run free, having being cooped up for most of the past twenty-four hours.

Skyler leans into me. 'Rose has a friend called Terry,' she whispers.

'Well, that's good,' I say, slightly nonplussed.

'Except Terry doesn't exist. Well, we don't know if he does or not,' says Skyler, looking back at her daughter, 'but we think it's one of those imaginary friends children sometimes have. We're worried that perhaps she hasn't integrated as well as Willow, which is odd as we thought she'd find it easier, what with her love of the outdoors and sports. And it has been almost two years since we moved.'

'She looks happy enough,' I say, looking round at her. 'Is she getting on well at school?'

'Oh yes, there's no problem there, it's wonderful. It's a tiny local school but with good teachers – some of them are from London themselves, mainly because they couldn't afford London prices,' she says.

'Rose looks happy,' I say, turning round and looking at her. She's talking to Hannah, describing in vivid detail the beach, the crabs, the old bits of wood belonging to pirate shipwrecks and about what we're going to cook for supper tonight.

'I've asked Willow if her sister has confided in her and she says that Rose definitely thinks Terry exists and that he's probably a ghost, but a nice one.' Skyler shrugs.

'Do you think Silver Trees is haunted?' I say more quietly, as I know Hannah has elephant ears. What I don't anticipate is that Skyler will give such a sincere answer.

'Yes, we think so,' says Skyler also in a whisper. 'It used to be a schoolhouse run by nuns, and when we first arrived and looked around, all the desks were still neatly laid out facing blackboards, and there were crucifixes on every wall. Upstairs there were dormitories, and we even found a dunce's hat, which we threw away because it's bad karma to keep something like that in the house.'

'What are you two whispering about?' interrupts Jack.

'Nothing important, sweetheart,' I say, keen to get off this eerie subject. Skyler grins conspiratorially.

'Thankfully, we've managed to find a good state school, but I still make an effort to go to the local church occasionally because it's a good way to get to know the community. We've also met a lot of people through the Tremontgomery tourist office. Helen Albertson's the tourist officer; and there's Peter, the local baker; Clare, who's our only full-time employee, and two girls who help us out cleaning the bedrooms when we're really busy.

'So you don't miss London just the teensiest bit? The traffic, the roadworks, the supermarkets, the nightlife?' I tease. We've come to a grassy clearing. I see a large stone cottage ahead and let out an involuntary squeal of delight.

Laughing, Skyler replies, 'I miss the convenience and edginess of urban life, though not the dirt and noise, and as for the nightlife, I didn't really see much of that because when George wasn't working endless hours, we were always in with the kids, watching TV and having dinner parties. In many ways we were more isolated there than we are here. Yes, it can be a bit parochial occasionally here, but you get narrow-mindedness wherever you go. Whitlow people always seemed to think they were the centre of the universe. At least here we realise we're not, but we're happy to be in the world we're in and, well, just be contented,' she says smiling. 'I miss teaching the boys, though. I loved that job. But when I first saw the schoolhouse I felt the place spoke to me, you know?' Skyler stops and turns to me. 'It said, "Buy me!" and I knew from the moment I walked through the front door that it was right. We had to completely gut it, and upstairs was mostly one big dormitory, so it needed partitioning off, but we've done it and I feel the house is thanking us for it, because so far we've been pretty busy, the guests have mostly been lovely, and fortune has shone on us.'

Before I have time to ask any more questions, Skyler stops at the front door of the cottage. 'Oh, one thing I forgot to mention: because Suzanne didn't tell me she was coming until so late, I'd already booked all the rooms in the main house and the other cottage, so you'll have to share this one with her for the first week or so. I'm really sorry, I hope you don't mind.'

I can feel the hairs on the back of my neck rise. It's not a voluntary reaction and perhaps I've just caught a cool breeze. I can see it's going to be close quarters for us all, but I don't want to put Skyler out or make her feel bad about the lack of room; after all, it was my idea for Suzanne to join us at the last minute.

'Don't worry, Skyler, that's not a problem at all,' I say, telling myself not to be ridiculous. 'Suzanne and I will be fine and the kids get on great.' Nevertheless, as we walk in I can't help but worry. Suzanne has a very different attitude to parenting and housekeeping to mine. She gets someone else to do everything in her house and has very little to do with Orlando. The poor boy goes to so many clubs and play dates at other people's houses that I marvel that he recognises his parents sometimes. In addition, Suzanne doesn't like dogs in her home because she doesn't like mess, so Hunter will probably have to stay outside.

It should be fine, though. Really.

'Cooee, Suzanne, are you in?' Skyler shouts from the tiny hallway. We hear Suzanne calling, 'I'm coming,' and she bounds down the stairs, dressed head to toe in classic country Burberry. She almost looks like something out of *Horse and Hound*. She stands on the lowest stair, her arms open as if welcoming us to her country manor. I can't help but chuckle and then she gives me a huge bear hug that I find quite touching, if a bit awkward.

'Oh, I'm so pleased to see you, Amanda,' she says, smiling broadly. 'I was really worried about you. I thought you'd been kidnapped by the Cornish National Front, or whatever they're called!'

'Kidnapped!' I laugh.

'Well, you never know. They don't want Londoners down here, do they? I thought they might hold you for hostage or something. But you're in one piece, you're safe and you're here. Come in. How about a Bloody Mary after that terrible trip? It'll calm your nerves and warm your toes! I've just made a lovely big jug for us all!' I must look surprised, because she laughs and says, 'It's my instinctive reaction to being surrounded by so much nature, Amanda.' I cannot imagine how the Cornish landscape inspires a need for vodka and tomato juice, but hey, we're on holiday, finally, so I nod and say, 'Why not?'

Orlando is standing to attention just behind his mother. Like her, he's dressed immaculately, in a striped blue and white Gant shirt and gilet with loose brown cords and Timberlands. He looks like a mini-banker.

'Hello, Mrs Darcey,' he says, as though I'm his schoolteacher, and offers me his hand. I ignore the hand and hug him, because I'm sure the boy doesn't get enough hugs. I'll be amazed if he grows up normal with parents like Suzanne and Howard. 'Don't call me Mrs Darcey, call me Amanda,' I say, hoping that if we're all living together he'll at least be able to relax enough to call me by my first name.

As I sip the perfectly chilled Bloody Mary Suzanne has given me, Skyler, who sensibly declined hers, shows me around. The cottage is charming, a smaller version of the house. It's made of stone, with wild roses and clematis growing up the side. There's a small kitchen, beautifully fitted out with a microwave, oven and a dishwasher (I say a silent prayer of thanks for that at least). There's also a little reading bench by a window with a stunning view of the sea. The sitting room has two large yellow sofas, a TV,

DVD player and mini hi-fi. At the far end there's also what looks like a stone pizza oven.

'Did you put that in?' I ask Skyler, as she lets my three in to have a look around.

'No. It's nice, though, isn't it? And very unusual,' Skyler replies. 'The other cottage has one as well, so perhaps the original owners were Italian. The cottages were for the men who worked in the school grounds, and they may have emigrated here, who knows?' She walks over to the other side of the room. 'Here's the bathroom,' she says, opening a door under the stairs. It's small, with a toilet, basin and shower, but alas, no bath. Jack will not be pleased. He likes his baths.

As if reading my mind, Skyler says, 'The children can use our bathroom at the main house if they want. It's huge, with two baths in it. They'll love it.'

Comforted by that thought, I head up the stairs behind Suzanne to have a look at the bedrooms. Suzanne's is well proportioned, with a large window looking over the woods and the main house. She's already put her clothes away, all colour co-ordinated on hangers or neatly piled up. Orlando is sleeping on a single mattress on the floor, despite the fact that the bed is a six-foot cherrywood bateau-lit with enough space for six. The duvet is cerise pink and the pillows lime-green, but the colours work beautifully. There are paintings of Venice and Rome and a large vase of sunflowers that look real but can't be. Over the window there's a striking curtain of red, orange and yellow cloth hearts. A door leads out to a terrace that overlooks the sea and beach below. There's even a small barbecue, round table and six chairs, as well as a large orange parasol.

'This is where we can have our afternoon Kir Royales, don't you think?' says Suzanne, as she looks at the view and then back at Skyler and me.

We leave Suzanne admiring the view, and having discreetly poured away the rest of my too-strong drink in the kitchen, I follow Skyler into what will be my room for the next few weeks. There's an identical bed, this one with a dark ochre duvet and deep maroon pillows. The room is enough for Nigel, me and all the kids to sleep in without feeling squashed. A mirror with brown velvet rims hangs on the pale-yellow walls, and there are large framed photographs of couples kissing and one of a very pert bottom. 'We call this the bottom room for obvious reasons,' Skyler says, 'and Suzanne's is the Venetian room.'

'This is stunning, Skyler,' I say, 'absolutely stunning; you really have put your mark on it.'

'Yes, we've worked hard. We've had to be quite resourceful, but we're very happy with what we've achieved so far. There's always more to do, of course, but we're getting there.' She lets Hannah, Jack and Jenny come through to see where they'll be sleeping for the summer.

'Are we all going to sleep in here?' asks Jenny, looking at the large bed.

'Well, I have mattresses for you if you want to sleep separately and there's still one more room,' Skyler says, perhaps aware that Jenny, being the eldest, might want her own room, 'although it's small and the views aren't as nice.' Jenny looks much happier at the thought of having her own bedroom, while Jack and Hannah are busy bouncing up and down on the bed, as if it's a huge trampoline.

'I'll leave you all to settle in,' Skyler says, walking back down the stairs. 'Come to the house when you're finished and I'll show you around the grounds. Perhaps Willow and Rose can take the children on a personal tour. Then we can all go to the beach. Does that sound like a good idea?'

We spend the rest of the morning unpacking the car, hauling our bags up to the cottage and finding places to put our clothes. I take another quick peep into Suzanne's room. She seems to have brought enough clothes to last her a year, while I've strictly limited everyone to five T-shirts, two pairs of trousers, five pairs of socks and pants and a skirt each for the girls, plus wellies, trainers and sandals. And we're here for five weeks. I'm anticipating doing a lot of washing. I just hope we won't be invited to too many smart dos, though Suzanne has obviously packed as if we will be.

Thankfully, Skyler has been true to her word and there are fresh towels for everyone, as well as soap, shampoo and conditioner. I know Suzanne gets her hair done once a week, so I don't know how she's going to cope, although I'm sure she'll track down the swankiest salon in Cornwall. Come to think of it, the Elysian had a hair salon in their spa, so perhaps I'll recommend she goes there if she feels a bad hair day coming on.

Downstairs, I find the kitchen is fully stocked with tea, coffee, fresh milk, hot chocolate, cereals, juices, a family-sized chocolate bar, and even a bottle of champagne.

Once we've all freshened up, we head towards the main house and find Skyler in the kitchen. I hand over the gifts we bought in Avebury and spend a few moments chatting about the place, which Skyler knows well.

'Come on, then, let's have a walk around the house and grounds,' Skyler says. 'Then we can have some lunch.' She leads us back through to the hall, and into the sitting room. It's huge, with a high, beamed ceiling, three enormous sofas and about eight large comfy chairs around coffee tables. On the far side of the room is a plasma-screen television. There's a bookcase set into the adjacent wall, and two more round mirrors.

As we walk upstairs, Skyler tells me about the guests. 'There's a Dutch family, the Schneiders, staying in the other cottage. They're always up at the crack of dawn. They have three children. The mother's called Penny and the father's called Maarten. They're a nice family and the kids are fun. They do loads of outdoor stuff with George. Then we have three women in these three bedrooms,' she says, pointing to three closed doors, 'who are escaping their families for a week. Nicola, Fay and Edina all come from London, and I think Nicola and Fay both have a soft spot for George, so he's quite in demand at the moment,' she adds with a wry smile. 'Next we have two gay lawyers, who are like peas in a pod, Peter and Paul Smith. They're charming and tease the three painted ladies, as they call them. You'll like them' – she winks at me – 'they've got a wicked sense of humour. We also have a couple of women from LA.' She drops her voice. 'They came last year and complained about everything, but they're back again this year, so they obviously liked something about the place. It's very tiring having them around, though.'

'As long as they make you money,' says Suzanne pragmatically.

'Yes, we need the money at the moment,' agrees Skyler. 'We're full, and we have to keep it that way all summer. Now, here's the family bathroom that you can use.' She opens a door into a large bathroom with two freestanding baths, two sinks, floor-to-ceiling windows and patio doors opening on to a terrace. A translucent red curtain is draped over half the window and an ornate mirror hangs over the sinks. Strings of crystals stream down from the high beams, and there's a big tapestry of horses and unicorns on the wall. The bare wooden floor has five or six rugs thrown about on it and the effect is deliciously decadent.

'We can't go into any of the bedrooms at the moment as the guests are still here, but Clare will be changing the beds soon, so you can take a peek then, if you like,' she adds, leading us along the corridor.

'I'm glad to see you have staff,' says Suzanne. 'It gives a good impression of professionalism you know.'

'Oh Clare, yes, she's wonderful, and what's even

better, she's local. She was born in Tremontgomery, so she knows all about the house, the area and everyone in it. She's been a mine of information about the area and has given us loads of useful contacts. She helps with everything: the cooking, gardening and cleaning, even does a bit of babysitting when we're busy with guests or trying to do the accounts. I don't know what we'd do without her. She doesn't like the painted ladies, though; she says there aren't enough good men to go around as it is, without having to compete with married women.'

As we walk down the stairs we see what must be the Schneider family standing in the hall, Penny and Maarten in front, and the three boys close behind. They look as though they've already been out for a morning hike. The children all have striking white-blond hair, shiny clean faces and piercing blue eyes. They look unnervingly like the children in *Village of the Damned* but they're smiling enthusiastically at my three, while the parents say a polite good morning. Penny is wearing a loose top in an attempt to camouflage her very ample bosom, and a pair of jogging pants that look a tad too small for her wide hips. This is in contrast to her husband, who is all taut, lean muscle, and is wearing tight dark-grey cycling shorts and a matching vest that leave nothing to the imagination. I can hear the girls giggling behind me while Skyler and I try to avert our eyes. Suzanne, meanwhile, blatantly stares at Maarten's crotch, positively transfixed by the man's evident charms.

'Have you enjoyed your walk this morning?' asks Skyler, beaming a winning smile at her guests.

'Yes, thank you,' replies Maarten, 'we all enjoyed.'

'Good. And can I help you with anything now?'

'Is the horse-riding arranged for after lunch? I think with Tom MacKenny and Matt, yus?' Maarten asks.

'Yes, that's it. George will take you to Tom's stables at about two,' Skyler says, looking at her watch.

'Goot, goot, that's goot,' Maarten says, clapping his hands, slightly agitated by Suzanne, who's still staring at his cycling shorts in blatant admiration. I nudge her and she looks at me.

'What?' she says, looking totally innocent.

Before I have time to answer 'You know what', the Schneiders bound back outside and head for their cottage.

'He was fit,' says Suzanne, still looking on as the door closes.

'Howard's fit as well, Suzanne,' I say. 'All those trips to the gym must be doing him some good.'

'Oh Amanda, that's very sweet of you, but he looks bloated and tired at the moment. Too many late nights with clients, drinking all the time. He's fat and out of condition. You saw him at sports day, he didn't even finish the dads' race. It was so embarrassing. At least Orlando could rely on me to win, and to be honest, it wasn't exactly challenging.'

'And as modest as ever,' I interrupt, smiling at her and knowing that I'd puffed my way to the finishing line – there was some tough competition this year.

She laughs. 'Yes, yes, I know, but anyway, Howard looked bloody awful, an utter mess. Orlando was terribly disappointed. He didn't show it at the time, but I could tell; after all, no one likes to see their daddy look like utter crap,' she says matter-of-factly.

'No, they don't,' interrupts Skyler, who has over-heard the last bit of the conversation and is chuckling to herself, knowing Suzanne's typically high standards all too well. 'Now, if you can stop letching over my guests, I'd like to show you the grounds.'

'Nothing wrong with window shopping,' Suzanne says, heading out the door, only to be called back by Skyler and told she's going the wrong way. We walk instead through the sitting room and out on to the terrace. There we find Paul and Peter Smith, the lawyers, who are dressed in matching blue sweaters and long grey shorts.

'Hello,' says Skyler, 'what are your plans for the day?'

'Oh, we thought we'd go into town for lunch and look around, though we heard there's a fair or some-thing on tomorrow, so we may leave it till then. We haven't had a chance to wander and explore properly yet. We've just been lazing around here and enjoying your beautiful home,' says one Mr Smith.

'We were thinking of practising some scenes from Wuthering Heights on the clifftops, but thought it might scare the birds,' says the other, who's slightly taller than his companion, with a chiselled face and a wicked glint in his eye.

'The fair's tomorrow. It starts at about ten, I think,' says Skyler.

On the corner of the terrace three women are sitting at their easels. 'Hello, Nicola,' says Skyler, greeting a tall, dark-haired women with a bottle tan. 'How's the painting going?' She peers over to look at the half-completed canvas.

'Very well, thank you,' replies Nicola, showing us a half-finished scene of the woods from the house. 'What do you think?'

'Beautiful,' comments Skyler as all the children gather round and admire her work. 'I like your use of colour and texture,' she says wistfully. I can sense how much she misses teaching art. 'I told you about the fair tomorrow, didn't I? Perhaps you'll be inspired by some of the scenes there,' Skyler says, passing them and leading us along the pathway.

'Skyler, can we have a word with you about the hot water?' One of the American ladies has appeared from nowhere and startles us all.

'Yes, of course, Ms Pepsin, how can I help?'

'It's too hot,' Ms Pepsin says, puckering her lips into a contorted smile so that her mouth becomes a mass of wrinkles.

'Oh right,' Skyler replies. 'Have you tried mixing it with some cold water?' she adds, trying very hard not to sound patronising.

'Of course I have, Skyler,' she says, retaining the fixed smile, 'but the hot water is so hot it's scalding; poor Adeline nearly burnt herself this morning and, well, back home we could easily sue for such things. It really isn't good enough.' Ms Pepsin shakes her head slowly, still smiling.

'Sorry to interrupt,' says Suzanne, stepping forward

unexpectedly, 'but I couldn't help overhearing. I wonder whether I can be of help. I've had exactly the same problem in the cottage and found that it works better if you run the cold tap for a few seconds before you add the hot, then it just seems to be the perfect temperature. It's worth trying.' Suzanne is calm but firm, and she doesn't smile.

'Oh, er right,' says Ms Pepsin, slightly taken aback, 'I'll try that.'

Suzanne continues to soft-soap her: 'We have the same problem where we live in London. It's the quaint plumbing we have in the UK; nothing as efficient as in the States, but it has a charm all its own.'

'Yes, quite,' Ms Pepsin replies, nodding to thank Skyler, then turning and walking away.

'Does that really work?' Skyler asks, turning to Suzanne.

'I've no idea, Skyler, but she's happy, and now we can go and have our lunch in peace.'

Chapter 5
Wish You Weren't Here

After lunch, the children disappear off with their divining rods and we spend a happy hour walking around the grounds, occasionally hearing screams when they think they've found gold. Skyler tells us the story of the renovation: arguments with builders over bills and schedules, cooking on a two-hob gas stove for three months and living without heating for six – fine in the summer but miserable in the autumn, which was particularly cold that year.

'It's never as easy as you think,' says Suzanne, whose own house has only just been finished.

'No, and we always knew it was going to be tough so we'd set ourselves a strict budget and timetable. But there's always something that comes up, no matter how many contingency plans you have – we always seemed to have to wait an extra month for the plumber to show up or pay a few thousand pounds more for something than we'd expected,' she says, looking tired but happy. 'We had a vision and we were enthusiastic and determined. We couldn't have done it unless both of us were totally committed to the idea.'

I'm pleased for her. I could sense her passion through the emails and postcards she'd written – about how lovely it was to bring the kids to the country, to live by the sea and get away from the big smoke. Whenever I'm stuck in traffic, drowning in road rage, I think of those notes and dream about doing the same with my family, weighing up the practicalities with the promise of fresh air and safe, open spaces. But if I'm honest, my family seems to thrive on an environment that's cosmopolitan and edgy. Whitlow, for all its faults, has the right combination of urban and rural. And who am I kidding? I have an overwhelming feeling I'd get bored in the countryside. Plus it may be wonderful in the summer, but in the long, cold, dark winters I think I'd get cabin fever.

As Skyler leads us down a path and through the woods to the lake, she tells us about some of the characters she's had to deal with since they opened.

'We've been lucky with Clare and the other girls, but we've had a few hiccups. We hired a guy called Colin to oversee the renovations, which were going well, but halfway through Colin became Colleen and started wearing dresses and skirts to work. He now lives in Brighton with his girlfriend. Then there was Dagmar and Eberhard, a Swedish couple who lived locally and helped us source the kitchen furniture and sofas. They had lots of great ideas about how to decorate the house, but they were also into swinging and kept propositioning us; it was hilarious, really, but when they didn't get the message we thought it best to politely tell them that their services were no longer required. And finally there was Leon the plumber, who wouldn't stop talking, moaning about his ex-wife mainly, and always brought his three-year-old daughter with him to work. I love children, you know I do, but she was a devil-child, always freaking out Willow and Rose. Other than that he did a good job. In the end, we got good contacts through friendly locals. Helen Albertson, the local tourist rep, put us in touch with Clare, and she introduced us to Tom MacKenny, who has the stables. Matt Charlton helps Tom; he used to be a fisherman and he's a fantastic surfer, so he also takes people surfing, sailing and coasteering.'

As we leave the woods and head on a narrow path towards the henhouse, the children rush up, finished with their gold exploration. 'There must be a huge ex-London community round here,' says Suzanne.

'Oh, there is,' says Skyler, taking Jack and Hannah by the hand and guiding them along the path. 'But they tend to keep themselves to themselves and we made a conscious decision when we moved to try to integrate with the Cornish locals.'

Skyler shows the children where they have to come to collect the eggs in the morning if they want to help out. Rose shows Jack and Jenny the runner beans and lettuces, allowing Jack to have a few strawberries, while Hannah and Orlando are led by Willow to pick some of the ripe cucumbers and tomatoes for supper.

'Your life here seems idyllic, Skyler,' says Suzanne, gazing at the children as they attempt to collect vegetables and fruit.

'In reality it's not quite as idyllic as we'd dreamed of, but we are so much happier here. It's hard work. My day starts at six in the morning, and my head doesn't usually touch the pillow till midnight, but I sleep well, I'm outdoors most of the day and have never felt more fulfilled. I'd like to paint more, but it's a small price to pay and I'm sure I'll be able to get down to it when it gets quieter in the autumn and winter.'

She leads the way through the vegetable garden on to a stunning but narrow coastal path.

'Lovely views,' says Suzanne nervously. 'I hope the children are going to be OK,' she adds as they run on ahead, totally oblivious to the danger, or perhaps excited by it. They can see the beach below and I know they're desperate to get to the sand and sea as quickly as possible. The beach is totally deserted, but as I look back for a second, someone I recognise is coming towards us. It's Deborah Banks, looking slightly incongruous in her immaculate suit against such rugged terrain.

'Hello, Skyler,' she says, 'I was just dropping off those spare lamps we had.'

'Oh, thanks so much,' Skyler replies. 'They'll be perfect for the blue room.' She gives Deborah a gentle hug and two air kisses. Deborah looks flushed and windswept. I introduce her to Suzanne, and they seem to warm to each other instantly.

'So you're not local,' says Suzanne.

'No, I moved here from London when I got married to Dennis. I used to live in Islington,' Deborah explains.

'Oh, do you know Roger Horton?' Suzanne asks.

'Yes. He's a good friend of Dennis's business partners. How do you know him?' I'm always astounded at Suzanne's ability to find a connection with anyone new that she meets. I guess that's PR for you.

'I work in the same bank as him,' explains Suzanne. 'He told me he was involved in a hotel development in Cornwall.'

'Do you have children?' I ask Deborah, noticing her expression as she watches our brood, who, led by Willow and Rose, are carefully picking their way down to the beach.

'Yes, a boy called Jeremy; he's twelve and he goes to boarding school. He's at a summer camp at the moment.' She looks a bit disheartened, but quickly changes the subject. 'We're having a party next week to launch our new cookery school. Skyler and George are coming, and I wondered whether you would both like to come too. It's going to be a lovely bash with loads of champagne – and good food, of course.'

'We would absolutely love to,' replies Suzanne before I even have a chance to react. 'What a kind gesture. I hope I've got something suitable to wear,' she adds, obviously forgetting the seventeen designer dresses she's brought with her.

'That would be lovely, thank you,' I manage to add.

'Well, I must dash, but look forward to seeing you then, if not before.' Deborah beams at us and quickly walks back along the path as we head down to the beach.

On the way down, Skyler points out the best places to see whales and seals.

'There's very little fishing here now – the fishermen sold all their rights, but there are two local families left who catch mackerel and lobster. Otherwise it's mostly yachts in the harbour these days.'

'Is business good all round?' I ask as we make our way carefully down the steps to the sand.

'In summer it is, but in the winter it's a bit slow, although there are high hopes for the Elysian bringing in a winter crowd.'

As we walk on to the beach, even Suzanne can't resist taking her shoes off and going barefoot. The sand is cool and soft, and it makes me think of my childhood holidays spent on numerous beaches, running back and forth to escape the waves, being hypothetically killed if I got caught out by one, and writing my name in the sand with my heel in large bold strokes. Nothing beats seaside holidays and I can see my children are as enamoured of its simple pleasures as I used to be. Even Orlando is laughing, and I've never even seen him genuinely smile before.

Suddenly Suzanne points to some people climbing over the rocks at the end of the bay.

'Who are they?'

'The Schneiders, I think,' says Skyler, peering for a few seconds at the figures scrambling over the rocks and wading through the water. 'They must have decided to do some coasteering instead of riding. They'll be with Matt. Do you think it's something the kids would like to try?' she says, looking at us.

'George mentioned it earlier,' I say. 'I don't see why we couldn't all have a go.' I turn to Suzanne, who looks horrified until she realises I'm joking and giggles.

'I don't see why not,' she says. 'We're both game girls.'

That evening we get properly settled into the cottage, finishing the unpacking and putting Hunter's basket and blanket in the corner of the sitting room. Suzanne seems to be OK with Hunter being inside, but he's under strict instructions to stay downstairs. The children are all happily playing outside and I'm in the kitchen when Suzanne's voice comes through from the sitting room.

'Do you mind putting our breakfast dishes in the dishwasher, Amanda? I'm crap at doing stuff like that. Tiff usually does it.' She's leafing through a *Newsweek* she's brought with her, along with *Harper's Bazaar*, *Vogue*, *Hello!*, *House & Garden*, *The Economist*, the *Telegraph* and the *Mail*. 'And we do have a washing machine here, don't we?' she asks, looking my way.

'No,' I say, letting the first comment go, 'but Skyler said she would do our washing up at the house.'

'Oh, that's good,' she says, picking up *Harper's* and having a quick browse. 'Although most of my stuff is dry-clean only, so that won't be a problem. And Orlando's got screw-upable T-shirts and shorts and only one shirt that needs ironing,' she says, stopping at a page containing a large Chanel ad. 'Ooh, I like that,' she enthuses.

'Mummy,' Jack walks up to me, 'I'm afraid Hunter got hungry and tried to eat one of your shoes,' he says, handing me a shoe I don't recognise.

'Oh no, that's mine, that's mine,' says Suzanne, throwing the magazine on the floor and grabbing it from Jack's hand.

'Oh God,' I say, 'we'll keep Hunter outside and just bring him in if the weather turns. I'm so sorry, Suzanne.' I'm silently praying they weren't too expensive.

'They were Paul Smith as well, but they were a few seasons old so no harm done really,' Suzanne replies.

'Will Paul mind that Hunter has eaten his shoes?' asks Jack.

'No, Paul won't mind,' I say, as Suzanne sighs quietly to herself and walks slowly up the creaking stairs to her bedroom.

I'm just about to go up to the house to see if Skyler needs any help when I hear Suzanne scream at the top of her voice. I rush back inside, bounding up the stairs three steps at a time, to find her almost in tears at her bedroom door.

'What on earth's the matter?' I say, looking for some sign of an injury.

'My shampoo and moisturiser! They've leaked over everything!' Suzanne's expensive shampoo and her Rene Guinot moisturiser have indeed leaked all over her toiletry bag. 'Everything's ruined, utterly ruined,' she cries. 'My skin will turn to crêpe if I don't moisturise every day. And my hair is like straw without the right shampoo. I can't do faint wrinkles and pretty freckles like you, Amanda. That's not me!'

I try very hard not to laugh. 'Don't worry, Suzanne. Why don't you go up to the Elysian and ask Deborah if her spa has any of the things you need? She has so many London guests she's bound to be prepared for all eventualities.' I manage to speak with a straight but obviously crêped face.

'Yes, yes, that's a good idea. I'll do that,' she says, reassured that she won't end up looking like me after three weeks in deepest Cornwall. 'Thanks, Amanda. And I must text Howard to let him know all is well,' she says, regaining her composure.

Which reminds me to call Nigel and find out how he's getting on, so I put off going up to see Skyler and go into my bedroom where I've left my mobile.

'Hello, honey?' Nigel sounds happy but a little flustered. 'So you made it OK, then?'

'Yes, we arrived safely and the house is wonderful. Skyler, George and the girls all look really healthy and happy.'

'And how's the cottage?'

'Lovely. We're sharing with Suzanne and Orlando,' I say.

I can hear him chuckling.

'What's so funny?'

'Oh nothing.'

'I don't know why you think it's so funny. When you come down here you'll be sharing with them, too. To be fair to Suzanne, it's not her fault that the cottage just isn't big enough for two families. And at least Orlando's coming out of his shell a bit here, which is great to see,' I say, watching him play tag with the others through the window.

'She shouldn't have had a child, she should have got a dog,' he replies, 'or better still a goldfish. Anyway, I don't want to talk about her. How are you? How are the children and how's Hunter – not still being sick I hope?'

'The children are loving it. Willow and Rose look as lovely and happy as ever. Rose has an invisible friend called Terry, and she and Jack are playing with him as we speak. Skyler thinks Terry could be the ghost of a boy that used to come to school here, so I hope he doesn't suggest they get up to anything naughty. Hunter seems fine too now, certainly has his appetite back as he just tried eating one of Suzanne's shoes.' I hear Nigel chuckle at that and it gives me a pang of longing for him to be here too. 'It's so beautiful here, darling. We can take lots of romantic walks along the coast and make love in the heather – not that I've seen any heather, but I'm sure there must be some about.'

'I like the sound of that. Don't worry about the heather, long grass will do. As long as there are no nettles or sand. Remember Corsica?'

'Yes.' I laugh, remembering us, fifteen years ago, thinking that making love on the beach would be so romantic, not realising that sand gets everywhere – and stays there for a very long time. Even our attempts at spontaneous sex in a meadow ended up with us getting stung by nettles and Nigel being chased by a hornet. I almost wet myself laughing as my naked boyfriend screamed his head off. We only made love indoors after that.

'When are you coming down?' I ask hopefully.

'I don't know, Amanda. Things are still pretty touch and go here and I don't want to let go of the reins at the last hurdle. I promise I'll try to get down the weekend after next,' he promises unconvincingly. 'Is Howard coming down?'

'Yes, I think so, but he's not here yet and apparently he's busy with work, too. The kids would love to see you and have a holiday with you, you know that. The beach is gorgeous and George has organised some lovely outdoor act—'

'Yes, I know, Amanda.' He sounds exasperated. 'I'm cross about this, too, you know, but I'm pretty bad company at the moment. You know the pressure I'm under – the pressure we're all under – and it's taking its toll. It's good that you're there with the kids and it's bad that I'm not. I'm missing you all like hell, but I'm doing this for us. You understand that, don't you?'

'Yes, I do,' I say, although I'm feeling very frustrated by the situation.

I've walked downstairs now and, not wanting to

discuss work and all the stresses of Nigel's job again, I call out to the children and hand the phone to Jack as they come running in from playing.

'Where are you, Daddy?' asks Jack, followed by, 'When are you coming down?' from Hannah. They obviously get the same non-committal reply because they hand the phone back to me looking unhappy. Jenny is the only one old enough to know it's not worth bothering to ask those questions.

'We're having a lovely time, Daddy. Hope you're having a good time, too. I'll hand you back to Mother now,' she says, handing the phone to me and walking off.

'Love you,' I say.

'Love you, too, and we will make love in the heather, Amanda. I promise. I don't care if there are nettles or hornets.'

This cheers me up again. Humming happily to myself because I'm on a promise, I head back upstairs with the children hoping to at least get them to wash before supper. It's almost time to go up to the house where Skyler's put on a huge welcome spread. Suzanne and Orlando have changed and wouldn't look out of place at a posh restaurant in Knightsbridge. I doubt if the same restaurant would allow us in the kitchen, the way we're dressed.

We walk down the cobbled path, Orlando and Suzanne slightly ahead, as though they don't want to be associated with us, although Orlando keeps looking back, realising it's much more fun back with us. As we come out of the woods, we see a long table set up on the lawn, covered with salads and cold meats. Skyler is putting plates of pasties and pies on the table and waves at us to come over.

'It seems everyone wants to eat here this evening. We normally offer a buffet on Saturdays anyway, and the guests seem to like eating in the garden when the weather's good,' she says, hurrying back towards the kitchen.

'I'll come and help,' I offer, walking after her as Suzanne wanders around the gardens.

In the kitchen Skyler stops a moment and says, 'You've asked me how I am, Amanda, but how are you?' She was always so good at sensing when I wanted to talk. But before I can say anything, Suzanne walks in with Jack. He's managed to fall in the lake, which thankfully is very shallow, though now he needs new clothes. Again. By the time we've been back to the cottage, got Jack cleaned up and returned, all the guests are milling around the tables, helping themselves to drinks and nibbles and enjoying the reddening sky. Swallows and swifts are skimming the lake, taking tiny drinks as they gracefully dive down and fly up again, creating haunting silhouettes in the sky.

Back in the kitchen, Skyler says, 'I've invited Clare and Matt along for supper too, as Matt was helping George with the coasteering this afternoon. I hope you don't mind?'

'Of course I don't. The more the merrier and I'm here to help anyway, I don't want you to feel you have to treat us like guests – after all, we're staying here for nothing so I want to earn my keep.'

'No, you're here to have a good time and a break from everything and I think you need it. Is it still full steam ahead with Nigel's big deal?' she says, looking at me as though she can read my thoughts.

'Yes, totally, that's why I'm not sure when Nigel will be down. He said he'd get here eventually, and he sends his love to you all. I've told him how wonderful it is here, which I suspect makes him feel even worse, but once it's done, it's done. I'm sure it'll all be worth it in the end.'

'I remember what it used to be like with George, so I completely understand what you're going through, Amanda. But it'll be over soon, I know it will.' Skyler smiles reassuringly.

I can hear Hannah calling out, 'They have bats here, Mummy, they have bats.'

'They're supposed to be lucky,' Skyler says, 'so we don't mind, and they eat the flies and mosquitoes, although we don't seem to have many round here.'

'That's probably why,' I say.

'Yes, but still, I must remember to tell Suzanne about them. Is she still obsessive about her skincare? She looks great.'

I tell here about the sponge-bag episode and she nods.

'Yes, thought so. Hopefully the holiday will loosen her up a bit. I already think it's starting to work on Orlando.'

We carry the salads out to the table. 'Clare's really worked hard on this with me, so I hope you enjoy it,' says Skyler. Tea-lights are scattered on the table and hang from the surrounding trees in large glass bowls, looking like fat glow-worms. 'For starters we've got chargrilled chicken with mango salsa; chicken patties with sesame seeds and ginger; chickpea salad with peppers and tomatoes; corn with lime and chilli butter; roasted vegetables and minted couscous,' she says with a flourish.

'That doesn't sound very Cornish,' Suzanne says. 'It sounds absolutely delicious, though,' she adds quickly.

'Well, it's not all Cornish, but I'll tell you what is,' Skyler says, starting at one end of the table. 'There's warm trout salad with orange dressing; Cornish cheese; bacon and sage omelettes; chervil new potatoes; potato jowdle, which is really just potatoes fried with onions; saffron cake and buns; and, of course, Cornish pasties – those have lamb in them and those have steak,' she says, pointing at another plate. 'For afters we've got Cornish strawberry shortcakes and special Cornish biscuits called fairings, made of golden syrup, ginger and cinnamon. We've also got creamed apples and a Cornish champagne cocktail, with locally produced sparkling wine and strawberry liqueur, plus fresh strawberries from the garden. We can even make up some mahogany for you – that's two parts gin and one part treacle.' She smiles at us both and giggles. 'Allegedly, Cornish fishermen used to drink it in the 1800s and it's meant to put hairs on your chest.'

'I don't need hairs put anywhere, Skyler, I pay enough to have them removed,' says Suzanne. 'You've really done us proud,' she adds.

'This would feed us for the whole summer,' I say. No wonder Skyler looks tired, the poor thing.

'We do this most Saturday nights, so it's no trouble,' she replies. 'And we always prepare Cornish food if we can – it's silly not to try some of the local recipes while you're here.'

Once the guests have helped themselves, the children fill their plates and sit on the lawn to eat. After they've finished Orlando and Jenny start chasing bats. Orlando does seem to be thawing nicely.

Clare comes over to ask us if everything is all right.

'More than all right,' I say, 'why don't you take a break?'

'The guests need to be served, but I'll come round and chat once they've gone,' she says. Then she turns to Skyler, looking indignant. 'By the way, I thought you should know that Nicola has been bothering George something rotten today. You saw how she was all over him at breakfast, and she's been pestering him with stupid questions about the local birdlife, even though Matt told them all about it when they went out with him yesterday. If I were you I'd slap her one.'

Skyler laughs. 'I don't think slapping the guests is quite the way to deal with it, but I'll tell George to keep away from her and cry rape if she tries anything,' she says, taking a sip of champagne.

'Well, if you want me to slap her, just say and I will,'

says Clare, crossing her arms. She turns and walks back towards the kitchen.

'She caught her last boyfriend in bed with her neighbour and threw him out the window,' Skyler explains. 'She's a black belt in karate.'

Suzanne and I laugh. 'This place is full of surprises,' I say.

'Yes, it's full of character and characters,' says Skyler, helping herself to a pasty.

An hour later, we've all eaten more than enough. The sun is setting and the tea-lights in the trees make everything look magical. I turn to see where Jack has got to, and see a very good-looking man in his thirties, who looks as though he's spent most of his life outdoors, walking towards us.

'Hi, Matt,' says Skyler, getting up to introduce him and give him a kiss. 'Come and have some supper.'

Matt helps himself to a large plate of food, then sits to join us. He starts chatting to the children about fishing, where they can catch the largest fish and why the surf in Cornwall is as good as anywhere in the world. Then he starts telling stories about pirates, sea monsters and storms that silence the children and completely enchant Suzanne. When Clare comes out to join us, having cleared up after all the guests and hopefully not sloshed Nicola, she helps herself to some food and sits down beside him.

Eventually, George and the two girls who are helping in the kitchen come out. Dorothy and Philippa – Dot and Pippa – turn out to be Clare's cousins and are both in their early twenties. Dressed in jeans, stripy shirts and cowboy boots, they wouldn't look out of place on a horse.

'I'm pleased you haven't eaten everything,' George says, helping himself to some trout and potato salad.

'It would take a month to eat all of this,' I say.

'The guests seem to eat a lot here, I guess, because they're outdoors so much. After all, that's what Cornwall is all about and it lets us get on with stuff in the house,' he says, his mouth full of potato.

'Nothing like banking days?' says Suzanne.

'No, nothing like banking days. We might have equally early starts, but there's no suit needed, no commuting and, best of all, no office politics or back-stabbing.'

'Yes,' interrupts Clare, 'they're more likely simply to punch you in the face if they don't like you round here.'

'Do you still get the office politics and back-stabbing at your place, Suzanne?' asks George, topping up her glass.

'Oh, yes, all the time,' she says dismissively. 'I'd love to suggest we put our boxing gloves on at the end of the day and whack each other instead. So much time gets wasted on petty arguments, and the men are worse than the women, but then again there's the excitement and social life, and the money, of course. What would we do without the money?' she says, taking a large slurp of champagne and leaving her glass nearly empty again.

'Yes indeed,' nods Skyler, deep in thought. I wonder if she and George have money troubles. Though she refused outright to let me pay anything towards our holiday here. In the end I at least persuaded her to let me pay for our share of the food. I wonder if Suzanne's paying her way at all? Perhaps we can have time to talk later on this evening, when Suzanne goes to bed.

Suzanne looks at her champagne flute, then leaps up. 'That reminds me, I have a little present for you, George and Skyler. No divining rods, I'm afraid, or essential oils – I wouldn't know where to start with them – but I know my bubbly.' She excuses herself, asking Orlando if he can do her a little favour, and they disappear for a few moments while I help Skyler relight the tea-lights that have blown out in some of the nearby trees.

'How are things financially?' I ask her quietly, as we move from branch to branch.

'A bit tight at the moment, but we're coping. It's great that we're full and can afford Dot and Pippa.' She turns round and nods towards the two girls, who are chasing the children around the table, pretending to be pirates. 'It's hard, but it's worthwhile. George and I never have those what's-it-all-about moments we had when we lived in Whitlow. I enjoyed my work, but was miserable for George, and when his health started to deteriorate that was it. He used to go to the gym, thinking he could exercise away the stress, but after a while he got addicted to it and found he was still thinking about stuff even when he was running on the treadmill. He visited a spiritual healer, who told him that running was a bad idea as it just made him think of his life as a treadmill, running hard and fast, but going nowhere. He started to feel like he was going round in circles. Now that we've moved here, he doesn't need the gym or alternative therapists. Anyway, everyone seems to be full of homespun wisdoms round here, although' – she looks at Clare, who's talking intently to Matt – 'some of them can be a bit OTT.'

I see Suzanne on her way back, carrying a box, Orlando trailing behind with a plastic bag. 'Suzanne fits into the big-city lifestyle, but I think even she gets tired of the politics at work,' I say, as we go back to the table.

'How about you? Are you OK money-wise?' Skyler asks, but before I have time to reply, Suzanne is beside us.

'A present from home,' she says, handing the box to George, as Orlando hands his bag over to Skyler. 'It's not local bubbly, I'm afraid, only six bottles of Tatty, and a few of Moët. They should last us tonight at least! Do we have any of that fab strawberry liqueur stuff?' she asks as George pops the first cork, which goes flying into the gardens. 'Or shall we have it neat?'

'Why don't we have it straight,' says George as he pours some into each glass.

'Can we have some?' asks Jenny.

'Yes, can we, Mummy?' asks Orlando, echoed by Hannah and Jack, Willow and Rose.

'I don't see why not,' says Suzanne, slurring her

words a bit; 'just a little, though. You don't want hangovers on your first morning here.'

I like Suzanne when she's slightly drunk. She comes out with outrageous stuff and can be wonderfully indiscreet. I remember one particular evening when she'd invited us to dinner. There was a City couple, colleagues of Howard's, and a couple Suzanne knew. The husband worked in advertising and the wife as a lawyer. I think her name was Barbara. There was also a newly divorced woman Suzanne had invited. I always thought lawyers were meant to be tactful, but Barbara kept asking her the most tactless questions: how would she feel if her ex remarried and had children, and how difficult was it to find a man if you had children. She was on the verge of tears by the time Barbara had finished with her. Suzanne was busy directing the Polish catering staff, who were having trouble under-standing her, and I wasn't sure if she'd noticed. By the time we got to dessert, everyone was slightly merry and we'd moved off sex and religion and on to office politics. It was then that Suzanne said: 'It's so important to be diplomatic and tactful. You've got to be pretty thick-skinned yourself, but you need to be aware enough to know if you're upsetting someone else. My problem is that I often speak before engaging my brain and can come across as rude. I don't mean to, I'm just speaking my mind. I think you're a bit like me, Barbara, aren't you?'

I wish I'd had a camera to take a photograph of the previously serene Barbara as she went bright red and pursed her lips so tight I thought they'd disappear completely. The divorcée couldn't help smiling and neither could I. The funny thing was that Suzanne didn't mean to be nasty or spiteful, she was just being brutally honest and, as she said, opening her mouth before engaging her brain. On this occasion, though, it couldn't have been better timed or her target more deserving. Barbara said very little for the rest of the party.

Suzanne stands up, wobbling slightly.

'I would like to make a toast: to George, Skyler and their wonderful girls and their amazing staff. Silver Trees is a credit to you all, and I speak for myself and Amanda when I say we're utterly chuffed to have been invited here and I'm only sorry we didn't come sooner. It really is the most wonderful place.' I notice that she's almost tearful, which for some reason makes me giggle, so perhaps I'm a little drunk too. 'The food is wonderful and I love your staff, they're wonderful too,' she says, turning round to Clare, Matt, Dot and Pippa and giving them a big grin. They all smile back and raise their glasses. George pours a thimbleful of champagne into the children's tumblers, together with lots of strawberry and apple juice, and we all toast Skyler, George and their team.

'What more could you want,' I say, 'than delicious food in a glorious setting with your friends and family – or most of your family?' I add, thinking of Nigel and Howard.

We all sit and drink and contemplate for a moment.

It's been a very long and a very good day, but as I watch the children chase fireflies, intoxicated by their new-found taste for Tatty, I can't help wishing Nigel were here to enjoy this moment too.

Chapter 6

Chelsea Tractors, Hippy Chicks and Cream Teas

'Who's farted?' asks Jack. 'Was it you, Hannah?' We're sitting in my bed the following morning, or rather I'm lying down trying not to open my eyes. Hannah tries to blame the dog, but since Hunter is outside it's highly unlikely. They both look at me.

'Don't you dare,' I say, sitting up indignantly and feeling ever so slightly hungover from the night before. I can't take my drink.

Jack has been awake for the past hour and has been quietly playing on the Nintendo DS while Hannah writes in her diary. She's been writing about everything she saw yesterday and what she hopes to do today on the beach, as well as some of Matt's stories about pirates and storms, which she admitted this morning did give her a few nightmares.

I don't hear a peep from Jenny's room, or from

Orlando and Suzanne, but then I hear the stairs creaking and suspect someone is either on their way to or from the bathroom. I get up and put on jeans and a shirt, then check to see if the coast is clear; I desperately need a pee. Suzanne is coming up the stairs, looking pretty and more relaxed than she did yesterday, in a white summer dress and cerise cardigan. She looks as fresh as a daisy, so perhaps all that office socialising has given her a tougher constitution than me.

'Hello, Amanda,' she says, 'the bathroom's free now. I tend to spend a lot of time in it, so I got up early. What time do you think Skyler will want us over for breakfast?' She's reached the top of the stairs and is peering behind me into our bedroom, which must look a tip.

'She said between eight-thirty and ten,' I reply.

'She's already up to get bread and papers and things. Orlando's been helping her collect the eggs, but we didn't want to disturb you.'

'That's a pity,' I say, disappointed for the children, who I know would have liked to have helped. 'Jack and Hannah were up, but were just doing their own thing. I'll check on Jenny.'

'Oh, Jenny's up already. She fed Hunter then helped Orlando with the eggs. I think she's helping Clare in the kitchen now. She's very capable, your daughter,' says Suzanne, tapping me on the shoulder and making me smile. That's a compliment indeed coming from Suzanne.

'She can be,' I reply, thinking of all the times I've asked her to clean her room, do her homework or help look after Jack, only to hear a tut, then 'Oh why, Mother?' and have to wait a good thirty seconds before she does anything.

I get Hannah and Jack into the bathroom and we share a shower. As there's three of us it's a bit of a squash, but the children don't seem to mind. Once we're all washed, with our hair brushed, and we're wearing fresh clothes, I put our dirty laundry in the linen basket and carry it up the path to the house, with Suzanne, Hannah and Jack following on behind.

'Hunter is very sweet, Amanda,' says Suzanne as we walk. 'I know he ate my Paul Smith slingback, but he's cute for a dog. And I don't like dogs in general. Orlando would love one and Howard doesn't mind one way or another, but Manuela would be the one to look after it and she has enough on her plate looking after Orlando. Can you imagine how disruptive a dog would be? The house would end up a mess despite our housekeeper's best efforts. Look what Hunter's done to yours, Amanda.'

I bite my tongue. I know she doesn't mean to be rude – it's just what she thinks – and I make a mental note to make the house look a little tidier next time she comes round.

'Did you speak to Nigel this morning?' Suzanne asks.

'No, last night, he'll have been up too early for work for me to call,' I reply.

'How was he? He must love having such a quiet

house.' I know all too well that Nigel hates it when the house is empty and misses the kids and me sorely, but I suspect this is something Suzanne just won't get.

'He's fine – stressed but fine,' I say, trying to keep my response as vague as possible. 'But he's definitely not going to make it down next weekend.' I'd been secretly hoping that, despite having planned to not come down for another two weeks, he might surprise us.

'Howey won't be coming down either,' Suzanne says. 'I spoke to him earlier and he said he's got an important meeting to prepare for on Monday, which is a pity, as I know he'd love being here and would really benefit from seeing more of Orlando – and vice versa. He said he was worried he'd be too distracted here to get the work done, but to be honest, I think he really needs the distraction at the moment.' She sighs.

Suzanne's a funny old stick. She comes out with some real corkers, like telling me my house looks a tip and I've got rubbish skin, then the next minute she's all soft and fluffy. It's only been a day, but we're getting on OK so far – although her directness can be slightly wearing. Then I think about the fact that I'm here with her for three weeks; as Nigel suggested, it's probably going to be a challenge. I don't know how many more spiky comments I can take before I start throwing a few punches of my own.

'So is Hannah looking forward to moving school?' she says as we walk through the back door into the kitchen. Orlando and Jenny are busy in the dining room serving toast and jam to the Smiths and the

Schneiders. Hannah and Jack have disappeared with Willow and Rose.

'Yes, she is. She's a sociable girl and she'll make new friends easily,' I say, sitting at the large kitchen table, on which breakfast has already been laid out. 'Morning, Clare, can we do anything?'

'Don't worry, we've got it under control. Help yourselves to coffee – there's plenty in the pot.'

We do as she says and sit, gratefully nursing our mugs.

'It's a good school, Dragons,' Suzanne continues. 'You've made the right decision. Hannah's a coaster, and coasters always manage to stay out of the teacher's way. Those at the top and bottom get all the attention, while those in the middle often get overlooked. I've listened to Ms Gooden talk and talk about how every child gets special attention, but it's rubbish, Amanda. In a class of thirty they're bound to get missed out; they know it and we know it and the system doesn't do anything about it.' Suzanne nods as though wholeheartedly agreeing with her own comment, which makes me smile. 'Jenny and Jack will be fine. They're brighter than Hannah,' she says, which wipes the smile off my face. How can she turn a compliment into a criticism in the same sentence?

'She's not stupid,' I snap. 'She's very bright, actually. She's got what her new teacher, Ms Appleton, calls a "wild intelligence". In fact, she's brighter than Jenny in many ways. Just because she doesn't conform doesn't make her thick, Suzanne.'

'Wild intelligence?' she says. 'Hmm, haven't heard of that one before. She's a maverick, then?' she says, looking at me askance.

'Yes,' I say, 'I suspect she is.' I'm not going to let her get away with that one. I don't mind biting my tongue about most things, but not my children. It's only the second day and I know I'll have to watch myself, so I change the subject. 'How's Orlando doing?'

'Orlando is doing well. We're looking into boarding schools for him at the moment in preparation for when he turns thirteen,' she says, buttering some toast. 'I think it's the right age for him to start; he won't be too young, and as an only child he'll make so many more friends there, being around his peers.' This is the first I've heard of her plan to send him to boarding school and I'm slightly shocked, although it is a few years off.

'Yes, but he loves being with you. Even after only a few days here, I can see how much he enjoys it, Suzanne.'

'Oh, don't be silly, Amanda, that's just him being excited about spending time with the other children on holiday. I'm just the taxi,' she says. 'I know your views on boarding school, but it's a very practical way of dealing with education and allowing yourself the chance to get back to work again. I know you really enjoyed the travelling you did. And I also know that having children restricted you and held you back in your career. I know how much Orlando restricts me – having to organise babysitters and the trouble we have if Manuela is ever ill and can't look after him when we've been invited to a concert or dinner party. It's a total drag.'

'But your work doesn't seem so demanding these days,' I comment; 'you've managed to find time to get away this year. I've never known you be able to have this much holiday before.' I smile at Orlando as he comes through from the dining room, and hope he hasn't overheard anything his mother's said.

'Well, to be honest, things at work are a bit touch and go at the moment.' Suzanne looks unusually embarrassed. 'I haven't really told you the whole story, Amanda, because it's a bit complicated. There was this ever-so-small mess-up at work, and I shouldered the blame to protect some senior executives, so they've given me more holiday as a sort of thank-you. I'd never have been able to take this amount of time off if it hadn't happened. It just goes to show that some good comes out of everything, doesn't it, even little mistakes.' She shrugs her shoulders, although I can see that it took a lot for her to admit her 'ever-so-small mess-up' to me. Suzanne is a perfectionist and would have found even a tiny one galling, especially if it wasn't her fault.

All the children have reappeared now, looking hungry. The elder children help to tidy up and all the guests are enchanted by the new additions to the staff. Jenny even manages to raise a smile from Candida Pepsin and Adeline Wenlock when, at her most charming and eloquent, she asks them if they'd like some more tea. Eventually, when they're done helping serve the guests, they all sit down to a breakfast of fresh eggs, collected this morning. Jack and Hannah have confirmed that it will be their turn tomorrow and have asked Willow and Rose to knock on the cottage door at five forty-five to make sure they get up in time. They're still a bit miffed that they missed out today.

Once the last guests have gone, George comes through and sits down with a sigh of exhaustion.

'Morning, all. Did everyone sleep well?' he asks.

'Yes,' says Jack, 'but I think champagne makes Mummy fart.'

I am mortified, but everyone laughs while I quietly scowl at my son. Luckily, everyone's soon distracted by Matt bounding in through the back door.

After he's got a cup of coffee and sat down, George says, 'Matt, I've worked out the activity schedules for today. It's just the Smiths and the painted ladies riding with Tom this morning. Given it's such glorious weather, this lot should all spend their first day on the beach,' he says, looking round at the expectant faces.

'I'll join you at lunchtime with a picnic basket,' says Skyler, 'then we can head on to Tremontgomery and check out the fair this afternoon. I think it's a New Age sort of thing,' she adds, as she clears away the last of the plates.

'What does that involve?' asks Suzanne.

'Tarot readings, spiritual healers, yoga, palm readings, numerology, all that sort of stuff,' she explains, though Suzanne doesn't appear to look any the wiser.

'It's all about astrological signs, then?' she asks.

'Yes,' says Skyler. 'You're a Taurus, aren't you?' She looks at Suzanne. 'I think I did your chart a few years ago when you came round for supper and I'd just done that course.'

'Oh yes, I remember that,' says Suzanne, looking a bit vacant.

'Yes, you're Taurus, with Scorpio rising and Venus in Aries.' Skyler smiles as the details come back to her.

'What does that mean?'

'You're a determined, ingenious leader, or an obsessive, possessive control freak, depending on which way you look at it.'

'Sounds about right,' I say, grinning at her. 'So, we'll meet you at the beach at about twelve, have lunch, and then head off. Shall we come back here first?' I ask, thinking about all the beach gear we'll have with us.

'Yes. You'll be full of sand by then, so come back here, then we can all wander into town, it's only a ten-minute walk.'

'Great. To the beach, then!' I say.

The children are well trained for beach trips. We have a family routine that makes me feel like we're the Brady Bunch, but the kids love it. Jenny is in charge of putting the sun lotion on Jack, Hannah and herself, Hannah is the towel collector and folder-upper and Jack carries the beach balls and bats. Suzanne, on the other hand, makes a big fuss and makes putting on sun cream a military operation. 'You're not putting it on right,' she moans at Orlando, when he seems to be doing it perfectly well as far as I can tell. 'You're not putting it on in the right order. Arms last, Orlando, arms last.' Then there are the towels. 'No, don't put them there, don't fold them that way, Orlando. That way is fine. Yes, that way, perfect!'

Poor boy. I know he is henpecked about school too; Suzanne is always bitterly disappointed when he doesn't get top grades. She made him do loads of entrance exams and he was so tired he fell ill. I can't believe she's like this with him on holiday as well, especially as he tries so hard to please her. I can tell by the way he always watches to see if she's looking when he does something helpful. He desperately needs praise and all she does is criticise him. I haven't heard Suzanne say 'well done' to Orlando since we've been here and he's been wonderfully behaved and extremely helpful. In the end I decide to bite my tongue again. I think I'm going to need to do that a lot this holiday.

While Jenny is finishing putting lotion on her legs, I ask if I can have a quiet word. 'Yes, what is it, Mother?' she says.

'Can you, Hannah and Jack try to include Orlando as much as possible?' I say, sitting down beside her.

'We do,' she says, continuing to rub the cream in.

'Yes, I know, but can you try to include him in games well away from his mum? I think Orlando would have a better holiday if he spent more time with you; I think his mum nags him a lot.'

121

'Like you do us,' she says.

'I don't nag,' I say. 'I advise constructively.'

Jenny smiles and continues to rub in the cream.

'Yes, Mother, we will.'

Our towels and lotions are sorted, the sun's still out and a light breeze is blowing as we head along the pathway, taking Willow and Rose with us. Orlando's in charge of Hunter and he looks back at me proudly as they negotiate the wooden steps down to the beach without any problems. The cliffs on either side act as huge windbreaks and the air is still and warm when we reach the sand.

'We should be in the sun all morning,' I say. 'We'd better find what shade there is to avoid getting burnt.' I look around for any overhanging rocks, of which there are several.

The children run down the steps and strip off T-shirts and shorts, leaving a trail behind them as they race towards the sea. I've already checked with Skyler that it's safe to swim here and that there are no rip tides or anything. She assured me this little cove was perfect for paddling about. Jenny, Hannah and Jack all swim well, having had lessons since they were two. I know Willow and Rose swim, because they used to take lessons at the same pool as Hannah, and Orlando has won school swimming championships – Suzanne wouldn't have accepted anything less – so we let them all run off, shouting after them not to go too far out. Suzanne and I fuss over laying out blankets and setting ourselves up for the morning.

They're barely up to their knees, though, before they all rush back, squealing at us.

'It's freezing,' says Jenny, grabbing the nearest towel.

'It's very cold, Mummy,' whines Jack.

'Oh, don't be such wimps,' says Hannah, gamely jumping up and down. 'Last one in the sea is a sissy. Let's all play pirates. Bagsy me be Blackbeard!' she shouts, with Willow and Rose following her back into the sea.

'Well, I'm going in,' I say, immediately regretting the announcement, but it's out there now and there's nothing I can do about it. Feeling I should lead by example, I take my T-shirt and skirt off, revealing a bikini I've had for over six years, but which still fits and looks good.

'Aren't you coming in for a dip?' I call to Suzanne, who looks horrified at the thought.

'No, darling, this bikini is not meant to get wet. It's Chanel.'

'Doesn't Chanel ever get wet?' I ask.

'Not this one, Amanda. You go and play with the children now,' she says, gently mocking me back.

The idea of being a kid again, free of responsibility and running into the water, freezing though it might be, is wonderfully liberating and I turn and run towards the sea, the salty air blowing in my face and hair, laughing aloud.

I remember dying to get into the water when I was a child, but getting distracted en route by the shells I'd collect and put in my bucket. There was so much to do in the wet sand by the shore. Here, I can see loads of tiny, terrified creatures darting into holes when they hear us heading their way. I guess the tide doesn't come up very high here all that frequently as there are still the remnants of sandcastles that were probably once intricate and magnificent, but are now in mushy mounds waiting for the next tide to demolish them completely. Mussels and broken shells lie in piles, rejected by child collectors who either found something better to do or whose buckets and pockets proved too small to hold all their treasures. Seaweed and bits of wood that Hannah claims come from pirate boats bashed on the rocks are collected in piles on the beach like smuggler's booty.

'There are dead bodies around here as well,' Hannah shouts to the others. 'Some are still bloody with lots of guts and intestines hanging out. Mummy, can you give a prize to the first person who finds a body part?' she asks, as the others half-heartedly go in search of severed limbs.

'No I can't, Hannah. Don't scare the others,' I say, scowling at my daughter. Ms Appleton was right: my daughter does have a wild intelligence.

The water is indeed freezing, but I don't say that out loud; I just look brave and strong as I rush in with the others, thinking of the time I spent in a sauna and freezing plunge pool at a five-star hotel in Austria, where guests paid £80 for the pleasure. I'm getting the same treatment here on the Cornish coast for free.

'It's fun, isn't it, Mother?' Jenny says, looking at the

goosebumps that have appeared all over my arms.

'Yes,' I reply through gritted teeth, though I'm determined not to let the cold get the better of me. I count, 'One, two, three,' and under I go, swimming for about five strokes before coming up again. The children are playing on the edge of the water, in and out up to their knees, racing against the waves, but at least I've done it. I may not repeat the experience but I'm feeling totally awake and refreshed. I swim a few strokes. The children are now oblivious to my existence as they see who can build the biggest sandcastle.

The sun feels strong today and I make sure all my lot and Willow and Rose have sun hats on, and Suzanne does the same with Orlando. I notice when Suzanne takes her cover-up off that she has a nice golden tan.

'You look brown already,' I say.

'Fake, darling. I went to the beautician's round the corner at home where they do a great tan, facial and body massage for two hundred pounds. I've had some extra training sessions, too, because bikinis are so unforgiving, aren't they?' She looks me up and down in the way she does, perhaps unintentionally focusing on my thighs, which don't suffer from cellulite but do wobble more than I'd like.

Suzanne looks trim, toned and anything but her forty-two years. With clothes on I look younger than my forty-three years, but once they're off I look every inch my age. Years of long- and short-haul travel, not exfoliating or drinking enough water and failing to protect my skin from the sun, have given me wrinkles and sun spots. I don't travel much at all these days, but my tan seems to have stayed with me, as have my freckles, so I look brown and healthy. I'm also, admittedly, a little weathered because I spend my life outdoors – but Nigel says he still loves me, so I can't complain.

As well as the Chanel bikini, Suzanne is wearing Prada sunglasses that are so large they make her look like a funky Joe Ninety. She's even lying on a Gucci towel – I had no idea that Gucci even made towels. She really does live in another world. While the children happily build their castles, she spends the next hour telling me how she takes care of her face, and all the new treatments she's been having, as recommended by Posh Spice or Cameron Diaz.

'I have oxygen,' she says, quite straight-faced, 'and then CACI. And then I have this combination treatment that deals with all my problem areas – you know, T-zone and so on.'

She lies down with her large (Dior) sun hat draped over her face, so she's a little muffled and I have to listen carefully.

'I go about twice a month and have my hands and feet done too. It's so nice to have pretty feet, don't you think, Amanda?' she says, twiddling her beautifully manicured pink-frosted toes.

I look down at my calloused feet and the hairs on my big toes and hide them under my beach bag. Then I realise the sun might do them some good and pop them out again.

'At least all feet look good when they're tanned,' I say.

'Yes, but there are areas you must always keep out of the sun, such as your hands and neck. They give your age away, darling. It's terrible, but you can't do anything about it, even plastic surgery doesn't work. I know some women who insist on wearing polo necks even in the summer because they have turkey necks. And of course women who've got a bit of weight on them – not too much, but just a bit – tend to look better than those who are emaciated. They may have a little puppy fat and cellulite, but they look younger; that's what I think, anyway,' she says, looking up at me, while I try very hard to bear in mind that this is intended as a compliment.

'Hello, girls!' It's Skyler, almost at the bottom of the steps. I must have drifted off, because it's already a quarter to twelve. She's carrying a basket in each hand. 'Clare has done us proud. More Cornish food, with a touch of Delia and even a dash of Jamie.' She looks at Suzanne. 'I know you said you're mildly wheat intolerant, so Clare's used gluten-free flour in the pasties.'

Suzanne looks touched.

'Why thank you, Skyler, that's very thoughtful of you.'

We help her unload the pasties, which are covered in clean white tea cloths and are still warm, as well as some fresh bread from the bakery and a small gluten-free loaf for Suzanne. There are also bowls of blueberries and strawberries fresh from the garden.

'It really is very sweet of Clare to do this,' says Suzanne, taking a bite of the pasty as the children, glowing with sunshine and sand, sit quietly and eat, ravenous with all their activity.

'This is great food, Skyler, thank you,' says Orlando.

'My pleasure,' says Skyler. 'Just help yourselves if you want any more. Clare told me to tell you that if you want to learn how to make the fairings we had last night she'll show you this evening. She said you mentioned you were interested in cooking.'

Orlando beams. 'That would be great. Can the others come as well?' he asks.

'Yes,' Skyler nods, 'the invitation was an open one.'

'I didn't know you were interested in cooking, Orlando,' says Suzanne, slightly surprised.

'Yes, I help Manuela with stuff sometimes,' he answers casually, taking a big bite out of a pasty.

'Well, would you like to go to catering school?'

'Oh no, Mummy, I'm just interested in cooking and making things, that's all. I don't want to be a chef,' he says, grinning.

'Not like Jamie Oliver then?' says Jack.

'No, not like Jamie Oliver,' Orlando replies.

There's silence for a while as the children concentrate on stuffing their faces. Even Hunter, who's been bounding in and out of the waves, has run out of steam and seems happy to sit and be petted by Willow and Rose.

After everyone's finished and we've packed up the remains of the picnic, Skyler says: 'Right, let's go into town and see the fair.' The children start to whinge about leaving the beach, but eventually they're enticed to leave by Skyler telling them they'll find the best ice cream in England there. With that, they reluctantly start to dry themselves, Jenny dealing with Jack, who wants to put his clothes on while still wet and who insists on using his sand-covered towel. Skyler packs away the remaining fruit and Suzanne fusses about folding and packing her Gucci towel, shaking sand over everyone in the process.

We walk back up and plonk the wet swimsuits and sandy towels in the laundry room at the main house, then make our way into Tremontgomery.

Skyler takes us the 'cross-country' route which she says is quicker. I'm glad I have taken her advice and wear my wellies as the fields are muddy. Suzanne clearly regrets not bringing a pair, as her Gucci flip-flops are now unrecognisable they're so caked in mud.

The whitewashed cottages I first spotted glistening on the horizon as we drove into Tremontgomery yesterday don't look as clean close up as they did from a distance, but the streets are busy and colourfully dressed up with flags for the fair.

I check Hunter's leash is secure: there are a lot of cars, it's a new place and he's more active and curious when there's something new to discover. Then I tell Jenny to keep an eye on Hannah, while Skyler tells Willow and Rose to keep an eye on Jack. Jack, however, has other ideas and insists on holding Orlando's hand.

'They seem to be getting on well,' says Suzanne, looking at the pair of them.

'Yes,' I say, smiling. 'Ask Jack what he wants for his birthday and he always asks for an older brother, even before a new Nintendo game. A younger brother won't do, he has to be older; so Orlando will be very popular this holiday. Ever thought of having another one, Suzanne?' I ask as she puts on her oversized glasses.

'Oh God, no. Had enough trouble giving birth to one. All that pain,' she says, although, if I remember rightly, she had an elective Caesarean. 'And where would poor Manuela find the time? She has enough on her hands with Orlando,' she says, totally oblivious to the option that she herself could spend time looking after the next one.

We turn the corner on to the high street and pass a few boutiques selling clothes that make Suzanne wince. There's a lovely children's toyshop selling knights, dragons and the castle to go with them, which Jack immediately spots and wants for himself, asking if he has enough pocket money saved up. He hasn't, having blown it on a new kite last weekend. There's a cluster of antique shops too, although Skyler says she's not sure how old or genuine the antiques are.

We walk towards the main square, which overlooks the harbour. There are about six or seven yachts moored there, a few of the owners are on deck pottering about or watching the people onshore. It reminds me a little of a less glitzy St Tropez, where my parents took me as a child. I used to look at the boat owners and wonder if they ever came on land when no one was looking. It was those holidays that got me hooked on becoming a travel journalist and being paid to travel the world. And when I read some of the poems and stories my three write about their holidays, I know I've passed my love of travelling on to them. I doubt any of them will stay in Britain after university, knowing there's a big world out there and only a short time to explore it.

'Why is no one catching any fish, Mummy?' asks Jack, slightly perturbed because he thought there would be at least one pirate ship in the harbour. 'And where are the sharks kept?' Matt has told the children that sharks have been spotted off the coast and they want to go out in a boat to find them.

'Perhaps we can go out with Matt later in the holiday, children,' I say, slightly hoping the opportunity doesn't arise as my sea legs aren't very good these days.

To the right of the main square is a smaller, cobbled square where the stalls for the fair have been set up. Tall stone buildings, including a particularly beautiful church, surround it. We tell the children to stick together as we walk past tables laden with rhubarb and ginger jam, orange and yellow gourds and little piles of home-grown vegetables and flowers. Other stalls are selling crystals, some round, some carved in the shape of angels, some in the shape of phalluses, which Suzanne quickly ushers the children past, although by the expressions on their faces they all saw them. The air is heavy with burning incense and scented candles.

Skyler stops beside the largest crystal stall and explains to the children what each crystal can do, how you're supposed to look after them and wear them. Willow and Rose seem to know as much as their mother, and tell us about how turquoise makes you stronger and tiger eye more focused. So convincing are they that Suzanne and I end up buying our lot a crystal each. We walk on, past stalls selling scented pillows, elixir drinks and other therapies that Suzanne and I might try out later if we have time. Skyler greets a tall man in his early forties, with grey hair and a round, open face.

'May I introduce Peter Williamson? He's the local baker whose bread we serve up every morning for breakfast.' He offers his hand to Suzanne and me. He's introduced to the children and hugs Willow and Rose, then, to my surprise, pretends to hug Terry, Rose's imaginary friend.

When he speaks it's with a firm but gentle voice. 'Would you like to try some of the scones I've just delivered to Aunt Sarah's? It's the tea shop in the corner of the square.' All the children nod enthusiastically, happy to leave the incense behind as it's making us all feel a little light-headed.

As we walk towards the tea shop, Jack listens intently as Peter tells him that he used to be a policeman and how it was far less dangerous than being a baker.

'But you always smell good,' Jack says, sniffing Peter's arm.

'Yes,' he laughs. 'Children and animals like me

because I smell nice.' His round face grins. 'I feel like the Pied Piper sometimes,' he says as the children follow on behind.

The tea shop looks like someone's front room. The round tables are covered with blue-and-white checked tablecloths, each with a red potted azalea and small handwritten menu. There are two other couples in the shop, drinking tea and quietly eating scones. We pull two of the tables together and sit looking out of the picture window at the busy cobbled square. Just then, Skyler spots another friend and brings her over.

'This is Helen Albertson,' she says, introducing a fifty-something woman who looks like a funky Ethel Merman.

'Hello, there,' Helen says in a raspy voice. 'Where do you all come from?'

'London, I'm afraid,' Suzanne says before anyone can speak. I'm annoyed she feels she should apologise.

'No need to be ashamed of that. Half the population of this town are from London. Without them I don't think we would have such a thriving community, although we're trying to persuade more of them to stay over the winter months too. It can be so quiet, can't it, Skyler?'

Skyler nods in agreement.

'Why don't you tell the tourists there are pirates,' says Hannah, 'but that you can only see them in the winter? Then you'll get more people coming down because they'll want to see what they look like.'

Helen claps her hands. 'What a good idea, and do

you think they would believe us, little girl?' she says, bending down so she's Hannah's height.

'If you looked them in the eye when you were telling them, nodded a lot and left swords, skulls and broken, bloodied bits of wood on the beach. I know I would,' she says seriously.

'Well, I must invite you to our next brainstorming meeting, young lady. Now what's your name?'

'Hannah,' she replies. 'And I like the sound of a brainstorming meeting, but can we have a scone first?'

We order scones, jam and tea from a young dark-haired girl who turns out to be Clare's younger sister, Francesca. They don't do wheat-free scones, so Suzanne has camomile tea and takes a gamble on an oatcake.

Peter is talking to the children, while Helen corners me to talk about her work at the tourist office, since Skyler's told her I'm a travel writer.

'We have so much to offer here,' she says waving her arms and hands about like an Italian mamma enthusing about her firstborn. 'We have the Minack Theatre, stone circles, legends and mines—' She stops herself mid-sentence and looks at Orlando and Hannah, who are just tucking into their scones. 'Do you know, they used to send children like you down the mines, Hannah,' she says.

'I know they sent boys like me up chimneys,' interrupts Jack, who's smearing too much jam over his scone.

'You must go and see the mines,' Helen continues. 'And there's the Eden Project, where you can learn about the planet and how to preserve it.' She nods at Jenny and Willow, who are trying to feed Hunter crumbs underneath the table without anyone noticing. 'The air is supposed to be cleaner in Cornwall than anywhere else in England, and we have some of the most wonderful chefs and raw ingredients, as well as all those wonderful tropical gardens full of amazing flowers and plants.'

'Do you have any triffids?' asks Orlando, who's obviously seen the film or read the book.

'No, we don't have triffids, but we have many other wonderful plants, and because of our climate everything grows really well here.'

'Do you have lots of witches?' mumbles Hannah through a mouthful of scone. I send her a warning glare so she knows I'm not impressed with her trying to talk with her mouth full.

'I believe there are many that live secretly among us. You'll find some witches out there behind the stalls, telling you things about yourself that you may or may not want to know.'

'Can we go to see a witch, Mummy?' shouts Rose as Hannah nods encouragement and frantically chews on her scone. Jenny and Orlando look a little sceptical.

'Yes, I'm sure we can,' I say, 'but first eat your scones.'

Five minutes later, we're back outside in search of witches. Skyler buys some incense, I buy some soap and candles, and Suzanne gets a rather lovely bound notebook which she thinks Manuela will like. For a brief spell I think I've lost Jack, but Peter finds him listening to a man bashing a gong, which he claims is a cure for headaches. We pass a woman balancing against another man – inversion therapy, according to the sign above the stall. A lot of the stallholders are dressed like yoga instructors or hippies, although there are a few who just look like ordinary people, which makes me think they're there to make a fast buck.

Skyler offers to pay for us mums to have 'Animal Magic', while Peter and Helen watch the children. I sit down at a table, and a young woman with light brown hair tells me to close my eyes for a few minutes while she waves her hands over my head and shoulders and then asks me to pick a card. I pick one with a dragon on it.

'You have the energy of a dragon,' she says, looking deep into my eyes. 'You must keep your energy, as others may want to steal it. You must enhance it by being close to nature, and learning to release your anger because it will hold you.' I try to think of the last time I was really angry but I can't remember. 'Your enemies should fear you,' says the woman, which makes me giggle because it sounds so dramatic. 'Once angered you will fly up in the air, hovering above the clouds out of sight' – as she speaks, she gradually raises her voice and lifts her hand into the air, allowing it to hover for a few seconds and then, dramatically, crashing her fist on to the table, making me jump out of my seat – 'and then you'll flatten them!'

This all sounds very unlike me, but I do rather like

the idea of landing right on top of my enemies and splattering them. Very Old Testament. The lady continues, completely straight-faced.

'Don't fear so much. You will regain all that you fear you have lost. You have a lot of power, you just don't know how to use it yet.'

She finishes and I stand up. I go back to the girls, thanking Skyler for the consultation that I'm dying to tell them all about so I can find out if it fits with how they see me. We agree to confide in each other what the woman tells us once we've all seen her.

Half an hour later, we sit down and exchange notes. After I've told my story, Skyler tells us she's an eagle: all-knowing, clear-sighted and objective.

'She also said I was a bit up in the air at times which, I suppose, being an eagle, I would be.'

Suzanne and I nod.

'Yes, I'd agree with that,' I say.

Suzanne is not so happy.

'She told me I'm a gnome, which isn't even animal,' she says, looking genuinely annoyed.

'It's only a bit of fun, and anyway, I'm not a *real* animal,' I say.

'It's OK for you to say that, Amanda, you're a dragon.' Suzanne scowls at me. 'Everyone wants to be a magical, mystical, fire-breathing dragon. Who wants to be a ruddy gnome?'

'Gnomes can't be all bad,' says Skyler, trying to keep a straight face. 'Nice things come in small packages.'

'That's a myth invented by chippy short people. How

about poison dwarfs? Or Semtex?' She huffs again, which makes us finally give out and laugh. I'm surprised that Suzanne has taken it all so seriously. She looks genuinely affronted by our reaction.

'Was it all bad?' I ask, desperately trying not to laugh any more.

'No. She told me I'm very grounded and materialistic and would always be financially secure. She said I should spend more time with my child, as he wants to see more of me, which freaked me about a bit as I didn't tell her I had a child. But then again, she could have seen me earlier with Orlando. And she suggested I should loosen up a bit, though I don't need to pay good money for some old hippy to tell me that.'

I'm surprised by Suzanne's reaction. Perhaps the woman told her some other stuff that came too close to the bone. I notice Skyler refrains from pointing out that it was her money, not Suzanne's that paid for the consultations anyway. It irritates me that Suzanne can be so ungrateful.

We check to see how the children are doing. They're enchanted by Helen and Peter, who are telling them about the stone circles all over Cornwall. I can overhear Jack telling the grown-ups that the stones are all to do with fraternity rites.

I notice a tarot-card-reader-cum-spiritual-healer called Doreen, and in a last attempt to cheer up Suzanne, who still seems to be sulking about being described as a gnome, I go over to see whether she can talk to us. Doreen looks exactly how you'd imagine a tarot reader to look; she has a gypsy's glint in her green eyes, and long, silver-white hair. In front of her on a bench rest a selection of stones and cards on what looks like a very old hand-crocheted shawl that jangles in the breeze as it's weighed down by brass coins. As luck would have it, she has three slots left for the afternoon and agrees to read all our tarots.

'This is my treat,' I say.

'That's very kind of you,' says Skyler. 'We're obviously meant to see this lady or there wouldn't have been any spaces.'

'Er, right,' quips Suzanne. 'As long as she doesn't tell me I'm a gnome or an elephant, I don't mind.'

I go first into what looks like a small Rajasthani tent. Doreen shakes my hand. She's dressed simply but elegantly in a white dress and light-green short-sleeved cardigan and she has kind eyes, though she doesn't smile as she offers me a seat. On the table that sits in the middle of the tent is a pile of different-sized, highly coloured cards. She asks me to shuffle a set of cards six times and then cut them into three piles, placing one on top of another before thinking of one or two questions I'd like the cards to respond to. I silently ask if we will have a good holiday this year, and if Nigel's deal will happen sooner rather than later.

'Now, what's your name?' she asks.

'Amanda Darcey.'

Doreen places the cards in a pattern, and one by

one, starting with the card she laid in the middle, she turns them over.

'You have very strong cards, Amanda Darcey. I don't know what you ask of them, but they have a powerful message for you,' she says, looking me straight in the eye and smiling for the first time. 'You have lost your passion for life. You are focusing on the petty and material, being pulled, being drained by the worry of it, and at the same time you are trying to dismiss the important and spiritual side of yourself. If you like, you have lost your voice.' She's looking at me intently. I say nothing, just stare back at her. 'You are going through a period of great stress, but you will soon face a challenge that will help you deal with this stress and allow you to take a closer, deeper, honest look at what makes you happy. You will rediscover your passion. You have had to be patient. Things are not what they seem, but your worries are unfounded. Well,' she pauses ominously, 'most of them.' She brushes the cards back into a pile and puts them back neatly with the others.

'That'll be a tenner please,' she says, which instantly breaks the spell.

As I hand over the money, I wonder what this challenge or journey is that I'm about to face. Is Nigel lying to me about how well the deal is going or is it something to do with Skyler and Silver Trees? I suspect Doreen says all this to everyone, though; it's so vague it could apply to any number of questions. Anyone coming here is on a journey of some sort, and everyone on holiday is there because they need a break from work, so it seems to me to be more logical than mystical.

Skyler goes in next, leaving Suzanne and I to wander around the other stalls. We meet Deborah again, who looks fragrant and elegant in a simple, beautifully cut yellow dress, which Suzanne can't help admire. Deborah introduces us to her husband, Dennis, who's slightly shorter than her but handsome in a Marco Pierre White sort of way. He is very tanned with shoulder-length, wavy hair, and dressed in white chinos and a white shirt, unbuttoned at the collar.

'Ah, Debs told me there were some beautiful ladies who had just booked into Silver Trees.' He has a deep, gravelly voice. 'I was scolding her for not making room for you at the Elysian. We could do with some pretty faces like yours at the hotel,' he says, his too-white, capped-teeth smile beaming at us. He hasn't blinded me with his flattery, but it seems to have worked on Suzanne.

'You've kindly invited us to the launch of the cookery school, which we're looking forward to,' Suzanne says, blushing.

'Yes,' Dennis nods, 'it will be a wonderful event. There are a lot of celebrities coming. Not local celebrities, you know, we're talking big London names, Hollywood names, know what I mean?' He taps his nose and leans towards Suzanne and me, so that we get an overwhelming whiff of whatever expensive after-shave he's wearing. He kisses our hands, then waves at a man who looks as though he's about to go sailing.

'Got to go, ladies. Let's be off, Debs,' he says, taking her firmly by the hand. Deborah smiles awkwardly and follows her husband.

'What a charming man,' says Suzanne, looking after the attractive couple as they walk towards the harbour, Dennis almost pulling Deborah along as he talks to the man in the sailing gear.

'Arrogant,' I say, watching them walk away, 'and too slimy for my liking.' Then I'm tapped on the shoulder by Skyler, who asks if she's missed anything.

'We just saw Deborah; she introduced us to her gorgeous husband,' swoons Suzanne.

'Oh,' Skyler says, obviously not wanting to comment. Perhaps she thinks he's slimy as well.

'So what did Doreen tell you?' I ask, wanting to change the subject.

'Mine was weird. I had the Lovers and the Devil, which suggest affairs, clandestine relationships and relationships not being what they seem. She said I ought to keep my eyes and ears open. I know a bit about tarot cards and they can all be interpreted in different ways, but that's how Doreen interpreted mine.'

'You're not planning to have a fling with anyone, are you, Skyler?' jokes Suzanne.

'Of course not,' says Skyler, flushing slightly.

'I'm surrounded by men having affairs,' says Suzanne. 'In fact, I doubt if any of the guys I work with are faithful to their wives. One had a string of affairs when his wife had a baby because he got bored with domesticity. He made her life so miserable that *she* had an affair, and then he divorced her on the grounds of her adultery.'

Before we can respond, it's Suzanne's turn to have her cards read. While we wait, Skyler and I people-watch the mixture of tourists and locals mingling around the stalls, keeping one eye on the children, who are comparing crystals with Peter and Helen. After about ten minutes I see Suzanne walking towards us, looking pale. 'What's the matter?' I ask.

'Doreen said there was death around me. Not to do with my family, but definitely death near me.' She pauses, but neither Skyler nor I know what to say. 'I've already called Howey to see if he's OK. He's drunk with the boys after a long City lunch. Orlando's fine, isn't he?' she says, looking round and seeing her son being swished around by Peter as the other children line up to take their turn.

'Your son looks perfectly well to me, Suzanne,' reassures Skyler, as she looks down at her watch. 'Look, let's forget about any deaths, or at least try to as I know Helen's promised to tell the children some of her Cornish ghost stories, if that's OK with you both,' she says. 'I know they've had a long day, but it's her speciality. I've got to go back and help prepare supper, but why don't you and Suzanne stay here with Helen?'

'Actually, if it's OK to leave Orlando with you, Amanda, I'll head back now with Skyler,' says Suzanne, still looking a little disturbed by Doreen's comment.

'That's fine,' I say. 'I'm interested in what Helen's going to tell the kids anyway.'

An hour later, as the last of the stalls is being cleared away and the light is starting to fade, Helen is at the centre of a group of children outside Sarah's café. The kids are hanging on her every word.

'This town is full of ghosts,' she says. 'Yes, ghosts. Not just of pirates and fishermen, but other ghosts as well.' The market square feels quite creepy in the half-light now that it's almost empty. 'There's one particular story about a girl called Helena de Beaufort. Helena was a very beautiful lady, the daughter of a local gypsy, but people thought she came from royal blood because she didn't look like her father or her mother.'

'Am I from royal blood, Mummy,' interrupts Jack, 'because I don't look like you or Daddy?'

'I'm afraid not, darling,' I say.

'May I continue?' Helen asks Jack in mock surprise.

'Yes, please do, Helen,' Jack replies, his chin resting firmly on his hands as he waits for the next instalment.

'Well, Helena de Beaufort was very kind and beautiful and every day she would help out the local fishermen and mend their nets for a few pennies. She would also serve behind the bar in the local inn, and was well known to the fishermen and pirates in the area. There was a fisherman called Tom Heath and a pirate called John Tyler who both fell in love with Helena. Every day Tom would ask her to marry him and every evening in the inn, John would do the same. Helena couldn't decide what to do as she loved them both, and would wander the streets trying to decide which man to marry and how to break the other one's heart.

'Tom was decent and loving and thoughtful and John was passionate and adventurous and dangerous and Helena loved and needed them both. So Tom and John decided to fight one another on the cliffs by the Minack Theatre. There they would fight to the death for Helena.'

There's an audible intake of breath.

'One evening, they went up on to the cliffs and fought with their bare hands. When Helena found out about the fight, she rushed from the inn and rode full pelt to the spot where they were fighting. She pleaded with them both to stop, but each one wanted to kill the other. She stood crying on the cliff while they fought, and as Tom was about to cast a deadly blow to John's head she threw herself off the edge. Both men ran down to the bottom of the cliff to see if she was still alive, but she had vanished into the sea and her body was never found. The ghost of Helena de Beaufort is still seen on the cliffs sometimes and John Tyler and Tom Heath still haunt the streets, inn and harbour of Tremontgomery in search of their lost love, a love that will never die.'

The children's eyes are like saucers. They clamour for more, so Helen tells an even darker tale of the pirates who would wreck ships by confusing them with lamps on the shore. By the time she's finished and we head for home, the children are convinced Tremontgomery is swarming with ghosts.

Fortunately, they're so shattered from the day's activities that we have no problem tucking them into bed that night. Jack doesn't ask where Fishbowl is and Hannah doesn't even want a story read before her head hits the pillow and she's asleep.

Once everyone is settled, Suzanne, Skyler and I go out to sit by the big old cherry tree near our cottage.

'Ooh, let's have a drink,' says Skyler. 'I don't have to cook for anyone – they all eat out on Sundays.' Suzanne goes inside our cottage for glasses and another bottle of champers (I think she's brought an entire cellar with her) while Skyler lights some of the incense she bought at the fair and puts tea-lights on the table. As the cork pops on a bottle of Tatty we all cheer quietly, then sip our glasses, watching the sun set and musing over the day.

'The Death card doesn't necessarily mean death in a literal sense,' Skyler eventually says, recognising that Suzanne has been quieter since seeing Doreen and still needs some reassurance. 'It can mean the end of a situation or a necessary change. Likewise, the Lovers doesn't always mean affairs. It could refer to a friendship, a new relationship or even a choice that has to be made, whereas the Devil can very well mean affairs and mischief. It's all to do with interpretation.'

'And it's probably a silly bit of nonsense anyway, like Ouija boards. Don't you remember messing around with them as kids?' I say. Skyler looks askance at me.

'Just because we may not agree with them doesn't mean they're wrong,' she says. 'There's a lot of truth in them. Tarot cards may help you manage your reactions and expectations for the future, hopefully for the better. Ouija boards, however, are another matter altogether. I wouldn't touch them. They waken spirits that should be left alone.'

'Why? Have you had a bad experience with one?' I ask.

'No, but I've heard stories of people I know who use them it round here,' she says, 'and I've heard about dinner parties back in Whitlow where they got them out.'

'Surely not,' says Suzanne, suddenly coming to life again.

'Yes. It was the latest party craze in some circles. It had taken over from Ann Summers and designer children's wear parties – now it's all about contacting the dead.'

'Can we talk about something else?' I say, starting to feel uncomfortable. The smell of incense, the overload of sunshine and fresh air today, and probably the champagne as well, are making me feel quite heady. I keep thinking about Doreen's words: 'Don't take things at face value; things are not what they seem', and wondering how Nigel is getting on and whether he's being totally honest with me. I tried calling him earlier but couldn't get an answer at home or on his mobile.

Suzanne obliges and changes the subject.

'Why don't you have a party here at Silver Trees, like Dennis is organising at the Elysian? Howey and I know loads of celebrities, so we could help you organise the event. It would be easy,' she says, getting quite excited by the idea.

'That's very kind of you, Suzanne, but we've managed to cope quite well without celebrities so far,' says Skyler graciously.

'No, no, I insist, Skyler,' Suzanne replies excitedly, getting carried away by the champagne. 'Howey knows the actor in *Ocean's Eleven*. We could invite him.'

'Who, Brad Pitt?' I ask incredulously.

'No, the other one,' she says, trying to think of the name.

'Must be George Clooney,' Skyler teases.

'No, no. It'll come to me.'

Soon we're talking about our favourite films, how I love *A Room With a View* because it's so romantic and *Howard's End* because it's so tragic and passionate, and that's how I've always wanted to live my life. Suzanne looks at me as though I'm mad, but Skyler says she feels just the same, which is why she loves *Jean de Florette* and *Manon des Sources*. She thinks the French understand tragedy so much better than the English, but Suzanne disagrees.

'What about *Brief Encounter*?' she says, to which both Skyler and I burst out laughing.

'So which friends have been down to see you at Silver Trees? Are we the first?' asks Suzanne, miffed.

'Well, yes, actually. We've been so busy. My mum and dad are coming down for the first time next month,' admits Skyler.

'Wow! You've been here for almost two years and they haven't been down yet,' I say. 'How are they?'

'Mum's been a bit poorly recently, but she's a bit

better now and I'm so looking forward to seeing them,' she says. 'We've been to see them, of course, but they're both in their seventies now, so there just hasn't been the right time to have them here yet, what with us working all the time and all the renovations we've had to do.' She beams with excitement.

'She'll be very proud of what you've achieved, Skyler,' I say as Suzanne nods in agreement. 'They both will.' I take another sip of champagne. I realise we've already almost finished the bottle, but for the first time on this holiday I'm starting to feel completely chilled. As we sit in friendly silence, I think about the long and unusual day we've had. I know I'll sleep well tonight and tomorrow, perhaps, I'll even find time to chat to Skyler alone.

Chapter 7

In the Saddle

I love morning sunshine. We've had almost a week of clear, warm, blue morning sunshine streaming into our bedroom as the sweet smell of lavender and rosemary wafts up from the gardens below. The children have all been getting up and dressed at the crack of dawn, without waking the grown-ups, and have made their way to the main house to keep Skyler company while she does the morning chores. This morning I manage to join them to collect the eggs with Willow and Rose.

I haven't had a chance to speak to Skyler's girls as they always seem to be either helping their mum or Clare in the kitchen, or playing with the other children on the beach or in the gardens. Willow is clearly closer to her dad and, whenever she can, helps him collect wood or do the gardening; Rose is more like her mum, very bohemian and feminine. Skyler puts them both in similar clothes, but Willow always looks more messed up in hers. On this lovely morning I find myself talking to them while we're gathering eggs. Both of them are in loose-fitting dungarees and Willow already has mud all over hers. She's dying to tell me a garbled version of a joke she's overheard involving O.J. Simpson and Monica Lewinsky, and proceeds to recite it in such a funny way, although clearly not understanding the punchline, that I find myself giggling uncontrollably with her. 'So,' I ask when we've both calmed down, 'do you like it here?'

'It's lovely. I like riding with Tom on the horses,' she replies, stopping to look at me while she's speaking. Willow is only ten, but she looks and sounds older than her years.

'Oh yes, I've heard about Tom. He's very good with horses, isn't he?' I say.

'Yes, he talks to them,' she says, almost in a whisper. 'They understand what he's saying and he always lets me choose my favourite, Favour.' She grins.

'And do you still want to ride when you're older?' I ask. When I last saw her she wanted to ride professionally and win a gold in the Olympics.

'Well, yes, that would be nice, but what I really want is to sail around the world like Ellen MacArthur. I'd like to see the world like you did, Amanda, but without having to write nice things about the places I visit,' she says, which makes me laugh.

Just then Rose drops one of her eggs, splashing yolk over herself.

151

'Be careful with those eggs, Rosie,' Willow says, looking on. 'The hens will get really annoyed if they see all their hard work go to waste. Then they won't lay for us any more. You know what Mummy says: waste not, want not.'

'What does that mean?' asks Rose. 'I've never understood what that means when Mummy says it.' She wipes at the yolk on her dungarees.

'If you don't waste anything, you won't want for anything,' her sister replies, smiling.

'That's what Terry says, too,' Rose says, nodding. 'He says we should be careful with everything, especially money.'

Willow smiles. 'Yes, he says lots of things, doesn't he, Rosie? Now let's get on with these eggs, then we can go to the beach or go riding, OK?'

'OK, Willow,' says Rose.

'So how did you meet Terry?' I ask as I fill up my basket.

'He was standing at the bottom of my bed and asked me to play with him in the garden,' she replies. 'Didn't you, Terry?' she says, looking over her shoulder.

'So he's here with us now?' I say, slightly startled.

'Of course he is.' Rose smiles as though he's answered.

'Does Terry like me?' I ask, not knowing what else to say.

Rose pulls back as though listening to what the boy is saying.

'Yes, he does,' she says, looking up at me, 'and he

tells me to tell you not to worry about money because it will be all right.'

At first I go cold, but then I think Rose must have talked to Jenny or Hannah, who may have overheard my conversations with Nigel.

It's still spooking me a little as I head back to the cottage to collect our riding things. Just then my mobile starts buzzing in my pocket. It's Nigel calling for a chat, so I tell him about the conversation.

'Oh, Hannah or Jenny probably mentioned that we were a bit worried about money at the moment,' he reassures me. 'That's all. We've just got to be careful what we say in front of the children. They're like sponges.'

'I know,' I say.

'Apart from that, how are things?' he asks. 'You've been down there for a week now and everyone seems to be getting on fine.'

'The kids are very well and very happy. They've been on the beach most days. Our lot have completely adopted the Schneider children now. They help even up the boy–girl ratio in the group, so at least now they can play football with fairer sides. And Hunter's in heaven. He has so many children cuddling and stroking him, and he's very patient with them, even when his tail gets pulled. He loves the beach as much as the rest of us, and the kids take it in turns to walk him every day; they fight for the privilege.'

'It all sounds perfect, Amanda,' he says wistfully. 'What are your plans for today?'

'We're going riding this morning, and then the children are going to learn to surf with Matt, the local instructor, who helps George and Tom with all the outdoor activities when they need it.'

'With all these handsome outdoor types around you, should I be getting jealous?' he says jokingly.

'Don't be silly. I forgot to tell you, us girls have been invited to a party next Friday by Dennis Banks, the owner of the posh hotel, the Elysian, but of course I didn't bring anything party enough to wear.'

'I bet Suzanne brought her entire summer wardrobe,' he laughs.

'You guessed right, although of course she claims she has nothing to wear!'

'How are you two getting on?'

'All right,' I say tactfully. 'I like Suzanne, you know I do, but she is precious, and she does very little around the cottage. I clear up, put the dishes on the table, load and unload the dishwasher, you get the picture.'

'You knew she'd be like that,' he says, laughing some more.

'Not this bad, though.'

'Why, doesn't she do anything?' he asks, starting to take it more seriously.

'I'll give you an example. Yesterday morning we had breakfast on the terrace. The kids and I laid the table, the sun was shining, birds were singing and it was all very nice. Meanwhile Suzanne was in the bathroom putting her face on, which seems to take longer and longer every day. When she appeared, she looked lovely, while we were all slightly less pristine, having been up collecting eggs, going to the baker's and helping out in the main house. Then Suzanne announced she would be making lattés. It seems Suzanne makes the best lattés in the world. So for the next half-hour she made lattés, even though neither I nor the kids like them. She made a dreadful mess in the kitchen, and when she delivered them, she expected a round of applause and a bloody medal. I burnt the toast, of course, so she looked like the hero and I was the villain.'

'Oh, it just sounds as though she wanted to do something nice, that's all.'

'That's not all,' I say, feeling annoyed that my husband's not backing me up. 'She's so mean, Nigel.'

'What do you mean? I thought she bought Skyler loads of champagne when she arrived.'

'She did, but since then she hasn't paid for a thing. She hasn't done any food shopping, or offered to pay her share. Skyler even paid for her to have her fortune told. It's not like she can't afford it, after all; she's loaded.'

'Well, from my experience, Amanda, the richer they are the meaner they are. I know, I work with a whole bunch of them; some of them even dress as though they're on the breadline. I guess that's how they stay rich. However, she does throw wonderful dinner parties,' he adds, trying to lighten the conversation.

'Her caterers throw wonderful dinner parties,' I reply petulantly. 'All she does is play the big "I am". She's great to have a dinner party with but lousy to share a holiday cottage with. I wouldn't mind so much, but neither Skyler nor I can afford to keep subbing her. I'm not impressed.'

'Don't worry, darling, she'll probably pay you back at the end of the holiday. The kids are getting along well, so at least that's something,' Nigel says, trying to change the subject.

'Yes, they're fine,' I say, 'but they miss you, Nigel.'

'I miss them, too. Can you call me back later so I can say hello to them all?'

'Of course, that's if I can pin them down for long enough! I barely see them – they're just constantly off exploring!'

'I'm hoping it will be just another week and then I'll be down. Aren't you moving into your own cottage soon?'

'Hopefully by the time you get here, once the Schneiders leave. Then either we or Suzanne and Orlando can move into their cottage. I can't wait, Nigel. I don't want to create a fuss and spoil it for the kids, but we're down to our last hundred pounds and we've still got four weeks to go.'

'Well, have a quiet word with Suzanne. It's perfectly reasonable to ask her to pay a bit towards the provisions.'

I'm silent; Nigel's always so damn sensible. He comforts me a bit by telling me things are looking good and that soon I'll be able to afford my own Gucci towel and Chanel bikinis.

'I'm not interested in designer labels, Nigel, I just want you here,' I say, only slightly mollified.

'I know, I know you do. Love you.'

'Love you, too.'

I put my phone back in my pocket and get my clothes ready for riding: jeans, T-shirt and trainers – they'll lend us boots when we get there. I'm a bit nervous about getting on a horse as I haven't ridden since I spent some time on a ranch in Canada, and that was only one day's riding. I know Jenny is nervous too because she used to have riding lessons but stopped after she fell off two years ago; she hasn't been on a horse since, so Tom will have his work cut out with her. The other children are all very excited. Suzanne, of course, has brought her finest riding gear – cream jodhpurs, riding boots, jacket and hat – and looks ridiculously over the top. I can't help giggling when I see her.

'Are we going to see the Queen?' asks Hannah when she sees Suzanne coming downstairs.

'No, no, Suzanne just wanted to wear her riding outfit. Rather splendid, isn't it?' I say, as all my children gawp.

'Do you think it's too much?' says Suzanne, aware of the reaction.

'You're fine, Suzanne. You'll put everyone else in the shade. Now, we'd better get going. George is taking us in his car, which is actually a battered-up old school minibus which he bought for next to nothing so he could ferry guests around – just as well, given there are so many of us.'

I've heard Skyler and George talk about Tom

MacKenny with great affection, and from the description George gives us en route, he sounds dreamy.

'Tom is a six-foot Paul Newman lookalike in his early fifties,' he tells me and Suzanne with a twinkle in his eye. 'He moved here from Calgary when his wife died of cancer, built his own place, and set up the stables, taking in ex-polo ponies and training them for the tourists to ride. He takes people all over, through the woods and along the coast. He's brilliant with kids and even better with horses – our guests always come back glowing with praise about the experience.'

We're driving up a long dusty track, past a field of contented and healthy-looking horses. After twenty minutes or so, we park outside a ranch house, which looks slightly incongruous in the Cornish countryside; it wouldn't look out of place in the Rockies. I can see Matt standing outside, waiting for us, then a tall silver-haired man comes out to greet us.

'Hi, everyone, I'm Tom,' he says as we get out of the car and line up in front of him. 'How're you all doin'?'

'We're all doin' fine,' says Willow, beaming away at her hero.

'Good to meet all you pretty ladies and handsome gentlemen. Can you please tell me your names and whether you've been ridin' before so we can get on the way.'

Jack starts the introductions with, 'My name is Jack, I'm six, I like cuddles and I've never ridden a horse before, so can I have a nice one, please?'

'You sure can. Let's see if I can find a cuddly horse

for you,' Tom says, winking at him. Jack tries to wink back.

'My name is Hannah, and I'm eight and like climbing trees,' says Hannah.

'Right then, Hannah, let's see if you'll be as good at ridin' as you are at climbin' trees.'

'I'm Jenny and I'm ten years old. I don't know much about riding, but and I want to travel the world like my mother,' says Jenny. I smile. I guess I can't be such a bad role model after all.

'Been ridin' before, Jenny?' asks Tom.

'Yes, back home in Whitlow Park, but that was a couple of years ago and I fell off, and haven't been on a horse since,' she explains.

'The secret is to get right back on again,' Tom advises. 'So we'll give you a very gentle horse, my favourite. A real sweetie called Bluebell.' He smiles and it lights up his whole face. Jenny instantly looks more relaxed.

'And who might you be?' he says, looking at Suzanne.

'My name is Suzanne Fields, I'm forty' – liar, liar, pants on fire – 'and I've ridden since I was a child, though I haven't been on a horse for ages, so I'll probably need lots of help in the saddle.' She giggles flirtatiously, perhaps expecting him to say she doesn't look her age.

Tom looks at her up and down and smiles.

'Married?' he asks.

'Why yes,' she says, blushing like a schoolgirl.

'Thought so,' he says. Suzanne, who's usually quick with the witty comebacks, is dumbstruck for once, and before she has time to think of a reply Tom has stepped in front of her son. 'And who might you be?'

'My name is Orlando. I'm ten and I'm really looking forward to riding and surfing today,' he says. 'Can you teach us how to talk to horses?'

'Anyone can talk to a horse, only people rarely do. And when they do, they don't listen to what they've got to say,' Tom replies. 'Very nice to meet you, Orlando.' He shakes his hand, which makes the boy swell with pride.

I'm last in line.

'My name is Amanda Darcey, I'm forty-three, and I want to tell on Suzanne, because she's actually forty-two.'

Suzanne doesn't seem to find this funny, although Tom certainly does.

'I rode a long time ago and am a little nervous about today,' I add.

'No need to worry, Amanda,' Tom says warmly, 'and you don't look a day over thirty-two.' Without looking at her, I can feel Suzanne bristle at this.

'Now, everybody, listen up. My priority here is for the horses to be well cared for and the guests to be safe – in that order,' he says, looking at everyone steadily. 'First I'd like to check out how well everyone can ride, and then I'll choose a horse that's right for you, because, believe you me, horses have characters too,' he says, looking at Jack and Hannah, who nod vigorously. 'They can be jealous and romantic, and if they mate and the mate dies, they can pine away and try to kill themselves. Did ya know that?'

All our children shake their heads, still looking serious.

We're riding with the Schneiders today, and they're waiting for us on the verandah, already kitted out. While Matt goes to get the horses ready, Tom shows us around briefly. Inside the ranch house there's a large open-plan sitting room and a large kitchen with a green Aga and a big oak table. There's a wonderful smell of fresh coffee and I see some cookies, obviously straight out of the oven, cooling on a wire rack.

'We can have some cookies before we go and when we come back, but no eating while you're riding, OK, guys?' Tom says, looking round at all of us. The children nod in unison.

He opens a back door. 'We don't have any suicidal horses here at the moment, but we have a few feisty ones, so we'll see how each of you sits in the saddle first of all,' he says. He leads us around the back of the house to an open clearing, with trails leading off in different directions. In the centre of the clearing are a few tree stumps, which are presumably used as benches, and a campfire waiting to be lit. To the right, there's what looks like a wooden horse.

'Now, this is Bud,' he says tapping the horse, which is little more than three pieces of wood with a saddle on it. 'I'm going to watch you each get on and see how you sit, and how you get off. Everyone got that?'

Everyone nods.

'Great, so who's first?'

Jack puts his hand up and runs over, ready to mount.

'Jack, you may need a bit of help,' says Tom, putting his hand out so that Jack can step on to it and climb up, which he does with ease. Jack receives a 'well done', as do Orlando, Hannah and Jenny, leaving them grinning with delight. As the Schneiders and Willow and Rose have done this many times before, Tom goes straight on to Suzanne and I me.

'Now for the grown-ups,' he says. I approach Bud tentatively, but find myself mounting the horse easily, getting a 'good posture' comment from the master. Suzanne, of course, mounts as if she's entering a dressage competition.

'I'll give you a horse that will loosen you up a bit, Suzanne,' he says. 'And you look as though you've ridden a lot, so one that will test you too.' Suzanne seems to ignore the first comment and beams enthusiastically at the second one.

Tom and Matt spend the next half-hour fitting those of us who need them with boots, hats and gloves and deciding which horse should have which rider. Then they gather the horses into the corral. My horse is called Sid, Jack's is called Favour, Hannah has Lightning and Jenny, as promised, has Bluebell. Suzanne has one called Thunder and jokes that she hopes he doesn't have a temper.

'You're a good enough rider to control Thunder,'

says Tom. 'He's a control freak and it takes another control freak to deal with him, so you're ideal.' Suzanne giggles nervously, not quite sure if that's a compliment.

For the next ten minutes everyone grooms their horse; Jack, Hannah and the younger Schneider children helped by Matt and Tom.

'How's your holiday been so far?' Tom asks, coming over to me after helping Jack with Favour.

'Very good, thank you. We've been on the beach most days because the weather's been so wonderful; we went to the fair in Tremontgomery last weekend and, other than that, we've just been relaxing, really. It's good to get out and do something active today, though,' I add, not wanting to seem too lazy.

'Is the Elysian party still the talk of the town?' he asks, making sure Sid's saddle is well secured.

'Yes, I believe it is. I'm told there will be loads of famous people there to schmooze with. Suzanne's particularly excited about it.'

He looks over at Suzanne, to catch her staring. She quickly tries to make herself look busy with Thunder. What is it with cowboys? Mind you, comparing Howard with Tom I can understand why she's attracted to him. Tom looks like a man who could easily whisk a girl off her feet and ride off into the sunset.

Finally, we're all mounted and ready to go.

'We'll take a break after a couple of hours,' says Tom, 'but we'll go at a steady pace so that no one gets left behind.'

We set off along one of the woodland trails. For the first hour or so, no one says much, although I can hear Jack occasionally 'whispering' to his horse. We ride through narrow pathways, between birch, sycamore and oak, a gentle breeze occasionally rustling the leaves. It's so beautiful and peaceful, with the sunlight filtering through the leaves. After a while, though, I become aware of Suzanne fussing behind me. I can tell she desperately wants to be up front with Tom, because I can hear her encouraging Thunder to speed up, though it doesn't seem to be working – the horse knows its place and wants to be at the back. Determined as ever, Suzanne digs in her heels and finally Thunder reluctantly breaks into a canter. She's overtaking everyone when suddenly Thunder rears up. She tries to get him back down and under control, but isn't strong enough. The horse rushes into the trees with Suzanne clinging on and shouting 'Stop!' in a determined voice. But Thunder's having none of it. Tom has been watching to see whether she can stop him by herself, but now gallops after her.

For a few minutes we wait in silence, listening to increasingly shrill cries of 'Stop!' Then there's silence. Has she fallen? Is she just out of range? I can see that Orlando's on the verge of tears when suddenly I hear Suzanne's laugh. She's obviously not hurt, and by the sound of things she enjoyed the excitement. A moment later we see Suzanne and Tom trotting safely back to us.

'Sorry 'bout that, people. Mrs Fields here forgot who

the boss was. You work *with* the horse,' he advises. 'Never think you're the boss, coz you're not. Got that, Suzanne?'

Suzanne, positively swooning, nods.

'Sorry, Tom, I forgot my place,' she says. I can't help smiling and glance at Matt, who raises his eyebrows as if to say, 'Not another one!'

I, on the other hand, get no such treatment. Tom has removed my stirrups because he's detected that I don't grip properly with my legs. But now my saddle seems to have loosened and I'm slowly starting to slip sideways. Fortunately, Sid is the antithesis of Thunder: as I dangle precariously, he turns his head and looks at me as if to say, 'What are you doing down there? You're supposed to be on top,' which is exactly what Tom says when he trots up beside me.

After a few hours we stop and take a break. Matt has brought along some cookies, which he hands out to the children. Tom and Suzanne are laughing together and already seem remarkably intimate. She touches his shoulder, removing a hair that isn't there, while he brushes some hair back from her cheek. I hope she knows what she's doing, especially as I can see Orlando is watching as intently as I am.

A short while later we're back at the ranch house unsaddling our horses. Jenny seems to have redis-covered her confidence and I feel I've improved – at least I haven't fallen off again.

'I guess I'll see you all at the party at the Elysian,' Tom says as we walk over to George's minibus.

'Yes, together with Howard, Suzanne's husband,' I reply, hoping he'll get the hint.

He smiles, takes my hand and kisses it.

'I look forward to meeting him. He must be quite a man to be able to live with a woman like that.'

He says this so sincerely that I'm not quite sure whether he means it as a compliment or criticism, but decide not to tell Suzanne either way.

Driving back to Silver Trees, everyone chats about their morning, except Suzanne, who's strangely quiet.

'That was quite a rescue,' I say to her under my breath.

'What?' she says. 'Oh yes. He didn't really rescue me, Amanda. I managed to stop Thunder by myself, but it was good to have the company on the way back to the rest of the group. Did you know his wife died?'

'Yes,' I reply.

'And he doesn't have a girlfriend,' she adds.

'I didn't know that,' I say.

Suzanne notices my somewhat disapproving expression.

'Yes, I know I'm married, but that doesn't mean I can't window shop,' she says defensively. 'And with so many handsome men to look at, who could blame me?' she says coquettishly.

'I've got no problem with a bit of meaningless flirtation, but do you think behaving like that in front of Orlando is such a good idea, Suzanne?' I say quietly, which wipes the smile off her face.

*

Skyler welcomes us back to Silver Trees, looking slightly flustered but telling us that she's left a picnic for us on the beach.

'Are you OK?' I ask as I follow her into the house.

'I'm fine, but I've just had some news from Helen. She's got wind of a hotel inspector who's coming down to grade Silver Trees. He's due to arrive on Sunday, and there are so many things that need checking for health and safety. We still need to repaint one of the bedrooms, but Ms Pepsin is staying in it this week, and we can hardly disturb her, can we?' Skyler says in a rush.

'Don't worry, Skyler, we'll help out.'

'Don't be silly, we'll be fine. You go surfing and enjoy your holiday,' she says smiling, 'and if I do need your help, I'll tell you,' she adds, hurrying off in the opposite direction.

After collecting our beach gear ready for surfing, we head down to the bay for another delicious picnic in the shade of our favourite rock. Matt and the Schneiders appear just as we're finishing, and Matt suggests we have half an hour to digest our food while he gets the kit ready. I have never been surfing before, but I've bungee-jumped in New Zealand, ridden an ostrich in South Africa and run with the bulls in Pamplona, so it would be churlish not to give surfing a go.

Suzanne decides instead to have a pampering afternoon at the Elysian spa, which doesn't surprise me, although I'm annoyed that yet again she assumes she can leave Orlando with us – not that we don't love having him there, but she doesn't seem to have an ounce of maternal responsibility or concern for him.

As she heads back up the path, I take the children over to where the boards are laid out waiting. They huddle round Matt, who makes sure they have their life jackets on and shows them how to position their boards at even spaces on the beach.

'Has anyone been snowboarding?' he asks. Orlando, Jenny, Willow and all the Schneider boys put up their hands.

'Great, well, this is sort of like snowboarding except that you're on water. It's all to do with positioning yourself on the board, balance and the ability to get upright and stay there.'

Orlando puts his hand up to ask a question.

'Isn't it more difficult because water moves and snow doesn't, and if you fall it's much easier to lose your board?' he says, all of which sound like valid points to me.

'Totally correct; that's why we do lots of practice before we get in the water. Has anyone been wind-surfing before?' he says, looking round. The same hands go up. 'Again, some of the same techniques are used: it's all about how you balance your body and use the waves. Everyone with me so far?' Everyone looks at Matt blankly and he laughs. 'Don't worry, you'll get it in time,' he says, stepping on to his board.

For the next half-hour Matt shows us how to jump on and off the board, how to stand up and what to do if we fall off. The kids, who have smaller boards, make light work of jumping on and off them and springing up to a standing position. I, on the other hand, find it difficult to balance even on dry land, so who knows what I'll be like on water. Maarten and Penny are having the same problems. Maarten has very long legs and Penny is rather portly, so springing up suddenly from horizontal to vertical is not proving easy.

After another half-hour of tuition on the sand, Matt takes the children one by one to the water's edge to see what they can do. Orlando is first and gamely wades into the water, looking like a sleek seal in his black wetsuit. Penny is standing next to me, obviously uncomfortable in a very tight wetsuit.

'I look like a beached whale, don't I?' she says.

'Not at all,' I lie. 'I think it's great that you're giving it a try. It's more than most mothers would do,' I say, thinking of Suzanne, who should be here to watch how wonderfully her son is doing, even if not to have a go herself.

Matt swims out and asks Orlando to get on the board, then try to stand up. On the fourth go he gets it right and manages to stand for a few seconds before falling off. All the time, Matt gives him loads of praise and support while we clap from the beach, although I'm not sure he can hear us. With each attempt, he manages to stand up for longer and longer periods, and then, on what must be his tenth attempt, he stays standing and everyone applauds.

We all have a go in turn, and eventually each of us manages to stand on our boards, thanks to Matt's patient coaching. We're all ridiculously thrilled by our achievement. Whilst we all splash about, exhausting ourselves paddling back out and straining to leap up on the board, Matt goes back to Orlando and takes him further out where the waves are bigger.

I pause on the shoreline as Orlando once again gets into position and, on Matt's command, jumps up as a swelling wave brings him towards us. For a whole five seconds he's properly surfing, the thrill of the speed marked on his face. He comes crashing down with a squeal of delight, and I just know he feels like a champion. I wish Suzanne was here to see her son – she would have been so proud. Dragging my board back to the rock, I go for my beach bag, then realise I've left my camera back at the cottage. I want to take a photo of Orlando and the others, so I yell to Jenny, Penny and Maarten that I'm popping back to the house and dash for the path.

I trundle along, my head buzzing with the adrenalin of surfing for the first time. Life was starting to feel rather monotonous in Whitlow, and I'm beginning to realise how bogged down I've been feeling, with all these irritating, draining financial worries. In the grand scheme of things money is so unimportant, but so often it takes over and supersedes all the much more valuable things in life, like the joy of being with my children and watching them grow up, or having fun by myself and with Nigel. I want to enjoy the simple pleasures in life, like being with friends and drinking wine, not worrying about what I could be doing with my time or how our money could have been spent, or, indeed, if I should be using my time to make more money. I felt alive today, riding and attempting to surf. At home, I feel like I've just been surviving, treading water emotionally and financially while going nowhere. I'm pondering all these things when I see something that stops me dead in my tracks.

In between some trees, to the side of the path, I can just make out a couple kissing. They're totally oblivious to me, completely involved with each other. My first reaction is to smile, because it's the sort of thing Nigel and I did on our holidays before the children. I'm about to walk on when I suddenly recognise the man. It's Tom MacKenny. He's leaning into the woman, who has her back to me. And suddenly, though I can't see her face, I'm utterly certain it's Suzanne. She's got the same elegant posture, the same mane of hair, and I'm sure I've seen that dress in her wardrobe, although she wasn't wearing it when she supposedly headed off to the spa. What is she playing at? And what should I do? I could make light of it – after all, I don't really know Howard all that well. Maybe they're having problems; maybe they have an arrangement whereby certain things are allowed. But no matter which way I look at it, Suzanne's a married woman on holiday with her sensitive ten-year-old son, and this is the last thing Orlando needs – what if I'd been walking back with him? I'm half considering making my presence known and just seeing what excuse she offers, when they walk off into the wood, out of sight and never looking back to see me standing on my own, stunned and speechless.

I decide to carry on back to our cottage to get my camera, not wanting to follow them into the wood and end up embarrassing both them and myself. By the time I come back down the path they're still nowhere to be seen, so I carry on to the beach, where Jenny is now practising with Matt and not doing quite as well as Orlando.

For the next hour Matt helps all the children, some more successfully than others. Trying to forget the encounter I have just witnessed, I take a few shots and then gamely jump back into the water with my board. The boys and Hannah seem to have the strength, balance and courage required, while the other girls and I are a little more nervous about being knocked about by the crashing waves and flying boards. But I do get some wonderful action photos of everyone. The consensus is that Orlando is the best surfer and has made the most progress that day, but once we see Matt in action, all our attempts look pitiful. He really is master of the waves, riding them as though they were a horse.

Later, as we carry the boards back up to the house for Matt, I can't stop thinking of Tom and Suzanne. I can't wait to get back to the cottage to see if she's there. After we've thanked Matt for a fantastic afternoon, I get everyone showered and dressed. Orlando is on cloud nine, talking about the surfing and how wonderful it was and could I show Mummy the photos. 'Of course,' I say, but inside I wish I'd managed to take a photo of Tom and Suzanne together – perhaps it might knock some sense into her. What the hell is she playing at?

Chapter 8
Going Green

'Mummy, I did really well at surfing,' shouts Orlando, as he runs up to the cottage.

Suzanne is sitting on the verandah, glowing and happy.

'Careful of my nails, Orlando,' she says, pulling away slightly as he hugs her. 'Mummy has just had a manicure, so try not to smudge them. I've been busy too, getting my hair done, having a massage and a facial. I feel like a new woman,' she says, her eyes sparkling as she smiles at everyone. I look at her, wondering if it's the wonderful massage or the wonderful man that's made her skin glow.

'I didn't see Deborah, but I did see Dennis and he's so looking forward to seeing us at the launch on Friday,' she says, waving her newly manicured nails in my face. 'It seems there might even be a few people from London who we'll know, or whom I will, at least. Oh yes, I almost forgot,' she says, taking a sip of herbal tea. 'Dennis suggested we all go sailing with him on his yacht this evening. He thought the children might like it. How does that sound?'

The children all jump up and down in excitement at the thought of going to sea.

'Aren't you all exhausted after riding and surfing?' I ask, feeling ready to collapse myself. But their faces are beaming. Where do they get their energy from? 'Well, I'd better tell Skyler, just in case she's preparing something for us this evening and she might want to come along too,' I say as I go to find her.

As I'm walking to the house I consider telling her about Suzanne and Tom kissing, but I think she's got enough on her plate with the inspector coming, so I decide it can wait. I find Skyler in the sitting room, plumping cushions and putting out fresh flowers ready for the evening. She looks exhausted, and I realise it's she who needs the break.

'We've all been invited by Dennis Banks to join him on his yacht in an hour,' I say. 'Can I persuade you to go and I'll look after the guests?'

'No, you go, Amanda, and have a good time. I've got too much to do for this inspection visit. Dennis's yacht is stunning; we went on it last year. You'll have a lovely time. Deborah is a great hostess, and it's nice to have a little touch of luxury occasionally. Maybe you could take Willow and Rose with you?'

I feel torn about whether or not to go myself. I still

haven't had any time with Skyler since I arrived, but she seems insistent.

'OK, and of course I'll take the girls, but only if you let us help you out more. Just let us know; that's what friends are for,' I say and hug her. She looks as though she needs it.

'Now everyone's got to be on their best behaviour,' I say as we walk into Tremontgomery. 'We're going on a lovely yacht and you've got to do exactly as Mr and Mrs Banks tell you,' I add, looking closely at Jack and Hannah, who are sulking because Hunter has had to stay behind with Skyler.

Suzanne and I walk slowly, my legs already feeling stiff from the day's activities. The kids have skipped along all the way, speeding up now the harbour is in sight.

'The Elysian is run so well,' says Suzanne. 'Skyler should really take note of how they do things. Silver Trees is charming in its own way, but it's a bit disorganised; she was never the best time-manager in the playground, if I remember rightly. How she's managed to make all this happen I'll never know, though George, bless him, has got his head screwed on.'

I can't help it. I finally snap. Every little comment and thoughtless action from Suzanne that I've suppressed over the last week boils up inside me.

'That's thoroughly unfair, Suzanne! Don't forget we're her guests. And she's looking after all her *paying* guests as well as us. She's got a hotel inspector coming this Sunday and she needs our support. She's put so much time, effort and love into Silver Trees and all you do is act like Lady Muck and compare it to the Elysian, which is a completely different enterprise. Try to be a little less thoughtless and a little more grateful, for once.' I've probably gone too far, but I don't care. In fact, I'm just about to ask what she thinks she's doing kissing Tom when Orlando comes back towards us.

'Mummy, can Jenny and I go to Aunt Sarah's or Peter's bakery so we can buy something to give Dennis and Deborah?' he asks. Suzanne's still staring at me in a mild state of shock, and in the end it's me who speaks.

'Yes, of course, that's very thoughtful of you,' I say, smiling and handing him some loose change.

Suzanne and I walk in frosty silence towards the harbour, but it's such a beautiful evening, with the soft light making the water glow, that we can't stay cross for long. There are four big yachts moored up today. Suzanne hires the odd boat for corporate entertaining, and perhaps to break the ice a little between us she starts to tell me about them.

'That's a Swan, and that one there is an Oyster, both cruisers,' she says as we pass two sixty-foot stunners, with tall, magnificent masts.

'I wonder if Dennis has one of those,' says Hannah.

'I don't think so, darling,' replies Suzanne. 'I suspect he has the money, but not the knowledge. He seems like the type to tell others what to do rather than roll up his sleeves himself,' she adds, looking at me askance and winking. 'These are wonderful yachts.'

I smile back at her. I'm feeling a little guilty for

snapping at her, but I don't think Suzanne has the faintest idea how hard Skyler and George have had to work. She might know what good looks like, but she has absolutely no idea how much work goes into making it happen, because she always delegates the responsibility to someone else.

Suddenly we hear a voice call out to us.

'Hello! Are you the Silver Trees group?'

We turn to see a tall, dark and very handsome man dressed in white walking towards us.

'Hi, I'm Terence,' he says with a light Scottish lilt to his voice. 'I'm here to collect you in the rib.'

'Great,' I say, gathering up Jack, Hannah, Rose and Willow and looking round for Orlando and Jenny to return. 'We've just got to wait for our elder children.'

'OK, well, let's get you into the rib in the meantime. We're moored just a few minutes away,' he says, pointing out to sea.

We turn and gasp at a huge motor yacht moored about a mile out, glistening white in the sunshine.

'Got them!' shouts Orlando, rushing towards us with Jenny. They grin and open a bag of delicious-smelling scones.

We board the tender one by one, and once everyone's safely seated Terence starts the outboard. As we head slowly towards the yacht, Terence says, 'While we're on our way, I'll run through the safety regulations, so everyone listen closely. Everyone has to wear a life jacket, and when we're on board you must be careful when you're walking on deck – absolutely no running. And if we ask you to sit down or go below, you do as you're told. Everyone understand?' The children all nod seriously, staring open-mouthed. 'We'll have a proper tour when we're all on board, and perhaps you can even help with the steering. Anyone interested?'

Four hands shoot straight up, together with cries of 'Me, me, me', until Terence raises his hand for silence. Wow! I wish I had that effect on my three.

As we approach, the yacht looks even more incredible.

'*Refined Beauty* is thirty-four metres long, with a beam of just over seven metres, a draught of one point nine five metres and a range of five hundred and twenty nautical miles,' explains Terence.

'What does that mean?' asks Hannah, speaking for the rest of us.

'Ah, we have landlubbers on board, have we?' Terence turns and grins. 'That means you may have to walk the plank!'

The children laugh and Jack asks if they really do have a plank and please can everyone walk it, but only with their swimsuits on.

'I'm sure you can, but you'll have to ask Captain Banks,' says Terence, winking at Jack. 'He's the one who makes all the decisions.' He steers the tender smoothly to the side of the yacht, and everyone is guided up the steps to be greeted by Dennis. He, too, is dressed in top-to-toe white and is red-faced from too much sun or alcohol, most likely both. Deborah is looking her usual elegant self in a light purple chiffon number. Beside them, a man holds a tray of drinks: champagne for the grown-ups and juice for the children.

'Welcome on board *Refined Beauty*,' announces Dennis proudly. 'First let me introduce you to Terence, my skipper,' he says, gesturing to Terence, who bows and winks at the children. 'I bet none of you have been on a boat like this before, have you?' he asks the children. Then he introduces two more of his crew, who are also in white and looking slightly bored. 'This is Ben and this is Jerry.'

'Like the ice cream,' comments Orlando.

'Yes, just like the ice cream,' laughs Deborah.

Dennis leads us round the boat while Terence, Ben and Jerry get ready to cast off. Dennis is very bullish.

'This boat was custom built for over half a million,' he says nonchalantly, expecting a gasp, but not getting one as the children are too distracted by the boat to be paying proper attention to what he's saying. Suzanne lets out a polite 'Wow!' but as she works with bond traders who earn that sort of money in a month, she's less impressed than Dennis would like her to be. 'It can cater for up to ten guests and six crew, so we'll have bags of room this evening.'

He leads us into a very comfortable salon and dining room on the main deck, which is all white leather and white cushions. All I can think of is sticky fingers over the pristine whiteness, but hopefully they haven't got anything vaguely messy on the menu for supper.

'This is the main stateroom, where I do all my

business and entertain celebrities and local VIPs. It's a nice way to smooth over deals, isn't it, darling?' He turns to Deborah, who is asking me where Skyler is and doesn't hear.

'Isn't it, darling?' he repeats angrily.

'Isn't what, darling?' I can't believe that he talks to her like that, and what's worse, she seems to be used to it.

'And where are Skyler and George?' asks Dennis. 'Didn't we invite everyone over?' He looks at Deborah, who nods.

'They're back at Silver Trees because they have a hotel inspector visiting soon and still need to get things organised,' I explain.

Dennis huffs and says, 'What a horrid bunch of nit-pickers they are. Those who can't, teach and those who can't teach, criticise. Skyler will be fine, though – they like those characterful places, even if they are a bit tatty round the edges.'

'I think it's got a lot of charm,' says Suzanne, 'and soul. Sometimes the larger hotels have all the facilities but lack character.'

I look at her and smile. Perhaps my earlier outburst hasn't fallen on deaf ears, although Dennis glares at her as if he's been betrayed by an ally. The children sense the tension and quieten down, watching the dynamics between the grown-ups. Dennis huffs again and walks on, telling everyone exactly how much everything cost, where he got it from, which celebrity sat on which chair and which politician looked through which window.

The children are behaving well, but they all look bored. Dennis Banks may be rich, but he is also dull. Deborah hasn't said a word and looks a little embarrassed at her husband's pomposity. She's a very different woman when she's with him. She doesn't sparkle in the same way as when I first saw her at the hotel. It's almost as if he drains her energy when he's around.

We hear the engine start up and Jack and Hannah immediately ask, 'Can we watch Terence steer the boat, Mr Banks?' interrupting Dennis just as he's about to tell us how much a painting of a horse cost.

'Er, yes, of course you can,' he says, pushing his way past us and up the stairs to Terence, who seems in control and happy to see us, although he only barely manages to hide his disdain for Dennis. I'm amazed they haven't mutinied. 'Everything in order?' booms Dennis, even though he's standing right next to Terence.

The pilot house is a mass of swirling lights, buttons and gauges, like some sort of nautical spaceship. Terence points at things and tells us what they are and what they do.

'This is a digital compass to tell us which direction we're going in. This is the radar to tell us what else is in the area.'

'Like pirates,' interrupts Jack.

'Yes, like pirates,' Terence smiles, 'but it can also pick up large fish like dolphins, which like swimming beside us and following in our wake. Perhaps we'll see a few this evening,' he adds.

'Or some sharks,' says Jenny. 'We heard there were sharks about.'

'Yes, we might even see sharks. You've just got to keep your eyes peeled,' he says, aware that Dennis is getting agitated by all the attention he's receiving.

'Can we have a look at the engine room?' asks Orlando.

'You'd better ask Captain Banks,' replies Terence tactfully.

'I'm sure you can at some point, little boy,' Dennis says to Orlando, 'but I need to know if everything is OK first. Everything OK, Skipper?' he asks again, tapping Terence on the head like a lap dog.

'Yes, everything's fine, sir,' he replies, 'although we've had weather warnings, so I don't think we should go out too far or for too long. We don't want to get caught in—'

'I'll decide what we'll do,' Dennis interrupts, his mouth tight, his eyes fixed on Terence, who nods in agreement, and says, 'Righto.'

Terence, aware that he still has an audience, continues to tell the children what's happening.

'We have two anchors on the bow. Jerry's winching them up electronically now as I move the boat slowly forwards to help dislodge them. Then when the anchors are up, off we'll go into the unknown,' he says mysteriously, leaving the children wide-eyed.

'Do you ever lose the anchor?' Jack asks, looking up at Terence as he steers the yacht out.

'No, but they can easily get tangled up when there

are lots of yachts moored close together, and then you have to hire a diver to untangle everything. I've never done it, Jack, and I hope I never will,' he says, looking round at Dennis, who has given up showing us the yacht and is walking back to his master cabin, huffing and puffing about something or other.

'Is there a hierarchy with yachting?' I ask Terence as the children wander about the pilot house under strict instructions not to touch anything.

'Oh my word, yes,' he says. 'The top-of-the-range sailing yachts that you find round here are Oysters and Swans. There were a few moored in harbour.'

Suzanne nods in an 'I told you so' fashion.

'I've been a full-time skipper on many a Swan. They're wonderful boats. Motor yachts are a different story. You tend to have a lot more seasickness on motor-boats, because the motion isn't as smooth and in general the guests aren't used to boats. But don't worry, ladies, any sign of bad weather and I'll get us back straight away, no matter what the captain says,' he adds with a wink.

As I watch the harbour gently slide away, I start to appreciate what a beautiful coastline Skyler lives on. The whitewashed buildings of Tremontgomery drift into the distance and I can see what we've come to regard as our bay and beach.

'There's Silver Trees!' Jenny shouts.

'And that's where we have our picnics,' calls out Willow.

The children point and shout every time they

recognise something until the coast is nothing more than a faint line on the horizon.

The sea is flat calm, and a glass of pink champagne, some smoked salmon, fresh oysters and mussels go down well. The children are watching the water avidly, and suddenly Hannah shrieks, 'Dolphins!' We all watch transfixed as five or six dolphins ride the waves around and behind us, racing faster and with more refined beauty than Dennis's half-a-million-pound yacht could ever muster.

Terence is telling Jenny and Orlando about St Andrews, where he was born, and the stunning beach there.

'Isn't St Andrews the place where all the best golfers go?' asks Orlando, who I know is learning to play golf at his dad's club.

'Yes, that's it. There's also a deer sanctuary nearby and a castle and dungeon you can visit. It's a lovely little place, you should get your mum to take you there,' he says to Jenny.

'My mother's a travel journalist,' says Jenny. 'She took us all over the world when we were little and she still takes us places now, though not as much since Jack was born because it's more difficult with three,' she explains, sounding very grown-up.

I've noticed the wind getting up a little as the light fades. The sun is low, casting pink and gold over the choppy waves.

'The weather is turning,' I overhear Terence say to Dennis as he comes back up to the cabin, but he brushes his skipper aside with, 'We've only just come out and our guests want to see the sea.'

Dennis comes over to us.

'So, Amanda, I understand you're a travel journalist?' He smiles warmly to me.

'Yes.' I nod.

'And what did you think of the Elysian?'

'I must say it's very impressive. I know Suzanne was particularly enamoured with the spa, and she really knows her spa treatments,' I say, looking over at her. She's trying to look calm and composed, despite the fact that it's getting rockier and rockier. There are definitely more grey clouds in the sky than when we first left harbour.

Dennis comes closer to me, invading my body space and making me feel rather ill-at-ease.

'Do you know what I like in a woman?' he whispers in my ear.

'No,' I say, feeling rather nauseous – and not because of the sea.

'Discretion, Amanda. I like a woman who can keep a secret. Are you discreet?' he asks, stroking the back of my hand.

'No,' I say loudly, laughing a little hysterically and jolting him. 'I'm afraid I'm terribly indiscreet. I would be the worst person in the world to tell anything to. I'm a journalist, for God's sake. Anything you tell me, I'll put down in print. Anything I can't put down in print, I'll tell someone else about it, so they can.' I smile sweetly at him. He looks rather shocked. Good.

He moves away and starts to talk to Suzanne. It's now decidedly rocky and the remains of the sun have been covered by thick grey cloud. All the children have come inside, and Hannah whispers to me that she's feeling sick. In the next second she's thrown up all over the cream sofas.

'Deborah,' I yell, 'we need some towels.' I grab a bowl of mussels and empty them into a salad bowl so that Hannah at least has something to throw up in.

'I think I'm going to be sick as well,' says Orlando, rushing to the bathroom.

'I'm not feeling too good, either,' says Jack, looking as though he's about to burst into tears.

'Dennis, I suggest we go back now,' Deborah says, looking alarmed and rushing around, fetching towels and bowls for everyone.

'It's a good way for them to gain their sea legs,' he snaps back, walking upstairs and barking at Terence to head back to harbour.

Hannah has filled the bowl and Suzanne's looking a bit pale too, but thankfully Terence manages to get us back to land in only ten minutes. The ride back is as rough as a fairground ride, but at least it's quick. The crew quickly drop anchor and Terence gets us all back into the rib. We manage to say thank you and wave goodbye to Deborah, who looks very concerned about everyone. Dennis has already gone down below, probably to fumigate the sitting room.

As we head back to the quay, Terence is more sympathetic.

After about half an hour I'm feeling stronger and have decided what to do. I wake Hannah and, with her leaning heavily on me, get her back up to the main house. There we find Clare, looking stressed but in control.

'I'm so sorry, Clare,' I say, 'but I think Hannah, Suzanne and I have a touch of food poisoning – that or we don't agree with yachts. Do you have a spare room I can put Hannah in? Suzanne is using the bathroom in the cottage and I'm worried about the others.'

'Oh bugger, poor darlings,' says Clare. 'I'm so sorry, Amanda, but all the rooms are taken. I'll ask Skyler if you can use theirs – they have their own bathroom.'

I sit Hannah down while we wait. After a few minutes, Clare returns with Skyler.

'You have our bedroom for the night, Amanda. I'm sure Jenny and Orlando will be fine in the cottage, and Jack can share with my girls. There's a study that doubles as a small bedroom, and George and I can sleep in there.

Clare leads us up to Skyler's bedroom. There are still no lights, so everything is lit by candle and torchlight which makes the room look even bigger. Hannah suddenly throws up all over me. I take her to the sink, and for the next few minutes we take it in turns to be sick. I feel weak and empty and I know Hannah does too. When we both think it's safe, we take off our dirty clothes, and I dampen a flannel, wrap us both up in the duvet, then hold the flannel against Hannah's forehead until we both fall asleep.

*

The next morning I'm woken by Skyler knocking on our door. I open my eyes. Hannah and I look and smell awful, but at least I don't feel so bad any more, and I don't think I'm going to throw up again.

'Morning,' says Skyler. 'How're you feeling?'

'Better, I think. Thanks for everything, Skyler. What with everything else going on, this is the last thing you need,' I say.

'Don't be silly. You're unwell, and that's what friends are for. You'd do it for me, I know,' she says and smiles.

Hannah is awake too, now, and looks up at me. 'I feel better, Mummy,' she says, sitting up.

Skyler has brought up a tray of dry toast and water.

'This is the best thing for you both in the circumstances,' she says, putting the tray down on a nearby table and opening the windows to let the sunshine in.

'The rain's stopped and the electricity is back on,' she says. 'Suzanne seems to be much better as well, though she still needs to rest. Jenny and Orlando have been helping out with Jack; they've been reading to him, telling him stories and baking cookies this morning, and the Schneiders thought it would be nice to take them to the Eden Project today. They'd planned to go anyway, so would it be OK for them to take Jenny and Jack along? I've asked Suzanne and she's OK about Orlando going,' she says, coming over with a glass of water.

'Yes, I'm fine with that, if they don't mind,' I say, taking a sip of water.

'Mummy, can I go, please can I go?' Hannah says in that whiney voice that always irritates me.

'Don't use that baby voice,' I say, 'or I won't even consider it.'

'Please can I go, Mummy?' she asks, quickly switching to her most polite voice. 'I feel so much better and the fresh air is just what I need. It's not good to be cooped up inside all the time.'

'Children always get over food poisoning quicker than adults,' says Skyler. 'Apparently there's a batch of dodgy seafood in the area, Peter told me when I went to the bakery this morning. You must have been unlucky.'

I beckon Hannah over and ask her if she genuinely feels well, to which she nods yes. Her eyes are shining again, and despite her messy clothes, I think she's fine.

'I'll take her down to get cleaned up in the girls' bathroom and she can wear some of Willow's old clothes,' offers Skyler.

'Thanks, I've got loads in the wash but I haven't ironed anything yet.'

'OK. And you stay in bed,' says Skyler. 'You and Suzanne probably ate more seafood than Hannah did.'

Hannah bounds out as though nothing ever happened and Skyler promises to return with some clean clothes for me and suggests I take a long bath.

I lie back against the pillows and look round the bedroom. There are old wooden printing blocks of angels' wings, treble clefs and a King and Queen of Hearts, all hung at random on the lemon-yellow walls.

There are clothes rails with matching colours hung together, just like in Suzanne's room, but the colours are mauves, purples and pinks rather than browns, blues and greys. There are three large paintings of nudes and lovers, one with 'Thank you, Skyler' scrawled alongside the date and the artist's signature. They're erotic and sensual and make me think about what I would do to our bedroom at home if I had the time and money. Suddenly my mobile chirrups. It's Nigel, sounding very cheerful.

'Everyone's got food poisoning,' I say. 'Well, not everyone, just some of us,' I add, explaining who's ill, who isn't and how we got it.

'Oh, you poor love,' he says, sounding very sympathetic. 'Make sure you take it easy today. Actually, things are moving on nicely here, so I should be down soon. How are you getting on with Suzanne?'

'Oh, OK,' I say, thinking back to the brief stand-off we had in Tremontgomery yesterday evening. 'I think it's safe to say we're very different people with very different values. And she is a control freak in every sense of the word. I really feel for Howard, and especially poor Orlando.'

'Well, it's a lesson learned. At least you won't go on holiday with her again.'

'No,' I laugh. 'I think it helps if you bring up your kids in the same way, and this is definitely an area Suzanne and I are at odds with. Luckily the sun's been shining so there's enough space for everyone.'

After we say goodbye I take a long bath, then change

into the fresh clothes that Skyler has left on the bed. The sun is hot by now, and with the children all occupied and nothing much for me to do, I decide to read a magazine on the big comfortable sunlounger on the balcony.

Next thing I know, someone's saying my name and Jack is smiling at me. I pull myself up, rubbing my eyes. My watch says five o'clock. Jack is laughing and holding my hand.

'Mummy was fast asleep,' he says, delighted by my confusion.

'You've slept for over seven hours,' says Skyler, bringing in a large bouquet of flowers and an entourage of Orlando, Jenny and Hannah, all carrying gifts. 'We've already been up here once, but you were sound asleep and we didn't want to wake you. You obviously needed it,' she says, sitting down on the other lounger.

'I think we all do,' I say, as Hannah and Jenny come over and give me a big hug.

'We've done some paintings and drawings of what we saw at the Eden Project today,' says Jack, 'and we've brought you some flowers as well,' he adds, handing over a loose bouquet of sweet peas and lavender. I immediately think of the poor lavender outside our cottage. I must remember to tell Skyler, though perhaps now is not the time.

'Deborah Banks sent these lilies for you, and another bouquet for Suzanne, together with a card.'

The lilies smell delightful and the note reads, 'I'm so

sorry for poisoning you, Amanda. I am mortified. Will make it up to you at the party, which I hope you will still come to. Your friend, Deborah, x'.

'Isn't she a sweetie,' I say, looking up at Skyler.

'Yes, she is,' Skyler says, taking the flowers back. 'I'll find a vase for them in a second.'

'How's Suzanne?' I ask.

'Oh she's fine, Amanda. She's had this lot visit her already with gifts and flowers, which cheered her up no end. I've already got a bag of her clothes to take to the Elysian for dry-cleaning. I think her main concern is what she's going to wear to the party!'

'Now, Amanda,' says Orlando seriously, 'we're going to tell you some amazing facts we learned today at the Eden Project.' He clears his throat. 'In just one year we fill enough household dustbins to reach from the earth to the moon,' he says, nodding seriously as he steps back in line.

'And did you know,' says Jenny, 'that recycling just one glass bottle saves enough energy to power a TV for one and a half hours?'

Next Rose and Jack stand forward and manage to say, almost simultaneously, 'And the biggest seed in the world is from the coco-de-mer in the Seychelles. They weigh up to eighteen kilos and they look like our bottoms.' And with that they turn round, pull their trousers down and wiggle their bottoms at me.

I clap my hands, delighted with the presentation and the moonies, as they all bow and beam at the applause.

'Thank you for that, children. All very useful,' I say.

For the next half an hour they excitedly tell me about all the other things they saw.

'It's very important to recycle *everything*,' says Jenny, 'although we don't in our house. We have a recycle bin, but Hannah and Jack use it as a wicket when they're playing cricket,' she adds. 'We learned about how nature is amazing and how each generation, but especially your one, is messing it up for the next. And even now we might not be able to stop it. Even when the electricity went off here and we all had to use candles, it wasn't so bad, was it? In fact, despite the fact that you weren't there, Mother, it was all rather fun.'

Chapter 9
Tissue-paper People

It's Friday, the day of the Elysian party. We spend a lovely day on the beach, the children practising their surfing with the Schneider boys. They have formed teams, and spend most of the day challenging each other to collect the most shells, build the biggest sandcastles, or play dungeons and dragons. They're like modern-day Swallows and Amazons. George has been wonderful with them, and so have Matt and Tom, who have been giving them more lessons in surfing and riding.

Everyone has gained in confidence with their riding, although Suzanne keeps letting Thunder gallop off into the woods so that Tom has to go after her. It's becoming so obvious now that even Jack remarked on it yesterday.

'Suzanne's not very good at riding, is she? Does she know what she's doing, Mummy?'

Despite her flirtation with Tom, and her happiness at seeing Orlando enjoy himself, I can sense that Suzanne is getting tired of living in the cottage and yearns for some five-star luxury. Just before we get ready for the party, I overhear her on the phone to Howard in her bedroom. I'm downstairs in the kitchen loading the dishwasher, again, but the cottage is so small, and her voice so loud that I can hear almost every word.

'I'm starting to get bored of all this back-to-basics stuff,' she says. 'It's all very cutesy with the children playing on the beach and all that, Howey, but it's not really me, darling. I need my space.' There's a pause while Howard says something, then, 'Yes, of course I knew it would be simple.' She sounds aggrieved. 'But, well, there's simple and there's *simple*. Mind you, I didn't think there would be anything formal to go to here but at least we've got this do at the Elysian tonight. I'm still at a loss for what to wear; everything I've brought with me is so last season, and there'll be people there who really count in my business. I just don't want to make a bad impression.'

There's another pause. Jenny walks in the door and is just about to ask me something when we both hear Suzanne say, 'Oh yes, yes, the people here are lovely. Not as backward as I would have thought, you know. Not too much inbreeding. They're quite an intelligent, creative lot really. The ones I've met anyway.'

'What a snob!' Jenny gasps.

I put my finger to my lips and whisper, 'Don't tell anyone what Suzanne just said, OK?'

'OK,' she says, though her expression suggests she doesn't understand why.

'Did you want something?' I ask.

'Only to tell you that Skyler says you need to leave by seven,' she says.

'Thanks, darling. And remember, not a word to anyone.'

Jenny taps the side of her nose, then turns and goes back outside.

After a few minutes, Suzanne walks down the stairs with her choice of dress and shoes in one hand and a make-up bag in the other.

'I'm just going to get myself ready now,' she says. 'I'll try not to take too long in the bathroom, but you won't need long to prepare, Amanda, will you?' She smiles, and before I have time to answer she disappears into the bathroom and locks the door.

I walk up to my room and look through my clothes. What does Suzanne have to worry about? If she had a wardrobe like mine she'd worry. The last thing I expected on a Cornish beach holiday was a posh do, so all I've come with is casual wear. I try on different combinations in front of the bedroom mirror. Everything makes me look like a busy mother of three with lots of common sense but little style. I decide to ask Skyler if she's got anything I can borrow; we're roughly the same size. I tell Jenny to bring the children up, then head for the house.

I find Skyler, as ever, in the kitchen.

'Just let me finish the salad dressing for tonight, and then let's go up,' she says after I've explained why I'm there. 'God, we've only got twenty minutes!'

Up in their bedroom Skyler starts to pick things out of the wardrobe.

'George is going to feed the kids supper up here, and then Clare's going to tell them stories about her ancestors, who were all pirates, or so she says. And she's just told me that Nicola has been flirting with George again, asking if she can paint him. So she's also going to protect him in case Nicola gets any ideas while I'm out.' Skyler giggles.

'I'm pleased you're so relaxed about it,' I say, finding a lovely dress and wondering whether it would suit me.

'Oh, you know how horny people get on holiday, especially somewhere as romantic as this. Whether they're single or happily married, there's always that idea at the back of their mind that they could have a holiday romance, even if the person they set their sights on is already taken. George had to ask one man to leave last year because he kept making improper suggestions to me. There's always an element of harassment that comes with this job,' she says.

I'm just about to tell Skyler that I think Suzanne and Tom are having a holiday romance when she suddenly says, 'This is it! This will look great on you, Amanda!'

Five minutes later, I'm dressed in an exquisite short satin skirt with a chiffon and net overlay, embroidered with semi-precious stones. With it I'm wearing two semi-transparent tops with yet more stones decorating them. I look at myself in the mirror and smile.

'There you are, Amanda,' says Skyler grinning broadly at me, 'you look like a fuckable fairy.'

Skyler quickly dresses in a large cream petticoat and skirt, and a thin white sleeveless top. We do our make-up in five minutes flat, then each grab a wrap and head downstairs.

'You look beautiful, Mummy,' says Hannah, as Jenny and Jack look me up and down.

'You look like an angel,' Jenny says.

'So do you, Mummy,' says Rose as Willow nods in agreement. Both girls run up to cuddle Skyler, who bends down to hug them back.

'You both look stunning,' says George, who comes in with Clare to say goodbye. 'Have fun and be good, and don't come back too late or too drunk,' he says cheekily.

'We won't,' says Skyler as her husband gives her a big kiss on the lips.

'Now come away, children, and let your mummies go to the party,' says Clare, ushering them into the sitting room. 'We've got lots of stories to tell you tonight and pirate cookies to make. Is everyone up for that?' They all shout, 'Yes,' and disappear into the sitting room.

No sooner have the children gone than Orlando and Suzanne make an entrance. Reeking of Jo Malone and looking as though she belongs on a catwalk, Suzanne is flawless in a pretty Paul Smith two-tiered stripy summer dress and delicate Laboutin kitten heels.

'Ugh, these shoes are just so last season, but they were bought to go with this dress. I really do hope no one notices, I look such a hotch-potch mess,' Suzanne complains before even greeting anyone.

'You look wonderful, Suzanne,' Skyler says graciously.

'Oh, so do you both,' says Suzanne.

'Everyone looks lovely,' says Orlando, who tries to hug his mum.

'Don't crinkle the dress, darling,' Suzanne says.

'The other children are in the sitting room with Clare. Why don't you join them, Orlando?' Skyler suggests.

He kisses me and Skyler goodbye, and we hug him warmly, not worrying about getting crinkled, then we all get into Skyler's car.

The drive of the Elysian is resplendent with fairy lights, which zigzag between the trees all the way up to the hotel, itself beautifully lit in subtle yellow and white. As we turn in front of the hotel, we see the windows lit by candlelight. Skyler parks her elderly four-wheel drive beside a line of Porches, Ferraris, Aston Martins and Beemers.

At the door we are greeted by two tall, attractive girls, their hair tied back tight. One of them I recognise as the rather brusque receptionist Lauren.

'Would you like a glass of champagne?' they ask in unison.

We nod and smile, quickly taking a glass each and walking in, sipping nervously. We're directed to the summer dining room, which is packed. Deborah greets us at the door, looking stunning in a white catsuit and huge sunglasses. Even Suzanne is in her shadow today, which isn't something she's used to, though she's gracious enough to gasp, 'Deborah, you look absolutely beautiful. Stunning.' She gives her a warm kiss on the cheek.

'Please, please come in,' Deborah says. 'Let me introduce you to everyone. And please accept my apologies for the awful seafood fiasco. You must have been dreadfully ill but you look wonderful now, you all do,' she says, holding each of our hands in turn. 'I'll take you around the room, and introduce you to the people I think you'll find interesting and get on with. Which aren't always the same people!' She winks, her eyes falling first on a twenty-something six-foot stick insect with high cheekbones and a sniff. She's wearing a long electric-blue shirt, short black skirt and thigh-high scarlet boots.

'Hello, Constance, may I introduce you to Suzanne Fields, Skyler Blue and Amanda Darcey. Skyler owns the wonderful bed and breakfast up the road, which used to be a schoolhouse and has glorious views of the sea, something we don't have, alas. Amanda is a travel journalist and Suzanne works for an international bank.'

Constance looks us up and down for a few seconds, completely spaced out. Suddenly she blurts out: 'Do any of you have a tampon? I forgot to bring mine.' Then she starts to laugh manically, which makes everyone a little nervous. Thankfully, she manages to stop.

'Sorry about that. My friend Mark told me a joke a few minutes ago and I've only just got it.' She starts to laugh again. 'But anyway, do any of you have a tampon?'

'I'll get one of the girls to find you one, Constance,' says Deborah, nodding to one of the waitresses and whispering in her ear. She leads us away, looking a little embarrassed. 'I didn't realise Constance was already flying,' she says when we're far enough away. 'Let's try again.' She leads us towards a slightly older, petite lady, who's deep in conversation with a man who looks as though he's come straight from his yacht. Standing with them is a slightly taller bored-looking woman in her twenties.

'Hello, Vivienne,' Deborah says, interrupting the woman, whose face I recognise from somewhere. 'May I introduce you to Suzanne, Amanda and Skyler,' she says.

'Oh, hello there,' says Vivienne. She reminds me of Carrie Fisher, but without the Princess Leia hairdo. 'Very nice to meet you. I work in TV; I'm the celebrity correspondent for *Good Morning UK*.'

'Ah yes,' Suzanne says, shaking Vivienne's hand. 'I recognise you.'

'Yes, everyone does,' Vivienne replies modestly, 'but it's usually a case of people thinking they know who I am but not being able to place me, so they tend to greet me like a neighbour or vague acquaintance.' She laughs. 'You do too, don't you, Henry?' she says, turning to the man, who's downed a glass of champagne in the few seconds we've been standing there. I do a double-take as I recognise him as Humpy Fartface. Perhaps he's too drunk to remember me, though, as he doesn't say anything.

'No, I don't get recognised,' he says. 'Except by ex-wives.' He laughs and offers his hand, introducing himself as Henry Foster. He tells us that he owns his own building company and loves to sail. 'Yes, sailing is my thing,' he says, throwing his champagne glass about as he speaks and spraying the last few drops over us. 'Mind you, I'm not much bloody good at it. I managed to lose my anchor off St Tropez last year, or rather my skipper did. Fired him, of course. How the fuck could he have done that? It's a bloody big thing to lose,' he adds, looking around as if we're supposed to have the answer.

'I heard it's actually quite easy to lose an anchor,' I say, remembering what Terence had told us. He looks at me po-faced, unable to respond as he's obviously one of those boat owners who don't know how to sail.

'Don't I know you from somewhere?' he says, looking at me closely.

'I don't think so,' I say and turn slightly to look over his shoulder at Deborah, who has slipped away to join Dennis and some other recently arrived guests on the other side of the room. Skyler is talking to Vivienne, who's looking decidedly less bored now, while Suzanne stands by my shoulder like a celebrity-spotting meerkat, scanning the room for someone more interesting to talk to.

'Oh, hello there, girls.' Dennis Banks comes over to us with two men, both of whom are in their late thirties and look rich and tanned. 'Wanted to see if you were both fully recovered,' he says, looking Suzanne and myself up and down a few times before saying hello to Skyler, whom he air kisses on the cheek. 'And I see that you are,' he adds. 'May I introduce you to Patrick Cardigan, who works in the City, and Mark Eggers, who lives in North Cornwall. I don't know what the hell he does; can you tell me, Mark?' he says, patting the man on the back.

'I'm in the music business. I've got my own studio, enjoy life and get on with people. I have a very high EQ,' he says.

I wonder briefly if he's boasting about his libido.

'What is EQ?' asks Skyler.

'Emotional intelligence,' interrupts Suzanne. 'EQ is emotional intelligence. It's a test to show how emotionally in tune you are with other people; empathy, if you like. But I'm surprised you have a high one; men don't tend to have very high EQs. In fact, you're lucky if you find one who has an EQ at all.'

Mark is speechless, but Patrick rallies to his defence. 'And how do you know that?' he asks aggressively.

'Because I am – or was until recently – PR director of ING Banking International. I worked closely with the HR department, and they have personality tests for potential employees, like the RATAR scheme . . .' She pauses briefly to take a sip of champagne and Mark interrupts.

Sarah Tucker

'There are loads of them. Corporations—'

'As I was about to say,' Suzanne says firmly, giving Mark a don't-try-that-again look, 'corporations can't afford to make mistakes when hiring candidates, especially at senior level. It's simply too expensive and, unfortunately, as universities are churning out kids who are superb at passing exams but have absolutely no common sense and an inability to think laterally, they need to employ these tests to detect personality defects. EQ is allegedly helpful if the person you're hiring has to work in a team, and particularly for those who have to manage others.' Suzanne is holding court: everyone in our group, which has now become quite sizeable, is listening. 'Personally, I believe it's a complete load of bollocks; I just trust my instinct. You can get people with high EQs who are complete arseholes,' she says, which makes all the women laugh, although the men remain tight-lipped.

'What's your last name?' asks Patrick quietly.

'Fields. Suzanne Fields,' she says, smiling at him.

'Oh my God, it's you, isn't it! You're the one who called some customers plebs, didn't you?'

I look at Suzanne, who's gone scarlet. More scarlet than Constance's boots. The others all stare, trying to recognise or remember her, while Patrick claps his hands in delight.

'Oh my God. Yes, it is. I was dying to meet you,' he says, as more people gather around, heightening Suzanne's embarrassment further.

'What's this, then?' says Dennis, looking at Patrick.

'Well, to cut a long story short, it was to do with bank charges. You know all the banks had to refund charges left, right and centre. Well, departments were set up to look for new ways of getting money out of their customers, and then Suzanne here said live on TV that all the customers were plebs, and it was a PR fiasco.'

'God, yes, I saw that!' Vivienne stares at Suzanne, who looks horrified. 'You did a live interview. And I don't think it was plebs; you called them idiots.'

Suzanne looks as though she wants the ground to swallow her up whole.

'But they are idiots,' says Henry, who's had too much to drink and is visibly swaying as he speaks. 'They're all bloody idiots not to keep their accounts in credit. Stupid twats,' he says, thankfully taking the focus off Suzanne long enough for Skyler and I literally and physically to stand by our friend, so that she knows we're there for her.

'Oh, don't be such a bigot,' says Deborah, who's walked over to see what all the fuss is about and has heard the last part of the conversation. 'Everyone needs financial help occasionally and if it weren't for borrowers the banks would go bust. Now, everyone, stop being so boring and come over here and listen to Allison Norfolk, she's about to officially open the cookery school.'

Everyone turns to look at the other end of the dining room, where a tall lady with long dark hair stands, her ample bosom trying to escape from a low-slung tight cream jumper. I giggle as I notice all the men ogling her nipples, which are clearly visible through her jumper.

'They're the size of fucking corks,' Patrick says under his breath. A thin, insipid-looking man is standing by Allison's side.

'Her husband,' whispers Vivienne. 'Bonks anything that moves, that one.'

'Ladies and gentlemen, it gives me great pleasure to be here today at this splendid hotel in this gorgeous location,' she says, pausing for polite applause and then continuing: 'Cornwall has become a foodies' paradise. From its wonderful cheeses to its excellent seafood . . .'

I notice Deborah looking our way and mouthing to Suzanne, 'Are you OK?' Suzanne nods and smiles back, still blushing furiously.

'From its excellent biscuits and cakes to its traditional beers and local wines, the Elysian is the perfect location for a cookery school. We will be attracting those who want to improve and perfect their cookery techniques and beginners who want to know how to boil an egg – I think there are many gentlemen here who might benefit from that,' she says to more laughter. She says a few more words that are drowned out by Henry and Patrick laughing loudly at some private joke, then she hands over to Dennis. These men definitely have low EQs.

'Thank you all for coming,' he says. 'I will be brief, as I know you all want to sample the food our local chefs have prepared for you this evening, but I just want to say thank you to all those who have made this possible. We feel the area has a lot to offer and we want to share it with the rest of the country and the rest of the world. Now, without further ado, let's go and eat!' Everyone applauds and we are ushered into the winter dining room, where tables of food are laid out for a banquet.

As we start to make our way through, I notice Tom MacKenny walking towards us, barely recognisable, and devastatingly good-looking, in black tie. He's taller than anybody else in the room, and seems to walk taller than them, too, so that the crowd parts for him and people turn and stare. Tom MacKenny may not be as wealthy as some of the other men in this room, but he has something they don't: presence.

'You look absolutely wonderful,' says Tom in his soft Canadian drawl, addressing himself to Skyler, Suzanne and me. I notice that Mark has quickly taken Constance by the arm, as has Henry his girlfriend, while Patrick ushers Vivienne away, all the women clearly annoyed not to be introduced to this tall handsome stranger.

'Why thank you,' Suzanne gushes, having recovered from her ordeal.

'I hardly recognised you out of the saddle,' I say, realising at once what I've said as the others burst into laughter. But it breaks the ice brilliantly as we walk into the dining room, Tom linking arms with Skyler and Suzanne as I hold on to Skyler's other arm.

The buffet tables are laden with hams, game, salmon – poached and smoked – terrines and pâtés. There are Middle Eastern lamb kebabs with cardamom, nutmeg, coriander and cumin; tamarind chicken skewers with red onion and green pepper; Cornish mackerel fillets served with pan-fried cherry tomatoes, wilted spinach and wholegrain mustard; chunky Moroccan chickpea pâtés; as well as broccoli and walnut bakes and butternut squash and cherry tomato tarts for the vegetarians. On another table are the sweet things, including some of the goodies we've already tasted at Silver Trees.

We're served by two dark-haired smiling young women, while Lauren offers cocktails from another table.

'We have Spanish sunrise and ginger refresher, with pomegranate and raspberry cordial, and honey and apple warmer made from a blend of Cornish honey, apples and cider vinegar,' she says, offering me a glass. But I'd rather stick with the champagne. I'm not driving tonight, so I want to make the most of it.

We help ourselves to food and start to mingle. Suzanne monopolises Tom, while Skyler speaks to Deborah and I get the short straw, Dennis, who's thankfully taken the hint and doesn't flirt. But after only a minute of stilted conversation, he spots a beautiful and infamous young rock 'n' roll couple heading our way.

'Kate! You look fabulous,' I hear as he abandons me without a backward glance. I'm feeling like a bit of a wallflower when to my delight I spot Terence coming towards me, a broad grin on his face.

'Hello, how are you, then?' he says. 'Have some smoked salmon.'

'No thanks, I'm keeping away from fish at the moment,' I say.

'Oh, of course you are. So sorry to hear about the food poisoning, but you're obviously much better now,' he says, putting the plate on a side table and sitting down on a sofa. I sit beside him.

'Yes, we're much better now, thank you. Only Hannah, Suzanne and I were ill. The others definitely just had seasickness as they perked up no end once we were on land. But what I had took me right back to the last time I had food poisoning.'

'When was that?' he asks.

'Oh, a long time ago. At one of those hippy music festivals.'

'I wouldn't have you down as a hippy, Mrs Darcey,' he says, his eyes glinting like a schoolboy's.

'I wasn't. I was a real swot at school, university and in my first years at work. I wore lots of navy, beige and brown and everything was polished and shiny. Then I met a guy who was very much a hippy and he introduced me to the festival scene.'

'That's what we need round here. There's been a literary festival at Port Elliott for a while, but I think this place needs more. It's a wonderful setting for it,' he says, taking a sip of champagne. 'There's so much beauty in the landscape, you know, real passion, and there's a wealth of creativity that hasn't been tapped. There are some incredible characters around, and plenty of people with the money to back it, providing they can see a return, of course.'

'They see everything in terms of cost and profit, don't they?' I say, looking around at the crowd. 'If it doesn't make money they're not interested.'

'Yes, but they also bring wealth to the area, Amanda. The farmers sold their land and the fishermen sold their rights willingly to these guys, so it's not all their fault, and if it brings in the tourist trade, then all well and good.'

'I used to enjoy literary festivals,' I say. 'The poets were always really angry and said "fuck" a lot, while the radio presenters would pick out bits from their best and worst books. I thought I'd made it when they picked something from one of my travel books.'

'Did they like it?' he asks.

'No, but it was funny anyway. And they were right to take the piss. I was a bit worthy about travel in those days,' I say, feeling nostalgic for the carefree days before marriage, kids and a mortgage.

We sit in silence for a few seconds while I sip my sixth champagne of the night.

'What was your favourite holiday?' I ask him, starting to feel more chilled.

'I have fond memories of camping,' says Terence. 'We used to go all over Scotland. I remember one summer on the west coast, spending every night in a sleeping bag listening to voices coming back late from a party, all drunk, some coming out with really funny stuff, others rude and abusive. Putting the tent up was a real pain, especially as we always managed to arrive after dark and had to do it by torchlight!'

'Oh don't get me started on camping,' I reply. 'I loved it. We used to go down to the South of France and spend the next six weeks getting to know the locals, climbing trees, collecting the most enormous pine cones and going to the supermarket for bread, milk and ice for the ice box. I remember always being in my rubber ring in the swimming pool because I didn't learn to swim until I was eleven.'

'God, that's late,' he says, leaning in a little closer as someone walks past and bumps into him.

'Yes, I know. I was always scared of the water, and of life in general, I think. I guess that's why I pushed myself to travel, get out more and never wear brown, blue or beige again. I suppose I wanted to be more like Skyler, my friend who owns Silver Trees,' I say, pointing to her talking with Deborah.

I notice that Suzanne is still talking to Tom, and that their body language is very intimate. Perhaps I should go over, but then Terence says, 'Yeah, funnily enough, I was scared of water too when I was a kid, so perhaps that's why I ended up being a skipper. I wanted to challenge myself. Confronting our fears head on is always the best way.'

'Do you have any fears now, Terence?' I ask.

'No, I'm happy now. I've found my peace. And you?'

'I have loads of fears at the moment. Financial and practical, but mainly financial ones that inevitably have an impact on everything else, even though they shouldn't. Hopefully, though, everything will be sorted by the end of the summer,' I say, taking a large slurp of champagne and making myself hiccup. 'I just need to put it all to the back of my head and get on with enjoying my time here.'

'Well, you have two wonderful friends over there; why can't you share your worries with them? It's never good to let these things stew,' he says softly.

'Oh I know, but there hasn't really been the opportunity. Skyler is always busy and Suzanne has her own stuff to worry about.'

'Maybe you think that if you offload on them, they'll do the same to you and you don't want that,' he says, looking at me as though he can see right through me.

'Oh, no, no,' I say, suddenly sitting up. 'It's not that at all. I'm here for Skyler, not just for the holiday, and Suzanne is too.' Although I realise as I say it that I'm here because I couldn't afford anywhere else and Suzanne is only here because her holiday fell through, which makes me feel a bit shitty.

'Holidays are a great time for being yourself and finding yourself, don't you think?' Terence says. 'I always find that holidays and travelling give me a new perspective on life; they re-energise me and help me focus on what's important because they take me away from the petty everyday-ness of work and responsibility. I love being at sea because it makes me realise that no matter how in control I think I am, I'm not. The sea is always in control.'

'You sound a bit of a dreamer,' I say, feeling slightly on edge; I'm not sure if he's flirting with me or just talking as he normally would. He's incredibly intense.

'Perhaps I am, but I've made my dream come true and here I am, living proof that dreamers can get paid. How many of the people here are living their dream? Are you living yours, Amanda? Are you where you want to be?'

I didn't expect to get involved in such a deep conversation at this party, particularly so early in the evening. I thought it would all be very *Hello!* magazine, but Terence has really made me think.

'I achieved what I wanted to achieve in a career. I have three healthy, well-balanced kids, I think,' I say, smiling.

'Your kids are wonderful,' says Terence, 'and so are Skyler's and Suzanne's.'

'I have a happy marriage, although I'd like to see more of my husband – at the moment we communicate mainly by phone, which isn't good enough – and I have lovely friends. So on paper everything looks great, but all of it takes money, and that's the one thing we're short of at the moment, though I haven't told anyone here that, not even Skyler, so please don't tell anyone,' I say, looking at Terence intently.

'My lips are sealed,' he says.

I take another sip of champagne and we sit in silence. 'Are you married?' I ask.

'No, but I've got a boyfriend.'

'You're gay?' I say, surprised, then clap my hand over my mouth. 'Oh God, sorry, I didn't mean it to come out that way!'

'No apology needed,' he says, grinning at me.

We can hear the DJ starting in the room next door and people are drifting in to dance.

'It's strange, but with the exception of my husband and a few other men I know, all the best men seem to be gay,' I suddenly blurt out. Oh God, I can't believe I just said that. I'm obviously quite drunk. Terence is still grinning at me. 'And you have all the best music!' I say, hearing one of my favourite tracks come on. 'Abba's gay. Donna Summer is gay. All the music I used to dance to in the seventies is gay!' I'm hiccupping quite violently now as I watch Skyler and Deborah approach.

'Would you like any pudding?' Deborah asks.

'No, I'm fine thank you,' I say.

'And I've got to get back to the boat,' says Terence.

'Oh no,' I cry. 'Can't you stay and dance?'

'Sorry, I've got to go, but I'm sure we'll see each other again.' He gives me a hug and a kiss. 'Deborah, thank you so much, it's been lovely,' he says, and he's gone.

The next few hours are a happy blur of dancing and more champagne. Skyler and I are taking a break after a particularly energetic Abba-fuelled session when Tom approaches, arm-in-arm with Suzanne.

'Can I leave Suzanne in your safe hands for one minute? I'm very keen to buy a horse from this gentleman here,' he says, indicating a small wiry man with jet-black hair to our left.

'Sure thing, cowboy,' slurs Skyler. 'Actually, I'm feeling a bit queasy,' she says to us. 'Do you mind if we go outside? I shouldn't have had any champagne.

Those two glasses have gone straight to my head and I'm supposed to be driving us back.'

'I'm sure Tom will give us a lift back,' says Suzanne, putting her arm around Skyler as we lead her outside. It's still warm and we walk slowly and none too straight through the Elysian's huge walled garden, with its magnificent greenhouse and neat lines of herbs, salads and vegetables. Through a door in the opposite wall we can see a wide sweep of lawn.

'How can I compete with this?' says Skyler as we sit down on a bench overlooking the lake. There's a small fountain in the middle with a statue of a little boy, water spouting out of his penis.

'You want a lake with a boy peeing?' slurs Suzanne in amazement. Skyler bursts out laughing.

'No, no, no. I mean all this,' she says, standing and swirling both arms in the air to take in the house and grounds and trees around us. 'The Elysian has so much.' She sits down again with a thump. 'Dennis and Deborah have the celebrity contacts, the staff and the money. They have a huge kitchen garden, compared to my tiny one. They have the spa, luxury toiletries – and the pond with a statue of the boy with . . . ' She starts to cry.

'But she doesn't have the view,' I say, giving her a hug, 'and she doesn't have friends like us, does she, Suzanne?' Suzanne is looking very drunk and a bit frazzled herself.

'No, she doesn't, Skyler,' Suzanne slurs, 'and this place is not unique, darlin'. You can find places like the Ely-shan' – she tries again – 'the Ely-si-an anywhere. You can. Silver Trees has magic. I know what good looks like, I do. Silver Trees has magic and this place doesn't. Do you hear that, Skyler?'

Skyler looks at Suzanne, and laughs at her attempts to comfort her.

'You are sweet, Suzanne, you know that? You're infuriating sometimes, but your heart's in the right place,' she says, hugging her. 'But the truth is we're really tight for money at the moment; we barely broke even last year and we desperately need every booking we can get. We're only able to carry on because we've got a big investor who's supporting us until we make a profit.'

'Why didn't you tell us?' I say, feeling guilty that Skyler hasn't felt able to mention this before. I've been so wound up in my own financial worries that I haven't had time to ask her how things are going with the business. I also now feel really guilty that Suzanne and I are taking up a cottage they could easily have rented out in high season.

'You just don't, do you?' she says, shrugging her shoulders. 'You put on a brave face, work hard, keep your head down, count the pennies and hope it will all work out. Silver Trees is George's dream as well as mine, and he so wants to make it work; he's so happy here. George has got his head screwed on; he knows it's a good investment and I trust him. It's not as if we didn't do the research, and we had a budget, but it cost more than even the surveyors expected and everything just mounted up. I know we've got the ability to make it work, but getting a good review from the inspector is all-important, so I've got to pull out all the stops,' she says. 'This was never just a pipe dream.'

'Strange,' I say, smiling and cuddling my friend. 'I was just talking to Terence about dreams and he asked me if I was living mine. I am, but everything is in the balance for us too, at the moment. I haven't told either of you, but if this deal doesn't happen we'll have to sell the house.'

'Oh, not your luverly house!' says Suzanne, putting her hand to her mouth.

'Yes, my luverly house. We've put it on the market, and if Nigel isn't successful we'll have to sell,' I say. 'The estate agent's already got someone who wants to pay the asking price, but I don't want to sell, so we're playing a waiting game. It's all about timing.' I hiccup. 'Nigel is trying to find financiers and get the banks on side.'

'Be careful who you go to. You've got to find people you can trust,' says Skyler uncharacteristically. 'They're all a bunch of blood-sucking wankers. Oh, God, sorry, Suzanne, present company excepted, of course.'

'Oh don't apologise to me,' slurs Suzanne. 'I'm not actually a banker. I think they're a bunch of wankers myself. Complete twats! Course I screwed up something rotten on TV. Fancy calling the customers idiots! Honestly. What a twit I am,' she says, nodding at us both, which makes Skyler and me giggle – Suzanne has never admitted her own failings.

'That was awful of that shitty man Patrick to make

you feel so bad back there,' I say, looking at Suzanne, who's still nodding.

'Yes, it was awful,' agrees Skyler. 'What actually happened?' she asks. 'I didn't see the programme.'

'Oh, you didn't miss much,' Suzanne replies more coherently, the memory clearly sobering her up. 'I was asked to do an interview about bank charges. The interviewer was very aggressive and they had phone-ins and everything, which I wasn't expecting, and it just came out. I called the customers idiots, and they had hundreds of complaints. I had to go to the boss and I was minuted in the board meetings. Actually minuted! In the end they decided to put me on to corporate events, so now I handle corporate entertainment and in-house presentations. I know all about corporate hospitality now, girls,' she says with a wry smile on her face.

I can tell it's not been easy for her to admit all this and to accept what was in effect a demotion. 'Oh, Suzanne, what did Howard say?' I ask, trying to comfort her.

'Howard said I was a silly cow and we haven't really talked properly since,' she says. 'But you don't need to hear me whine about my marriage problems.'

'No, really, I understand how tough it can be. Nigel's work has put a strain on my marriage as well,' I admit. 'But I'm hoping the holiday will help – if he ever gets here,' I say, looking back at the house. Tom MacKenny is walking towards us.

'Now, I don't really think any of you ladies are in a fit state to drive, so I'd be very happy to take you all home,' he says, smiling at us as we stand to greet him and sway in a non-existent breeze.

'Oh, is it time to go already?' asks Suzanne, losing her step a little until Tom gently catches her.

'All the other guests are leaving – it's three in the morning,' he says, looking at his watch.

'Is it really?' I ask. 'God, I completely lost track of time. The kids will have us up at the crack of dawn tomorrow. Do you have a good hangover cure?' I ask Skyler, who's faffing beside me with her wrap.

'Bacon sandwiches,' she says, looking up.

We make our way back to the winter dining room, which is now being cleared of the last few stragglers, and head to the main entrance, where Deborah, still looking fresh and lovely, smiles at us warmly, kisses us all goodbye and waves us off.

'Do you think that was a good evening?' I ask the girls.

'Very good,' says Suzanne, falling into the car so that we have to push her over and lodge her against the door. 'I really enjoyed it and I'm pleased we've had some time just the three of us. We're always surrounded by people, aren't we?' she adds.

I tell the girls about Terence and how lovely I thought he was and did everyone know that he was gay, to which everyone replies, 'Never!' – rather sarcastically, I think – and Suzanne says, 'I knew from the first moment I met him! All the handsome ones are, except for you, of course, Tom,' she adds, giggling.

Then we're all gabbling about our childhood

memories of holidays – me under canvas, Suzanne feeling unwanted in hotels and resorts, always cared for by nannies, and Skyler allowed to run wild so that now she thinks children need barriers, even on holiday. Tom listens to us rattle on without saying a word, just laughing occasionally at some of our comments.

When we get back to Silver Trees, he parks at the front entrance and turns round to us.

'D'ya know, ladies, your kids are very lucky to have you as their moms,' he says.

We all nod drunkenly, Suzanne burps loudly, Skyler giggles and I manage to fall out of the car head first and fart. If our children could see us now, I don't think they would feel that way.

Chapter 10

A Death in the Family

I'm sitting in the cottage, at the kitchen table, my head banging from the hangover to end all hangovers. The last time I remember feeling this bad must have been in the eighties. Suzanne is in an even worse state, but she's promised to unload the dishwasher this morning and she's damn well going to do it.

'It's your turn to do the dishwasher, Suzanne,' I say through gritted teeth as I sit, clutching my cup of tea. 'You haven't done it once since we arrived.' The children scurry out of the cottage, anticipating a confrontation that's been building for some time now. 'I know it's not really your thing, Suzanne,' I add, 'but I'm not your servant and neither are my children, and it's time you pulled your weight around here.'

Suzanne is sitting opposite me, looking grey.

'I've just done my nails,' she whispers, looking up at me mournfully.

'I don't care,' I say, standing up and throwing a tea towel at her. 'It's our holiday too and we're not your skivvies!' And with that I storm off into the gardens.

Suzanne follows, throwing the tea towel back at me.

'Sorry, I'm not very good at washing up, but then I haven't had much practice,' she says sarcastically. 'At least I know how to manage my money, so I can afford to get someone else to do it.'

All the children are within earshot, so I calmly walk up to them and tell them to go to the main house.

'Mummy's just got to have a few words with Suzanne,' I say as they turn and walk away. Jenny looks back briefly – she senses that Mummy is going to have more than a few words. As they disappear up the path, I turn to Suzanne, who looks at me, hands on hips, as if to say, 'What now?'

I take a deep breath before I let it all come tumbling out.

'Who the fuck do you think you are, you stuck-up, inconsiderate, ungracious cow? You swan about the house as though you're some princess to be waited on hand and foot!' Suzanne steps back into the cottage and nearly falls over the sofa. 'And how dare you mention something I told you in confidence last night in front of the children! And you forget that Skyler is also in financial difficulties, which her children may be aware of. You're bloody lucky to have a friend like Skyler, who will give you somewhere to go for your holiday because your plans got screwed up. You're lucky to have any friends at all with your pompous, holier-than-thou attitude. You know your problem, Suzanne? It's not just the customers you think are idiots: you think everyone is! You treat us all, even your own child, as servants to fetch and carry for you. Your son is like a pet you expect to perform and behave. You do fuck-all in your life because you delegate it to everyone else. You have someone to cook for you, someone to shop for you, someone to clean for you, someone to raise Orlando for you now; if you could you'd get someone to wipe your arse for you! And you have the audacity to criticise those of us who have to live our own lives and don't go around living them by proxy. You're a spoilt bitch!'

Suzanne looks in a state of shock, and I'm shaking. I don't think anyone has ever spoken to her like that before. She's just about to speak when I stop her.

'Don't say anything. I'm so angry I need to get out of here. I'm just pleased this is the last day you and I have to share the cottage.'

I march along the path away from the main house; I don't want to bump into anyone. I head towards the beach and along the coast, passing by the spot where I saw Suzanne and Tom kissing, which only reminds me again how angry I am with her. I walk on in the hope that the breeze will calm me down. I love the wind on my face; it feels as though it will blow all the anger away and I'll be left calm and in peace, but there's a part of me that hopes the wind will be strong enough to blow

Suzanne Fields out of the cottage and into the sea. Why did I suggest she accompany us down here?

Nigel was right: of course we wouldn't get on. We have different values, different budgets, different parenting styles. I stop and look out over the cliffs, watching Matt, already out surfing with the Schneiders, making the most of their last day. He turns and waves as he sees me standing there.

'Oh, this is too silly to think about,' I say out loud. 'It's my holiday and I'm not going to let anything, even Suzanne Fields, spoil it for me and my family.' I take a deep breath and head back to the cottage, all too aware that Suzanne will probably have gathered her thoughts and be spoiling for a fight.

When I get back I can hear Suzanne talking loudly on her mobile in the bedroom.

'I can't deal with this any more, Howard, I really can't. I feel so dreadfully ill, the cottage is a state and Amanda, the children and that dog of hers are all right in small doses, but she's a bit square, a bit dull, Howey, and ever so worthy about herself and the way she's brought up her brood. She definitely doesn't like people with money, I can tell from the way she looked at the guests at last night's party. They were all the usual types, Howey, and they're fun in their own way. But she doesn't see that. She just sees the negative and it's very draining being round someone like that. And what's so great about her contribution to the world? Travel writing, for goodness' sake. The way she goes on about how shallow some of those party people were, but she's not exactly deep herself. And it's not even as if she was a good travel writer. I've read some of her stuff and I could write better on a bad day. Most decent journalists do something with their work, but she hasn't written anything substantial for years. She's just stagnated. No ambition, that woman, and that's where it's left her and the family. And having three children is too many, especially when you can't really even afford one of them. It turns out that Nigel's business is having a bad time, by all accounts. And she just called me a stuck-up cow and a princess. I'm not a princess, am I?' she says, sounding wounded.

There's a pause. Then, 'She told me last night that she was short of money and they've got to sell the house. These people, don't they know how to manage their money? They're just jealous of us because we can—'

There's silence for a few seconds and all I can hear is the sound of my heartbeat. I was calm a few minutes ago, but now I'm all wound up again.

'Yes, yes, the party was good. Although someone knew about the TV thing . . . yes, I know, very embarrassing, but I held my own. I've called Deborah this morning to see if there's any room at the Elysian, but she says they're full after last night. The other cottage is supposed to be free tomorrow, so at least we'll have our own space, darling. It's been dreadful. Amanda doesn't know how to keep house and the place is an utter tip. I do wish Manuela was here to help out.'

I can't believe what I'm hearing. Part of me doesn't want to hear any more while another part does.

'Oh, and when you come, make an excuse that we have to go back early. Amanda's here for the full five weeks, but I don't think I'll make three. I'm not surprised she couldn't afford anything else. She even buys the cheap stuff in the local supermarket and moans at me for buying all branded goods. It's not *my* fault they're skint.'

There's another brief silence, then, 'Yes, yes, the children are getting on very well. Orlando has really come out of himself, which is one thing, although he's catching some of the other children's bad habits. He looks scruffier these days, but then again, he's been on the beach a lot and I don't want him to spoil his good clothes. Amanda lets her three drink fizzy drinks and they eat far too much chocolate. Skyler's two aren't much better.'

Thank goodness Skyler can't hear this; she'd hit the roof.

'They're very sweet,' Suzanne continues, 'but the youngest has an imaginary friend, so she's obviously desperately lonely or not quite all there, if you know what I mean. Skyler's also admitted that there are financial problems at Silver Trees. You know, all these creative types may baulk at us with our office jobs, but at least we can pay the mortgage and buy things for us and our children. You should have heard Skyler and Amanda last night, talking about living their dreams. What are they going to live on – air?' I hear her start to pace. 'So, Howey, when you come down, say your mother or aunt has died or something, and that we've got to go back . . .'

There's a slight pause and then she screams, 'Well, make something up, then! That's what you do for a living!'

I'm really upset, but what good will it do? I've already made my feelings clear and it's apparent from her call to Howard what she thinks of Skyler and me and her holiday so far. I make up my mind to have nothing to do with her again. I got to know her at the school gates, and though I knew she was a snob, I always thought she had certain qualities that made her likeable. The fact that she screws up and isn't perfect, despite her attempts to be, is endearing, as are her spontaneous acts of kindness. And she's funny and has a lot of spunk. But she's also two-faced and spoilt, and she doesn't think much of me either.

How could she be so mean to Skyler when Skyler's opened up her home to us? Skyler shared her problems and now Suzanne's thrown it all back in her face. I hope she does go when Howard arrives. She's a shitty person, and, although I've grown fond of Orlando, I'll be glad to see the back of her.

I turn round and head towards the door, but as I open it I'm confronted by a sobbing Skyler.

'Amanda, I've just had some dreadful news,' she says, weeping so much I can barely make out what she's saying.

I wait until she's able to draw breath and suggest she

comes in. Hearing the commotion, Suzanne comes down the stairs, but I don't turn round. I'm too worried about Skyler.

'What is it, darling?' I say, cuddling her and getting her to sit on the sofa. I would ask Suzanne to make Skyler some tea, but she probably wouldn't know how.

'My mother's dead,' she says through the sobs. 'She had a stroke this morning. She died before an ambulance even arrived. She never saw the house and there was so much I wanted to show her. I wanted to show her everything we'd achieved.' We're utterly shocked and neither Suzanne nor I can think of anything to say. I can sense Skyler doesn't even want to be touched; it's as though she's in physical pain. 'I know she was in her seventies and had had a good life, but she'd also had a hard life. She always said that our generation want everything and that for us enough is never enough. And she was right. She was right.'

She's babbling now, so I put my arms around her.

'Do you want a cup of tea?'

She smiles faintly through the tears.

'No, thank you, Amanda. You are a sweetie. I'm sorry for breaking down like this. I just came to ask you both a huge favour. You're the only ones I can really trust.' I feel the hairs on the back of my neck prickle as I sense Suzanne standing behind me. 'You know how important this place is to George and me, and we've got so much riding on it.' She takes a deep breath and wipes the tears away, sniffing heavily. 'We've got to go home to help Dad organise the funeral, which means,' she says, looking at me and Suzanne, who is now standing by my shoulder, 'I need someone to run Silver Trees while we're gone. Clare, Matt and Tom are all brilliant, and I know Peter and Helen would help any way they could, but I need someone staying here and co-ordinating everything, especially with the inspector coming tomorrow. We really need a good review – not just a good one, but an amazing one – and I need you to help me.'

I'm stunned and feel quite sick. Last night I would have had absolutely no hesitation in saying yes, but after my showdown with Suzanne, and what I've just heard her say on the phone, I know it's not going to work. We would kill each other. Skyler can see the hesitation in my face.

'Please, Amanda,' she says, starting to sob again, 'I really need you to help me.'

'Of course we'll help you out,' says Suzanne, leaning over and giving her a hug. 'Of course we will, won't we, Amanda?' she says, looking at me.

I look straight back at her, wanting to say so many things, but it's almost as if the last few hours haven't happened. Suzanne looks completely calm.

We follow Skyler to the main house, where we find George, Willow and Rose busy packing their car for the journey. George looks apprehensively at us.

'It's OK,' Skyler says, 'they're happy to help.'

'Oh, that's great – thanks, girls.' He still looks stressed, but in control.

Willow and Rose look upset, although I think it's more because of their mum.

'Terry is very sad,' Rose tells me, 'so he'll be coming to the funeral too.' She wraps her arms around my shoulders as I bend down to hug her goodbye.

Skyler must be feeling completely numb now, I think, as she goes through a quickly written list of things Suzanne and I need to think about. I know she had a special bond with her mum; it was as though they were on the same wavelength, and I envied her that, because I don't have that sort of relationship with mine.

I have a quick look at the list: it has the daily routine and what the inspector will be looking for. Skyler suggests the guests be told what's going on only if they ask.

'As long as Ms Pepsin and Ms Wenlock have someone to whinge to, I don't really think they care who it is,' sighs Skyler, managing to raise a brief smile.

George hurries us round the house, going through a checklist of what we need to do each day.

'Dusting has to be done every day; Clare knows the routine. Believe it or not, we even get sand blowing up from the beach,' he says on automatic pilot. 'Beds are changed every three days, and each room has its own colour scheme; sheets are in the laundry room. They're not labelled, unfortunately, but it doesn't really matter, if you can just try to remember what goes with what, it will make it look nicer.'

I'm taking notes and Suzanne is asking questions

that I haven't thought of, so perhaps between the two of us we might cover everything.

'I'll take photos of each room,' Suzanne says. 'That way we'll remember the colour schemes and how things should be.'

I'm still furious with her, but I must admit it's a good idea.

The Schneiders, Smiths and the painted ladies are leaving on Sunday, and an Italian family and a couple, also called the Smiths, are arriving.

'So one Smith in and one out,' I say.

'Yes, but I think it's their real name this time. So that's ten out and seven in, which means you can move into the other cottage, Suzanne, so you'll all have some more space,' he says, perhaps aware that we haven't been getting on too well. He has no idea. 'All the floors need to be cleaned and the flowers checked every day,' he says as we walk down the stairs. 'The mirrors also need cleaning once a week, but there are special ladders for that, and hopefully we'll be back in time to clean them.'

'I'm sure Howard or Nigel will help out when they arrive,' I say, looking up at the mirrors, which look very large and heavy.

We walk into the kitchen, passing Candida Pepsin who, like a sniffer dog, has sensed that something isn't quite right.

'Is anything the matter?' she asks George.

'Everything is fine, Ms Pepsin. Are you having a good morning?'

'The toast was cold and the milk was too warm, and it's so windy today,' she says coolly.

'Would you like some more toast?'

'No, thank you, we're going walking along the coast. Well, that was the plan anyway. What's happening? Everyone seems very stressed, and your wife looks as though she's been crying.'

'Well . . .' George hesitates, not sure if honesty is the best policy with this guest, but then Suzanne interrupts.

'She's just had some bad news. Her mother died of a stroke earlier today.'

Candida Pepsin looks shocked.

'I'm so sorry to hear that,' she says, looking genuinely sad. 'Can you please pass on my deepest sympathies? Do you want me to tell the other guests?'

'No, but thank you, Ms Pepsin,' Suzanne replies.

Candida nods.

'If the other guests ask we will, of course, tell them, but we don't want them feeling that they're getting anything less than one hundred per cent.'

'Why? Is she going?' Candida asks.

'Well, obviously she has to arrange the funeral, but in her absence there will be plenty of other staff to look after the house and we will be overseeing everything. Please, Ms Pepsin, feel free to come to me at any time and ask questions and I will be delighted to help,' Suzanne says, sounding her most gracious self. She should have been an actress.

Candida nods.

'Please pass on my commiserations to your wife, will

you?' she says to George and walks away, leaving the three of us totally nonplussed by her response.

'Her bark is worse than her bite, that one,' says Suzanne. 'I work with types like that all the time,' she adds, brushing herself down.

George takes us into the sitting room, where Candida is now telling her friend Adeline Wenlock the news. They both look up as we pass by and nod their heads reverently.

We go over to the large patio doors.

'Clare cleans all the windows,' George tells me, 'but Skyler often helps out. And soot may come down into the fireplace, so that will need cleaning out. The books on the bookshelf also need to be dusted – the spiders seem to like this particular area. The patio needs to be swept of any leaves, although there aren't many at this time of year. We've got menus planned and Clare will give you a list of what's needed each day.' He quickly walks us through the vegetable patch, saying what each crop is, although some of them are obvious. They have different types of potato for different dishes and none seem to be labelled, so I take notes.

'All the pathways need to be cleaned of debris each morning for health and safety reasons, and there are some loose steps on the pathway going down to the beach which I needed to sort, but which I haven't had the chance to yet, so maybe you can get Matt to give you a hand with that,' he says.

'The wisteria needs trimming back this week as well, otherwise it gets so unruly,' he says as we walk around the front, 'and the entrance area always needs sweeping. If it rains, all the tables that are currently al fresco need to be taken in, as well as the umbrellas. Guest umbrellas are available in the lobby, and if they want any more soap or shampoo you'll find it in the larder. Laundry is collected each morning and delivered that evening or the following morning, unless urgency is specified,' he says as I continue to scribble. Suzanne isn't writing anything down, so I hope she's not going to get me to do all the work. At least I know Clare, Helen, Peter and the rest of the gang will be supportive.

We go through to the laundry room, where he shows us a scary-looking industrial ironing machine and the two washing machines. In the room beyond he shows us where the wine is kept: 'We don't really use our cellar as we haven't had the funds to develop a good range of wines yet,' George says.

'Pity,' says Suzanne. 'I think that would add something to the business, offering local wines as well as the champagne you gave us on the terrace,' she suggests, making a note.

'I know, Suzanne,' says George, 'but we've had a lot of other things to focus on, such as leaking roofs, and damp and dangerous electrics, so a limited wine list is the least of our problems.'

Back outside, he says, 'Now, the inspector is called David Torey, and should be arriving sometime tomorrow afternoon; that's all we've been told.'

'I'm surprised they even told you someone was coming,' says Suzanne.

'Yes, they give you a few days' notice usually,' I tell her, 'to give you a chance to get your act together.'

George nods nervously, clearly praying that he's put his livelihood in safe hands.

'He'll ask to see all the reception rooms and guest bedrooms, and he'll check every nook and cranny for dust. He may speak to some of the guests, and ask how they've been served, about the facilities and how friendly everyone has been – if we listen and act upon their requirements, that sort of thing.'

Finally, George gives us a list of the guests who have food allergies, and the phone numbers of Tom, Matt, Peter and Helen, as well as Clare, Dot and Pippa, all of whom know about Skyler's mum and are on their way to help.

I can feel my heart racing. This is all so sudden and I've heard so many horror stories from inspectors, hoteliers and guest-house owners, so I know how much can go wrong. I remember one inspector telling me she took a whole star off because her egg was hard and not soft boiled.

The car is packed and ready to go, Willow and Rose are already in the back and Skyler, still puffy-eyed and dazed, is in the passenger seat.

'Are you sure you're going to be OK?' she asks, getting out to say goodbye.

'Yes,' we both lie.

'I know everyone will be helpful; I'm so sorry to do this to you, girls. I know you needed a holiday and now this has happened.' She starts to cry again, and we give her a collective hug.

'Everyone will help out,' I say reassuringly. 'The inspector will think this place is the best he's ever been to, and I know everything there is to know about travel critics, for goodness' sake!' Skyler smiles at me as I brush away her tears.

Orlando, Jenny, Hannah and Jack are all standing at the door, waving their friends goodbye.

'Will Willow and Rose be back soon?' asks Hannah, looking up at me.

'Yes, they will, but they've got to be with their mummy and daddy because their grandma has just died,' I say.

'She's gone to heaven,' says Jack.

'Yes, she's gone to heaven,' I say, waving them goodbye and turning to the children, who, although a little more sombre, still want to play on the beach as originally planned. They're crestfallen when I tell them that's not going to be possible today.

As we wave the Blues goodbye, Suzanne and I look at each other properly for the first time since the argument. At that moment, I think both of us want to cry.

Chapter 11
The Cavalry Arrives

'So are you going to stay or go when Howard arrives?' I ask bluntly as soon as I see the car turn the corner.

'What do you mean?' Suzanne says, looking totally nonplussed.

'I heard every single word of your conversation with Howard, Suzanne. You didn't sound as though you wanted to spend another day here. That's not exactly supportive of our friend, is it? You remember, the one who can't afford to pay the mortgage and has to live off air to fulfil her dreams?'

Suzanne looks suitably chastened.

'Things have changed. Skyler needs our help and that's that. If we can work out a rota for everyone to get involved, the kids included, then this *can* happen, but if we don't work together, it will all fall apart. We've got to put our differences behind us,' she says, crossing her arms.

'Yes,' I say, crossing mine, 'and everyone has to do their bit, which doesn't mean one delegates and the other does all the work. We'll both have to get our hands dirty. There's no Manuela here, so you'll have to help change the beds, serve the food and wash up with me and Clare.'

'We'll have a rota,' she says.

'We had a rota in the cottage and you didn't stick to it,' I say. 'But this time it's important, Suzanne, because it's for Skyler and she really needs us to make this a success.' Then I look up at the house and realise that we have six rooms to clean.

'Who's got the toilet brush?' I call to Clare, who's in Candida Pepsin's bedroom changing sheets. Suzanne is taking photos of the rooms while we work, which I was expecting, but if she thinks I'm cleaning out all the toilets at Silver Trees, she's got another think coming.

'It's under the sink,' I hear Clare say. I look and find an orange and green toilet brush and holder. Clare is brilliant. She's a real grafter and so down to earth. While we're working, she gossips about all the guests, especially the painted ladies, who are always moaning about their husbands.

'Fay is going out with a married man who's just about to leave his wife for her, except that she's not interested. Edina thinks her husband's gay, although having her as a wife, I can understand why. And there's

Nicola, who's been after George since she arrived. She moans about her husband non-stop, wishing he would have an affair so that he'd leave her in peace.'

Listening to Clare is certainly making the chores easier.

'And don't get me started on the LA whingers. Candida Pepsin's about fifty-eight, I would say; she's had a lot of work done on her face and is a class-A bitch. Still, with a name like that she's on to a loser. I thought Candida was a vaginal disease – and I'm sure my mum gave me something called Pepsin when I had worms. She talks about her perfect daughter all the time, and then criticises how you and Skyler look after your kids, allowing them to run around as you do. I've sneezed in her food a few times,' she says, quite straight-faced.

'Please, Clare, no sneezing in food while the inspector is here, OK?' I say.

'OK, as it's for Skyler and George,' she promises. 'Now, Adeline's a bit younger. She told me she had a boob job in South America and thinks it's gone wrong – one is bigger than the other. She even asked me to feel them! What do I want to feel her boobs for?'

I laugh. I'm tired and stressed, but Clare is excellent company. With her help the challenge will certainly be easier.

'Have you got a boyfriend?' I ask as we go through to the next bedroom.

'No, I've been looking for ages, but to be quite honest there aren't many decent ones out there, are there? All the hunky ones are married and there's so much competition for the rest, without having to worry about married women who are bored of their husbands. I've got my eye on a few people, though,' she says, smiling.

'Matt?' I say.

She blushes.

'Well, he's cute, isn't he?' she says, suddenly coy.

'Yes, he's very nice and very good with kids. And he's a talented horseman, too. He knows Tom quite well, doesn't he?'

Clare nods as she folds some blankets.

'Yes, that he does.'

'Is Tom a ladies' man?' I ask, wanting to know if Suzanne is one of many he's seduced.

'Actually, between you and me, I think he's seeing a married woman at the moment. I heard Pippa chatting about it, saying he'd been seen with this woman, but that's all I know.'

'How many more bedrooms have we got to do?' asks Suzanne, coming into the room with an A4 pad.

'Just two more,' says Clare, 'and then we need to start on dinner.' It's three in the afternoon and we haven't stopped since George and Skyler left at eleven.

As soon as they'd gone I'd phoned Helen to take her up on her offer of help.

'Helen, are there any good kids' clubs in the area? We just need the kids out of the way if we're going to have everything ready for the inspector,' I said breathlessly.

School's Out

'There are no kids' clubs round here,' she replied, 'but I can have them, if you want. I'm organising another trip round Tremontgomery for children and I've got extra help at the tourist office this week, so it won't be a problem to take the four of them.'

'Are you sure?'

'Honestly, it'll be fun. They need some extra help in the kitchen at Aunt Sarah's, too, and I know they'll enjoy making scones there. It will keep them amused for the afternoon and give you a break. So sorry to hear about Skyler's mum,' she added.

'Yes, and the inspector arrives tomorrow, so we've got to do our best for her,' I explained.

'Oh my word,' she said. 'What a time for it to happen! Not that there's a good time for your mum to die. Look, I'll try to come over every day and see what I can do, and I'll double-check about kids' clubs, although I think they're all connected to hotels and the nearest one is in Falmouth.'

'Whatever you can do, Helen, will be greatly appreciated.' Well, that was one job ticked off the list. Only ninety-nine to go.

Five minutes after I'd put the phone down, Helen arrived and took the kids and Hunter. I waved them goodbye, then I called Tom on his mobile.

'Hi, Amanda, how you doing?' he asked calmly.

'Oh, panicking somewhat. Having never run a bed and breakfast, and having spent most of my life criticising them, to be on the other side is proving quite an eye-opener. I've got twenty toilets and sinks to clean,

245

not to mention the dusting and polishing and then supper to prepare.'

'But you've got Suzanne and Clare, haven't you? And I'm sure Pippa and Dot will pop by when they can,' he said.

'Yes, everyone's mucking in,' I said. 'Suzanne's come up with some great ideas, although I haven't seen her change a bed yet.'

He laughed.

'Yes, Suzanne strikes me as a lady who likes to have things done *for* her.'

This surprised me; I'd have thought he would have wanted to defend her.

'Well, I'm out riding with Peter, Paul and the three painted ladies, but when I bring them back I'll come in and see how I can help out. I know Matt has taken the Schneiders surfing this morning and then they're having a picnic on the beach, so at least everyone's out of your way.'

'We'll have to have everything ready for when they all come back. And thanks for offering to pop by,' I said.

Four hours later, most of the bedrooms have been cleaned. Suzanne's been taking photographs and notes, but actually *doing* sweet nothing.

'Suzanne, do you think you could help, please?' I say as she swans into the last bedroom. My back is sore from bending over baths, scrubbing sinks and cleaning out toilets. She looks like an events co-ordinator with her clipboard, officiously ticking off rooms as Clare and I get stuck in. I want to kick her.

'I've been making notes about how we can do this efficiently. I've got a rota for everyone and, although you may scoff, Amanda, it will make things easier in the long run.'

'We don't have a long run, Suzanne,' says Clare, standing up. 'This is all short-run, skin-of-your-teeth stuff. If we had a month, great, but we don't, so can you get your finger out of your backside and do some work? You agreed to help Skyler and you've done nothing since she left.'

'Well, I could help now, I suppose,' she replies, looking quite shocked by Clare's tone. 'I've made all my notes – but take a look at my suggestions later and you'll see I haven't been wasting my time. Now, what would you like me to do?'

I stand up, toilet brush in one hand, scrubbing brush in the other.

'I suggest you look at Skyler's menu for this evening and collect all the vegetables and ingredients we need. She said they usually do a buffet on Saturday evenings as we had before, so it should all be pretty straightforward. I think we have to go to Tremontgomery for the fish and there's also a vegetarian option marked in her recipe folder. Can you actually cook, Suzanne?'

'Of course I can cook,' she replies, scowling at me. 'I've done dinner parties for twenty.'

'No, you've had caterers do dinner parties for twenty. Skyler prepares afternoon tea for when everyone arrives back from their day's activities too, so we need warm scones and jam ready for five o'clock. Then there're the pre-dinner welcome drinks, so you need to organise those as well. So, get the menus, check the ingredients and start co-ordinating,' I say, staring at a woman who looks as though she wants to get in her car and drive back to Whitlow this instant.

'OK,' she says nervously. 'Where did you say the menus are?'

'Downstairs,' I answer.

'Well, carry on the good work,' she says, turning and heading for the kitchen.

One hour later, we're starting on the stairs and landing, dusting photos, paintings and skirting boards that don't appear to have been touched for ages.

Cleaning and tidying the bedrooms has been interesting. Peter and Paul's room had been left in immaculate condition, but there were some very odd sex toys lying around in the bathroom, which Clare and I had a giggle at. The three painted ladies were all as messy as each other and had left their dirty laundry strewn everywhere. Cleaning their baths took ages because of the oils they use and their dressing tables were covered in creams to make their skin look younger, brighter and tighter.

I'm just straightening up from carefully dusting every inch of the banisters when my mobile rings. It's Nigel and I'm so relieved as I've been trying to get hold of him all day.

'Hello, darling, how are you?' he says innocently.

'I have so much to tell you, Nigel, but the first thing is I love you,' I say, sitting down on the landing and feeling overwhelmed just to hear his voice.

'I love you too, darling,' he says, 'and I have some wonderful news.'

'That's good,' I say, feeling weary now, and unsure whether or not I've got the energy to stand up again. 'What is it?'

'The deal's gone through! We don't have to sell the house – in fact, I've taken it off the market today. I'm not saying we're going to be millionaires, but we can certainly worry less about money. The business can go global and we'll comfortably be able to afford Hannah's school fees.'

'Oh, Nigel, that's fantastic!' I manage to say, before bursting into tears. After everything that's happened over the past weeks, not to mention the years of waiting for the deal itself to happen, I want to laugh and cry at the same time. He starts to tell me more of the details and it becomes clear that all our worries really are over and, most importantly, we can keep our home and I'll be able to see more of my wonderful husband. The sense of relief is overwhelming and I want to jump for joy, except that I'm so tired I don't think I could manage a hop, let alone a jump.

'Oh, that's fabulous, wonderful, brilliant, amazing,' I gush. 'The best news ever, darling. Well done. Very well done, my clever, wonderful, hard-working, brilliant, perfect husband.'

He's been working so hard on this for what seems like an eternity and now at last it's happened and he's probably in a state of shock himself. I know he never gave up hope, but I also know he had moments of doubt.

'So why all the phone calls earlier. I was worried, but you didn't leave a message. What's going on there?' he asks.

Where do I start?

'I have news, too, but it's not good,' I say. 'Skyler's mum died this morning and she and George have had to go to London to organise the funeral, so she's left Suzanne and me in charge.' I explain about the changeover of guests tomorrow and about the inspector coming, and a bit about what I overheard Suzanne saying in the cottage, but I don't go into too much detail as I don't want Clare to overhear. Nigel listens in shocked silence.

When I've finished he says, 'Well, the cavalry is coming, Amanda. I know Howard's coming down this evening and I was going to come tomorrow, but I'll come down with him instead. We'll share the driving. It sounds as though you need an extra pair of hands and we might be able to help with the kids, at least, while you get on with your stuff. And anyway, I want to celebrate with my gorgeous wife!'

'That would be lovely,' I say, 'and a wonderful surprise for the children. They've missed you, and so have I. They've had some great times on the beach, but it'll be so much better if you're here. And you'll be able to spend more time with us now anyway.' I get to my feet and start brushing myself down.

There's a slight pause.

'Well, it's not quite that simple,' Nigel says.

'What do you mean, it's not that simple?' I say, feeling myself go tense.

Nigel's voice sounds hesitant.

'Because I've been focusing on getting this deal signed, there's a lot of everyday business I've let fall by the wayside and which I haven't delegated to anyone else. There's still an awful lot to do,' he says rather sheepishly.

I've gone into an empty bedroom so that Clare can't hear.

'Nigel, we made a deal that you would slow down once this was done, and it's not going to happen, is it?' I say, feeling tearful. What an anticlimax. 'That's what we agreed. You've missed so much with the children already; you haven't been able to share stuff with them.' I try to choke back the emotion.

'I work hard for them, for us, for you!' I can hear Nigel's voice hardening; it's the same voice he uses when he's speaking to business clients, but I'm not going to let him do that with me.

'You will make yourself ill, Nigel, and your health and your family are what are most important. We've said it time and time again. And what do you remember about your childhood, huh? The toys that your parents bought you or the time they spent with you? Especially the time they spent with you on holiday. That's what we all remember, and that's what our three will remember. Except that you weren't with us, so they'll remember you *not* being there to see them surf for the first time, and that's not a shame, it's a tragedy. Buck your ideas up, Nigel Darcey, and think about it on your drive down here, because your family needs you.'

Then I put the phone down on him. I've never done that in my life. I'm just so cross, tired and upset that I don't want to say something I'll bitterly regret. That's the last thing that would help right now.

I look at my watch. It's four o'clock. I'm expecting the guests, Helen and the kids to return any time in the next hour, and I'm concerned that Suzanne won't have got far with the food.

I go back out to the landing.

'Clare, can I leave you to finish off here and in the sitting room? I want to check to see how Suzanne's doing. Are you OK?' I ask, looking at the girl who's worked flat out since Skyler left.

'Oh don't worry about me, Amanda,' she says, smiling. 'This is what I do every day. As for Suzanne handling the cooking, we can all do it. I usually help Skyler, so I know most of the recipes now,' she adds breezily.

'Yes, but I don't want you cracking under the pressure,' I tell her, 'you're invaluable.'

'Skyler and George have been really good to me. That's why I'm doing this. Don't worry. I'll call Pippa and Dot. I know they'll be willing to help out if I explain the circumstances.'

'That's a great idea,' I say. 'Thanks, Clare.'

I go downstairs to check on Suzanne, who's making a din in the kitchen. I walk in to find bowls of ingredients all over the island. Lettuces are washed and sliced in one, tomatoes in another; there are green beans topped and tailed, carrots sliced into batons, pastry rolled and ready to bake, piles of scrubbed new potatoes, a small bowl of red chillies, herbs and a large cheeseboard. Outside on the terrace, the table is already laid out with a cloth, plates and pickles.

'You've been busy,' I say, looking around, although I still think Clare and I have done most of the work today.

'Yes. I've done all the usual Cornish fayre that Skyler normally serves on a Saturday. I've called Peter and he's bringing the fish and bread over in a few minutes. Candida is allergic to wheat, dairy, shellfish and tomatoes, according to your notes, but she'll be fine with the trout.'

'Are you sure?' I say, thinking how fussy Candida Pepsin is and how we don't want to get on the wrong side of her, especially with the inspector coming.

'Amanda, I have cooked for so many neurotic eaters – or rather had catering for them – that I know what this type like. I once had a guest who would only eat off square plates, so leave Candida Pepsin to me,' she says decisively, continuing to read from her notes. 'Now, all the rest of the guests eat everything,' she says, wiping her hands with a tea towel.

'Thank God.'

'Helen is bringing over a selection of veg and non-veg crostini to have with drinks, plus the kids have made scones and cakes at Aunt Sarah's which they're bringing back for tea, and apple crumbles, which we can have with cream and ice cream for dessert. Helen promised they'd be here shortly, so that everything can be got ready in time for the guests returning, which' – she looks at her watch – 'should be in forty-five minutes' time.'

'That's cutting it a bit fine,' I say, realising it's four-twenty already. 'While we're waiting we can get the tea trays ready in the sitting room for when everyone gets back. And napkins—'

Suzanne taps a pile of orange linen napkins, all ready to put out. 'I thought the children could do that when they get back,' she says with a smug smile on her face.

There's a knock on the door, and I'm hoping it's Peter and Helen with the kids, but as I open it I'm greeted by the scowling faces of Candida and Adeline. They obviously went on their coastal walk as they both look utterly windswept and are in no mood for pleasantries.

'We'll be down in ten minutes,' says Candida. 'Could we have two green teas in the sitting room with some of those gluten-free scones, please?' And with that she stomps up the stairs, Adeline following in her wake.

Thankfully, Helen and Peter are next to arrive with the children, who want to show us what they've made and what they've been doing.

'We saw bees today, Mummy,' says Hannah. 'And we saw them make honey; they make it out of their bottoms. Isn't that clever? We make poo and they make honey.' Hannah giggles, which makes all the other children laugh. While I hug my three and Orlando rushes up to Suzanne and gives her a tight squeeze that makes her watery-eyed, Helen brings in the scones and crostini and Peter, like some latter-day saviour, brings the bread and fish.

'Now, children,' says Helen, 'you've all got to go to the cottage and get tidied up. Could you big ones look after the little ones while we sort out the food for the guests tonight? And don't make a mess because your mums have spent a long time clearing up after you.'

The children head off to the cottage while Helen and Clare get the afternoon teas ready. I'm preparing the trout, and Peter starts to slice the bread, telling Suzanne which is which so she can label them. I hear the front door open again, and Matt and Tom returning with the Schneiders, the Smiths and the painted ladies. I go out to greet them. Everyone looks happy and refreshed, hungry, tired and thirsty. They seem bemused to see me and not George or Skyler, but they all say hello and head off to their rooms to freshen up.

'How's the day been?' Tom asks, coming into the kitchen and looking at all the food.

'With any luck we might pull it off tonight. We're just hoping we'll have it down pat by the time the inspector calls tomorrow,' I say, filling the kettle.

'Well, Matt and I are happy to help with all outward-bound stuff,' says Tom, 'so don't worry about that.'

'You must be hungry,' says Suzanne, smiling up at him. 'Do you want a bite to eat?'

'I'm not sure we have enough, Suzanne,' I say gently.

'Oh, don't worry about me,' says Tom gallantly. 'I've got a stew going back at the ranch.'

'Is there anything else we can do?' Matt says.

'No, thanks. Everything's done. The only thing we might need help with is any DIY stuff. George mentioned some loose steps and I spotted some trellis out the back that's hanging precariously by one nail, and you know, if there's a plumbing emergency or another power cut,' I say, trying to sound feminine without coming across as completely pathetic.

'We're on call all the time. We'll keep our mobiles on and I'll pop over tomorrow morning to take a look at those steps and trellis,' Matt says, as he and Tom make their farewells.

As we warm the scones and put out the jams and cream, I realise I haven't told Suzanne any of our news.

'Suzanne, I forgot to say, I spoke to Nigel earlier and he said he's coming down with Howard this afternoon. Did Howard tell you? They should be here by about nine or ten, all being well.'

'Yes,' says Suzanne, 'I had a text from Howard.' She pauses briefly. 'Amanda, we haven't really had time to talk about our argument and my conversation with Howey. I want to apologise about what I said on the phone today and to say that you're right about me. I am a bit of a prima donna, but I've always been like that and you know I'm like that. I realise it's one thing to be with someone like me for a few hours and quite another to live with me for weeks. And I'm sorry I haven't tried to make things easier for you,' she says.

'It's very big of you to admit that, Suzanne,' I say, feeling slightly shocked. 'I really appreciate you apologising and I am sorry for calling you a bitch.'

'A stuck-up spoilt bitch,' Suzanne corrects, half smiling.

'OK, a stuck-up spoilt bitch,' I repeat, 'but it's been tough for me, too, as you know. But that's all over now. Nigel's deal has gone through so our financial problems are over.'

Suzanne claps her hands and squeals with delight. She comes over to hug me.

'Oh, well done, well done. I know that has put a strain on everything over the past few years, but I didn't know quite how much until this holiday. You should have spoken to Howey. He would have helped,' she says, although Howard would be the last person Nigel and I would have gone to. I know Suzanne trusts him, but I wouldn't.

'And I'm sorry about what happened with your job,' I say. 'It must have been very difficult adjusting to the change.'

'Well, I can't blame anyone but myself. It's my own stupid fault,' she says.

I smile.

'Of course, Nigel tells me that he's still got to work

long hours, so I'm not pleased about that,' I say, standing up and shrugging my shoulders.

'No, that's not good. You and Nigel aren't like Howard and me. I get on with Howey *only* if I don't see him too much. You have a different relationship with Nigel. You genuinely enjoy each other's company. There is only so much I can take of Howey in one go,' she says, 'and he of me probably,' she adds.

'I doubt that,' I say. 'He loves you very much, and so does Orlando, Suzanne. Your son adores you. You should spend more time with him. He really is an amazing boy, and that's all because of you, you know.'

'Yes, I know that,' she says. 'Or rather I've realised that this holiday. I was considering sending him away to boarding school, but after this, no way. Unless, of course, he *wants* to board, but I realise now I'll miss him terribly if he does.' She comes over to me, squeezing my shoulder. 'Thank you for understanding.'

'Thank you for agreeing to help when you did, Suzanne. I didn't think you were going to when Skyler asked.'

'Well, you may wish I hadn't after the inspector has been,' she says, laughing.

'We're doing our best,' I say, 'and we're Skyler's only hope.'

Just then Clare comes in with the apple crumbles from Peter's van.

'Do you need any help?' I ask her.

'Nope. Why don't you have a cup of tea? You guys haven't stopped, and you're the ones who've got to be fresh to greet the new guests and the inspector,' she says.

So for five minutes Suzanne and I sit down on the sofa at the top of the stairs.

'You don't know much about my family, do you, Amanda?' Suzanne says. 'We meet at the school gates and chat about unimportant nonsense and go to each other's dinner parties, but that's about it. This will probably seem strange, but you have no idea how I envied Skyler when she burst into tears this morning. I was never that close to my mother. My parents divorced when I was three, and they're both dead now. I can't really say I knew my father at all. I suppose that means less for a girl than it does for a boy, but I'm scared that Orlando's going to grow up feeling the same way about me and Howey, and that I'm going to miss his childhood altogether.'

'Well, you've caught up with a little of it here,' I say. 'I always think parents who dump their kids in clubs from morning till noon every day of the holiday are missing the plot a bit.'

Suzanne nods. 'Although my mother allowed me to see my father and grandparents as much as I wanted, she didn't feel welcomed by my father's family. So I was very protective of her, because his family was large, with three brothers and sisters and lots of cousins and second cousins. My mother was an only child, like me and Orlando.'

'Is Howard like your dad?' I ask. 'A lot of women marry men who are like their fathers. I know Nigel is similar to mine.'

'Howey's a little boy, just like my father was, and yet not like my father. My father was a bully. You know, spiteful to my mother and really controlling. He regarded everything as a possession, including his family. He made her life hell, or tried to after they got divorced. He accused her of all sorts in the courts and was really petty. He once got his solicitor to write her a letter complaining that she didn't send enough pants with me when he had me during the holidays and that I always had head lice. I used to feel so sorry for her, bringing me up all by herself, and yet I had to be civil to my father who, as I grew older, I realised wasn't a good man at all. He accumulated vast wealth because he felt it validated him in the eyes of those around him, but I could see right through him and so, in the end, could my mother. Fortunately, when she married again it was to someone who was kind and brought out the best in her. She was a strong woman, but I never forgave my father for being the way he was and for the way he treated her.'

'And yet, you're attracted to that type, aren't you?' I say.

'Yes, I've always been attracted to arrogant men. I want to impress them, just like I wanted to impress my dad, even though he only valued someone or something in monetary terms.

'He was really proud when I got my job at the bank. He said I could earn a lot of money there and he saw me as being worth something then. My husband is slightly different. Howey might be like a little boy, but he's naughty, not nasty. Transparent, if you like. You know, he actually rang me at work one day and told me that he'd met someone else and would I mind if he went off with her for a few months, sort of a marital sabbatical, and then if it didn't work out, he would come back to me and all would be the same again.'

'God, Suzanne! What did you say?' Maybe her and Howey have got an agreement then and that's why she sees no harm in having a holiday fling with Tom.

'I was a bit stunned, as you can imagine. I asked him to clarify what he'd said and he said that that was exactly what he had meant and that he was very lucky I was so understanding. I told him to fuck off. I slammed the phone down and he never mentioned it again. I don't think he met her, either, but you see what I mean when I say he's a child. At least you can see it coming. With my father, you couldn't. He was devious. Yes, Howey sulks and is petulant, but he's not nasty or deliberately cruel,' she says, teary-eyed.

I put my hand on her shoulder, wondering how I hadn't known all this, when we were supposed to be such good friends. Suzanne was right, it was just about the playground and dinner party niceties.

'I'm OK,' she says. 'I haven't spoken about this to anyone, since . . . since I don't know when. The recent faux pas at work has made me feel a little insecure about myself, but it also made me realise what's important and that I've fallen into the same trap as my father, thinking that money is what life is about. It's strange, you and Skyler worry about not having enough, but you're so much happier than the saps I work with, do you know that? For all their wealth, they're unhappily married, dependent on drugs and drink, and see very little of their kids. You and Skyler have got it right.'

'Do you love Howard?' I ask, aware that some guests are starting to arrive, but knowing that Clare can handle them for the minute.

'Yes, I do love Howey. Even if we divorce – and we have talked about it – I will always love him. I know that every time I look at Orlando. My mother told me that her divorce lawyer commented on how charming it was that she had loved my dad when she married him, almost as though it was an added extra, the icing on the financial and social cake in their life contract. I guess he was just cynical, having dealt with thousands of divorcées. But my mother still loved my dad, albeit in a very different way to the romantic love she'd first felt, and she told me that that love was all due to me. I had kept the ties between her and my dad strong and constant, and I had shown them both the meaning of unconditional love.'

She pauses, then says, 'You remember when I went to see Doreen at the fair?'

'Yes I do,' I say, slightly confused as to why she's bringing that up now, although realising that an alarming amount of what Doreen said has come true.

'I didn't tell you everything she said, Amanda. She told me that I was considering divorce and had discussed it, but that I should think again. She said,

"Despite everything, you still love him and you always will. And he will you." I couldn't tell you then because I haven't told anyone about what Howey and I have been considering. We look like a happily married couple who bicker a lot, but we haven't been happy for a long time and we've both buried ourselves in our work lives. We have a set of friends who are all happily married, or perhaps they're just pretending like us, and are comfortable in their rut. I don't think he's seeing anyone else and I'm certainly not,' she says.

This surprises me and I so want to ask about Tom, but realise that given the leap of faith she's just taken with me, perhaps now is not the time to interrogate her.

Suddenly we hear a little voice at the bottom of the stairs.

'Is tea ready?' It's Jack peering up at us, with Jenny, Orlando and Hannah bringing up the rear. Hunter bounds in behind them.

'It is,' I say, still dazed from Suzanne's speech. Suzanne and I get to our feet and make our way downstairs. Despite the wind that's been blowing all day, it's still warm, and most of the guests have moved out of the sitting room and congregated on the terrace for tea. Clare has laid out scones, jam and honey on one table, and is serving pots of tea.

'If you'd all like to help yourselves to the scones,' she says, then goes inside to look after Nicola, Fay and Edina, who are still in the sitting room.

Maarten Schneider comes to tell me that they've

decided to head back to London this evening, so they won't be needing supper.

'Sorry for the late notice and to inconvenience you, but our flight is very early, so we've decided to stay in a hotel by Heathrow,' he explains.

'We are very sad to go,' says one of his sons, looking up at me. 'We like very much playing with the English children,' he adds, making me smile because he looks so intense and serious for one so young.

'We're ready to go now, but we would very much like to keep in touch,' says Maarten, shaking Suzanne's hand violently. 'Do you have a guest book we can sign?'

'Yes, over here,' Suzanne says, presenting a beautiful book with a blue, pink and gold marbled cover.

'Isn't that the book you bought at the fair?' I whisper to her.

'Yes, but I couldn't find a guest book – I'm not sure if they even have one – so this will have to do. I'm sure the inspector will ask to see one, and it won't look good if there's nothing in it,' she says.

'Perhaps we can make up a few of our own,' I say mischievously.

The children all hug each other and promise to keep in touch.

'I hope the children do stay in touch,' I say to Maarten. 'They got on so well, didn't they?'

'And please pass on our commiserations to Skyler and her family; Matt told us the news. We're very sorry to hear it,' Penny says.

As I wave them off, I remember wistfully how

many times I promised to stay in touch with friends I made on holiday but never did. Holiday friendships are so special, but they generally only work on the beach, by the pool or on the campsite, and rarely back at home.

There's a lull of an hour or so before supper, during which Suzanne, Clare and I go over the menus for the next few days and fine-tune the cleaning rota. Then we're all flat out getting supper ready for seven.

At six-thirty, the guests are beginning to gather in the sitting room for drinks and nibbles. The crostini are all laid out, as are the ice, sliced lemon and drinks bottles. Dot and Pippa have appeared from nowhere – Clare must have summoned them, I assume – and are already beavering about in the kitchen, helping Suzanne and Clare put the finishing touches to the buffet. It all seems to be well under control, so all we have to do is get the children to put out the napkins and offer the guests a glass of chilled champagne, which they do very charmingly. I quickly whizz outside to light the tea-lights and make sure that there are enough tables.

As people drift back out to the terrace with their drinks to enjoy the last of the day's sun, we are all rushing around putting the finishing touches to the dishes and carrying them out to the buffet table. Finally, everyone tucks in and, for a brief moment, there's only the sound of cutlery clinking against the plates and the odd 'mmm' of appreciation.

'Do you know what this place needs?' says Suzanne quietly as we stand by the kitchen door. 'Some music. A place this enchanting and engaging needs a certain type of music; there must be some talented local musicians nearby who could play guitar or flute or something while people eat. I think Silver Trees would like it and Skyler would approve,' she says, smiling as Clare and I nod in agreement.

The dessert is a real success, although there's a brief panic when Suzanne thinks we've given Candida a gluten crumble. In fact the labels have been mixed up and everyone gets gluten-free – but no one's complaining.

As the guests get up and go through to the sitting room for coffee, Dot and Pippa start on the washing-up.

'I'm going to head home now, ladies, but don't worry about breakfast tomorrow. I'll be back at the crack of dawn to sort all that,' says Clare, 'and if the children would like to come with me to the bakery in the morning, that will be fine.'

'Thanks, Clare, I don't know what we'd have done without you,' I say and we send her off with leftover crumble.

I go through to check that everyone's happy, and sit and chat to Fay, Edina and Nicola who, despite the whining, aren't quite as awful as Clare has reported. I discover that Fay has her own interior design business, Edina is a translator and Nicola has her own nanny agency. They all wanted a creative break from their lives, which they say is exactly what they've had.

'We've enjoyed it here very much,' says Nicola. 'It's been a really good break. We rarely have time to ourselves at home and we've been able to get away from everything, although we seem to spend a lot of the time moaning about our men, so they obviously still take up most of our energy,' she says, smiling.

'Well, I've seen your painting and it's great. You should do more of it,' I say.

Paul and Peter Smith have also had a wonderful time and want to book for the following year and to bring some friends.

'This is a fantastic place for a house party, you know,' says Paul. 'Do you have a guest book I can say thank you in?'

I hand him Suzanne's book, grateful that she so thoughtfully donated it.

Back in the kitchen, I discover Clare has laid out some supper for us; she thinks of everything. The kids have eaten with the guests, but Suzanne and I haven't stopped to eat anything since breakfast. Realising how famished I am, I sit down next to Suzanne who's talking to the children about their day. I've never seen her look so relaxed and happy.

'We need to decide which jobs we'll be doing for the rest of the week,' I say.

'What jobs?' asks Jack.

'Well, for a start, Clare suggested you could collect the eggs in the morning for breakfast. And I need help picking and cleaning the vegetables each morning. We only just had enough today, and although there'll be fewer guests tomorrow, we will still need help. Can you do that, children?' she asks.

They all nod sleepily. Suzanne and I look at each other, suddenly realising how tired they are.

'Well, let's worry about that in the morning,' she says.

After we've tucked the children into bed, Suzanne and I head back up to the house to have our supper and go through everything for the next day. We sit with Pippa and Dot who have finished cleaning up and, clutching coffee and mint tea, look through George's notes together.

'The new guests and Mr Torey are all due to arrive at about midday,' I say.

'We'll put the new Smiths in the old Smiths' room,' Suzanne says, 'the Grossettos can have the two big rooms at the front of the house, and the inspector should have the one with the best view.'

We all nod.

'Oh, and we've already cleared out the Schneiders' cottage, so either you or Suzanne can move into that one,' says Pippa.

'Thank you,' I say and then before I can ask Suzanne whether she'd like it, she interrupts.

'You take it, Amanda. It's larger than ours and you need the space more than we do,' she says graciously.

'Thank you, darling,' I say and give her a hug. I get the feeling Suzanne doesn't get hugged enough.

'Right,' says Dot. 'So tomorrow morning we'll be over

early, like every Sunday, to help with the changeover. We'll need to change all the beds and clean all the rooms, do the tea trays and flowers, then there are the paths to sweep and some light bulbs to change in the main hall before the inspector arrives.'

'Our husbands are supposed to be arriving later tonight, so they can make themselves useful, too,' says Suzanne. 'We should have fresh flowers in the hall, too – everything must look wonderful.' She looks down at her list to see if she's missed anything.

'I don't think any of the new guests have any allergies or food dislikes,' I say, 'so we're having lamb tomorrow. I'll collect it when I get the bread from Peter in the morning.'

By the time we're happy that we've thought of everything, it's nearly eleven. Pippa and Dot finally head home and Suzanne and I are laying the tables for breakfast when the doorbell goes. It's Howard and Nigel, looking surprisingly fresh and raring to go after their journey.

'Your heroes have arrived,' Nigel says, hugging me and giving me a long passionate kiss, which would normally embarrass me, but by now I don't care. And as I look over his shoulder, to my surprise I see Howard kissing his wife just as passionately.

'We've brought some bubbly for you girls,' says Howard, 'to celebrate Nigel's deal and the fact that we're going to run this place for a few days. We've been talking about it on the way down, and we're both up for helping out in any way you want us to. Cutting trees, helping outdoors, mending fences and cleaning bedrooms, though we've both drawn the line at cleaning toilets. Is that OK, hon?' Howard looks at Suzanne, who's so tired she'd agree to anything at the moment.

'Yes, darling, that sounds great. It's lovely to see you. We've missed you, Orlando especially. We've got a full day ahead of us tomorrow, but one glass of champagne would go down nicely,' she says.

'Where are the children?' Nigel asks.

'Oh, they're tucked up in bed, of course,' Suzanne replies. 'They wanted to stay up, but we didn't want them to be grouchy tomorrow as they're helping out,' she explains, looking at Howard, who now looks a bit grouchy himself.

'We expected a welcoming party!' he says, pushing his bottom lip out in a mock sulk. At least I hope it's a mock sulk.

'Tough, you've got us,' says Suzanne, 'so we'll show you where to put your bags, then we'll have some champagne. Hope it's Tatty.'

'Of course it is,' he replies, bringing out two large bottles and chinking them gently together.

I've got a feeling the men are keen to get hammered. The first time I met Howard he and I were quite drunk. It was at one of Suzanne's dinner parties and the girls had moved places between courses so that I was sitting beside him for pudding. I remember thinking how good-looking he was, like a young Michael Douglas. We'd quite quickly covered religion and politics, and had moved on to sex. One of the other women had just started to list her menopause symptoms, when Howard piped up: 'Don't you just love the word "menopause"? It makes me think of a Grecian god or a cat with very big feet.' He hiccupped and then continued, 'What I don't like are the phrases "medium to heavy flow", "sanitary towel" and "panty liner", although for some reason I don't mind "tampon".' The woman was looking thunderous, but by now I was laughing so much I'd got stitches.

When he was sober, though, I had always found him rather petulant, still playing on his golden-boy looks to get his own way. With Suzanne having two little boys to contend with, it's no wonder she's always needed domestic help.

'The last thing we all need is hangovers tomorrow, Howard,' I say carefully, 'so it'll have to be a glass each and then bed.'

We go into the sitting room and Suzanne and I start to fill in our husbands on what's been happening. I leave out the bit about seeing Suzanne snogging Tom, and she leaves out the bit about me calling her a stuck-up bitch.

'How's it been working out so far?' asks Howard.

'We've had our ups and downs,' I say, looking at Suzanne, who raises her glass to me.

'But we're OK now,' says Suzanne, 'and we do need your help, gentlemen, so although you might be expecting a lie-in tomorrow, I'm afraid you're going to be up with the lark, like the rest of us.'

'Five-thirty wake-up call,' I say, grinning.

'No way,' says Howard, nearly choking on his champagne.

'Yes way,' says Suzanne. 'So drink your drinks and let's get to bed, shall we?'

Howard and Suzanne head off to their cottage and I show Nigel to our new cottage, which is twice the size of the last one, with four bedrooms and a bathroom with a real bath. The children are asleep in the other cottage as we'd tucked them up in their usual beds before Pippa told us they'd cleared out the Schnieders' cottage. So, given that we have an empty house, I would desperately have loved to have had wild holiday sex with my gorgeous husband, but I'm too exhausted to do anything other than fall into a deep, restful and well-earned sleep.

Chapter 12

An Inspector Calls

'Daddy, my daddy!' yells Hannah, racing into our room at five o'clock the next morning. I groan and turn over. Who needs an alarm clock when you've got kids? I don't have to get up for another half-hour, but of course now the adrenalin's pumping and I think of all the things we need to get done. I might as well get the kids dressed and fed before we go to the morning market to get the food.

'Honestly,' says Nigel jokingly, 'I thought holidays were all about long lie-ins and late nights. What's with this up-with-the-dawn stuff?'

He's silenced by Jenny and Jack rushing in and leaping on him. They'd all been directed over here by Suzanne when they'd not found me in my usual bed.

Nigel's now buried under a mess of children, all of whom are struggling to kiss and hug him. It's rather lovely to watch and they have seen so little of him recently that I feel churlish about hurrying them up.

'That's enough, children,' says Nigel, finally extricating himself from the mass of arms and legs. 'It's lovely to see you, and Mummy says you've all been doing wonderful things which I'm sure you want to tell me about, but you know it's a big day today and that we all have special responsibilities – you have to collect a lot of eggs this morning and help serve breakfast, don't you?' he says, nodding in the hope that they will all nod back.

'No, we want to be with you!' shouts Jack, jumping up and down.

'No, Jack, it's an important day today,' says Nigel, doing his mock-stern voice and face. 'The hotel inspector is coming and everything has to be perfect for Skyler and George or they won't get good marks. And we don't want that, do we?' he says, getting more serious as he goes on.

'Yes, we'd better go,' says Jenny sensibly. 'Come on, you two, we have lots to do. Everyone get dressed. Hannah, make sure Orlando is up and put cereal out for everyone.' Then she turns to me, smiling: 'And you stay in bed for another five minutes, Mummy, and cuddle Daddy.'

The children bound out of the room, leaving Nigel and me in a state of bemusement. I don't know whether I'm more shocked by the fact that Jenny realises we need some time on our own or that she's called me Mummy for the first time in ages.

'So have you missed me?' Nigel says, enveloping me in his arms. He hasn't done that for such a long time. He's been too busy and I've been too tired.

'Of course I missed you,' I say, giving him a kiss on the lips, which has the potential to turn into something else, though not even we can have three-minute sex.

'So why did you put the phone down on me?' he asks, pulling away and looking me in the eyes.

'Because when you told me the deal was successful I was on the most amazing high because I thought we'd be seeing more of you. And then you dropped the bombshell that that wouldn't be the case. Can't you see how I felt? The children miss you and I miss you and you're still going to be doing the same routine of late nights and early mornings, just for a different reason. Is it all worth it? You're missing your children grow up. You've missed some amazing stuff already this holiday, Nigel. They've learned to bake scones and surf and ride. This place is magic, even Orlando has come out of his shell. And you've missed all of it. Yes, I've taken photos for you, but it's not the same.'

'I know, darling, I've got to do something about it,' he says, 'but one step at a time, and at least we know our home and Hannah's education are secure; that's the main thing,' he adds, snuggling up to me and kissing me again.

I snuggle back, then look at the clock in the room and realise that we've got to make a move. Today is going to be a long one.

*

Downstairs, Hannah has overfilled the bowls with cereal, but Jack and Jenny are eating it anyway; we can all feel the tension in the air. I haven't felt this much adrenalin pumping round my body since I did my first ever bungee jump twenty years ago and nearly wet myself.

'Does everyone know what they're doing today?' I say, feeling as if I'm about to teach an exercise class and am getting them ready for the warm-up.

'Yeah!' they all shout back.

'Yeah!' shouts Nigel, grinning at me.

'Good. Well, everyone, let's go. We have work to do.'

Last night, Jack had the fabulous idea of using Matt's walkie-talkies to communicate. He's still so excited about the prospect of playing with them he's in cloud cuckoo land today. There's a hiccup as he can't find his trainers, but five minutes later we're racing to the house. The wind has died down overnight, and it looks like it's going to be a gorgeous day. The sun is already warm on our backs as we make our way up the path. We find Orlando, Suzanne and Howard dressed and waiting in the kitchen. It's too early to start preparing the breakfasts, so Suzanne is on her way out to cut flowers for the rooms, and the children are immediately sent back out to collect eggs.

Howard is busy making a pot of coffee. 'Morning, all,' he says. 'I'm told I'm mending the path steps with Matt today. I gather he and a woman called Helen are coming over later this morning.'

'And Tom will be along too,' I say.

'Ah yes, Suzanne's mentioned him quite a bit,' says Howard smiling. 'He sounds like a very nice guy.'

'He is,' I say, wondering briefly what will happen when they meet.

Clare rushes in. 'The Grossettos have just called to say they'll be arriving earlier than expected. They want to know whether they can have breakfast. That means we'll need extra bread and rolls, Amanda, and here's the list of ingredients I need for dinner tonight. Hi, I'm Clare,' she adds, introducing herself to Nigel and Howard.

'OK. And after breakfast, who's supposed to be helping you with the rooms?' I ask.

'Suzanne's rota says Howard,' she says doubtfully.

Howard is sipping coffee, seemingly oblivious to what's going on. He looks up.

'What have I been seconded into doing now?' he asks.

'Changing beds,' I say.

'That's completely out of my comfort zone,' he says, smiling. 'Can't Suzie do it?'

'Can't Suzie do what?' says Suzanne, who's just come back in.

'Change the beds, darling. You can do that, can't you?' says Howard with a little-boy smile.

Suzanne doesn't flinch. 'No, Howey, it's your job. I'm co-ordinating everything today. There's got to be someone making sure everyone is doing what they're supposed to be doing, otherwise everything will fall apart,' she says.

'Well, I don't care who it is,' says Clare, exasperated, 'as long as someone helps me.'

'We will,' say Orlando and Jenny, who've just come in with baskets of eggs. 'We've collected loads and the others are still collecting. We'll help you, Clare.'

'Thank you, dears,' she says and smiles. 'Trust the young 'uns to teach the grown-ups how to get things done, eh? Come on, you two, let's get your hands washed. Then we can start on the breakfast orders, and as soon as the guests are sorted we can do the beds. We've got to be quick, OK?'

'Right, well, Nigel and I will get going,' I say, doing a mock salute to Suzanne, who salutes me back.

As I drive us into town, I fill Nigel in on some of the holiday gossip, including the visit to Doreen at the fair and my suspicions about Tom and Suzanne.

'Never,' says Nigel, suddenly waking up when I tell him about seeing Suzanne and Tom kissing. 'Not Suzanne. Not with a cowboy,' he says, half laughing.

'Why not?' I say.

'Because that's not Suzanne's type. Suzanne goes for smooth charismatic charmers. *Wealthy* smooth charismatic charmers, at that. She's more likely to go with that guy from the Elysian you were telling me about,' he says, staring out the window and admiring the scenery. It's a beautiful, clear summer's morning and the sea and sky are a striking blue against the greens of the surrounding countryside as we drive into Tremontgomery.

'No, I think even Suzanne thinks Dennis is a bit creepy,' I say, and fill Nigel in on what happened at the party and how his friend embarrassed her.

'That wasn't very nice, but Suzanne could do with a bit of humility now and then. She's certainly queening it over everyone at the moment,' he says.

'Yes, but she's good at it. She's bossy, but at least she keeps things in order, or that's the idea anyway,' I say, turning into the high street, which is now partly cut off by market stalls. I still haven't managed to get to the market, as there's always been something else to do – such as clearing up the cottage, loading the dishwasher and making sure Hunter hasn't chewed up any more of Suzanne's designer shoes. Once we've parked the car I look at the list and decide that as Nigel is still not completely with it, we'd better work together, then he can take stuff back to the car as and when we get overloaded.

'Don't Skyler and George have a veggie patch?' Nigel asks, as he sees the list.

'Yes, but it doesn't provide enough for the number of guests they've had this year, so they have to buy extra,' I explain. 'Skyler's learning as they go along and she didn't expect so many people to want supper in the evenings as well as breakfast. After all, they are technically only a bed and breakfast, so the supper is optional. It's just that Clare and Skyler's cooking has become so popular the guests prefer to stay in.'

I get the vegetables and ask Nigel to take them back to the car while I head for the meat stall. Clare has told me that it should be outside Aunt Sarah's, but when I get there it's a cheese stall.

'Excuse me, where's the butcher's?' I ask the man on the cheese stall.

'They've moved pitch to the high street,' he says, pointing to a stall up the road, which has a long queue in front of it.

I decide to get the cheeses now. Clare's listed lots of regional cheeses, including Cornish Yarg, Cornish Blue and some local goat and sheep cheeses that she thinks will impress David Torey. I look at my watch, realising with a shock that it's almost seven-thirty. Breakfast starts at eight and I haven't even got the bread yet. Nigel returns and I ask him to wait in line for the lamb, giving him strict instructions for what he should ask for. Nigel has a tendency to over-buy or get sidetracked when I send him on the occasional visit to the supermarket. It's an endearing quality, but frustrating when I've asked him to get a large chicken for a Sunday roast and he comes back with lamb chops because they looked nicer and the guy on the meat counter said they were a better buy.

'Just the lamb, OK?' I say. 'Because it won't be me shouting at you, it will be Suzanne and Clare. And Clare's even more scary than Suzanne,' I add, running off to the bakery.

'I expected you half an hour ago,' says Peter. 'Helen's just been in and taken some croissants and loaves up for you, but you'd better take this lot too. I've done you some cakes and buns. I thought it would help if Clare didn't have to make them.' He hands me more bags than I can carry. 'Let me help you with those. I expect your car's parked up the high street?'

'Yes, it is. Thanks so much for this,' I say, suddenly realising that I've given Nigel my purse to pay for the meet and won't be able to pay Peter.

'Don't worry, pay me later,' Peter says after I've explained. 'You've got far too much to think about. Just let's be on the way with this or you'll be late.' He opens the door and puts a 'Closed' sign up.

Back at the car, which is now packed full of food, I thank Peter and look around for my husband.

'I've got to get back to the shop,' Peter says, 'but I'll come over and help out as soon as I can.'

'Thanks, Peter, you're a star.'

It's nearly eight, and the guests will be coming down for breakfast. Where has Nigel got to? I call his mobile but there's no reply. After another five minutes, when I've almost given up, Nigel finally appears with a woman who's carrying what looks like a box of lobsters.

'What the hell have you bought?' I say, looking at him tight-lipped.

'Cornish lobsters,' he says, grinning, 'but I've paid for them myself and not out of our kitty. And I got the lamb as well,' he adds quickly, realising I'm furious.

I thank the woman and pack the lobsters, still very much alive, into the car. The lamb, thankfully, is dead.

'Silly question,' I say as we set off at top speed back to Silver Trees, 'but why the lobsters?'

'I just had to stop at the fish stall, it looked so amazing, and the lady said it was very unusual to have lobsters here – they're mostly sent out to the Med. I just thought—'

'No, you didn't think, Nigel,' I say. 'We're late with the breakfast stuff and the guests will be waiting. How are we going to cook the lobsters? Do we even have time to cook them? And a lot of people don't even like lobster.' I'm aware that I'm ranting a little now. 'It's lamb on the menu, not lobsters, and we'll have to eat them today as we've nowhere to put them.'

I turn off the lane rather too sharply and skid into the driveway. A big four-wheel drive and a green Honda are parked at the door. The Grossettos and Smiths must have already arrived. It's a quarter past eight.

'Help me take the bread and rolls into the kitchen by the back entrance,' I say. 'That's our priority. The rest can wait.' Together we grab the bags of bread and race around the side to find Helen and Clare busy frying sausages and bacon. Through the door into the dining room I can see Candida and Adeline, both smiling for a change.

'So sorry we're late,' I say. 'Thank God you brought stuff up for us, Helen. Thank you.'

'No problem,' she replies. 'Clare thought you were cutting it a bit fine, so she rang me. You're just in the nick of time, though,' she says, spearing some sausages on to a plate. 'There's been a rush on toast.'

'The children have been very helpful,' says Clare, laying a tray of bacon and scrambled eggs out for Jenny to take through. Jenny's looking very smart in a white apron and little chef's hat.

'They're our little helpers,' says Helen. 'I think we've got enough eggs for tomorrow as well. I don't know what those kids did to make the hens lay so many, an egg-laying dance or something.' She smiles as she puts another round of bacon in the pan.

'Did you get everything on the list?' asks Clare.

'Yes, we managed to get everything, and Nigel thought it would be a good idea to buy some lobsters.'

'You fucking what?!' says Clare, forgetting that some of the guests might hear her.

Nigel tries to explain himself, while Helen laughs. Clare tells him off, saying all the things I told him she'd say, and a few more. Suitably chastised, Nigel goes out to collect the rest of the food.

'Oh, and Pippa and Dot are on their way, Amanda,' Clare says. 'They're going to get started on sorting the bedrooms while the guests have their breakfasts,' she says, handing Orlando a plate of scrambled eggs on toast and a small pot of home-made tomato chutney.

In reception I find Suzanne in her element, telling the new guests all about the house, as though she's lived here for three years rather than a couple of weeks.

'Yes, the main building dates back to the nineteenth century,' she's saying to a round-faced woman dressed casually but stylishly in jeans and top. 'Ah, there you are,' she says. 'Please let me introduce you to my assistant, Amanda Darcey.' Before I have time to open my mouth, the woman grabs me and kisses me on both cheeks.

'Hello, I am Eliana Grossetto and this is my family,' she says, as three very charming, beautiful children come forward. 'This is Frederic, he ees twelve and likes Daveed Beckham but not eeze wife. This is Isabella, she ees ten and likes English boys. And this is Luigi, 'oo ees four and ees a leetle monstur,' she says, pointing to her youngest, who doesn't look like a little monster at all.

I smile, still a bit miffed that I've been demoted to assistant, then bend down so that the children can kiss me on both cheeks.

A tall, dark man in his mid-forties, with big brown eyes and long eyelashes, walks in with two large pieces of designer luggage.

'Hello. I'm Paulo, Eliana's husband. Very nice to meet you,' he says, shaking my hand. Unlike his wife he has only a wisp of an accent.

Suzanne turns to me.

'I've explained to the Grossettos that their rooms aren't quite ready yet. We're going to put their luggage under the stairs while they have breakfast.' She turns back to the Grossettos. 'Amanda will take your luggage and I'll show you to the dining room.'

The little Grossettos trail behind their parents, Luigi cheekily sticking his tongue out at me as he passes. I put the bags under the stairs and turn to find another couple, who look unnervingly like the rock 'n' roll couple at the Elysian party. Both are wearing jeans and black jumpers, and look more like brother and sister than man and wife.

'Hello,' says the man. 'I'm Mr Smith and this is' – he smiles at the woman, who looks a bit sleepy – 'Mrs Smith.'

I smile. 'Welcome to Silver Trees, Mr and Mrs Smith.' I remember when Nigel and I used to go to hotels and I'd be his Mrs, even though we hadn't yet married. We couldn't think up silly names as the credit card always gave it away. 'I'm afraid your room isn't ready yet, but you can leave your bags here and have some breakfast with the other guests while you wait.'

Mr Smith looks furtively at Mrs Smith and she nods. He hands one large Louis Vuitton suitcase over to me and they walk, almost touching hands, into the dining room, where I hear Suzanne say, 'And you must be the Smiths.'

Nigel comes into the reception area.

'All the shopping is packed away in the kitchen. What can I do now?' he asks.

'I know Matt needs help with mending and sweeping the steps as Howard's been roped into room cleaning – it's a health hazard at the moment with those loose stones, and he said he'd be starting this morning. I'll get him on the walkie-talkie and see if he needs you yet,' I say, looking at my handset. 'Hello, Matt, hello, Matt, can you hear me?'

There's no answer, just a lot of buzzing.

'Hello, Matt, can you hear me?' I shout this time.

'Yes, I can,' a voice laughs. 'I'm out here, Amanda.'

Matt walks in through the front door, grinning at me. 'I should get started with the steps as the guests will want to go to the beach later. Howard here says he'd rather help me than do the beds, if that's all right with you, Amanda.'

'As long as you check with Suzanne, she's the co-ordinator, after all,' I say, realising Howard may be more of a hindrance than a help when it comes to the beds, especially as we have to do the rooms in breakneck speed.

As the three men head off towards the path with tools and sweeping brushes, Peter and Paul pop their heads round the door to say they're all packed and ready to go.

'We just wanted to say how much we've enjoyed staying here and how sorry we were to hear about Skyler's mum. I hope she's OK. Please tell her we had a wonderful time.'

'I will,' I say, very happy that they've enjoyed themselves, and even more happy that we can now get into their room. Just as I'm waving them goodbye, Nicola, Fay and Edina appear from the dining room.

'We'll be about half an hour, OK?' says Nicola. 'We didn't have time to pack this morning. Do you mind if we take a walk in the grounds before we go? It's so beautiful this morning.'

'If you could pack and bring your bags down first,' I say, 'it would be really helpful. Then you're welcome to stay as long as you like.' I'm not letting us get behind schedule any more than we already are.

'Yes, that's fine,' Nicola sighs. 'I noticed two very handsome men have just arrived,' she says, smiling.

'Yes, but they're both taken,' I say, smiling back.

Nicola looks at me as if to say, 'So?' – then walks up the stairs, followed by Edina and Fay, who look a little hungover.

Suzanne returns from the dining room.

'Right, everyone who's leaving has eaten and is now packing. The new guests are having breakfast, then they can go for walkies around the grounds,' she says, rather as if they were wayward pets. 'Clare and Helen are preparing lunch and supper, and you can join Pippa and Dot who are meant to be doing the rooms once they arrive. And what's this I hear about Nigel buying lobsters? Stupid bloody thing to do. Why did you let him?'

'I wasn't there when he did it. And he did still get the lamb as requested,' I say, feeling I should defend him as it was a generous thought.

'Well, I don't know what we're supposed to do with them,' she says, throwing her hands up in the air. 'Clare said she won't kill them and I'm certainly not volunteering. Though I guess if someone can face it we could do a lobster cocktail or something as a starter. David Torey should be impressed that we've used local produce, so perhaps it will all work out. Has Tom arrived yet?' she says, just as Tom walks through the door, accompanied by Pippa and Dot. The cavalry have truly arrived.

'Hello, ladies,' says Tom, sounding as though

everything is under control and we have all the time in the world. 'How's everythin' goin'?'

'Fine,' say Suzanne and I in unison, although neither of us sounds convinced. I hear Eliana shouting at Luigi in the dining room, '*Basta*, Luigi, *basta*,' which I think means stop it. There're some more shouts and cries, then everything seems to calm down. Neither Suzanne nor I want to go in. Whatever is happening, Clare, Helen and the children seem to have it under control.

'I'm gonna round up the new guests in the sittin' room and give them a talk about the riding and other activities we have to offer,' Tom says, 'so Matt has time to finish the path, then he can come in and talk to them about surfin' if they wanna do that, OK?'

'That sounds great,' Suzanne replies as we hear another loud crash from the dining room and Adeline and Candida scuttle out, looking harassed.

'The Italians are a bit too noisy for us, Suzanne, but your children are such charming waiting staff, they really are,' Adeline says. 'We're going up to our rooms and then we're going to walk along the coast, OK?'

As Adeline and Candida walk up the stairs, Pippa and Dot follow on behind, intending to get started on the Smiths' room. Suzanne and I look at each other.

'If we pull this off,' she says, 'it will be a miracle.' And with that we hear another crash from the dining room and another child being scolded; this time it sounds as if it's Frederic. We finally pluck up the courage to go in. We're met with a scene of chaos: Paulo is chasing Frederic, who's chasing Luigi round the central table.

Jenny, Hannah, Jack and Orlando are busy tidying the other tables, trying hard to avoid the flailing limbs of the Grossetto family. We go through to the kitchen, where Clare is loading the dishwasher and Helen is already preparing the lamb for tonight.

'Do you need any help?' Suzanne asks.

'No, we're fine,' says Clare, 'just get the bedrooms done and then get Pippa and Dot to do the dusting. We're OK on the food and the kids can go out and play in the garden.'

We head back to reception to see Nicola, Fay and Edina coming back down the stairs.

'We've got a few other bits and pieces to collect,' says Nicola, 'but this is the bulk of it.' I draw a deep breath, thankful that we can get to the new rooms so the little Grossettos can trash their bedroom rather than the dining room.

'We wanted Skyler to have this,' Fay says, carrying a large canvas.

Suzanne and I look at a beautiful view of Silver Trees from the gardens.

'We thought she'd like it,' Fay says, 'and that it might help cheer her up a little after her sad news.'

'She will love it,' I say, giving Fay a hug.

'We've had a great time,' Nicola says. 'Is there a guest book we can write in to say how much we enjoyed it?'

'It just so happens there is,' says Suzanne, pulling out her book, which is already getting nicely filled up with praise and promises of return.

'Please say our goodbyes to Tom and Matt. They

were amazing,' says Nicola, with a sparkle in her eye. 'And Skyler and, especially, George. Lovely man, that George,' she adds.

It's a good job Clare isn't around as she'd probably say something scathing, but Suzanne and I let it pass, although we both notice that the cheeky minx has put her mobile, home *and* work numbers in the book: 'Just in case George ever wants to get in touch when he's in London,' she writes.

We wave the women goodbye and then, as if on starter's orders, I race upstairs to the bedrooms.

Peter and Paul's room, as before, has been left in immaculate condition, and Pippa and Dot have already stripped the beds, cleaned the bathroom and hoovered; after they've changed the flowers and the soap they're ready to help me on the painted ladies' rooms.

Nicola, Fay and Edina have all left their rooms in a right state, so the girls and I have our work cut out for us. We have to open the windows wide as each room stinks of perfume. From Fay's window I can see the boys still busy on the path, and hear Tom on the terrace, giving the Grossettos and the Smiths a lecture on the joys of riding. There's also the sound of pans clattering in the kitchen, and I suspect that Clare and Helen have given the children jobs to do before they're allowed to escape and play for the rest of the morning in the grounds.

We're almost done with Fay's room when I see Adeline and Candida head downstairs for their walk. I hope the boys realise the ladies are on their way.

'Hello, Matt, can you hear me?' I say into my walkie-talkie. 'Hello, Matt?'

'Hello, Amanda, can hear you loud and clear, over,' he says, using the right jargon.

'LA ladies approaching. Handle with care and make sure you don't trip them up, over.'

'Copy that. We've finished now. Nigel and Howard are going to sweep the path and then fetch the surfboards for the beach. I'll head back with the tools. Over and out.'

Good, at least that's one job done. Half an hour later and Nicola and Edina's rooms have been completely cleaned and are ready for the Grossettos. I rush downstairs to let them know, only to be greeted by Suzanne, who is standing in reception with a tall blond man in his thirties.

'Sharon!' she says, smiling a little too brightly. 'This is David Torey. Mr Torey, this is Sharon Darcey, my housekeeper. I couldn't cope without her.'

I just manage to hold back a look of horror and confusion – why Sharon? Not only have I been demoted to housekeeper, now I've lost my name.

'Hello, Mr Torey,' I say, trying not to falter at Suzanne's bizarre introduction. 'Very nice to meet you.'

'And you,' he replies, shaking my hand. 'I'm a bit early, but as I explained to Skyler' – he gestures towards Suzanne, which confuses me even more – 'I found Silver Trees more easily than I'd anticipated . . . although the sign is rather obscured by vegetation.'

'Yes, we'll have to sort that out,' says Suzanne quickly.

'Your room is just being made ready. Would you like some tea before you go up? After that we could start your tour of the house and gardens.'

'That would be very nice,' he says. 'I'll just collect my luggage from my car.'

'Would you like some help?' Suzanne asks.

'No, that won't be necessary.' He smiles. 'And I'll start the tour upstairs, if that's OK. I realise the maids must still be cleaning the rooms, but I like to see the quality of work as they do it; it gives me a better impression of the standards you adhere to,' he says as he turns and goes.

'Fuck and double fuck,' I say, staring at Suzanne, but she's already on her way into the sitting room, where Matt has arrived back and taken over from Tom. He is telling the Grossettos and Mr and Mrs Smith about the local surfing.

'Sorry to interrupt, Matt, but I just wanted to let everyone know that your rooms are now ready whenever you'd like to go up. Please ask my assistant when you're ready to be shown to your room and she'll help you with your luggage.'

God, I'm confused. Who am I? A housekeeper, assistant or a bell boy? Amanda or Sharon? How bloody ridiculous; we're bound to be found out. Still, I'd better keep my mouth shut until Suzanne explains what she's up to.

'Now don't forget, you need to be ready for riding at the main door in half an hour if you want to go,' says Matt. 'Picnic lunches have been prepared and will be in the kitchen if you want them. Surfing pick-up is at three and I'll meet you at the main entrance so we can go down together. Everyone clear?'

Everyone nods and Luigi shouts in his loudest voice, 'No!' provoking a clip round the ear from his dad.

Suzanne goes into the kitchen as I lead the guests up to their bedrooms. Paulo and Mr Smith are carrying their own luggage, so it's no great hardship. I show the Smiths their room, and they immediately put a 'Do Not Disturb' sign on their door and shut it firmly. Perhaps they've had too much of the Grossettos already. I show them into their two rooms and then rush back downstairs and dash into the kitchen.

'What the hell are you doing, Suzanne?' I say, interrupting her as she briefs Helen, Clare and the children. 'What were you thinking, pretending to be Skyler?'

'I'm sorry, Amanda,' she replies calmly, 'but when David arrived he thought I was Skyler and it suddenly dawned on me how bad it would look if I explained, even under the circumstances, that Skyler had left her guests and friends to run the business. It wouldn't have looked good.'

'We should have discussed it last night and that still doesn't explain why you're calling me Sharon!'

'We didn't think of it last night,' she replies, 'and anyway, it's done now. I've just been telling Helen, Clare and the children about it, so hopefully they'll remember to call us by our pretend names. Let's hope we can get to the boys and Pippa and Dot before David does. The only ones I'm worried about are Adeline and Candida, as they know our names and I don't think they're game enough to go along with the ruse. As far as everyone else is concerned, I'm the boss and you're the assistant and they don't need to know any more. David is only here for a day and a night, then he goes. We can hold our breath for that long, surely?'

I still have an overwhelming feeling that someone, somewhere, is going to blow our cover, but there's very little I can say or do now. 'OK,' I say, 'but don't forget, we've got to give him a tour of the house and he'll expect Skyler to know all about it.'

'I can help with that,' says Clare. 'I know all about the place. Why don't I come round with you?'

'Hello,' says David, his head peeking round the door. 'Am I interrupting something?'

'Oh no, no,' says Suzanne, 'just a morning meeting with the staff. Would you like to meet everyone or see the bedrooms first?'

'Rooms first would be fine,' he says and everyone quietly sighs with relief.

As Suzanne shows David upstairs, I hear Jack asking Hannah, 'Can I be someone else, too? Can I be called John instead of Jack?'

'No,' I say, turning round, 'that would make everything too confusing. We'll have enough problems remembering that Suzanne is Skyler and I'm Sharon – but only to some of the guests. Keep things simple, be yourselves and say I'm your mummy.' Jack looks a little disappointed, but cheers up when I tell him he can go riding and surfing with his dad for the first time today.

In fact, all the children look absolutely delighted when they hear their fathers will be spending the day with them, while their mothers make sure that Silver Trees is everything David Torey would expect it to be, and more.

I head upstairs to join David and Suzanne/Skyler.

'Shall we begin, ladies?' he says, gesturing with his clipboard.

We show him Candida Pepsin's bedroom first, which Pippa and Dot have just made up. It's a charming room, with large windows overlooking the garden, where we can see Howard and Nigel have returned from the sweeping and are playing happily with the children. At least they're having fun.

'So, how long have you had the hotel?' David asks, starting to take notes.

Suzanne knows less about this than I do, so I speak for her. 'Skyler's had the property for just over two years now, I think, isn't that right?'

Suzanne nods.

'And you must have spent in excess of twenty thousand pounds renovating it,' I continue. 'It was a Catholic schoolhouse when they bought the place, and it was still full of desks and a blackboard, and had one huge dormitory upstairs,' I say, desperately trying to remember all the things Skyler has told me. 'We've tried to retain the character of the house and to use colours that enhance the natural brick rather than mask it.' I can't believe I'm coming out with this bullshit. 'The guests seem to enjoy the character of the place; it has a genuine feeling of warmth, don't you think?' I say, trying to remember some of the lines I've used to describe charming hotels in the past.

'It certainly does have something special, as you say, Sharon,' David says, looking slightly puzzled. 'How many beds do you have?'

I say seventeen and Suzanne says eighteen, correcting herself by explaining that there's a camp bed in one of the cottages. He asks about the number of en suites and we disagree on that as well, which is harder to get out of, but he seems to let it pass.

We know we must look and sound very awkward. I find it hard to believe we're going to get through this without being found out.

'Do you have any plans for a swimming pool or any other facilities, such as a tennis court?' he asks, walking into another of the bedrooms.

Suzanne has completely frozen up on me.

'No, we have no plans to do that,' I say, hoping Skyler hasn't applied for planning approval and not told us.

'So what do you offer guests that makes you different from anywhere else?' David asks.

'We offer the best of what Cornwall has to offer,' Suzanne suddenly pipes up confidently. 'We offer families an opportunity to holiday together and enjoy spending time together. So many family holidays these days offer kids' clubs from morning till dusk so the parents see too little of their kids; with the surfing, sailing and riding here, as well as the wonderful walks, there's lots for families to do together.'

I'm left slightly dumbfounded, but manage to say, 'And for those who don't have children there's the peace and tranquillity of our grounds and the setting.' Unfortunately, I happen to say this just as we're passing the Smiths' room, where a lot of groaning is going on.

Even David smiles.

'I know what you mean, Sharon,' he says, raising an eyebrow.

'But don't just listen to us, David, have a look at the visitors' book,' says Suzanne.

'Later, later. First I'd like to look around a little more, if I may.'

Clare comes upstairs to tell us that everything is now prepared for lunch and supper.

'The girls and I will be tidying up the sitting and dining areas, Skyler,' she says. She's even better at this than Suzanne.

'Now, where are your fire exits?' David asks as Clare turns to go.

Suzanne and I look blank, but thankfully Clare says, 'Upstairs, it's through the main bathroom and down the fire escape to the terrace, and downstairs there's one for each room, and we congregate on the same terrace. We have safety drills once a month, according to fire regulations, and each room has instructions in case of fire and a small fire extinguisher, as do both cottages. There's also a first-aid kit in every room.'

David looks impressed and we discreetly nod at Clare to stay with us for the rest of the tour.

We walk around each of the empty bedrooms, with

David checking and asking questions, which, between us, we manage to answer. Clare has the technical knowledge and knows how many staff there are, the room charges and the sort of food that's offered, while I know what sort of selling-spiel David is looking for, and Suzanne provides the charm and the professionalism.

After we've viewed the bedrooms, we walk downstairs into the sitting room and leave David wandering around on his own, looking out of the patio doors on to the gardens beyond.

'Lovely views,' he says, making another note. He goes into the dining room, walking around the tables, and then has a really good look around the kitchen. As we're walking towards my cottage I try to remember if I've left anything out which might give the game away. It's very weird looking around the cottages as if they're inhabited by complete strangers when they're full of all our stuff. My mobile, which I've left on my bedside table, starts ringing, and although I'm itching to pick it up, I manage to resist.

I leave Clare and Suzanne to accompany David to the other cottage, as the entourage seems a bit excessive now.

I watch them disappear down the path then head back inside to see who the call was from. Skyler's left a message: 'Hi, Amanda. Just wondered how everything is. Hope all is going well and that you're handling the inspector if he's arrived. The funeral is in a few days' time, but I just wanted to say a huge thank-you for everything. I love you all. Willow, Rose and George also send their love.'

I juggle the pros and cons of calling back. Skyler's got enough on her plate, but in the end I give it a go, wanting to put her mind at rest about things here.

'Hello, Skyler,' I say when she picks up, trying to sound relaxed and cheerful.

'What's up?' she asks, immediately worried.

'Everything's fine. The new guests have arrived, the old ones have gone and they've all signed the visitors' book.'

'I don't have a visitors' book,' she says.

'You do now. Suzanne donated the notebook she bought at the fair. Everyone has put lovely things in it and Fay has left you a beautiful painting of the house as a gift. They all say they want to come back next year and were very sorry to hear your news.'

I can hear Skyler start to cry down the phone.

'It's horrible, Amanda,' she says through the sobs. 'There's so much stuff to go through, and Dad is a mess. George is being brilliant looking after the girls, and they've been so great, but I'm the one who has to ring round all Mum's friends. We've got over a hundred coming to the funeral, and I've had to organise the catering, flowers and cremation. God, they make a killing, those funeral parlours, don't they?'

I laugh and so does Skyler when she realises what she's just said.

'Death and taxes, the only certainties in life,' I say.

'I'm really pleased to hear everything's OK down

there. Did Howard and Nigel arrive safely?' she asks.

'Yes, they did. And they brought more champagne. They're playing with the children now, and they're going riding with Tom in about an hour once the Grossettos have finished their first session. Then they're all going surfing with Matt this afternoon.'

'I wonder how Tom will get on with Howard,' she says.'

'Why do you say that?'

'Oh, I'm not blind, I see how those two look at each other and the way Suzanne looks when she's talking about her riding. They're round each other all the time, the little flirts,' she says. 'Tom's such a ladies' man. There's always a rumour about him, and he likes the married ones, I'm told.'

'Well, I think you're probably right,' I say, weighing up whether I should tell Skyler about Tom and Suzanne kissing, but just as I'm about to say something I hear George's voice in the background, calling her away, and very abruptly she tells me she has to go.

I start to walk back up to the house, when suddenly I hear Jack, sobbing, somewhere in amongst the trees. With my mother-radar on high alert, I stumble through the trees towards him. I find him standing at the foot of a big Scots pine. Howard is crouching in front of him, drying Jack's eyes with a large handkerchief and saying, 'Now then, no harm done. You just got a fright.'

'Jack, what's happened, baby?' I say, kneeling down and clasping his hands. He's still crying, but not so loudly.

'We were playing hide-and-seek and I think he was trying to climb this tree,' says Howard. 'Look, that branch has snapped – he's only fallen a yard or so.'

'Does anything hurt, Jack?'

'Everything!' he says between sobs.

'Oh, Jack, bad luck,' says Howard, trying not to laugh. 'Do we need to bandage you up like an Egyptian mummy?'

Jack smiles through his tears.

'I don't think so. I wouldn't be able to surf then, would I?'

We laugh, which makes him laugh, and very soon he's stopped crying and is begging Howard to help him find another hiding place.

'OK,' says Howard, grinning, 'now, let's see . . .'

I leave them crawling into the middle of a huge rhododendron bush, and head on up the path, smiling to myself and thinking how good Howard is with the kids, despite his own behaviour sometimes.

Then I remember David, and my mind is immediately racing, running through all the things I know inspectors look for: quality of service, warmth of welcome, facilities, health and safety, cleanliness, suitability for families and pets. Skyler should be fine on all those things, surely.

I meet David, Suzanne and Clare just by the house. David is looking very happy with what he's seen.

'The cottages are lovely,' he says; 'they're very tastefully decorated and the paths are clear and safe. Yes, it all looks good. Now, if you'll excuse me, ladies, I need to go to my room and make some notes and calls, then I'm going to take a walk down to the beach.'

But just as he's about to walk up the stairs, Deborah comes through the door. Before we can drag her to one side, she says, 'Hello, Suzanne; hi, Amanda.'

'Hello, Deborah,' we both reply weakly, and introduce her to David.

'Ah, hello, David. I think you're due to see us tomorrow afternoon. I'm Deborah Banks, co-owner of the Elysian Hotel. But I mustn't interrupt your inspection here. Silver Trees is wonderfully unique, don't you think?'

David Torey looks at her and then at us.

'Yes, I must say I've never been to a place quite like it.'

'Can I have a word with you, Deborah?' whispers Suzanne as we leave David in the hallway, still looking bemused.

'Before you say anything, I want to apologise about that "other thing",' Deborah says mysteriously, 'and also to invite you to the Minack Theatre tomorrow evening; they're doing a production of *Romeo and Juliet*. It's being sponsored by Henry Foster, whom you met at the party. Would you like to come?'

'We would love to, Deborah, but first, could I explain something? Please could you not call us by our names in front of David?' I explain our charade, which seems increasingly silly.

Deborah is mortified that she may have spoilt our deception.

'I'm so sorry,' she says, hand over her mouth.

'You weren't to know!' I reassure her. 'And don't tell anyone else, please.'

'No worries, my lips are sealed.' She smiles. 'About tomorrow night, unfortunately there's no room for children.'

'How about husbands?' Suzanne asks. 'Ours have just arrived.'

'Oh dear, I only have two places. Could the men possibly look after the children? You both looked as though you were having so much fun at the party, perhaps you'd like another girls' night out.'

'After a day like today,' Suzanne says, 'it sounds just what we need.' She grins at me. We're both praying we might just have got away with it.

Chapter 13

Outward Bonding

It's the morning after, and David Torey is leaving the building. Thanks to Matt and Clare, last night's supper was a triumph. Matt came up with the brilliant plan of barbecuing the lobsters – thankfully taking care of killing them, too – and the guests were suitably impressed. The rest of the food was delicious, and even though we were all exhausted by the time the last guests had disappeared upstairs, we couldn't keep the triumphant grins off our faces.

Now we just need to wave goodbye to the inspector, and we can relax.

'Thank you, Skyler and Sharon,' he says as we escort him out. 'It's been a pleasure. The supper was delicious and I had a very comfortable night. I would love to stay longer but, as you know, I'm due to stay at the Elysian tonight. But you certainly offer very special accommodation and have wonderfully warm and knowledgeable staff.' He shakes Suzanne's hand and then mine. I'm so relieved we've managed to get away with our little white lie. He must have just decided he'd heard wrong. I just hope he doesn't quiz Deborah about it once he gets to the Elysian. He doesn't look like the sort of man who would have a sense of humour about things like that.

As I wave him goodbye with one hand, I call Skyler from my mobile with the other. She answers on the second ring.

'Amanda, how did it go?'

'Good, I think. He's just gone and he seemed to love the place.'

'That's great news. Sorry I had to cut you off yesterday, Amanda, but there was a lot going on. Thank you so much for everything, and would you please thank Suzanne and everyone else too?'

'Yes, of course. How's it going there?'

'As well as can be expected, I'd say. What's everyone up to today?'

'The men are planning on some hiking and beach games with the children and then they're babysitting for us tonight so that we can go to the theatre. Deborah has invited us to the Minack.'

'Oh, you'll enjoy that.'

'She told me to say that she was sorry about the "other thing", but I've no idea what she meant.'

'Oh, OK,' she says, but I sense from the tone of her voice that it's not.

'Is it something you can tell me?' I ask quietly.

She groans.

'Deborah must have assumed you already know. Well, I'll tell you, but you're sworn to secrecy.'

'I swear,' I say, although I'm not sure what I'm swearing to.

'George and I bought Silver Trees with Dennis's help. We thought we had enough money but with all the unexpected costs, we needed more. Dennis agreed to lend us the money for a set number of years at a set rate of interest, but then he had to ask for the money back early to pay for the Elysian's renovations.'

'But a deal's a deal, so he's reneged on his agreement,' I say angrily.

'He didn't know he'd need the money,' Skyler explains, 'so it's not his fault. But that's why Deborah was apologising.'

'How are you going to manage?' I ask.

'One step at a time,' says Skyler. 'I've got my mother's funeral tomorrow.'

'If there's anything we can do to help—'

'You've done more than enough, Amanda, now just go and have fun with your family and at the theatre tonight, and look after my guests. We'll be back soon. Love to you all.' And she goes before I've got time to reply.

I don't have time to think about Skyler's revelation for the rest of the day. The morning rush of chores goes relatively smoothly, although the girls couldn't get into the Smiths' room until after eleven. The other guests seem happy. Even Adeline and Candida were humming over breakfast – I think enjoying the special attention Jenny and Suzanne were giving them. The Grossettos have settled in nicely, although Luigi has managed to smash one of Skyler's lovely vases, scrawl on their bathroom wall with a felt-tip pen, and is terrorising Hunter by growling at him every time he sees him. Tom has told him off for trying to scare the horses and Matt has had to ask Eliana to keep hold of him on the beach after he picked up a boogie board and tried to hurl it at another child. Despite all of this, he's somehow managed to charm Adeline and Candida, and is now sitting with them on the terrace tucking into a large plate of scones. It's five o'clock and Clare and Pippa are quietly beginning the preparations for supper whilst Dot serves tea.

Suzanne is already down at her cottage preparing herself for the theatre. I'm just about to head off to do the same when I see Deborah's car sweep into the drive. She jumps out and rushes over to me.

'Hi there, Amanda. I've brought the tickets over for this evening. Is everything OK here? David Torey certainly seems very impressed with Silver Trees, although of course he's not allowed to say too much,' she says seriously. 'Tom said he'd take and collect you from the theatre to save you having to try and park your car,' she adds, 'so see you in a couple of hours. Pick-up is at six and it takes about an hour to get there; the performance starts at seven-thirty. I must rush back. See you later!' and she leaps back into her car and drives off. She looks the happiest I've ever seen her.

I check that Clare is OK, then run down to the cottage to change. Nigel is there, but about to rush back to the children.

'We've planned a treasure hunt for them,' he says as he quickly changes his shirt.

'What a good idea,' I say, already running up the stairs to the bedroom.

'Oh, it wasn't my idea,' he says, following me up. 'It was Orlando and Jenny's, and they've roped in Howard and me to search for clues. They've even got the Grossettos and the two LA ladies involved, so we should have a lot of fun after supper.'

'Probably more fun than us,' I say.

'Oh don't be silly, you'll enjoy it. You've always talked about the Minack and how wonderful and romantic it is.'

'Yes, but I thought I'd be going with you, Nigel.' I'm wearing smart jeans and a warm but smart sweater as I know it'll be too cold and blustery at the outside theatre for anything more frivolous. Nigel watches as I pull a hairbrush through my hair a few times and quickly dab on foundation and mascara and put my compact and lipstick into my bag. I can do the rest in the car.

'Go and enjoy yourself, and by the way, you look lovely,' Nigel says, kissing me on the lips. Which reminds me, we must have sex sometime this year.

Nigel and the children insist on escorting me up to the house. We're standing at the front door as Suzanne,

Howard and Orlando approach, Suzanne wearing a beautiful full-length dress of midnight blue.

'You look stunning,' I tell her, 'but you should bring a jacket or something. I think the Minack's got stone seats and it's probably quite breezy.' But we're running late and Tom's Land Rover is already coming through the gates, so Suzanne just dismissively waves her hand at my advice and says not to worry. We clamber in, and Howard, Nigel and the children wave us goodbye as we speed off.

Suzanne's sitting beside Tom, and I suddenly feel like a gooseberry, particularly as Howard shouts out, 'Have a wonderful time, and make sure no one gets off with my wife!' Sure enough, Suzanne spends the next hour flirting with Tom, saying what a wonderful rider he is and how masterful he was with the Grossettos that morning. I try to concentrate on the beautiful scenery. The sunset is lovely, with purples, blues and reds scarring the sky, promising another warm day tomorrow. We drive down the endless narrow roads, curving between high hedges and drystone walls. I can't help thinking how good the walls would look at Silver Trees along the pathway to the beach, but that would cost money the Blues clearly don't have.

When we arrive, there's already a car park full of four-wheel drives, Volvos and BMWs. Tom manages to find a space, and we walk towards the theatre. It's amazing; a striking stone construction perched precariously on the edge of a promontory, with large stone monoliths acting as a backdrop to the stage. What an incredible setting. Nigel would have loved this.

I spot Deborah and wave.

'We've saved you some seats,' she says, walking over and kissing each of us warmly on the cheeks. 'Vivienne and the rest of the crowd you met at the party are here.'

I can tell by Suzanne's face that she hopes she isn't seated next to Patrick. Then, just as we get to our seats, the wind catches Suzanne's dress, and it flies up to reveal knickers, stockings, the lot, much to her embarrassment and everyone else's amusement. She looks as mortified as she did at the Elysian and tries to regain her composure as we take our seats.

The performance starts shortly afterwards, and for the next hour Suzanne and I are entranced by the tale of forbidden love and bigotry, the atmosphere only enhanced by the wild setting. The actors, who, Deborah whispers in my ear, come from London, are brilliant. Occasionally we can hear waves crashing against the rocks which only heightens the tension, and I forget that my bottom is starting to go numb despite the cushions provided.

The interval comes before we know it, and I get up gratefully to stretch my legs and get some feeling back into my bottom. There's a small bar for the audience, but Dennis has kindly provided a picnic of champagne – Cristal, no less – and nibbles for us. I wonder how he can justify the expense and still be asking for his money back from Skyler and George. I can't stop thinking about how he's let them down and how they don't deserve such bad fortune as I look at the group of hangers-on: Constance still giggling and sniffing, Henry boring her with his talk of boats and Patrick and Mark looking smug, arrogant and bloated with alcohol. Vivienne is talking to Suzanne, so I decide to make my escape and take a walk along the coast.

But just as I'm turning to go, Dennis comes up to me.

'Are you enjoying the performance?' he asks.

'Yes, I am, thank you,' I reply. I wonder why he always targets me for a chat. I'm sure he knows I dislike him and can see straight through him, yet he seems intent on winning me over. He's looking even more puffed up than normal, his jowls exaggerated by the lighting.

'I expected to see Skyler here. Where is she?'

'Oh, I thought Deborah would have told you. Her mother died and she's had to rush off with George and the children to sort out the funeral.'

'Who's looking after Silver Trees?' Dennis asks, looking bemused.

'Oh, Clare, myself and Suzanne, and we're getting loads of help from Tom, Matt and Helen, so we've managed to cope admirably and all the guests are happy.' I don't want to get into a conversation with a man I have so little respect for. I'm dying to mention the fact that I know about him calling in his loan, but I bite my tongue.

'That's odd. David said Skyler was there to greet him when he stayed at Silver Trees.'

I don't want to tell Dennis about Suzanne's deception, so I lie, 'Oh, he must have been confused. Suzanne and I showed him around. He probably thought one of us was Skyler,' I say.

'You most likely did a better job anyway. They're lovely people but in my opinion they're not exactly capable of running a business.'

I'm so stunned that all I can do is smile weakly and say, 'Well, I'm just off for a little walk, Dennis. See you in a while.'

The interval is long so I have enough time to walk quite a way along the coast. As I turn to head back, with the ocean to my left, I see a couple kissing inland a bit near a cluster of trees. The romantic story has obviously caught the imagination of some lovers. I can barely make them out from this distance but I have a strange feeling of déjà vu. Then I realise why. It's just like when, a few days ago, I spotted Suzanne and Tom, standing on the edge of the cliff and kissing like star-crossed lovers! After giving me a big speech about loving Howard and staying with him despite everything, I can't believe Suzanne's behaviour, especially now that Howard's arrived.

'Suzanne, what the hell do you think you're doing?' I shout, turning off the path and heading inland towards the couple. I've had enough off her false promises and her pretending that she can confide in me. She's got to realise that she can't go sneaking around like this.

The woman doesn't turn round. Perhaps the wind's blowing in the wrong direction or she's just choosing to ignore me, or maybe she's so wrapped up in Tom she doesn't hear me.

'Suzanne!' I shout again as I get closer. 'Suzanne!' This time I get a response, but confusingly it comes from behind me.

'Amanda!' I hear a voice as someone comes running up behind me. 'Amanda, what do you want?'

I turn round and see Suzanne approaching. Just then her dress rises up around her waist again, which makes her stop and shriek with embarrassment, not that there's anyone around to notice other than me.

I feel immensely relieved that the woman isn't Suzanne; perhaps the man isn't Tom either, but as I turn round I see the couple have stopped kissing and are looking in the direction of all the shrieking and shouting. It's getting dark now and there are lots of shadows being cast by the surrounding trees and bushes. The wind is warm but strong and there are clouds scudding across the full moon. As I turn to go, I take one last look. The man walks slowly towards me, holding the woman's hand. It's definitely Tom. I can't mistake that walk or his distinctive silhouette, and I'm sure it's the same one I saw on the cliff that day. And now, although the light is dim, I can just make out the woman's face, too.

'Amanda, what are you doing here?' Suzanne has finally reached me. Now I finally know who the mystery couple are, I don't want a scene, so I turn and walk towards her.

'I'm coming. Sorry, I got lost out here and couldn't find my way back.'

'Well, follow me back, Amanda – the second part is about to start. Are you enjoying this?' she says, trying to keep her dress and dignity in place and failing on both counts.

'Yes, very much so,' I say, still dazed by what I've just seen.

Suzanne prattles on about the production and how Vivienne thinks she would make a good presenter and wants to know if she has a show reel. I'm only half listening, trying to work out the implications of what I've seen.

The wind has picked up. Deborah returns to her seat beside me just as the third act starts, and the passion and tragedy on stage seems to affect both her and Suzanne. As the play ends with the bodies of the two lovers sprawled in a pool of light, the audience rises as one to give a standing ovation. Suzanne, Deborah and I – and most of the women in the audience, I'm sure – have tears running down our cheeks.

Even Dennis seems impressed.

'Wonderful, wasn't it? The actors are down from London, the next Leonardo Di Caprio and Clare Danes, don't you think?' he says proudly. 'They're only here for this performance, but perhaps we'll have time to have a quick word with them now.' Most of the crowd are wandering back to their cars, but Patrick and Mark are mucking about on the stage, talking about Mark's latest music deal, and how he gaffer-taped his drummer to a tree overnight because he couldn't get the beat right. Suzanne and I wait around with Constance, who seems on edge, perhaps because there's no bathroom to disappear to.

'Why don't you go behind a bush?' Suzanne says, trying to be helpful. 'Or can you wait until the hotel?'

Constance ignores her and goes in search of Mark. They disappear behind some scenery and she returns five minutes later, her normal giggling, hyper self.

I walk towards Tom's car with Suzanne, who's as eager as I am to get home.

'I want to say my thank-yous and goodbyes to Deborah. Where's she got to?' she asks, looking around.

'I'm sure she'll turn up,' I say. 'Perhaps we should wait by the car for Tom – we don't want to miss our lift,' I say.

For ten minutes we wait in the dark as the last guests disperse, still talking about the amazing performance. Eventually Tom turns up, looking his usual calm self, and Deborah follows a few minutes later.

'Sorry we're late,' Tom says. 'We're taking Deborah home because Mark's car's broken down so Dennis has got to take two extra bodies with him.'

'Great,' says Suzanne. 'I wanted to thank you for the invite anyway, Deborah. Wasn't that wonderful?' she remarks as Tom starts the engine and we wave goodbye to the others. 'So atmospheric with the backdrop of the crashing waves and the wind howling round the theatre, even though it did play havoc with my dress.

And I also wanted to say I so enjoyed the party at the Elysian, Deborah, it really was splendid. I think Skyler should have a party like that; it would be great PR for Silver Trees, don't you think?' She doesn't leave Deborah any time to answer. She seems high on the night's experience and the sea air. 'You're quiet, Tom. I suspect that wasn't really your thing, was it?' she says, squeezing him on the shoulder. 'Too much romance and not enough action?'

'I think there was a fair bit of action in that story,' replies Tom drily.

'What did you think of it, Deborah?' Suzanne asks.

'I thought it was very stirring and evocative,' Deborah says simply. 'It's a very moving play with powerful themes.'

By the time we reach the house, Suzanne has discussed the entire works of Shakespeare, while Deborah, Tom and I have been allowed to say very little.

'Thank you so much for a wonderful evening,' I say to Deborah, as I get out of the car, 'and thank you, Tom, for the lift,' I add.

'My pleasure,' he says as Suzanne gets out of the front seat, allowing Deborah to take her place. We wave them goodbye and head inside. The lights are still on but it looks as though everyone's gone to bed. I take a quick look at the dining room to check everything's clear for breakfast, then go through to the kitchen.

'Pippa and Clare have laid out the tables for breakfast. They've been amazing,' I say, looking at

Suzanne, who's examining her dress to see what damage the wind has done to it.

'Well, I'm calling it a night,' she says and gives me a hug. 'It's been a full-on day today, hasn't it?' She yawns.

'It certainly has,' I reply. 'I'll close up and you go to bed, Suzanne.' I check in the sitting room to make sure everything is tidy. The kitchen looks fine and upstairs is quiet, so I walk slowly towards the cottage, the full moon shining its unearthly light on to the pathway, spotlighting our cottage, where Nigel has hopefully exhausted the children with a treasure hunt – or, more likely, the other way round.

As I walk towards our door, I'm finally able to think clearly about the secrets I've been privy to today. Skyler and George's livelihood hangs in the balance, and I've just been partying with the man who's swept the carpet out from under them. I stop and smile. Dennis is a man who thinks he has everything: celebrity friends, houses, cars, a son tucked away in boarding school and an adoring wife; who spends half his life out at sea and the rest, it seems, with his head in the clouds, because for someone who prides himself on being so astute, he has missed what's right in front of his nose. His adoring wife is having an affair with Tom MacKenny.

Chapter 14
Jump

The next morning I'm woken by Hannah and Jack, still overexcited by the previous evening's treasure hunt. It's early, and I decide to make the best of it and go and get the bread. It's a beautiful morning, the sun already blazing out of a clear blue sky as I head for Tremontgomery. Once I've been to the bakery, I head back to Silver Trees, singing along to the radio and wondering whether I could fit in an early morning swim before everyone appears. After the stress of the last few days, I can feel my mood lifting as I drive down the pretty lanes.

I park the car and get the bread out of the passenger seat, still singing to myself. I bounce through the front door – and stop dead in my tracks. David Torey is standing at reception, looking incandescent with rage. Suzanne is behind the desk, red-faced and apparently unable to speak. Clare, who's come out to the hall to see what's going on, is backing swiftly into the kitchen.

'Well, then, who are you?' David is saying. 'I know that you two are not who you say you are and that Skyler Blue and her husband are away. This has serious implications, not only for the grading of the property, but also for insurance, and I am absolutely horrified that I have been lied to like this.' He pauses, and I can sense from Suzanne's demeanour that she's about to deny everything. Realising that to dig ourselves in deeper would only make things worse, I quickly step in.

'I will explain everything, Mr Torey. My name is Amanda Darcey and this is Suzanne Fields. We are very old and *trusted* friends of Skyler and George. We came here on holiday and to help out a bit, and when Skyler's mother died suddenly a few days ago we offered to look after the guests so that she and George could return to London to organise the funeral. She didn't ask us to help her, it wasn't planned or anything, it was just a spontaneous offer made in difficult and traumatic circumstances. It seemed like the best and least disruptive solution for the guests and we're terribly sorry for misleading you, but we felt that, under the circumstances, it was our only option.'

'The best option is never the dishonest one, Mrs Darcey, you should know that. A deception like this could have serious long-term ramifications. It's not a case of you offering; she should have said no. For Skyler to leave the property and the safety of her guests in the hands of people who have never run a bed and breakfast before is extremely irresponsible. I'm not sure whether I should grade this property at all now.' He pauses and I can't help but think he's overreacting and enjoying the power of his job. After all, anyone's allowed to run a B&B, the only fault we made is that we didn't tell him the whole truth up front. But there's no point me arguing any of this, it'll only make things worse.

'I'm afraid I must go away to reconsider my grading. I will call back in a few days to let you know my decision.'

And with that, he turns and goes.

We're both stunned into silence. Then Suzanne says weakly, 'I wonder how he found out.'

'That's hardly the point, is it? We should never have lied in the first place. How are we going to explain this to Skyler and George?' I'm furious with myself for not dealing with the deception earlier on.

'I'm sorry, I – I – I just panicked. I felt I had to do something,' says Suzanne, looking totally deflated.

'I know,' I say, patting her on the shoulder. 'I suspect he probably would have blown up about it either way; he's just that type of person. Look, don't beat yourself up about it, maybe one of the guests let it slip during the day and it took some time for him to put two and two together. Or maybe Deborah told him when he was over there.' After last night's revelation, I realise I'm not sure we can trust Deborah, and as she's the competition, she'd have the motivation for spilling the beans on our charade.

'Deborah wouldn't have done it on purpose. She's too nice,' Suzanne insists.

I laugh. 'Well, it turns out we know nothing about Deborah Banks,' I say, walking into the kitchen with the bread.

'What do you mean by that?' she says, following me.

'Your dear friend, whom you wanted to stay with a week ago when you'd got so sick of me' – I turn to see a very shame-faced Suzanne – 'well, your friend is having an affair, and do you know with whom?'

'Who?' she says, as though she's about to learn the meaning of life.

'Tom MacKenny.'

Suzanne laughs. 'No, not Tom. Tom's not her type.'

'Why not? You flirted with him, so why can't she fancy him? I'd say he's perfect because he's so completely different to Dennis. I saw them kissing last night at the theatre, and I was just about to confront them when you turned up.'

'Never,' says Suzanne, her face dropping to the floor.

I'm aware that Clare is listening to every word.

'Ooh, I haven't heard gossip like this for ages,' she says, grinning as she puts the rolls into the baskets. 'We all knew he was seeing someone. Are you sure?'

'Definitely, and they know I saw them. Why don't you confront them when you next see them? Who's to say that one of them didn't snitch on Skyler when she left?' I say, lowering my voice. The children have come in with the eggs and I don't want them to hear.

Suzanne looks shocked, then humiliated. She obviously had a soft spot for Tom and feels foolish, but at least she knows the truth about him now.

'Mummy, can we go coasteering with Daddy and the older children?' asks Hannah.

'Only if Daddy lets you,' I say, 'but you might be a little too young,' I add, thinking of the huge waves I saw last night.

Suzanne leaves the room, obviously still shocked by the news, though I'm not sure what's shocked her more: Tom and Deborah's affair or that Skyler is now in serious trouble after our white lie.

'Are you OK with breakfast this morning?' I ask Clare, feeling in need of some fresh air myself. I'm so wound up by everything and already regret having exposed Deborah and Tom's affair. It's not usually in my nature to react so hastily and spitefully. It's none of my business, really.

'We're fine, Amanda,' she says. Then, obviously noticing how anxious I look, she adds, 'And don't worry about the inspector. Things will turn out OK. You did a good job for Skyler and she'll understand.' She turns to my three and Orlando to give them their orders for the morning. I look at the children and realise how much they're enjoying the responsibility and how they've thrived on being out in the open air. At least they're oblivious to the mess their parents have made of things. It's Skyler's mother's funeral this morning. I hope she doesn't ring until tomorrow – I know I can't keep any more secrets to myself and

I certainly don't want to give her more bad news on top of everything else.

I walk along the coastal path, grateful for the wind on my face. I close my eyes and breathe in the sea air, desperately wanting our luck to change. Everything seems to have gone against us just when we thought we were getting things right and starting to enjoy the challenge. I open my eyes again and turn to walk back, but something, or rather someone, stops me in my tracks. I can see a figure about two hundred yards away standing precariously close to the edge; as I walk closer I can just make out that it's a woman. She's got her back to me, but I know it's Deborah and I think of turning back, unable to face her after having been so indiscreet about her private affairs. But suddenly she starts to shake and crumples to the ground. I run up to her.

'Deborah,' I say softly, trying not to give her a fright.

She turns and stares at me, her face red with tears.

'Amanda? Oh, I'm sorry, I've—' She breaks off, covering her face with her hands. She looks so desperately sad that I go right up to her and hug her. Has Tom dumped her? Or has Dennis found out about them?

When she finally stops crying, we sit down on a nearby rock.

'Oh God,' she says, 'what must you think of me? I'm such a mess. My life is such a mess.'

'Why?' I ask, putting my arm around her.

'My life looks so glamorous and privileged, what with all the parties and the Elysian, but the truth is Dennis just uses me as some sort of corporate hostess. He's a bullying, arrogant snob. The only friends we have are Dennis's hangers-on, who have their own homes in Cornwall, but choose to stay at the Elysian because Dennis gives them a ridiculously reduced rate.'

I want to tell her that I guessed as much, but I don't.

'I've always admired and envied Skyler for her friends and lovely family. When she came down to take over Silver Trees I wanted to help her out. The house needed a lot of work doing to it and I loved the idea of helping them restore a traditional Cornish house and turning it into a family-run business, so I persuaded Dennis to invest in it, and that's how our involvement began,' she says, choking back the emotion. 'I never got as close to Skyler as I wanted because they don't run in Dennis's circles, mainly out of choice on their part, I'm sure,' she adds, smiling.

'Knowing Skyler, I think you're probably right,' I say.

'But now Dennis's mean streak has come out. It's stupid, really, because they're not even in the same market as the Elysian, but he's started seeing Silver Trees as competition. Skyler and George are getting more bookings, while we always seem to be full of Dennis's non-paying friends.'

'We're not paying,' I admit.

'Well, you're the first, though in fairness I think what you're doing now for Skyler is payment in itself.'

'So does Dennis really need that money back?' I ask.

'I don't think so. He could get it from other sources but he'd lose interest and that infuriates him. And he didn't like seeing George and Skyler doing well. They see right through him and he knows it. Dennis told David Torey that Skyler and George had left Silver Trees in your hands. He just dropped it into conversation this morning over breakfast. Something along the lines of George and Skyler being at her mother's funeral. I was horrified but I couldn't stop him.'

'It's not your fault,' I say, realising how distressed Deborah is by the incident and feeling guilty for even suspecting for a moment that she was to blame.

'I could have kicked him in the shins or something,' she says, half smiling. 'I know I should have at least tried to defend my friends. But I didn't. I said nothing and just sat there like a lemon. I could see David was confused and then incensed because Dennis was laughing about how easily he'd been duped. Have you seen him yet?' she asks.

'Yes, we have and we've explained everything,' I say, 'and he seems to have understood – well, sort of – but we don't know where that leaves Skyler and George. Hopefully, he'll calm down and see reason before we have to say anything to them.'

'I hope so,' Deborah says, looking down.

'And what about Tom?' I ask when she's calmed down a little, fearful that she'll start blubbing again at the mere mention of his name.

But instead she smiles.

'It's simple, really. We're in love, and have been for

some time. He's so different from Dennis in every way. And he realises how much I miss my son.'

'So it wasn't your decision to send him to boarding school?'

'No, that was Dennis's decision, and for him to go to this wretched summer camp. He's always kept Jeremy at arm's length, just as his parents did with him. It breaks my heart that he won't even try to connect with his own son and I miss him dreadfully,' she says, starting to cry but managing to stop herself. 'Tom wants me to divorce Dennis and bring Jeremy back home to move in with him, but Dennis has this ruthless streak. He knows how much I love Jeremy, and he'll use that. He'll try to take everything. He'd try to destroy me, I know he would. I've seen him do it in business, destroy people's reputations on a whim, play devil's advocate at dinner parties just for the hell of it, and reduce guests to tears. It's all a power game with him. Just look at what he's doing to Silver Trees.'

'He can't be all that bad, though. You loved him once. You must have done – you married him,' I say.

'Yes, I did love him once, before I realised what he was really like, and now we have Jeremy, which makes it all worthwhile. It's not that I haven't tried to be a good wife, Amanda. I have. But it's been hard. I remember a dinner party we attended once with all his friends, all in business. We were just married and he was lecturing me on the way there, telling me not to tell people where I came from.'

'Where *do* you come from?'

'Hackney,' she replies, smiling.

'What's wrong with Hackney?' I say incredulously.

'Nothing, but . . . well, he told me not to mention it, and not to get drunk because when I'm drunk he says I'm stupid, and to hide my watch because it's not worth showing and not to talk to Henry because he'd flirt too much with me, or to Gerard because he'd want to fish for business gossip, and not to talk about holidays as we weren't having any that year, and not to mention the fact that I couldn't ski, surf or dive.'

I am so dumbfounded at how anyone can live with someone like this for so long that I'm speechless.

'I was on the verge of tears that night, and then Dennis turned to me and said . . . do you know what he said?' She's in tears again. 'He told me to remember to be myself, after all that. That's what he said and it's been like that ever since. He's told me what to do, how to behave, whom to befriend, even what to eat and drink sometimes, and then he always tells me to be natural and be myself and, do you know, Amanda, I started to forget who I was. I lost all sense of my own identity, but being with Tom, well, I think that's helped me find it again.'

'Deborah, you are not right for Dennis. You can take the man out of the City but not the City out of the man and he's still the same Dennis, even down in Cornwall. His friends are all corporate pompous twits, full of their own self-importance, knowing the cost of everything and the value of nothing. He'll always expect you to put him first. To be a corporate wife for any duration you need to be thick-skinned and even more ruthless than the men. And you don't strike me as ruthless, Deborah.'

'You mean like Suzanne?' she says.

'Well, sort of, but she's different. Anyway, their marriage isn't all hunky-dory either, but Howard is fundamentally decent,' I say, surprising myself.

'Dennis really changed when he left the City and started to play with his own money rather than somebody else's. He used to talk about money with such flippancy, because none of it was his own. But he didn't have to ask for Skyler and George's loan back, he could have borrowed what we needed elsewhere. I think he just doesn't like to see others doing better than him. He's like a spoilt child who's never been allowed to fail. I think that he chose me for his wife because he felt he could take charge and perhaps change me, iron out all the things he didn't like about me. He almost did. Then I met Tom and what started as a friendship with someone I could talk to, be myself with, became something so much more meaningful and intimate.'

'I understand. No one can hold their breath emotionally for that long. Christ, I can't even do it for a month on holiday. I've had to bite my tongue on so many occasions with Suzanne. I couldn't do it for weeks. You've had to do it for years.'

'You're very different people,' comments Deborah. 'I wouldn't really have put you two together as friends. You and Skyler, yes, but not you and Suzanne. She's more . . . well, more the corporate woman you were talking about.'

'Yes, but she's got a soft centre. I've found out a little more about her on this holiday. She's OK once you break through the layers,' I say, thinking back to our rows and our heart-to-heart earlier on. 'So what are you going to do?' I ask, looking out to sea.

'I'm not sure. I know Dennis would see divorce as a failure and he could react really badly.'

'He'd probably regard it as your failure, not his,' I say wryly.

'Well, I am partly to blame. But so is he,' Deborah sighs.

I sense that Deborah is terrified of Dennis's reaction.

'But that's no reason to think about ending it all,' I say as softly as I can.

Deborah looks startled.

'Oh no, you thought I was going to jump! Oh no, no!' she says, almost laughing. 'I just needed some space to think and I always think more clearly by the sea.' She pauses. 'And this is where I used to meet Tom a lot. It was our meeting place.'

'Yes, I guessed as much. I saw you kissing Tom not long after we arrived. In fact, I thought you were Suzanne,' I admit, blushing a little.

Deborah laughs. 'Tom knows what Suzanne's like – fun when she wants to be but a lot of hard work.'

'Yes, Nigel thinks that too. But it's amazing no one else knew about you and Tom.'

'Well, Tom flirts with lots of women, so he kept

everyone off the track. No one really knew for sure who he was dating, only that she was married.'

I smile, remembering that Clare had mentioned this rumour.

'And Dennis never suspected?' I ask.

'Dennis wouldn't consider Tom a rival. He has no money and isn't a suit or a celebrity. He would never imagine I would go for someone like Tom.' She shrugs her shoulders.

I stand up. 'Why don't we go back to the house and we'll sit down with Suzanne and see if we can work something out?'

Back at the house, I'm immediately confronted by Candida, and it's clear she's on the warpath.

'Will you please tell that couple in the room next to us to stop bashing the walls all the time?' she says to me, totally ignoring Deborah. 'They're at it all hours of the night and day and even with our earplugs we can still feel the vibrations; it's most off-putting!'

'I'm so sorry,' I say, 'I'll go up and deal with it right away.' I walk up the stairs. The sound of bedposts banging rhythmically against the wall can be clearly heard down the corridor. I thump on the Smiths' door and say loudly, 'Will you *please* stop having sex! You're disturbing the whole house!' There's a brief silence, then laughter, and the banging stops. I walk back downstairs to find Suzanne and Deborah grinning at me and even Candida Pepsin managing a bemused smile.

'Perhaps I should have tried that one,' she says, nodding approvingly as she goes into the sitting room.

Deborah and Suzanne hug each other.

'How are you?' asks Suzanne. 'You look very red-eyed.'

'Oh, I'd rather not talk about it right now if you don't mind.'

'Well, we had a visit from David Torey this morning. He's discovered we aren't who we said we were, so now we're all in deep shit,' Suzanne says.

'Yes I know. Dennis told David this morning,' Deborah admits, looking shamefaced.

'Why would he do that?' asks Suzanne, bemused.

I quickly explain to Suzanne about the loan. She listens in silence and when I've finished she blurts out, 'Well, that's bad business sense. And, what's more, he's an arsehole.'

'I agree,' Deborah says, nodding back at her.

Suzanne and I sit Deborah down in the kitchen. Clare pops her head round the door.

'Everything OK?' she mouths.

'Yes, fine thanks, but can you find the men for us? We need them,' I say.

'I'll get Jack to go and find them,' she replies.

Half an hour later, Howard, Nigel, Suzanne, Deborah and I are sitting around the kitchen table, drinking tea and eating the scones Clare made this morning. The children are happy playing 'Love King' with the Grossettos, which is, according to Jenny, a modern version of Kiss Chase.

'Right, now everyone's here I'd better fill you all in,' I say. 'Skyler and George have borrowed money from Dennis, who now apparently needs the money back to pay the bills at the Elysian. This obviously leaves Skyler and George up the proverbial creek without a paddle, and we need some ideas to help them out.'

'How much do we need?' asks Howard.

'Dennis lent them about twenty thousand, I think,' says Deborah.

'But that's peanuts!' says Howard, laughing.

'It's not to Skyler and George, Howard,' says Suzanne. 'And if you have that sort of money lying around I'd like to know about it,' she adds, looking at her husband with one eyebrow arched.

'Well, I've got plenty of contacts,' Howard says, ignoring her. 'The money's definitely out there, it's just a question of finding this place's unique selling point to make it attractive to a potential investor. After all, there are loads of B&Bs in Cornwall. What's so special about this one?'

'Lots of things: the view, the ambience, the staff, its family friendliness. Why don't we ask some of the guests and use what the others wrote in the guest book too?' I suggest, getting up to fetch it, but Clare, who's been listening at the door, has beaten me to it and hands it to me. 'Thank you, Clare. Shouldn't you be seeing to the teas?' She disappears, a rueful grin on her face.

I open the guest book at the first page.

'Right, this is what Peter and Paul Smith said: "We

loved everything about this place. The style, the people, the way we were treated. There is so much to do, everything is close by and the food is phenomenal. Can we please come next year and bring our friends? Great party place."'

'Well, there are a few ideas,' says Suzanne.

'But they're not money-spinning ideas,' says Nigel. 'The Blues need something that makes them stand out, that will guarantee them a regular income. That's what will attract an investor.'

'How about two-for-one offers?' I say.

'That's a loss leader so you could only afford to do it for a time,' says Howard.

'How about inviting schools to come here on field trips?' I suggest.

'Not enough money in it, and far too much effort,' says Suzanne. 'It's chaos with just our children, can you imagine what it would be like with twenty-five of them?'

We sit and think and drink more tea. The children have kissed each other to death and now want to play with their dads on the beach.

'Well, it's almost time to start getting supper ready, so let's sleep on this and chat about it some more tomorrow,' I say, 'but think hard, because Skyler and George have invested everything in Silver Trees and they really need our help.'

'We know, darling, and we do want to help too,' says Nigel.

As we get up, I hug Deborah once more and whisper to her, 'Everything will be all right.'

'I know it will,' she says.

'Howard or Nigel, can you give Deborah a lift back to the Elysian?' Suzanne asks.

'Thank you, but don't worry.' Deborah smiles. 'The walk will do me good.'

I walk with her to the front door. As I watch her disappear along the path, my phone rings. It's Skyler.

'Hello, Skyler, how are you? Did everything go OK?'

'I'm holding up, but my father isn't, I'm afraid. He collapsed at the funeral and had to be rushed to hospital.'

'Oh God, Skyler, I'm so sorry. You've got to be there for him, so don't worry about anything here,' I say, realising that means we'll have to hold the fort for longer.

'Can you look after the place for another few days?' she says timidly. 'I hate to ask, but I don't know what else to do, I just can't leave him and I don't think I'd cope on my own with George and the girls.'

'Of course we can. We've got Nigel and Howard here now and they and the children seem to be enjoying their new-found responsibilities. Matt's got them cutting down trees, mending fences and everything,' I say, trying to sound positive.

'And what are the new guests like?'

'The Grossettos are noisy and friendly. The Smiths bonk a lot. And Candida and Adeline are as happy as they will ever be,' I say.

'That sounds good,' she replies. There's a brief pause. 'I have something else to tell you,' she says. She sounds hesitant and for a brief moment I panic that somehow David Torey has been in touch with her directly.

'I'm really sorry to land this on you, but a Scout troop of fourteen boys are due to turn up on Friday for the weekend. They're expecting to pitch tents near the house and have all their meals provided, as well as all their outdoor activities laid on for them. George would have done the activities and Clare and I were going to do everything else; do you think you'll be able to cope with that?' she says, sounding more desperate than I've ever heard.

At that moment I remember what David Torey said: that I should have said no and that perhaps I'm in too deep already. But her dad's just collapsed, her mum has died and she's on the verge of losing her life's dream – the last thing she needs now is for her friends to let her down, so instead I say, 'Of course we'll manage, Skyler. Don't worry about a thing. We're here to help however we can. That's what friends are for.'

I put the phone down and return to the kitchen, where everyone's still debating what to do. They all turn and stare at me, wondering at the look of horror on my face.

'For goodness' sake, Amanda,' says Nigel. 'What now?'

Chapter 15
Dib Dib, Dob Dob

Our feet haven't touched the ground since I told everyone the latest news. Howard thought I was joking, laughed, then realised I wasn't laughing back. Nigel put his head in his hands. But after a few moments Suzanne stood up and announced, 'I was a Girl Guide. This will be a piece of cake.'

'What do you mean, a piece of cake?' I reply. 'It's going to be a nightmare.'

'No, it's not,' says Suzanne. 'I've organised hundreds of events for grown-ups who behave like adolescents. This will be fine. We'll have to ask if Clare, Pippa and Dot can work full-time for the weekend, and Tom and Matt too, but I'm sure they'll enjoy it.' She paces up and down as she speaks, ideas flying into her head every time she puts a foot down. 'First of all, the men need to draw up a plan of action, detailing what they're going to do with the boys each day. Are you happy with that, Howard and Nigel?' she says, looking at both of them as though they're Orlando's age.

'Fine, as long as we can have Orlando to help,' says Nigel. 'He was indispensable with the treasure hunt.'

'Good. You can get to work on that then,' she says. 'They'll need to be active from nine in the morning, with a break for a snack mid-morning, then lunch, then another mid-afternoon snack, then supper at about six, on both days. You'll need to give them something to do when they arrive, as well. We need to exhaust them completely.'

'Orlando wanted to make a raft with me today. Why don't we get them to do that as well?' says Howard.

'Oh, we should get Terence to come and help!' I say. 'He's bound to have all the right qualifications.'

'Great idea,' says Suzanne. 'Is someone writing all this down?'

Three days later, I'm standing on the drive with Suzanne, hoping that all our preparation will pay off. It's three o'clock, and the scouts are due any minute. We warned the other guests of the impending invasion, so they're all eating out this evening. Five luxury portaloos and porta-showers have been delivered and are strategically positioned out of sight from the house, at the end of the field, thanks to Suzanne's careful negotiating and ruthless manipulation.

With the help of Matt, Nigel and Howard have found

an appropriate field for the Scouts' tents and checked it for any debris, such as broken glass. Tom has the stables ready and the horses primed for their young riders; the clues are in position for the treasure hunt; the wood and barrels are waiting to be made into rafts, and the prizes have been bought – although Howard, as extravagant as ever, went overboard and bought £50 book vouchers for the winners. Clare has bought two huge catering tins of hot chocolate, sixty currant buns and seven large bags of marshmallows for toasting on the campfire. In fact, I found out quite late from Helen that we can't have a campfire in the field – something to do with preserving the wildlife – but they can have one on the beach, where we've set up a barbecue for lunches and suppers.

Jenny, Orlando, Jack and Hannah, with the help of Frederic, Isabella and Luigi, have made banners for the two teams: Surfs and Turfs. Surfs have a boy riding on the crest of a wave and Turfs have a boy climbing an oak tree. They're really rather good.

'If it rains, we're screwed,' says Suzanne as we watch two minibuses coming up the drive.

'No, if it rains it'll be more fun. These boys want to be men and it will make the challenge even tougher,' I say, ready to go into battle – I feel this is do or die, for Skyler's sake.

A fifty-something man dressed entirely in green, so that he resembles a smiley leprechaun, gets out of the first minibus, which is marked South Bristol Second Scout Group, and walks up to us. Both vans have large roof-racks piled high with luggage, most of which appears to be tents. Another man gets out of the second and waves to me.

'Hello, there,' says the first, his Bristol accent hitting us both in the face. 'My name's Edward Tempest, and I've got fourteen young lads here wanting some adventure. We've had a long drive, what with the traffic, so I'll get the boys to introduce themselves once we've settled in and got the tents up.'

We offer to show them where they can set up camp. As we walk, I explain to Edward who we all are, where Skyler and George are, and hand him an itinerary of the events we have planned, the names of the teams, who will be leading each and a brief biography (Suzanne's idea), including their qualifications.

'I'm impressed,' says Edward, looking through it. Remembering various press trips I've been on, we've tried to make it busy enough so they don't get bored, but not too hectic. We've taken the kids' advice too, especially Orlando's. Howard had suggested we take them to the Minack Theatre one evening, but Orlando quickly put the kybosh on that, and I think he was right. Boys that age and Shakespeare just don't mix, especially on a windy cliff.

Edward looks at the area we've marked up for the teams to pitch their tents, makes a few adjustments, then says, 'Great, well, I'll let you get on with it. They're a good bunch, and they've got lots of energy and a strong sense of adventure, so I think this competition you've planned will really fire their imagination. Were you two ever Girl Guides?' he asks.

'I was a Queen's Guide,' I say.

'You never mentioned that,' says Suzanne, looking surprised.

'You didn't ask,' I reply. 'I was patrol leader for the White Rose Patrol and wanted to get all the badges. There was even the stalker's badge where I had to stalk someone round the high street, wearing a wig and everything. You couldn't do it now, of course – you'd be stopped by a security guard on suspicion of pinching something.'

They both laugh.

'What were you like as a camper?' Suzanne asks as Edward walks back to the vans and starts to get the boys out.

'Absolute crap. I couldn't put a tent up if I tried. They weren't like the tents you get these days, where all you have to do is pull a toggle. All the poles and tent pegs were made out of wood, and the tent had to be put up in a certain order or it wouldn't work. There were a thousand and one guy ropes and they had to be tied in exactly the right way. I remember doing my camper badge with three other girls who hated each other and kept storming off. We did it in the end, although not exactly in the Girl Guide spirit.'

The boys are all in the field now and line up with their tents to be given their orders. I can hear a few mumbles from dissenters, but Edward just silences them with, 'Be quiet and listen. Each of you boys will be put into one of two teams, Surfs or Turfs. The winning team will get prizes and there will be non-stop challenges throughout the weekend to test your agility, your brains, your strength and your stamina. After the teams have been chosen, the first challenge will be to get your tents up as quickly as possible. You've all practised putting them up before, so you should be able to do it easily, but I'll be on hand in case you need help.

'Can I be in the Turfs?' shouts one boy at the back.

'Just wait and see, Kevin,' Edward responds firmly, 'and don't shout without putting your hand up first.'

'Are we still in England, sir?' asks another boy.

'Yes, Wayne. Now, enough nonsense, let's get you into teams. Luke, you'll be captain of the Surfs, and, John, you're captain of the Turfs. I want you to choose your teams, so stand there.' He points a few hundred yards away and the boys take it in turns to choose their team.

'I used to hate this,' Suzanne whispers to me. 'I remember it at school in netball and I was always the last one chosen. It was horrible.' I'm surprised to hear she wasn't the one doing the picking, to be honest.

One by one the boys are chosen, and each member seems happy with the choice, apart from Kevin.

While the Scouts are busy setting up camp, Howard and Nigel have brought out a trestle table on which Clare puts rolls and currant buns and jugs of water and apple juice. I go back to the kitchen with Clare to find Eliana busy making meatballs. 'I thought I could 'elp,' she says, smiling. I feel like kissing her, especially as she's also made her special tomato sauce. Pippa and Dot are busy peeling potatoes for the piles of mash that we'll need.

'How are the desserts coming along?' I ask.

'All done,' says Clare. 'We've made huge apple crumbles and blackberry and apple pies and we're doing a fruit salad for tomorrow lunchtime, which we can prepare in the morning. We've also made a carrot cake, fruit cake and sponge cake for snacks, and Aunt Sarah's have made a huge batch of chocolate-chip cookies, which should go down well,' she says, smiling.

'Phew, hope we've got enough,' I say, realising how it could all go horribly wrong at any moment.

It's almost five o'clock and we've done everything we can for now in the kitchen. The meatballs are bubbling gently in their sauce, the puds are ready and there are three huge bowls of mash being kept warm on the hotplate.

'How about some champagne?' Suzanne says. 'I think we deserve it.'

We walk out on to the side terrace, to find Nigel and Howard already sitting there drinking beer.

'What are you doing here, why aren't you working?' I ask in mock horror.

'Oh, give us a break,' Nigel groans. 'We've been working all day and we've covered everything,' he says, getting a list out of his pocket and showing us a long line of ticks.

'Do you mean we actually have nothing to do for a whole evening?' I ask incredulously.

'Yes, apart from be with your family and your husbands,' says Howard, pulling Suzanne on to his lap and giving her a squeeze.

'We've got a bit of time,' she says, 'but the kids are doing a presentation for the Scouts this evening and I think we should watch.'

'Where are they now?' I ask.

'They're practising in front of the Grossetto children, although I'm not sure how much they understand,' Nigel says.

I walk over to my husband and give him a kiss on the lips. 'Do we have time for S-E-X?' I whisper playfully.

'Could we do it in ten?' he asks.

'Hope not, but perhaps twenty,' I say, pulling him up by the hand and leading him to our cottage while Howard and Suzanne giggle at us.

Walking through the woods I take a moment to take in just how beautiful Silver Trees is. The gardens and the house are glowing in the early evening light.

'Wouldn't you like this sort of country life, away from it all?' I ask Nigel.

'We could have it if we wanted,' he says. 'We have the money; we can sell up and move out here if you want.'

'Yeah, but would it make us happy? The thing is, when you achieve your dream, what happens next?' Nigel is silent, so I continue. 'I used to think like that all the time, but when I was working there was always somewhere new to go. Then suddenly I started to be sent to the same places, see the same faces, the world seemed to get smaller and I felt smaller in it,' I say, feeling my spirits sink for reasons I don't understand. Perhaps I'm just tired.

'What makes you happy, Amanda?' Nigel asks.

'My children, my husband and my friends. And orgasms. And champagne. In that order,' I giggle.

He grabs me by the waist, laughing.

'Well, you have your children here, your husband here and your friends here. You've already got the champers, so let's see what we can do about the orgasm, shall we?'

But as we enter the cottage, I can hear someone upstairs and remember Dot saying she meant to change our sheets this evening, because she hadn't been able to do it earlier.

'Oh bugger,' I say, getting frustrated.

'We'll find somewhere else,' says Nigel.

'Where?' I ask, feeling like a schoolgirl who wants to sneak off with her boyfriend. 'The place is crawling with children on the lookout for anything that moves, thinking it could possibly win them some points. Can you imagine how many points they'd win if they spotted us at it?' I say.

'Well, we'll have to just make sure they can't find us, won't we?' he says, kissing my neck now as we stagger along the path back towards the main house. 'How about the greenhouse?' he asks.

'Where, in amongst the tomatoes?' I say.

'One of the bedrooms?' he suggests.

'All the bedrooms are full. Skyler's rooms are free, but I'm not having sex in her bedroom, or in Willow and Rose's.'

Nigel pulls me round the side of the house and pushes me up against the wall.

'Too open,' I say before he starts to kiss me. 'Anyone can walk round here,' I protest between kisses.

'Exciting, though, isn't it?' he says.

'When you're twenty, yes, not when you're forty and you're supposed to be looking after your friend's B&B with fourteen Boy Scouts and nine guests in your care.'

'Then where?' he says, exasperated.

I take him by the hand, walk him towards the car park and stand by our Espace.

'In the car?' he says.

'Why not?' I say.

'Why not use Howard's Porsche?' he says jangling some keys he's just retrieved from his pocket with a glint in his eye. 'He gave me the keys to run some errands earlier and I've still got them.'

'Because it's naughty,' I say.

'Exactly,' he says. 'And snotty Suzanne would never know.'

'She's not all snotty, Nigel, she's got a heart too,' I say in her defence.

'Yes, but she's also got an attitude, and besides, I've never done it in a Porsche before. I bet even Suzanne has.'

He beeps the car alarm and opens the door. I look around, anxious that Howard would have heard the beep and recognised it, but no one comes out so I wriggle inside. 'It would help if I was five foot nothing,' I say, squeezing into a seat that's designed for driving, not bonking.

Nigel gets into the driver seat, turns on the ignition and heads, very slowly and quietly, out along the drive towards the main road. It seems we see everyone we know heading the other way: Peter in his van, Helen in her car and then Clare's sister, Francesca, in hers. We head towards Tremontgomery, through the high street, past the harbour and cobbled square and out towards the Minack.

'I saw loads of smaller roads on the way to the theatre,' I say.

Nigel spots a tiny single-track road with a dead-end sign, turns in and slowly drives along it. Tall hedges curve and meander for half a mile, then the tarmac comes to an end at a small, dusty parking area. Surrounding it is a narrow band of trees, below which we can hear the sea.

We look round, but there's no one. Just us. Finally.

Nigel kisses me on the lips and cups my face in his hands, and for the first time I feel I can let go. And before I know it I burst into tears. I sob uncontrollably, almost unable to breathe.

'My God, Amanda, what's the matter?' Nigel says, looking worried. 'We won't have sex here if you don't want to, darling.'

I want to smile but I can't stop crying. Eventually I manage to explain.

'I guess I've been so focused on helping Skyler and being strong for everyone, that I've just been bottling this all up. I've had a wonderful, dramatic, challenging experience, but not a holiday. And a holiday is what I needed, Nigel.' I take a breath.

'It must have been difficult,' Nigel says, holding my hand.

'It has, more than I realised. And then when you came down and said the deal had been a success but that you'd have to work even harder now, I felt like my bubble had burst – my bubble of hope, of having time with you again and being a family. I just keep asking myself, what's it for? So we can have holidays like this, which are even more stressful and challenging than being at home? At least at home we have a routine and the kids have school and I can close the door on everyone and be in my own home. It's lovely here in Cornwall, but I feel as stressed as fuck,' I say, almost hysterical now. I hadn't realised I'd been so pent up about it all and now I don't know how to stop myself dissolving into an uncontrollable mess of tears.

'Then you definitely need sex,' he replies.

'That's all you can say? I need sex? The answer to all the problems in the world is to have sex? With your wife, someone else's wife, anyone, but have sex? NO!' I scream, making Nigel jump. 'I want sex, but I need a break. I need you to stop working, I need you to stop putting pressure on me and the family and to realise that you will lose us, and lose yourself, if you don't realise what you're doing to us. We'll become like Suzanne and Howard if we're not careful.'

'Never,' Nigel says, looking horrified.

'Oh yes we will. We'll become just like them: cold and distant from our children while the kids become cold and brittle themselves. But I'm not going to let that happen. You either give up that job or I leave you,' I say, unstrapping my seat belt and trying, in an ungainly fashion, to get out of the car, but the seat is so low I keep falling back. Eventually I manage to haul myself out, but not before I notice that Nigel is laughing at me. I promptly whack him across the face, get out and storm off towards a path that seems to run down to the beach.

In fact, it runs along the top of the cliff. I go about three hundred yards and stop. Nigel doesn't seem to be following. I sit on a dry tussock of grass and gaze around me at the dramatic landscape, looking for inspiration, trying to control my breathing again. I suddenly feel so out of control, and feel that my whole family is set on a destructive course from which there is no return. I want to know what I should do, if I should continue to hold my breath and hope for the best like Deborah, if I should continue to follow the route Suzanne has taken until all it's about is money. At least I love Nigel and know he's not a liar, but I feel like a liar myself, continuing to live a life I'm not happy with and can't keep pace with. Skyler can't keep pace with her life, either, even though she's trying desperately hard. Even Suzanne, the ball-buster, isn't as thick-skinned as she pretends to be. She's even more vulnerable, in her own way, than the rest of us.

I look out at the endless, calm blue, the light just beginning to dim, leaving the water glowing. I can understand why Deborah wanted to come to the sea when she was so upset. Just looking at it soothes my mind until I'm thinking of nothing at all.

After a while I'm conscious of Nigel standing behind me, then sitting down by my side, not hugging me, just looking out to sea.

'You've been under a lot of pressure too, haven't you, Amanda?'

'Yes, I have,' I reply, hoping he doesn't say anything stupid, because then I might have to throw him off the cliff.

'So have I,' he says.

'I know!' I scream. 'Everyone knows you've been under a lot of pressure because that's all you do, that's all any of you men do: go around in your own little world saying you're under pressure. But I'm under pressure, too,' I say, getting up again, 'and I can't do this any more. I can't be on tenterhooks about money all the time. Happiness is about having someone to love – and I have that: I have you, my family and friends. But it's also about having something to look forward to, about having hopes and dreams – and that's the problem: I have nothing to look forward to, except you working longer and longer hours and a few brief phone calls while you're travelling the world. I'm not one of those wives who gets on better with her husband when she doesn't see him. I'll walk away if it comes to that, Nigel. This holiday, if you can call it that, has really taught me what's most important in my life, and do you know what that is?'

Nigel doesn't dare speak. I'm so angry I don't blame him.

'Me. I'm important,' I say.

Nigel looks up at me.

'Of course you are, darling.'

'You think I'm mad, don't you?' I say.

'No, I just think you've had years of frustration, with me, your life and your desire to work; it's just like Skyler wanting to paint more and waiting for other people to get their lives sorted so that she can. I promise things will change, because the last thing I want is for you to leave me, for you to be unhappy and unfulfilled. You needed this break and all you got was more anxiety, more stress – and other people's stress at that – and you've handled it brilliantly, but now you want to scream. So scream, my darling, scream.'

I stand up and walk to the cliff edge, breathing in and out and in and out until I let rip. As I scream, my whole body shakes with emotion; I let the anger and sadness and frustration go far out to sea until my mouth is open but no sound is coming out.

I stop and look round at Nigel, who's still smiling at me, who knows me and loves me and wants me, and who knows I want and love him, too.

'You know, if you'd made me come I might have screamed that loud,' I say.

'Damn! And I missed my chance.' He laughs.

'Well, perhaps you haven't,' I say, walking towards him. 'Now, what were you saying about sex in a Porsche?'

We've reclined the passenger seat as far as it will go, but I get cramp as Nigel tries to pull down my jeans and explore. I'm laughing despite the pain because I realise how ridiculous it might look if someone were passing by, but the laughter rather destroys the moment and then I get cross with myself, which definitely does. Then we manage to turn the hazard lights on when Nigel tries to unbutton his trousers, and then we press something else which lights up a sign saying 'Operation not fully completed', which makes us both hysterical. Still, we persevere, and with a bit of imagination and a lot more laughter, we somehow manage. Fifteen minutes later we're both smiling.

We drive rather fast back to Silver Trees, aware that we've been gone for over an hour. They could have sent out a search party; the Scouts could all have packed up and gone, and we'd have such bad PR that even Suzanne won't be able to help Skyler recover from it.

When we get back, though, everything seems to be going nicely without us. Jack, Hannah, Orlando and Jenny are nearing the end of their global-warming presentation to the Scouts, who all seem transfixed, although some of the boys are clearly getting fidgety and hungry for their dinner.

After the presentation has finished and copious notes have been taken, meatballs and mash are served and silence falls over the campsite. Later, as I go to help clear the pudding dishes, Edward comes up to me.

'Wonderful afternoon, Amanda,' he says. 'The boys love it. They can't wait till tomorrow. Really looking forward to the raft-building, surfing, riding and coasteering, and especially the treasure hunt. Thanks for pulling out all the stops. And the food is great. Really great.'

I walk back to the main house, thinking that perhaps we've finally started to get it right for Skyler and George. We can rest easy tonight, although I don't think I'll have a proper night's sleep until Skyler returns, and I'm dreading telling her about the fiasco with the hotel inspector.

I find the children, Howard and Suzanne on the terrace eating leftover meatballs.

'Why didn't we have this earlier, Mummy?' asks Hannah. 'It's so much nicer than fish and chicken,' she says ungraciously.

'We might have leftovers tomorrow as well,' I say. 'Now go into the kitchen and help yourself to crumble, and take the plates with you, please.'

The children return with plates of piping-hot apple crumble and we all sit quietly, thankful that today we've managed to keep our heads above water.

The treasure hunt on Saturday morning is a manic scramble of boys trying to find clues and remember what they'd been told by the Global Warmers the previous night. It seems the Surfs were listening more carefully because they manage to beat the Turfs hands down, although some of Jack's hiding places are so good that two clues are never found. The raft-building session with Terence is also eventful as they have to cross the bay once they've made them and only the Surfs manage to stay afloat. Tom is the star of the day, and now all the boys want to work with animals. After that, it is just the coasteering, and here Matt leads the Turfs to an outright victory. They jump, wade, swim and run for two hours, and are so high on adrenalin that it takes endless hot showers and Peter's fabulous Cornish pasties to bring them fully back down to earth.

By late Sunday afternoon, the Scouts have eaten all the food, drunk all the apple juice and, bless their hearts, cleared up after themselves too. The Turfs are presented with their prizes, to much clapping and cheering, and then the whole troop set to work packing up their camp. I'm just about to head back to the house, when Kevin rushes up to me.

'Thanks for lookin' after us,' he says, his eyes shining; 'it's been the best weekend ever.'

Chapter 16

Handover

'We're so sorry to be leaving,' says Candida Pepsin, looking pristine in a black-and-white polka-dot two-piece. Adeline is standing alongside in an orange dress with white frilled cuffs.

It's nine o'clock on Monday morning, and I've let Suzanne and the men have a lie-in. The children are up and in the kitchen helping Clare prepare breakfast. Peter has delivered the bread and pastries this morning, so I've been manning reception and enjoying being by myself for once.

'It's been quite an adventure for us both,' Candida says, looking at Adeline, who gazes earnestly back at her. 'We so much enjoyed meeting the other guests, and thought the Scouts were very entertaining. Even Mr and Mrs Smith behaved in the end.' She smiles. I'm rather taken aback by her warmth. Perhaps we've managed to thaw two of Skyler's toughest customers after all.

'We just wanted to thank you for a wonderful stay,' says Adeline. 'We'll be telling our friends all about it and if we're able, we'd like to book two weeks next year as well. I know how these special places get booked up way in advance.'

The Smiths appear half an hour later, having lived off fresh air for the past week as far as I can see. As they walk down the stairs, I suddenly recognise them as the actors who played Romeo and Juliet at the Minack.

'Didn't you perform at the theatre a few days ago?' I ask as Mr Smith comes to the desk.

'Yes,' he says, 'but please don't tell anyone. We've enjoyed the privacy here so much. They wanted to put us up at the Elysian, but they tend to court publicity there and you don't. This is a secret gem and I hope you keep it that way.'

'The problem with having a secret gem is that no one gets to hear about us and then we can't afford to go on,' I say.

'You can,' he says, 'by word of mouth. That way it's almost like a retreat for artists, where you choose the guests as much as they choose you. You're bound to get only a certain type of clientele here anyway, like a more boho Soho House in Cornwall.' He smiles. 'Can we have breakfast before we go?' he asks, almost embarrassed.

'Of course you can,' I say. 'You must be starving!' I cheekily add.

The Grossettos are staying for another week and we welcome two more couples: a silver-haired, tweedy pair in their seventies, whose bags are laden with binoculars and books, and two elderly women from Wales who've known each other for sixty years. Marian has been married five times, 'always to men in oil', and Sheila, who is widowed and knew Skyler's mother, wants to see more of Cornwall.

I've just finished showing the new guests to their rooms when I hear a cheer from the hallway. I rush down the stairs to find Skyler, George and the children standing at the door. It seems so long since we last saw them, and so much has happened. Skyler looks tired but calm, and is dressed in her usual pink and mauve.

'Oh Amanda,' she says, rushing to hug me. We hold each other tight for quite some time and I'm aware of the children milling around and talking to each other. I have so much to say I don't really know where to start.

'Wanna go out and play?' says Hannah as the noise reaches a crescendo, and they all dash off outside.

Sensing Skyler and I want to catch up, George excuses himself. 'I'm just going to unpack the car and have a look around. I'll leave you girls in peace.' But he pokes his head into the kitchen first and Clare instantly drops the potato peeler and rushes out to greet him.

'Hello, George,' she says, almost jumping on him like an overzealous chimp. 'It's so good to see you. How are you both?' she says, seeing Skyler and coming over to hug her tenderly.

'We're fine. Tired but fine. Very happy to be back.

Amanda tells me she and Suzanne couldn't have done this without you, Clare,' says Skyler.

'Nope, that's true,' she says, winking at me, 'but they didn't do too badly, considering they're out-of-towners,' she adds. 'You sit and chat and I'll make you both a cup of tea, OK?' she says and heads back into the kitchen with a spring in her step. George heads back out to the car.

'How have you been?' I ask now that Skyler and I are on our own.

'Can we sit outside?' she asks.

'Of course.' We head towards the terrace, where we sat happily all those weeks ago, and collapse into two sunloungers.

'The funeral was very moving and I think a bit too much for Dad,' Skyler says.

'How is he?' I ask.

'Better. George is driving up to London in a few days and bringing him back, then he'll stay with us indefinitely. We'll install him in one of the rooms so we can keep an eye on him. I think Cornwall will do him good.' Tears well up in her eyes. 'I don't know how to begin to thank you for all you've done.' She leans over and takes my hand. 'I know this hasn't been much of a holiday for you, Amanda, but I couldn't have done it without your help.'

'It was a team effort. We all did our bit,' I reply. 'The men thrived on the outdoor stuff and really came into their own when the Scouts arrived. Suzanne was in her element bossing everyone around, making lists and co-ordinating us all. We even borrowed Matt's walkie-talkies and everything went according to plan,' I say. I don't want to spoil the moment by mentioning David Torey's visit yet. 'Tom, Matt, Helen, Peter, Pippa, Dot, and especially Clare, have been invaluable. They're amazing people. There's so much more sense of community here than in Whitlow, you know. All I ever do is whinge about Mr Durning's extension and have the odd dinner party. I think I know people, but I don't. You really get to know your neighbours here. They're not just acquaintances, they're real friends.'

'That tends to happen when the shit hits the fan, though, doesn't it?' she says, smiling. 'You find out who your real friends are and the hangers-on just drift away. Sometimes the people you least expect to be supportive are the ones who are there for you. I'm not saying that of you, Amanda, but it did cross my mind that Suzanne might think this was all too much for her to handle. She's not used to doing her *own* cleaning, let alone someone else's.' She laughs.

'Well, when push came to shove, even she stuck it out, in her own unique way . . .'

I won't tell Skyler about Suzanne's phone conversation with Howard, saying she wanted to go home early, because that would be unfair. After all, as soon as she saw Skyler in distress, her attitude completely changed, even after I'd shouted at her and called her names. It took a lot of courage to do that. Clare brings the tea out to us with some of Aunt Sarah's cookies that have somehow outlasted the weekend's feasting.

'How have the guests been?' she asks. 'Did you have problems with Candida and Adeline?'

'None at all,' I say. 'They just like things done their way, and they got on very well with Suzanne and Jenny in particular. They've written something in the guest book, as have all the guests, but you can have a look at that in your own time. Now don't you want to have a lie-down after that long journey?' I ask.

'That's the last thing I want to do,' she says. 'It's just so good to be home and to see you and have an opportunity to talk. Do you know, we haven't had a proper talk since you arrived? How about the children? Have they enjoyed the holiday? And how did it go with the Scouts?'

'The children had a whale of a time and they got on really well with the other children staying here. Orlando in particular has really come out of his shell and I think my lot have had the best holiday ever.'

'And have you seen much of Dennis and Deborah?' she asks.

'Where do I start?' I say. 'To be very brief, Deborah is having an affair with Tom and wants to leave Dennis.'

'No!' Skyler says, looking genuinely surprised.

'Yes, and guess what? I thought he was having a fling with Suzanne,' I say.

'So did I,' says Skyler. 'They were flirting non-stop. What dark horses the pair of them are.'

'Anyway, Deborah wants out of the marriage,' I say.

'I'm not surprised,' Skyler replies.

'She was mortified about the business of the loan from Dennis. I know you're worried about the future of Silver Trees, but we want to help out and between us we've thought of a few ideas. Actually, some of them came from your own guests,' I add. 'So you mustn't worry, Skyler. You'll be fine and Silver Trees will be fine. But we can talk about that later. I just wanted to say how lovely it is to have you back home.'

'It's lovely to be home,' she says, giving me a hug.

George, Nigel, Howard, Suzanne and the children join us at that moment. Soon the verandah is crowded as Grossettos appear, too, and Clare goes to get coffee for everyone. People are laughing and re-enacting some of the funny things that have happened to them over the holiday. Jenny is telling Rose how much she's learned in the kitchen from Clare and how she wants to be a chef when she grows up, Hannah is telling Willow how they can build their own raft and Jack is trying to tell Luigi and Isabella all the pirate stories he's heard. Even Matt and Tom have turned up to welcome the Blues back. Clare, Pippa and Dot return with pots of coffee, and some saffron buns. Then Suzanne decides that we need some champagne.

'Who cares if it's the morning; we can mix it with orange juice and have Buck's Fizz!'

She's just got up to go and fetch it, when she sees something over my shoulder and stops dead. I look round to see Deborah walking towards us. Suzanne and I go quiet and look over at Tom, but Deborah goes straight to Skyler, looks at her for a few seconds, then says, 'It's *so* good to have you back, you know. Your friends have done you proud. I, on the other hand, feel I have let you down.'

'You haven't let me down,' Skyler says, smiling at her. 'You're one of my friends and you've done me proud too. How could I have kept Suzanne happy enough to stay on if she didn't have the hook of a posh party and a posh night at the theatre to go to?'

Everyone laughs, including Suzanne, who admits, 'I would have stayed anyway, but it did help soften the blow of all this work.'

Tom has walked over to Deborah and now he boldly kisses her on the lips. It's the first time I've seen them be affectionate in public and it looks so natural, as though they belong together, whereas Dennis and Deborah never did.

I turn to say something to Suzanne, but she and Howard are both listening intently to Orlando as he tells them what he's most enjoyed about the holiday.

'Can we come back here again next year?' I hear him ask.

'I should think so,' says Suzanne, 'and hopefully we won't have to work as hard, although I admit I did rather enjoy getting stuck in. I've never had such an active holiday and I think it's done me good.' She turns to Howard. 'And do you know what, Howey, it's done you good too. You're in better shape than you've ever been, what with all that manual work and playing with Orlando and the Scouts in the fresh air. You actually look quite handsome at the moment.' She kisses him affectionately on the cheek. Howard smiles and kisses her back.

'It would be really good if you could spend more time with us on holiday next year,' Suzanne continues. 'I've realised that I'd like to see more of you, and so would Orlando, wouldn't you, darling?' she says, looking down at her son.

'I would, Daddy,' he says. 'I miss you.' This brings a tear to Howard's eye, something I've never seen before.

Clare has used her initiative and has brought out two bottles of champagne and jugs of orange juice. Matt is helping her pour the drinks and telling George about all the outdoor stuff he's been organising. We're all drinking and getting rather merry and I'm just about to pull Skyler aside and break the news about David Torey, when Clare walks round and tells me the man himself is at the door.

Before I have time to explain, Skyler says, 'I'd better go and see what he wants, then.' All I can do is follow helplessly as she goes to greet him.

David is standing at the door with his notebook open, looking decidedly less angry than the last time I saw him. He looks Skyler up and down as she approaches.

'Skyler Blue, I presume,' he says, shaking her hand.

'Yes, that's me. Very nice to meet you,' she says.

'And very nice to finally meet you too.'

'I want to explain why I couldn't be here and how dreadfully sorry we are, but—'

'You don't have to, Mrs Blue,' interrupts David. 'Mrs Darcey and Mrs Banks have explained everything to me in detail and although this is far from the norm, and we would normally frown upon such deception, in the circumstances, and in light of the death of your mother, we are prepared on this occasion to overlook this error of judgement.' David is looking intently at Skyler, who is now looking quite confused.

'Deception?' she repeats.

'Oh, your friends haven't told you. I'm afraid that when I came round they told me they were . . . well, that one of them was you, perhaps thinking that I wouldn't be impressed you had left the property in the hands of amateurs. But Mrs Banks explained that your friends were professionals in their own right. You are indeed fortunate to have such loyal and talented friends, Mrs Blue.'

Suzanne has joined us.

'A peace offering,' she says, handing him a glass of Buck's Fizz.

'How nice,' replies David, 'but first I am sure you would like to know how you have been graded.'

Skyler looks horrified and I'm suddenly very nervous.

David clears his throat, looks down at his notes and says, 'Despite the little charade, I've decided to give Silver Trees four stars. It is unique in both its ambience and service, and I think you've renovated and decorated the place sympathetically and beautifully. You have the benefit of wonderful views and you have used them to their fullest potential. Your staff are obviously very loyal to you, which speaks volumes, and all your guests couldn't speak more highly of you. In fact, one guest said yours is the best accommodation they've ever stayed in.'

'Really?' says Skyler in amazement. 'Was that one of the Mr Smiths?'

'I don't think so,' says David, looking down at his notes and now accepting the glass of bubbly from Suzanne. 'It was a Ms . . . Pepsin.'

Epilogue

'It seems only yesterday that we were on this terrace, drinking champagne,' I say as I sit with Skyler and George. Nigel and Howard are playing with the children, Clare is banging pots in the kitchen and Suzanne is chatting to Deborah about this season's fashions as they walk about the garden. It's almost exactly a year later and while it looks as if nothing has changed, I know that things are very different indeed.

'So much has happened in a year,' says Skyler, taking a sip of the Tatty that Suzanne and Howard have brought down. 'I never thought I'd be in this position this time last year.'

'What? Drinking champagne on the terrace? You were in exactly the same position last year, I seem to remember!' George jokes.

'You know what I mean. I feel so much more secure

now and it's all down to you guys,' she says, looking over at me.

'Not really, it was actually your guests who did most of the thinking for us. The Grossettos suggested you get yourself a proper website, which you've done. The Smiths suggested that you turn yourselves into a secluded artists' retreat for the low season, and now that you've done that you get all your resting actors and artists staying in the winter. And the Scouts were so taken by their weekend that they're coming back and have told other Scout troops about it, so you're now fully booked with weekend activity breaks. And you're building two more cottages for families. All of that's nothing to do with us, Skyler, and everything to do with you.'

'I know, but you bought the guest book.'

'Suzanne bought the guest book, but Silver Trees is and always will be your dream. You made it the place it is. You, George, the girls and your team. All we did was maintain it for you while you were away and try to help out where we could. Remember, we almost screwed up with David Torey?'

'But it worked out in the end,' Skyler says.

'Yes, just as I said it would. And you've even had time to paint,' I say, noticing how many more of Skyler's paintings are now hanging on the walls.

'Yes, I've made a point of finding the time for myself. When all the stuff happened last year, everyone in the town was so helpful. We've always got people willing to help in the kitchen now, so I've been able to paint more and even teach some painting classes myself. Nicola, Fay and Edina are coming back this autumn for some tuition,' she says. 'Remember them?'

'Yes, the ones that fancied George.' I smile.

'That was only Nicola, and this time, believe it or not, she's coming with her husband – although it might actually be her lover, I'm not sure. Anyway, my mum always used to say I should paint more and when she died I felt I owed it to her as much as to myself to do it because it's something I'm genuinely passionate about.'

We sit in silence for a while, watching the children rush around. They're beginning to get tired, and mine have collapsed on the grass for a rest. Orlando walks over and crashes down on to a chair next to where his mother and Deborah have sat down.

'Hasn't he changed?' Skyler says. 'And Howard and Suzanne seem to be getting on very well.' She watches them as Howard walks up behind Suzanne and massages her shoulders, while she visibly melts into his touch.

'Yes, mind you, both of them have changed pace considerably. I couldn't believe it when Suzanne resigned from the bank, but her new PR consultancy seems to be going really well. And she put her foot down with Howard, so he's travelling less and rather enjoying seeing more of his family. And Orlando's thriving. He's started playing tennis at school and on the weekends with his dad, and is doing really well. We might have quite the pro on our hands!'

'Yes, that was the first thing Suzanne and Howard told me when they arrived yesterday. They're very proud of him,' Skyler says.

'They should be. And he was so much help last year. The experience definitely brought the best out in him.'

'I think it brought the best out in everyone,' Skyler replies, cutting herself a slice of one of Clare's cakes.

'And how is everyone here?' I ask.

'Well, if you mean what's the gossip, Clare and Matt are going out with each other, finally.'

'That was on the cards for ages.'

'Yes, but they really only started talking to one another the day we got back from my mum's funeral,' she says. 'It's amazing how they'd known each other for such a long time, saw each other nearly every day, but never really spoke. The rest of us could see how well matched they were, but neither of them seemed bold enough to make the move.'

I laugh. 'That sums up the community back in Whitlow,' I say, 'although Mr Durning's extension has now finished and I must admit I'm trying to get to know my neighbours better. Is your dad enjoying living with you?' I ask.

'Yes, he is. He never moved back after Mum's funeral, and seeing Willow and Rose all the time has given him a new lease of life. He's even replaced Rose's imaginary friend. She talks to her granddad in exactly the same way she used to talk to Terry. He loves the area and is off birdwatching as we speak – it's a new-found passion, I think.'

'I hear Deborah has moved in with Tom,' I say.

'Yes. The divorce has been very acrimonious, though.'

'I know. She's stayed in touch over the year. I couldn't believe what Dennis put her through – accusing her of being a bad mother! And it seems he knew about Tom all along and even kept notes on her behaviour. Then he claimed she was bad with money, even though he never allowed her to spend a penny without his say-so. He really is a horrible bully. He's been haggling over every penny – but I suppose it's in his nature to trade everything in his life, not realising the cost of what he's losing in the process, silly man. She's best free from him.'

'She'll always let him see Jeremy regularly, won't she?'

'Of course she will,' I reply, 'and he needs his dad – well, until he prefers to spend time with his friends and Tom, that is.'

'All he ever cared about was money. But Jeremy's left his boarding school and is living with Tom and Deborah now. He seems to be very happy there, and is especially fond of the horses. Matt tells me he's got a lovely disposition but is rather sensitive.'

'Like his mother,' I say.

'Quite.'

'And how are you and Nigel?' she asks, looking over at my husband, who is now chasing the children again around the garden.

'He's fine. We're fine. Really. He's finally cut back on

work. I think he also realised while he was here that he was missing seeing the children grow up – that Matt and Tom had had more of a holiday with his kids than he had. The business is blooming and he's been able to take a step back from it which of course has freed me up to finally get properly back to work, so it's turned out well all round.'

'Yes, it's so exciting, your writing again – I read your pages every week.'

'Well, as the travel editor, I've got much more control about what I cover. I haven't had to fly long-haul this year, but I intend to next year and I hope to take the kids, too. They're all young explorers at heart and I want to nurture that sense of adventure in them, that sense that Nigel and I had when we first met.

'Hannah's joined the Guides and Jack has joined the Cubs, so thanks to this place I and my family have an energy and determination we'd lost, bogged down with the day-to-day paying of bills and getting from one place to another. Seeing the children enjoy themselves so much last year made me appreciate what I had, and also what I'd lost when I'd given up on my career. I'm a good writer and I'd lost my edge.'

We sit in companionable silence for a few minutes. Then Skyler smiles.

'You know Candida and Adeline are coming next week,' she says. 'They're bringing three other ladies from the States with them, which should be fun. I would never have said that a year ago, but now I think it will be.'

'Are any other guests returning?' I ask.

'Yes, they're all coming back. The Grossettos and the Schneiders are here for a fortnight in two weeks' time. They're dying to go surfing with Matt again. The Smiths are back next month.'

'Which ones?' I ask.

'Oh, the charming gay ones. The actors are here, too. In fact, the Minack recommends us to everyone that performs there, so we have quite a few off-the-cuff theatrical performances on our lawns. It's rather lovely for the other guests. And, of course, we get the bird-watchers, the romantic couples who won't leave their rooms and the families who are all cross at the beginning of the holiday and look so much happier by the end of it.'

'How's Tremontgomery?' I ask. 'Can we pop in later?'

'I don't see why not,' says Skyler. 'That fair we went to last year is on again. Fancy going to see that woman again? Doreen, wasn't it?'

'I'm up for it, but I don't think Suzanne would be keen. Wasn't Doreen the one who called her a gnome?'

'No, I think that was someone else,' Skyler laughs.

An hour later, Suzanne, Skyler and I are in my new four-wheel drive heading for the fair. The children have chosen to go riding with their dads, which sounds much more appealing than a boring old market, but we've been given a list of things they'd like us to bring back all the same, including some of Aunt Sarah's cookies.

Cecile the satnav has been replaced by Errol, who has a deep brown voice and calls everyone babe.

'Turn right and make a smooth journey straight on, babe,' Errol says, making everyone giggle.

'Where on earth did you find him?' asks Suzanne.

'Oh, Nigel got talking to Paulo Grossetto about cars last year and he works in the satnav business. He recommended this company who offer alternative voices to download,' I say.

Little has changed on the road to Tremontgomery. We drive into town and park behind the bakery. There are still yachts in the harbour, and the fair is just as buzzing and full of scent, colour, and mystique. As we get out and walk down the high street, we see Helen in the tourist office and wave. Aunt Sarah's has expanded into the next-door shop and now offers salads and quiches as well as cakes – all organic and home-baked, of course. We search for Doreen's stand, but can't find it.

'Silly to think she would still be here,' I say.

'There she is!' shouts Skyler, noticing the silver-haired woman sitting and smiling at passers-by.

'Who's going to be first, then?' asks Suzanne.

'I think Skyler,' I say; 'after all, she went second last time.'

As we wait, Suzanne and I sit on the harbour wall, just as we did last year. I remember having the same view of Aunt Sarah's and thinking how colourful and lovely it all was.

Skyler comes out grinning.

'So,' I say, 'what did she say?'

'That all my dreams have been answered and they always will be.'

'Well, you can't get much better than that!'

'Mind you, I could have told you that for free, Skyler,' says Suzanne drily. 'Your turn next, Amanda.'

I walk into her little Rajasthani tent, its purple and red lining just as it was last summer.

'Hello, do you remember me?' I ask.

'No,' she says, 'but I will. You've had an interesting year, haven't you, my dear? A good year. A year of discovery. You've made a journey and realised you're on another journey. Whereas before you only saw clouds on the horizon, now you can see the light, and there's a lot to be thankful for. You need to be by the sea. It's good for you. It's good for your energy and it gives you peace and focus. Think about moving closer to the sea, my dear. It will do you and your family good.'

Back outside, I say, 'She told me to move to the sea!' surprised by the excitement in my voice.

'Come and live here!' says Skyler, clapping her hands.

'We'll see,' I say, trying to be sensible. 'She got it right last time. Perhaps Nigel will get work down this way, then everything will fall into place.'

'I do love it here, but I'm a townie at heart,' says Suzanne, 'and I always will be. I must admit, though, I need my breaks here. I couldn't survive without them, and I know the same goes for Howard and Orlando. Skyler, do you mind us coming down here for the summer every year?' she asks.

'I'd be disappointed if you went anywhere else,' Skyler replies, 'but that's enough stalling, Suzanne. Go on, it's your turn now.'

'OK, but it's only a bit of fun, right?'

'Right,' we say.

While we wait, we sit and watch the crowds go from one stall to another, hoping to be told their destinies or to improve the ones they've got, without realising that the future is in their hands and that all the problems they face are just challenges from which they can grow and learn.

Suzanne returns after five minutes, ashen-faced and with tears on her cheeks.

'What's she told you?' I ask in alarm.

'Oh, only that I'm pregnant,' Suzanne replies.

There's stunned silence. Then Skyler asks quietly, 'And are you?'

'Well, I'm late, but only by three weeks and at my age, I just assumed it was early menopause.'

We don't say anything.

Suzanne sits down and looks at us both.

'To be honest, girls, if that woman had told me last year that I would be pregnant this time next year I would have laughed at the ludicrousness of it. I hardly saw Howard and I wasn't a very good mother to Orlando.'

'That's being harsh on yourself,' says Skyler.

'No, that's being truthful. I wasn't a good mother, and that's not by other people's standards, that's by my own. I was even considering sending him to boarding school. Now I'd never consider that, and I know Howard wouldn't either – I've told him he wouldn't,' she says, not realising how funny it sounds. We both laugh and she pokes her tongue out at us playfully.

'A year ago, I'd have considered having a baby an inconvenience, something I had to squeeze in between work and my hectic dinner-party schedule which, as you both know, I've toned down considerably, mainly because I've learned to do my own cooking and also because I only invite people I like now instead of people I want to impress. The first group is much smaller than the second. When she told me I was pregnant, do you know, girls, I cried because I was happy. I was in denial about it because I thought I'd left it too late but when she blurted it out I thought, hey, the pregnancy tests can't all be wrong.'

'So you did hope you were pregnant? Just how many tests have you taken?' I ask, surprised at this turn of events.

'Oh eight . . . double packs . . . but they can be dodgy,' she says, shaking her head.

'No they can't! They're ninety-nine per cent accurate! Congratulations!' She flings her arms about Suzanne in excitement. 'But you are happy about it, aren't you?' she asks, pulling away suddenly.

'I'm very happy about it. I really am. It may be my last chance to give Orlando a brother or sister, and I don't want him being a spoilt brat like his parents. We can't have three selfish people in the family, can we?' Suzanne's expression breaks into an ecstatic grin. 'So it looks like some of that trusting-to-fate and going-with-the-flow stuff has rubbed off on me. So many people don't realise what makes them happy, but we're the lucky ones because we did.'

'I couldn't have put it better myself,' I say, never thinking that Suzanne and I would still be friends and enjoying another holiday together.

We all hug each other for a moment. Then we get up and walk back past the stalls and Aunt Sarah's, which is as busy as usual, until we reach the car, where I turn to the girls and say, 'Shall we go to the place I went last year to have a really good scream? It's beautiful up there and we can just make sure we've not got any pent-up anxiety or frustration by having a good old yell at the sea. It's probably more therapeutic than all these stalls put together.'

'Why not?' says Suzanne. 'As long as it doesn't scare the baby!'

I drive us up to the place where Nigel and I parked last year, making the girls laugh as I describe our attempts at car sex, after which they both recount the times they've tried al fresco sex and how it's always been the best, despite the cold or mosquitoes or sand.

We get out and walk along the cliff. It's still the peaceful place I remember, with its wide-open horizon of sea. Skyler screams first, an almost joyful yelp. I can sense the relief in her voice. It's the anniversary of her mother's death and she's been through a lot this year. Suzanne screams, louder than I've ever heard her before, then laughs, surprising herself.

'That's at least two hundred pounds' worth of therapy in one yell!' she says, grinning. 'I should do that more often.'

'Wouldn't they consider it antisocial behaviour in Whitlow?' Skyler asks, laughing at her.

'Don't care,' Suzanne replies. She ponders for a bit, then says, 'I could start the latest craze, screaming parties. Everyone can just sit and scream in between courses and let it all out. It's much less tacky than Ann Summers and less expensive than designer handbags. Just think of it, girls' – she turns to us – 'you could have a legitimate excuse to scream at your husbands, someone else's husband, the school bully, the tax inspector, the parking attendant, the Prime Minister, your mother, your mother-in-law, anyone or anything that really makes you angry. All over a lovely three-course meal and a good bottle of wine.' She claps her hands in delight at the idea and then tries to find a pad and pen in her bag to make a note.

'I like the sound of that,' I say.

'Yes, and I could charge for it as well. Everyone could pay fifty pounds or something to let off steam in the dining room and they wouldn't have to explain why. Just the sort of thing that would go down well.'

'Ever the businesswoman, eh, Suzanne?' Skyler says.

'Yes, leopards can't change their spots,' she says, shrugging her shoulders. 'But perhaps it had better wait. I want to be a good mum to Orlando and to this one here,' she explains, rubbing her tummy.

'Orlando loves you,' Skyler says.

'Orlando loves me now, but that's easy, he's still only young.' She smiles. 'Anyway, your turn, Amanda,' she says, turning to me.

I open my mouth and try to shout, but find that I can't.

'Oh come on, Amanda,' says Suzanne, folding her arms. 'It was your idea to do this in the first place!'

I try again but I still can't.

'What's the matter?' asks Skyler, putting her arm round me.

I smile and look at them both – Skyler pretty in her brown, orange and purple layered outfit, and Suzanne in her jeans and crisp Paul Smith shirt.

'I don't think I've got anything I need to scream about. Isn't that a good thing? I've shouted out my anger, my hopes and frustrations about all the money worries we've had, and the ambitions that I've put on hold for so long. I'm just happy to be here with my friends and family where I can at last, for once, be completely myself.'